J.N. CHANEY
JONATHAN BRAZEE

LAS VEGAS, NV

Copyrighted Material

Undead Marine Copyright © 2024 by Variant Publications

Book design and layout copyright © 2024 by JN Chaney
This novel is a work of fiction. Names, characters, places, and incidents are either products of the author's imagination or used fictitiously. Any resemblance to actual events, locales, or persons, living, dead, or undead, is entirely coincidental.

All rights reserved.

No part of this publication can be reproduced or transmitted in any form or by any means, electronic or mechanical, without permission in writing from JN Chaney.

www.jnchaney.com

www.jonathanbrazee.com

1st Edition

CONNECT WITH J.N. CHANEY

Don't miss out on these exclusive perks:

- Instant access to free short stories from series like *The Messenger*, *Starcaster*, and more.
- Receive email updates for new releases and other news.
- Get notified when we run special deals on books and audiobooks.

So, what are you waiting for? Enter your email address at the link below to stay in the loop.

https://www.jnchaney.com/federation-marine-subscribe

CONNECT WITH JONATHAN P. BRAZEE

Visit his website
www.jonathanbrazee.com

Sign up for Jonathan's Newsletter
http://eepurl.com/bnFSHH

Follow him on Amazon
https://www.amazon.com/Jonathan-P-Brazee/e/B007E4W0GC

Connect on Facebook
https://www.facebook.com/jonathanbrazeeauthor/

JOIN THE CONVERSATION

Join the conversation and get updates on new and upcoming releases in the awesomely active **Facebook group**, "JN Chaney's Renegade Readers."

This is a hotspot where readers come together and share their lives and interests, discuss the series, and speak directly to J.N. Chaney and his co-authors.

facebook.com/groups/jnchaneyreaders

CONTENTS

PART I

Chapter 1	3
Chapter 2	13
Chapter 3	23

Part II	47

Chapter 1	49
Chapter 2	57
Chapter 3	73
Chapter 4	83
Chapter 5	87
Chapter 6	91
Chapter 7	97
Chapter 8	103
Chapter 9	111
Chapter 10	121
Chapter 11	143
Chapter 12	179
Chapter 13	197
Chapter 14	205
Chapter 15	213
Chapter 16	217
Chapter 17	227
Chapter 18	235
Chapter 19	239
Chapter 20	247
Chapter 21	255
Chapter 22	283
Chapter 23	297
Chapter 24	331
Chapter 25	339

Chapter 26	347
Chapter 27	359
Chapter 28	365
Chapter 29	369
Chapter 30	379
Chapter 31	387
Chapter 32	399
Chapter 33	405
Chapter 34	421
Chapter 35	425
Chapter 36	439
Chapter 37	447
Chapter 38	455
Epilogue	467
A short story in the Undead Marine Series	477
Situational Awareness	479
Connect with J.N. Chaney	505
Connect with Jonathan P. Brazee	507
Join the Conversation	509
About the Authors	511

PART I

1

The blast shot dirt into the air, the clods pelting the team as they fell back down.

"They're trying to flush us," Sergeant Paxton Alejo, League of Humanity Marine Corps, told the Boracay militiamen under his command. "The pedes don't know where we are yet."

A wide-eyed Private Agustin Mabong stared at Pax with nervous concentration, the side of his face plastered in the dirt. The boy looked far younger than his stated seventeen years. Four weeks ago, he was a scaler in a fish factory. Now, he was a soldier tasked with holding back the Tucanan Horde as the enemy tried to take his homeworld.

With twelve years and eighteen battles under his belt, Pax knew a thing or two about warfare, and the planet Boracay was already lost. The Corps wasn't coming—there was no reason to waste valuable lives over a done deal. The only thing the militia could do was delay the Tucanans long enough so that more humans could be evacuated before the inevitable outcome.

"Are we going to die, Sergeant?" Mabong asked in a quiet squeak.

There's a good chance of that.

But he wasn't going to leave it at that. He wasn't going to lie. Things were serious, and Mabong had every right to be anxious. But as a leader, he had to give the young man hope and a reason to fight.

"Maybe. But maybe not. And hopefully not right now," Pax said. "It depends on what we do over the next few hours. I'm counting on you, son, to do your part."

He hoped that his words weren't hollow. It was asking a lot of his charges. When the planetary militia had been quickly overrun, civilians like Mabong were drafted, given a weapon, and with almost no training, were thrown into the fight.

It wasn't until Pax and the rest of the League of Humanity Marine Commandos had arrived nine days ago that they'd gotten any training, and that was out in combat where mistakes could be fatal.

Pax heard two soft beeps over his bonebud, the tiny subdermal communicators set against his temporal bone. He did a quick check and noted the number with a small sense of satisfaction. The beeps were sent by D-6, the monitor he'd set up along what he thought was the most likely enemy avenue of approach.

"The pedes are right where I told you they'd be, four hundred meters out. Get ready. Do not, I repeat, *do not*, fire until I give the signal. I want thumbs-up from everyone that you understand."

He pushed his torso off the ground and waited until each of his eleven militiamen gave him the thumbs-up.

"This ain't no thing," he said. "A simple ambush, then we pull back."

In a way, what he'd just said was true. The ambush itself *was* simple, and even with a green unit like this, they should bag some Tucanans, who the military called "pedes" after their rough resemblance to giant Earth centipedes. The retreat would be the hard part. Pax had chosen an ambush site that maximized the kill zone and a retreat that favored humans more than Tucanans, but that favoring was relative. A Tuc warrior could move quicker on its sixteen or eighteen legs than a human on their two.

"Heads down until I give the go-ahead. The pedes can spot you if you expose yourself."

Mabong's eyes got even wider. He looked like he'd burrow into the dirt if he could. The kid was frightened, as he had every right to be.

Pax took one more look at his team. No, not *his* team. Technically, it was Staff Sergeant Kraus's team. But everyone knew that he was the one in command.

I hope I've done enough.

His job was to train them to be effective fighters. He'd only had eight full days with them, but if they weren't ready, that was on him, not them.

Pax lowered his head below the lip of the little ridge that was providing them cover. He'd already woven his snake-eye along the back of one bush, leaving only the 3 mm lens exposed. The pedes could pick that up, but they'd have to be looking specifically for it. Pax was willing to take the chance.

He pulled down his goggles and slipped the male end into the jack. He could use his naked eye to look through the snake-eye, but his battle goggles' AI provided him a broader scope of data. He gave the command, and the image of the kill zone was projected onto the inside of the goggle lens.

Pax could have lowered the opacity of the projection so that he'd be able to see the real world "behind" the image, but he wanted every detail of the enemy force. And with the eleven militia, it wasn't as if anyone was going to sneak up on him.

He settled in. The Tucanans could move quickly when necessary, so they might be in the kill zone within a minute, but he was betting he had four to five minutes. While they were willing to spend lives when necessary, they still took precautions not to needlessly waste their soldiers.

Heart rate increasing ran across the bottom of his goggles.

"No shit, Sherlock," Pax muttered.

No matter how many times he'd been where the bullets were flying, adrenaline still pumped, and his heart raced. He didn't think he'd ever calmly face an engagement. Some Marines thought fighters should be calm in a battle. Pax disagreed. Adrenaline had developed to keep early humans alive. It was a survival trait. It didn't matter if the danger was a sabertoothed cat or a Tucanan soldier.

Pax took a detailed look at the kill zone, then momentarily switched his goggles to real view and checked the charge on his trident, the weapon specifically designed to kill Tucanans. The weapon was exactly what it sounded like—a trident with three forked tines, fired from a launcher, and connected to a powerpack. Once struck, the enemy soldier would receive a 330 kilojoule jolt. That would spoil any Tuc's day.

Nothing had changed in the four minutes since he'd checked the trident last. The LED was a dim green—fully charged and ready to go.

His C-12 Denon, the hypervelocity mag rifle, with its 2 millimeter flechettes, wasn't fully charged, and he'd already expended most of the heavier ARs[1], but he'd be OK for this engagement at least. And if it came down to it, he had his Hokker-2, with its big 8 mm rounds. The handgun wasn't Marine-issue. It was Caanan-made. But what good was being an LoH Marine Commando if he couldn't get foreign weapons? The Hokker was a sweet piece of gear with a powerful punch.

He shifted his attention back to the kill zone. Birds flitted in the underbrush alongside the trail, oblivious to the alien presence heading their way. The irony of "alien" wasn't lost on Pax. Boracay had been certified as fully terraformed over three hundred years before, but there was still native life hanging on. That rendered all Earth-based life as technically alien. The difference was that the Earth birds weren't trying to take over the galaxy one system at a time, like the Tucanans were.

Suddenly, the birds bolted away through the trees. Pax felt an adrenaline spike as he searched for signs of movement.

And there it was.

The point Tucanan was at third mast—two-thirds of its body was prone on the ground with the front third upright. This allowed it to move quickly but still keep a reasonably secure posture.

Tucanans were metameric, which meant they had multiple body segments, like the Earth centipedes they resembled. But the number of segments on the different types of Tucs varied, and that number could determine which type the humans were facing.

Pax counted the leg pairs as it emerged down the trail. Eight.

Scouts, then.

Which was probably good, all things considered. Aside from

---

1. **AR**: Active Rounds. Ballistic flechettes with small explosive charges that detonated upon impact.

having one fewer segment than the infantry Tucanans, they massed about twenty percent less.

The first Tuc paused a moment at the beginning of the kill zone. Rays from Boracay's sun pierced the canopy and glinted off its exoskeleton, revealing iridescent blues, greens, and purples as the light hit it right—beautiful, in its own way, that belied their deadly danger. The Tucanan raised another segment to the vertical, giving it a slightly higher viewpoint. The thing didn't have eyes in the same way that humans did, but Pax knew they were adept at their version of sight, and he was very aware of the snake-eye lens in the bush a meter over his head.

His hand shifted to the stock of his Denon mag rifle, which was the carbine version of the venerable C-8, the primary weapon for the Marines as well as half a dozen other militaries. The Tucs were vulnerable to the weapon, but only to an extent. A flechette that penetrated the body armor could "kill" that segment, and it might put the Tucanan out of action for a bit, but unless all segments, each of which had a brain node, were destroyed, the Tucanan was still alive. The trident, with its charge, was the preferred weapon, but the lead Tucanan was too far away for it to be used.

Another Tuc emerged and came alongside the first. It was a scout, too, which meant this was probably a screening force. There would be four more of them, and anywhere from five hundred meters to a klick behind would be the main body of the larger, eighteen-legged infantry soldiers.

Whatever had alerted the point must not have mattered. The Tucanan dropped back down to third-mast and started forward again, followed a moment later by the second.

With only six here, we might have a chance. But let's make sure they haven't thrown us a curveball.

A third emerged into his sight, then another three more. It looked to be a normal scout team.

Pax watched them approach and looked for any sign that the ambush had been spotted.

"Don't even breathe," he started to pass to his team, but a quick glance showed they were as still as statues and ready to engage.

Despite being about to enter combat, he had to smile with the pride of a father watching his child run out onto the football pitch for their first ever match. He hadn't had much time with them, but it seemed he'd trained them well.

Closer and closer they came. The first two were within his trident range, but the rear four hadn't fully entered the kill zone yet. Pax didn't want any survivors. He didn't need Tucanans harassing them as they retreated. And if his team had to stop and fight, that would give the infantry time to move forward and join the battle.

That would spoil Pax's day to no end.

He kept his attention on both the point and Tail End Charlie[2] as he tried to pick the optimum time to spring the ambush. He could feel his pulse increase, but mercifully, his biobot didn't scold him about it.

And then it was time.

Pax toggled the powerpack on, pushed up his goggles, and passed, "Now! Open fire!"

In one smooth move, Pax rose to a knee, raised the launcher, and fired a single trident at the third Tucanan in the column. And here was where his gambler instinct took over. He only had one

---

2. **Tail End Charlie**: The last person in a patrol, or the last ship in a line.

powerpack, and instead of letting it power the single trident, he'd decided to go for a double when he saw they were scouts.

He immediately levered the second trident into the launcher and fired at the fourth Tuc just as the first trident hit his target and stuck at the second to last segment. The soldier immediately twisted around and reached with leg-hands to yank it out—Tucanans were well aware of what a trident was.

If it managed to get it out before the charge hit, then the effort would be wasted. But a second and a half after the initial one hit, and while the first of his team started firing, the second trident struck its target, and with the connection made, the powerpack sent its charge into the enemy bodies.

If the Tucs were the larger infantry or engineers, there might not be enough power to kill two of them, but Pax thought it could take care of scouts. And he was right. Both bodies stiffened into rigid boards as the electricity poured through them for two seconds. The current quit, and the bodies tipped to the side and started to curve into the spiral that was a sure sign of a dead alien.

But Pax was only peripherally aware of that as he dropped his launcher and grabbed his Denon. Another Tuc was down, but the remaining three were charging forward, their Buzzers blazing.

Facing down the demonic apparition that was a charging Tucanan soldier could break seasoned human fighters, and this was the first time his team had seen a Tuc in the flesh. But they kept up their fire, even as the enemy scouts filled the air with their deadly 8 mm blades.

One after the other, the Tucanans quickly went down. Down, but not out. The final two continued their fire for a few moments until both collapsed.

"Cease fire!" Pax shouted.

Beside him, Mabong was flushed with excitement. "Those pedes aren't dead, Sergeant!"

"Close enough for government work, son," he said, before passing on the net, "The infantry will be on its way. Time to bug out. Reyes, you know the route."

"I think Reyes's dead, Sergeant," Dizon passed.

Shit. Do your job right.

"Give me a head count," he shouted aloud as he rushed down the line to Reyes's position.

"One!" Chua said, followed by Toledo with "Two!"

Pax barely listened as he ran up on Dizon standing over Reyes, who was most certainly dead. A single Tuc blade had hit her just above her nose. While much smaller than an actual buzzsaw, the sharpened, spinning metal projectile had destroyed most of the forebrain before passing through and coming out of the back of her skull.

The head count finished. Reyes was the only KIA, while two of the others were WIA,[3] but still combat ready.

Pax barely knew Reyes, but as always, any loss of a person in his unit was a kick in the gut. What he'd told the team about the infantry coming was true, though. He couldn't let Reyes's loss affect him now.

"Dizon, you know the way, right?"

"Yes, Gunny."

"OK, you're on point. Lead off. Everyone else, fall in behind."

He looked down at Reyes. She'd been full of vim and vigor that morning, ready to kill Tucanans. Now, her body seemed so small.

---

3. **WIA**: Wounded in Action

"Toledo," he said to the largest one of his team. "You take Reyes. But if we have to run, leave her."

"I can't leave her, Sergeant. She's my cousin."

Pax understood the big militiaman's position, and he admired what that said about Toledo's character, but as their leader, Pax's job was to get as many of them back alive as possible. He didn't have time to explain himself, so the situation called for some tough love.

Pax grabbed the big militiaman by the shoulder. "I said, you drop her. I'm not going to lose you too because the pedes caught up to us. She'd want you to leave her if that meant saving your life."

Toledo's eyes blazed, but he bit his tongue. Pax knew he'd have to keep an eye on him if it came to it.

He took one last look at the ambush site. At least two, maybe four, of the Tucanan soldiers could still be alive. But there was no time to destroy each of the segments, and he wasn't going to waste his last powerpack and trident on an incapacitated scout.

If the gods of war had told him before the ambush that they'd drop six Tucanans with only one KIA, he'd have gladly accepted that. The mission had been a success.

This fight was over. Now it was time to beat feet and move onto the next one. Pax fell into his position as the team moved out.

2

"I don't think they're still following," Pax said as he scrolled through the readouts of his goggles.

"Can we trust that?" Staff Sergeant Kraus asked. "You said the pedes can knock down your drones."

Kraus didn't have any military experience. He was assigned his rank solely because of his advanced age of twenty-seven.

"Yes, I did. But the skeeter's still up there a klick behind us, and it's picked up no sign of them."

"But couldn't they be, you know, messing with us? Not shooting down your drone just to make us think they weren't after us?"

Pax flipped up his goggles. He could have just run the shield to transparent to look at Kraus, but he wanted him to see his eyes.

Yes, the Tucanans were not above a little subterfuge, but Pax's gut said this wasn't the case. The infantry had barely hesitated as they reached the ambush site before pushing on. It had all the makings of a priority target for them—probably Puerto Princesa, if he had to guess, which would take this group out of their AO.[1]

And if they had broken off a unit to chase them, then as long as the skeeter was up there and communicating with him, they had a klick cushion.

All eyes were on him, awaiting his response. They were exhausted, he could tell. Half of them were breathing hard, and sweat streaked down their faces and stained their fatigues. Only Toledo, who refused to let anyone else help with Reyes, looked adequately refreshed.

They'd only marched eight klicks so far. He'd pushed them hard, he had to admit, but not *that* hard. Any Marine could have done it without too much of an effort. But he had to remind himself that these weren't Marines. Four weeks ago, they'd been soft civilians. Now, they'd been pressed into service with essentially no training other than the on-the-job-training Pax had been able to pound into their heads since he arrived a week ago.

He knew he could push them for a while further, but that risked a complete collapse.

"If this is a trick, we still have a cushion. I think we can afford to take a fifteen-minute break."

There were sighs of relief, and several of them started to drop their gear.

"Combat ready," Pax said. "If the enemy is messing with us, we'll need to move out immediately. Keep your gear on and spread out like I taught you. Weapons outboard."

He watched to make sure they complied, then said, "Everyone drink and eat one combat ration. You'll need the energy."

---

1. **AO**: Area of Operations

There were some grimaces at that, and Pax suppressed a smile. Gone were the exclamations of "These aren't so bad" when they'd first sampled the Fordyce rations. Now, six days later, they were sick of the nutritious, if bitter meal.

Pax sat on a rock at their six o'clock so he could keep watch to their rear. He didn't expect anything, but complacency had probably killed more soldiers over the millennia than anything else. He pulled out one of his own rations, popped the end of the tube, and sucked in the paste. He'd long ago gotten used to their weirdly sour and slightly bitter aftertaste. Give him his old San Marcos Marine rats any day.

Unfortunately, Fordyce was the main supplier of combat rats to the LoH Marine Corps, and he didn't know if that was going to change anytime soon, no matter how many Marines complained about them.

He was very aware of the bag of sour pusses in his right cargo pocket. They might as well be burning a hole in his thigh. He was tempted, to be sure, but there were only four of the candies left, and once they were gone, that was it until he got off this planet. With a sigh, he tried to put them out of his mind.

Pax gave Toledo a sidewise glance. He hadn't wanted to force the issue with the young man, but the Militiaman seemed OK at the moment.

I'd better talk to him before we move out, though, and see where his head's at.

Dealing with civilians was difficult. It wasn't their fault, of course. They'd been yanked from comfortable lives, given a weapon, and told to go fight. The fact that they were still here with him was a testament to their fortitude. But it was also a fact that without the months of training that Marines received, more of them were bound to pay the ultimate price, and Pax hated that, just like he hated these missions.

This was the fourth battle where he'd been a member of a civilian contact team sent in after a Tucanan invasion with the mission to try and rally the local defenses to buy time for a major Navy-Marine Corps counterattack. And it looked like it was going to be the fourth time they'd lost the planet.

Even with planets that had a standing army, it was an almost impossible task for them to stop a Tucanan invasion. It took time for the League of Humanity to send in a task force, and the Tucs didn't dally. They were aggressive and quick, taking over planets in weeks, not months, and preparing defenses that rendered their positions too costly for a counterattack.

As a member of the First Marine Commando Brigade, Pax was one of the elite of the elite, trained to take the fight to the enemy and prepare the way for the main fleet. The Commandos were also the unit trained to penetrate Tuc defenses and make planetfall, so they had the civil contact mission as well. Pax understood the reasoning, but that didn't mean he had to like it, and he took every life lost as a dagger to his heart.

"Think they'll come, Sergeant?" Mabong asked, interrupting Pax's thoughts.

Pax squeezed the last of the paste into his mouth, then took a swallow of water before answering.

"This pod? No, I don't. But we'll meet some others. You can count on that."

The private seemed like he was going to ask something else, but with a slight shake of the head, he went back to the tube that he was slowly consuming.

After a moment, Pax said, "Like a bandage, Mabong."

"Sergeant? A bandage?"

"You keep playing with that tube like that and you'll never get it down. You've got to treat it like a bandage. Just tear it off. Or in this case, suck all of that gunk down. It'll only taste bad for a moment."

He looked back down the trail they'd made, so he couldn't see if Mabong complied, but after a moment, he heard a gasp, then the private sucking in air. Facing away from him, Pax didn't think the militiaman could see him smile.

Mabong sucked noisily at his water, but evidently, he wasn't through.

"Can I ask you a personal question, Sergeant?"

Pax really didn't want to get into his personal life. He'd rather forget everything before he enlisted, and since then, what mattered was being a Marine—first, a San Marcos Marine, and then seven years later, the LoH Marines after the Tucanans invaded and the League of Humanity was formed, absorbing most of humanity's standing armies.

At least Pax went from one Marine Corps to the other, so he could pretend there wasn't a difference. He'd have hated becoming a soldier or some other military type, even if the only difference was a title.

He wasn't going to reply to Mabong, and the private evidently realized that because he didn't repeat the question.

But then, for reasons he didn't understand, Pax said, "Go ahead, son. Ask."

"Well, um . . . it's . . . I mean, when we left Blue Creek, that other sergeant . . . he told his team that you were Sergeant Quad Bod. What does that mean?"

Pax gave a small snort. That wasn't the question he'd expected.

He felt more than heard the rest of the team turning toward him to hear the answer.

"Eyes outboard. The pedes are out there, not in here."

He heard the rustling as the militiamen faced outboard again. He knew, though, that their attention was still locked on what he was going to say.

"It's just a nickname."

"But what does it mean, Sergeant?"

"Damn, Mabong. You don't give up easily, do you?"

"Sorry. We're all just curious."

"And yet you're the one asking."

He paused a moment, then asked, "You've heard of the Marine Raiders, right?"

"Uh . . . no?"

What the hell? Never heard of the Raiders?

"Marine Commandos?"

Blank faces.

"Well, what about the SEALs?"

There was an excited murmur, then Mabong said, "Oh, yeah. We know about the Royal Charter SEALs. They were in *Point of the Spear*."

Pax rolled his eyes. Of course, they know about the Royal Charter SEALs, what with their publicity team going all out. They weren't even the premier SEAL force, but they had the best PR team.

He was used to the SEALs getting the attention, even if it was a burr under his saddle.

"That holovid was pure crap," he muttered. "It wasn't all true."

Come on, Pax. Don't demean the SEALs. You know better than most how capable they are.

"They're good. But Marine spec-ops are better. Especially San Marcos Marine Raiders."

That part was chest thumping, he knew, but he still had the SMMC—for the "San Marcos Marine Corps"— tattoo on his right arm. In truth, the five main Marine Corps all sent their special ops—Recon, Raiders, or Commandos—to REC, the Reconnaissance Evaluation Course on Nicholson, and now the LoH Marines did, too, combining all the various graduates as Marine Commandos. Pax still thought of himself as a Raider, despite the official Commando title in the LoH Marines.

He could almost hear the doubt in Mabong.

"But your nickname," Mabong insisted.

"Before the pedes came, I graduated from both REC and BUD/S.[2] Uh, REC is Reconnaissance Evaluation Course, the school for Marine spec-op forces, and BUD/S, the Basic Underwater Demolition School, is for the Imperial and Terran Union SEALs. Less than twelve percent make it through BUD/S, and fourteen percent through REC," Pax said with an unmistakable sense of pride in his voice.

"So, you're 'Quad Bod' 'cause you went through the two courses? Doesn't 'quad' mean four."

This guy's quicker on the uptake than I thought.

"You've heard of the Varangian Brigade, right?"

Crickets.

Sometimes it still surprised Pax how little the civilian population knew about the military. But then again, he'd never heard of these units before he'd enlisted, so why should they have?

---

2. **BUD/S**: Basic Underwater Demolition School, taken from the name of the Twentieth Century school for US Navy SEALs.

"The Varangian Brigade. Elite arctic shock troops for Uusi Turku's Army? The school is nine months in extreme conditions."

"You went through?"

Pax couldn't suppress a shudder. The school was as tough as REC, but while he thought he'd been cold at BUD/S back on Earth, that was nothing to how it had been at SSSC.[3] Of the four elite schools he'd graduated from, the Triple SC had been where he'd come the closest to quitting. He swore he could still feel the ice in his bones.

"After the NH Marines were formed, some of us went through other elite screening courses for cross-training. I went to Triple SC. And before you ask, yes, that's only three. But then, before I got back to the fleet, I was chosen to attend the SAS Selection Course."

Pax had been pretty proud of that. Very few Marine NCOs were sent to the course, and he knew he'd been selected because with three other elite courses under his belt, they were confident that he would make it through and not embarrass the Corps.

"SAS. I've heard of them," Correra said.

"I don't get it," Toledo said. "There're all these different super troopers? I thought that with the pedes, there're just the LoH Navy and Marines."

Pax gave a wry laugh. "Not hardly. The LoH Marines are only seven years old. We don't have the boot camps and all of the schools for that. So each government runs their draft and puts recruits through their own form of basic training and into their military specialties. That includes some of the spec-ops like

---

3. **SSSC**: Sissi Screening Course. The Sissi Brigade is the official name of the Varangian Brigade.

Raiders and SEALs. They'll hold back no more than twenty percent to keep the pipeline running. The rest are sent on to the LoH Marine Commandos. Two months of integration, then it's off to the fleet."

"I think I read that," Staff Sergeant Kraus said. "I guess no local government wants to give up all their militaries."

Another one who understands political realities. These guys might not be skilled soldiers, but that doesn't mean they're clueless about everything else.

For all the kumbaya and "we're all in this together," humankind was often at war with itself, and the various governments did not want to be caught without a strong military if and when the war with the Tucanans was over.

"You said all of you foreign soldiers got put into the LoH Marines . . ." Toledo started to say.

Pax automatically bristled at "soldiers." He was a Marine. But there were soldiers and Legionnaires who'd been absorbed into the Marines, and he let it slide.

". . . but didn't you say you were all San Marcos Marines when you first came?"

"OK, I probably said that. Technically, we're LoH Marines. But for special ops and some other branches, we tend to be grouped together by our parent units. Our brigade's mostly from San Marcos." He paused for a moment before adding, "That's beginning to change more now, though."

Which wasn't something Pax liked. He'd been with other services, mostly at his four schools, and he strongly preferred being in an all San Marcos unit.

"So, you made it through all four. That's what Quad Bod means," Mabong said, bringing it back to the original question with the tenacity of a terrier. "How many other quad bods are there?"

"Eleven, at least the last I knew," Pax said. "Five of us have the same four as I do."

"Is there a five bod?" came from Mabong at the same time that Kraus asked, "What other courses qualify?"

"There's one Penta Pope. A SagFed captain. And there're two more courses that qualify."

Pax had dreams of going through those two—the Geomeun Beremo of the Hangul Republic Army and the San Zhi Zhu Dragons Den—as well, but with the ongoing war, he wasn't sure he'd ever get the chance.

"So, you're kinda special?" Toledo asked.

Pax couldn't tell if the militiaman was being sarcastic or not, so he chose to ignore the question.

"You can't keep asking me questions to rest longer. One minute, and we're moving out. Form up."

There were a few groans, but his team got ready.

As they moved out, Pax could swear he could feel a soft warm glow emanating from the four pips tattooed in a line just under the SMMC on his upper arm.

3

"New mission," Pax told his team.

"I thought we were evacuating," Staff Sergeant Kraus said.

He looked around as if he could see Tucanan soldiers coming out of the trees.

"Hopefully, we still are. But we've got something to do before that."

The team was exhausted. The planetary defense was collapsing, and no one was coming to the rescue. Facing the hard reality, the general evacuation order had been given. All military forces were to return to their assigned evacuation points.

Pax didn't know how much of the civilian population had made it off the planet. With a pre-invasion population of over eighty million, that would be a logistical nightmare even without an invasion to contend with. It had been twenty-nine days since the Tucanan Army made planetfall, and nine days since Pax and the rest of the Raiders/Commandos had landed. Unless there had been a massive number of ships in the area that he hadn't been briefed about, there would still be large numbers of survivors scattered around the planet.

This is what he hated. Four civilian contact missions, four times retreating from the planet in defeat, four times leaving behind fellow humans to their fate. Pax was a Marine. They took the fight to the enemy and drank mead from their skulls. They didn't run away and abandon those they were supposed to protect.

But as humanity struggled against their tenacious enemy, seasoned military personnel—even lightly trained militias and planetary armies—were more valuable than civilian refugees. They wanted to evacuate the Raiders and other forces to live and fight another day.

Way back in the Twentieth Century under the old year system, during WWII, the Japanese had a small core of highly trained pilots who had initial success during the war. But as more and more of them were shot down, the training pipeline couldn't keep up. The Japanese production of airplanes continued, but there was a lack of pilots to fly them. In the final stages of the war, some pilots went into combat with only a few hours of stick time.

In a way, Pax's group of militiamen were the Japanese pilots of their time. They had the weapons, but not the training. They were being thrown into combat with the equivalent of a few hours of stick time.

Modern military planners took that long ago lesson from Imperial Japan to heart. Pax and the others were highly trained and experienced fighters skilled at their jobs. According to those in charge, they were worth more than the average civilian—or barely trained militiamen.

The concept stuck in his craw. That wasn't the case when he first enlisted. They served the civilians, those who couldn't defend themselves. But the Tucs changed the calculations. And a Marine obeyed orders. As much as it bothered him, he'd take his team to their evacuation point and board the shuttles, all while trying to put his imagined screams of the Boracayans left behind to their fate.

To the LoH, it was a matter of numbers, but to Pax, each of those numbers was a person, someone with a family, with dreams and aspirations.

"It looks like the pedes are setting something up about five klicks from our LZ. Intel thinks it's got antiair capabilities."

"And we've got to take it out?" Kraus asked.

"It's closest to our extraction point. Who else is going to be given the mission, Sergeant?"

Kraus frowned. "We're the only ones using this LZ?"

"The only military. The location had been previously disseminated, so there could be some civilians heading there hoping for a lift off the planet."

"Wait a minute, Sergeant Pax," Mabong said. "They sent the location out earlier? I mean to everyone? Won't the pedes know where it is then?"

They already know, or they wouldn't have set up along the most probable approach for our shuttle.

"Well, if that antiair asset is any indication, yeah, then maybe they know. All the more reason for us to take them out before our ride gets here."

He paused for a moment to let that sink in before continuing. "We don't have much time. Maybe ninety minutes, so we've got to get moving. Dizon, you've still got point. Coordinates are eight-six-eight-four, two-nine-three-six. That's just under four klicks.

"I know we never specifically rehearsed this type of mission, but it's an assault when you boil it down. Nothing more. Give me ten minutes to come up with something as we march, and I'll let you know what to do."

He nodded to Dizon. "Head on out."

It was easy to just say he was going to come up with something. With almost any military, he could pull out SOPs for the mission and adjust to the enemy situation and terrain. But his team? They just didn't have any experience.

These are the cards you've been dealt, Pax, so just get it done.

SEVENTY-TWO MINUTES LATER, the team was prone on the ground some 130 meters from their objective. Pax studied it the best he could through his snake-eye. It was an AA-33, code-named "Wanda." The weapon had the capability to shoot down a Navy fighter, much less a shuttle. They could be spoofed, but that was nowhere near a sure thing, and Pax didn't want to be at the mercy of the type and capabilities of whatever shuttle was coming to pick them up.

There were six tech Tucanans frantically working to get the Wanda assembled. Slightly shorter than the soldiers, their wider segments and longer foot-arms identified them.

It looked like a platoon of soldier Tucs were setting up in a tight security perimeter around the Wanda.

Pax was familiar with both of these types. He'd seen four of the many forms of Tucs during the war so far. What freaked him out more than a bit was that the xenobiologists had analyzed at least nine types of them. But that wasn't exactly correct. From a biological standpoint, there was only one type. That was clear from their convoluted version of DNA. Yet somehow, they manifested themselves in the nine forms. More, if the rumor mill had any truth to it.

The enemy had come from the direction of the Tucana Dwarf Galaxy eight years ago, intent on conquest. Enough of them had been taken, both dead and alive, to create an entire xenobiology industry. And while much about them was known, there was still more to be learned about their different forms and life cycles.

The biology of the enemy didn't matter now, though. The platoon of soldiers around the Wanda was his main concern. Even a squad of seasoned Marine infantry would have a difficult time with the Tucanan platoon. His militia wouldn't stand a chance. And that didn't even take into account the six techs. They might not be soldiers, but they'd fight if they had to.

And what that meant to Pax was that he'd have to trash the plan he'd come up with during the movement to contact. They'd be cut down before anyone could place the mini-magna incendiary grenades on the weapons system.

Pax thought there was about an even chance that he could infiltrate close enough to throw the grenades. He'd gone through the San Marcos Marines' Scout Sniper School, and he was quite skilled at infiltration, if he did say so himself. But that would take hours of painstaking movement—hours he didn't have.

If there was a full task force on the planet, he'd have numerous options, from arty to missile batteries to orbital fire. The problem was that he had to knock out the Wanda with what he had.

He pulled back from his snake-eye and set his goggles in place.

"Give me the Wanda schematics," he subvocalized.

Immediately, a line drawing of the antiaircraft system was projected onto the lenses.

"Vulnerabilities and potential weapons."

Arrows pointed at various spots of the schematic, highlighting areas of greater vulnerability. Above each spot was a list of Navy and Marine Corps weapons with the probability of a kill for each one targeting that spot.

Pax could barely make sense of all the data. He certainly didn't need to know that a *Kitan*-Class Heavy Cruiser's ten petajoule main gun had an almost one hundred percent projected kill rate against the Wanda, seeing there wasn't a *Kitan* anywhere near the system.

"Limit to light ground weapons."

Eighty percent of the weapons listed disappeared. It didn't make much of a real difference, though. He didn't have an M-303 launcher. Or a Hawkeye. Or a T-43-Bravo. He did have the mini-magnas, which had a ninety-two percent probability of a kill. That had been his original plan. But he couldn't get close enough to emplace the grenades with that platoon in security.

A thought hit him, and he flipped up his goggles and pulled out his trident launcher. But after a quick examination, he realized that was a dead end. There was no way he could adapt either the launcher or the mini-mag to marry the two together.

Back to the goggles. He zeroed in on each arrow and list of weapons, then eliminated one after the other. A VWA-2 would work, but he'd already expended the three he had.

He made his way around the Wanda schematic when he saw a potential solution.

Pax pushed up the goggles again and turned to Toledo.

"Do you have that tube rocket you showed me?"

The militiaman patted his cargo pocket.

"You said it's a fifty millimeter?"

Toledo nodded.

He went back to his goggles for a moment. The Boracay rocket was homemade, something put together from odds and ends. The Marine Corps had a fifty-millimeter rocket, the PR-443 Saber. It was much higher tech and had limited terminal guidance, and more importantly, his battlebot gave the Saber anywhere from a sixty-two to a seventy-nine percent probability of a kill when targeting any of four points along the Wanda.

He tried to get the probability of a kill if they used the Boracay rocket, but his battlebot didn't have the data on it. But while the homemade weapon was far more primitive, he figured a warhead was a warhead.

Time was ticking, and he had to make a decision. The cobbled-together rocket was his best bet. And if it failed, well, he had one last ditch plan that he didn't want to implement.

"Are you good with that thing?" he asked.

"Reyes was better."

Pax wanted to snap out that Reyes was dead, but he bit his tongue.

"Are you the best one with that?"

"I am," Mabong said.

Once again, Pax was surprised by the young militiaman. He looked at the rest of them, but no one took issue with the private's claim.

"OK, get it from Toledo and come here. Keep your head down."

Mabong crawled to the bigger militiaman, who handed him the rocket, which didn't look like any Marine Corps weapon Pax had seen. It was a simple tube, like the one Christmas present wrapping paper came on. There were two wires running along the length that were taped into place. Staff Sergeant Kraus had assured him that the rocket inside the tube, which started life as fireworks, would fire, and that the jury-rigged warheads they had ginned up had detonated during testing.

The private, belly in the dirt, squirmed up to Pax with an eager smile on his face. The fear from before the ambush was gone.

The kid's enjoying this, he realized.

There might have been a time, long ago, when he was excited about the prospect of action. But he'd seen too many battles and lost too many friends since then. His adrenaline might still flow, but it wasn't really enjoyment, per se.

He handed Mabong the eyepiece of the snake-eye.

"The Wanda is up ahead, a hundred and thirty meters out. Can you hit it?"

The private started to raise his body, and Pax had to pull him back down.

"The snake-eye is so you don't have to expose yourself. Don't blow it."

Mabong looked suitably chagrined. Keeping as low as possible to remain in defilade, he peered through the optical device.

"The best chance for a kill is at the power box. That's the round protrusion about a meter off the ground and to the back."

Mabong studied it for a moment before turning away from the eyepiece and looking at Pax.

"That's a pretty long shot. The most we did back at the camp, before you came, was a hundred meters."

"What're your chances, son? This is important."

The private shrugged. "Thirty percent?"

Shit. I was hoping for better.

"If I can get closer, like farther up this wash, I'm sure I can hit it."

"Farther up, the wash gets shallower. No more cover."

"I only need to get to a hundred meters. I know how far the rocket drops at that range. I can hit it."

Pax took the snake-eye again, and this time, he angled the lens to look at the ground ahead of them. Even as small as Mabong was, he'd have cover for only ten or fifteen meters at most. Then he'd be exposed.

Still . . .

"Can you get yourself forward? There's a tree at the edge of the wash that's about a hundred meters from the Buzzer. But the last ten meters are in the open."

Mabong didn't hesitate. "Yes, Sergeant Quad Bod. I can do it."

Pax gave a sharp, if quiet laugh at his nickname, then cut it off.

Tucanans didn't have ears. They "heard" through thousands of thin, short hairs, almost indivisible, that emerged from their shells. And at short ranges, they could use these hairs to pinpoint a noise source. While this created excellent short-range hearing, their range wasn't as good as humans', especially in the lower registers. At 100 meters, though, that was within their "excellent" range, and he didn't need to give them a chance to zero in on him.

"We'll cover you. You get up there, fire, then hightail it back."

Pax took a moment to pass the word to the others. They'd let Mabong edge forward until he ran out of the wash. On command, the rest would rise up and fire upon the Tucanans. Mabong would let loose with the rocket, and the team would perform an immediate and hasty retreat as the Tuc soldiers would undoubtedly give chase.

"And if he doesn't take out the Wanda?" Kraus asked.

"You get the team to the LZ as fast as you can," Pax said.

"But what about you . . ." the staff sergeant started to ask before understanding dawned on him.

Pax nodded. If the rocket didn't work, enough of the soldiers leaving their perimeter to chase the team might leave an opening for Pax to get in close. The techs would stay with their weapon, and they weren't pushovers. But they were *on* the Wanda, whereas the soldiers were out on a perimeter twenty-five or thirty meters from the weapon. That difference might just be enough of an advantage to let him get close enough to throw his grenades. All he needed was one not to bounce off and instead ignite on the weapon.

Pax gave his last-minute orders, then looked at Mabong.

"You ready?"

The young man was gripping and releasing the rocket tube, his pulse clearly visible on his neck as his heart pounded.

Pax reached out and grabbed the private's shoulder.

"Calm down. Do you know what buck fever is?"

Mabong shook his head.

"You might have been good with that thing back in the rear on whatever range you created. But there was no one shooting back at you. This is different. I can see that your heart is racing, and that can pull you off target."

Mabong grimaced, but he didn't say anything.

"Slowly count from ten to one, taking a deep breath at each number. Go ahead, son. Do it," he said, keeping his own voice calm.

His adrenaline was surging, but having been in more than a few battles, he'd had many more years' practice controlling that.

He watched as Mabong started counting. Time was slipping away, and a side of Pax wanted to urge the private to hurry, but he knew this had to be done if they had any chance of hitting the Wanda.

Mabong got to the end, and Pax asked him, "You ready?"

The young man's face was still flushed, but he looked calmer, and he nodded.

Pax stared at him for a moment. The pulse in his neck was still there, even if not as pronounced. The kid wasn't as calm as Pax would have liked, and for a moment, he considered taking the rocket and firing it himself.

He quickly dismissed that. He'd never fired one, and with Mabong mentioning the drop, this was something that needed practice to be any good with it.

"Get ready," he told the rest of the team.

The line of militiamen tensed as they prepared. In a moment, they were going to stand and expose themselves to the Tucanan soldiers. There was a very good chance that some of them would be killed. Yet he saw no hesitation.

They might not be trained Marines, but there was nothing wrong with their hearts. Pax was hit by a sense of pride that he was leading them.

"On three. One . . . two . . . THREE!"

Pax rose and then immediately engaged the peripheral soldiers, knowing that in the heat of the engagement, his militiamen would be targeting the closest soldier to them. He scored a direct hit on the fourth or fifth segment of the soldier on the Ballista, the Tucanan version of a heavy machine gun. It wasn't dead, but it was out of action for the moment, and that was what Pax wanted.

A split second later, the Tucs started returning fire. The soldiers were not in the "one shot, one kill" school of military. They swept their rifles across their fields of fire, using them almost as long-distance swords.

In his peripheral vision, he saw the trees getting chewed up in a line reaching to him. Pax waited until the last second before dropping to the ground as the sweep of Buzzer blades zipped just over his head.

It was a deadly version of old-time matadors timing the rush of the bull, and this wasn't the first bullfight. Marines trained in simulators to practice the timing. But all it took was one miscalculation.

Dizon never had that training. The Tucanan rounds hit him high in the chest, pulverizing flesh and bone.

Pax stood back up and shifted his aim. When under fire, the Tucs tended to lower most of their body segments to the ground. At only twenty-five to thirty centimeters in girth, that meant they presented fairly small targets, about the same as a prone human. But they liked to use their second segment to fire their weapons, so their heads and at least two segments were usually upright, giving the humans more area to target. Pax aimed at another and hit it at least four times before one of his ER flechettes blew off a foot-arm.

The Tuc recovered, lifted another segment off the ground, and picked up its Buzzer with the next foot-arm. Pax shifted his aim and squeezed off a single shot that hit the soldier square in the tiny head. The upper three segments fell over backward while its remaining foot-arms flailed. A head shot wasn't a kill shot. The brain nodes were distributed to all segments. But the thing was now blind, essentially out of the fight.

A three-beep alert sounded in his bonebud, and a small yellow triangle appeared in the upper right corner of his goggles. Pax couldn't afford the time it would take to pull up the details, but between the two alarms, he knew his battlebot had detected an energy weapon powering up.

The Tucanans had the same issue with energy cannons on the ground as humans did. The man-packed cannons fired beams that were quickly dissipated by air, dust, smoke, or even foliage. But his team was only 130 meters away, and the Tucanans had several that would be deadly at that range.

"Hurry, Mabong," he shouted to the still-crawling militiaman.

The private was not even halfway. He gathered his legs under him, stood, and sprinted to the tree, then he dropped to the ground, his back up against the trunk where he sat, his chest heaving.

"No time, Mabong. Fire!"

The militiaman stood, using the tree trunk as cover, then spun around, with just his head, right shoulder and arm, and rocket exposed. Pax thought he was going to snap off a shot, which would probably miss. But Mabong leaned up against the tree, using it to steady his rocket, took three deep breaths, then triggered the home-made weapon.

This was no hyper-velocity Marine ordnance. Pax's heart sunk as the rocket rainbowed up in the air, so slow that he could watch its agonizing arc. It was going to miss, flying over the Wanda.

Shit!

But over the last ten meters, it was almost as if the rocket dropped out of the sky. It fell . . . and impacted on the top of the protrusion. There was a surprisingly large explosion. Pax held his breath for a second, but when the smoke cleared, there was a significant hole in the side of the Buzzer.

Most of the weapon was intact, the missiles still live, but Pax knew it was dead. It couldn't fire again until the power source was replaced.

Rounds whizzed by his head, yanking Pax back to their reality. The Wanda might be out of action, but there were still now-angry Tucanans trying to kill them.

Tucanan SOP was for the nearest soldiers to fix the human attackers in place while the others maneuvered to flank them. And Pax could see movement to their right side. It was time to bolt.

"Cease fire!" he shouted. "Retreat!"

For the first time since the fight kicked off, he glanced along the line. Five were down. He could see Kraus helping Fuma to her feet, but with the other four, it looked permanent.

"Pull back to the RP,[1] now!" he shouted.

Staff Sergeant Kraus turned from Fuma toward Pax, looking like he was going to argue, when the side of his head exploded into a red mist. His body fell over onto Fuma, who pulled away in horror.

"I said now!" Pax shouted.

Mabong rushed past him, encouraging everyone to move it, and the dam broke. Some dragged bodies, and Mabong helped Fuma as they started a mass rush to the rear.

Pax took a moment to report to command that the Wanda was out. That would free their ride to descend to the LZ.

Even if they were retreating, the militiamen were still in the Tucs' sight, and Yolo took only two steps before he spun around, blood arcing away from his upper arm. But he jumped back up and kept running.

---

1. **RP**: Rally Point. A location with cover and/or concealment where Marines can reform and move out from after an engagement.

Pax took partial cover behind a substantial tree, and, ignoring the base of fire, started firing his Hokker at the enveloping force. The range was pretty far for the handgun, but the heavier round could penetrate through the brush and trees better than his flechettes. He'd love to drop a couple of them, but his intent was to slow them down.

With his team rushing out of sight, that left Pax as the most obvious target. Enemy rounds started chewing up his tree, and he half expected the energy cannon to fire, but with his right hand on the Hokker firing at the flanking Tucanans, he raised his Denon with his left hand and around the tree to fire blindly at the fixing force.

A blast knocked a heavy branch free. It fell, hitting his head and right shoulder. He dropped the Hokker under the force of the blow. A few centimeters to the left, and he could have been knocked out. Regardless, it was the reminder that he wasn't superman, and he needed to go.

He swept up the Hokker, bent low, and sprinted to the rear. He was hit twice, his body armor hardening to take the blow, before he was down the far side of the wash enough to be back in defilade. Then he broke into an all-out sprint.

RPs were usually well back from hostilities, but Pax just needed a spot for a quick head count and reorganization for the retreat. He'd selected a hollow they'd passed two hundred meters back, mostly surrounded by bamboo.

Bamboo was ubiquitous and used often and early during terraforming. It was a recon Marine's friend. A dense grove could provide visual and audible screening, and it could help block energy weapons and small arms, at least for a while.

Pax caught up with the last of his team, Mabong and Fuma, as they entered the hollow. It was a little tighter getting in than it had looked when they passed it, and the ground was marshy. Their feet sank in six or seven centimeters.

Seven sets of eyes locked onto him as they waited for him to tell them what to do. The mission had been a success, despite the cost, and he could see their confidence in him. He wasn't going to stomp that out, but the fact was that they were in a shit sandwich. If the Tucs decided to pursue them to the end, they had little chance of surviving long enough to catch their lift off the planet.

If they had any chance, they needed to move now.

It took him only a few seconds to assess the dead and wounded. Kraus had joined Reyes as a hard KIA, as had Manug. Pandora was a soft KIA—an SKIA. Dizon was still alive but barely hanging on and probably wouldn't survive the trek.

Yolo's arm was gone below the elbow.

"You hanging in there?" he asked.

The militiaman gave his arm a dismissive glance. "I know I should be freaked out, but I'm actually OK."

That's what drugs will do for you.

The moment his arm was shot off, his medbot would have poured anti-shock nanobots through his system.

"You two," he told Yolo and Fuma. "You're just going to have to keep up."

Then to the others, he said, "We all have the coordinates for the LZ. We need to move now. If we get hit and I say scatter, do that and make your way however you can."

Pax hated the idea of splitting up his small force, but if it got to that, they couldn't make a stand. By scattering, maybe some of them could make it.

"Leave Kraus, Manug, and Reyes. Toledo, you take Dizon—"

"No! I'm not leaving Lia!"

It had already been thirty seconds, and Pax didn't have time for this again. For the good of the team, he had to take tough action.

He splashed to the big militiaman, yanked Reyes's body off his shoulders, and put her on the ground. Toledo's eyes widened in shock, then anger before Pax grabbed him by the collar and yanked him until their faces were millimeters apart.

"You *will* take Dizon. Reyes is dead," he said, his voice as sharp as steel.

Toledo tried to pull back, but Pax was far stronger than he looked, and he had the younger man in a death grip.

"She's not dead, not until the brain cells deteriorate!" he said in a whine, anger suddenly gone.

Pax let up on his grip a bit, and in a slightly softer voice, said, "It's already been too long, and her injuries are too severe. She's gone. But Dizon's still alive. Are you going to kill him just to keep your cousin's body?"

Pax was aware of the others staring at them in silence, and he was tempted to slap some sense into Toledo, but he needed the big man's cooperation.

"Are you killing Dizon?" he asked again.

Toledo broke, and his shoulders slumped. He didn't say anything, but he nodded and stepped over to where Dizon was sitting in the water.

Pax looked around. Other than Toledo, he wasn't sure if any of the rest had the ability to carry Pandora.

"I'll take Pandora," he said.

He was their commander and best fighter, and he shouldn't be burdened with a body. But if the SKIA militiaman was going to have a chance, it would have to be him. And Pax was hardened enough to death that if the Tucanans reached them, he could drop Pandora and fight, as cold as that sounded.

"We've been here too long. The pedes will be on our asses. Timbol, lead off, and everyone, keep it up as fast as you can."

Before Pax picked up Pandora, he reached into his thigh magazine and pulled out three MP-9s. The small mines had a powerful blast, enough to take out a Tuc soldier or two. Normally, he'd carefully emplace them, but there was no time. With the standing water, though, maybe he wouldn't have to. He set them to arm in twenty seconds after being emplaced, then picked up Pandora and slung her over his left shoulder. With his right hand, he tossed the first mine, then marched off. He dropped the next two while still in the bamboo, before stepping out on the other side.

Now it was a race.

Given the terrain between them and the LZ, Pax thought that if it were just him, then he could beat them to it, maybe with enough cushion to load the shuttle and have it take off. But it wasn't just him. There were seven militiamen, three seriously wounded, and one SKIA. No matter how he twisted the situation in his mind, he couldn't see how they'd make the pickup without a fight. At least not all of them.

It was possible that they wouldn't pursue them. But these Tucanans were different. *They* were the Tucanans' mission. Pax knew they'd be coming.

As if on cue, there was a muffled explosion behind him. Part of him wanted to gloat that his little present had made its presence known, but it was also confirmation that they were coming. The mine might delay the Tucanans a bit, but not much. Pax listened with half an ear as he pushed forward.

"Come on, Fuma. You've got to keep going. The pedes are coming."

She grunted and tried to speed up with Mabong supporting her right side.

A second blast sounded behind him, and Pax could help but smile.

Marines would almost never follow a target's trail precisely because someone might do what Pax had done and mine it. The Tucanans, for as similar as their military tactics were to humans', could often be caught doing it.

He listened for a third blast, but it never came. That wasn't surprising. They weren't that dumb. Frankly, Pax was pleased to get two detonations. He'd taken out a few Tucanans, and he'd bought them a little more time.

He was tempted to fly his last skeeter, but he knew he might need it later. Instead, he forged on, urging Mabong and Fuma while listening for sounds of pursuit.

Pax was fitter than most people, but carrying a limp body was more difficult than carrying a pack of the same weight. His shoulder started to ache, and he shifted Pandora to the other. He had flashbacks to SAS screening and climbing Pen Y Fan during the Fan Dance as he concentrated on putting one foot in front of the other. They covered a klick, then two, before the indirect rounds started impacting. Under the cover of the trees, the Tucanans didn't know exactly where they were, but they could guess.

Several of the rounds came close, but not enough to hit them. And if the Tucs thought that would slow them down, they had the opposite effect. The humans had been slowing down, but each arty round spurred the militiamen forward.

"Charlie-Eight, this is Evac-Six," came over his bonebud. "Confirm that the antiair is out."

I reported it already.

But he could understand the pilot wanting to make sure.

"Roger that. What's your ETA?"

"Good to hear that. ETA is fourteen minutes, twenty seconds. What's the load?"

"Ten and an SKIA. And we've got a platoon of pedes on our asses."

"Let's make it quick, then. In and out before they get there."

"Roger that. Looking forward to seeing you."

Fourteen minutes was pushing it considering their condition. It was doable, but the longer it took, the more likely that the Tucanans would reach them before they could take off.

He was about to relay the information to his team, when someone shouted, "Contact front!" which was followed by both the sound of firing, and a moment later screams.

"Cease fire! Cease fucking fire!"

He sprinted to the front with Pandora's body bouncing on his shoulder.

Another C-8 joined in before everyone else repeated the cease fire call. A moment later, one, then the other weapon stopped.

"Hear the screams?" he shouted at Timbol. "They're humans!"

The point man's eyes got round, and his mouth dropped open. "But . . . I thought . . ."

Pax didn't have time for recriminations. "I'm an LoH Marine. Show yourselves."

An older woman rose from the ground, her hands up.

"There're five more of us. Don't shoot."

Pax looked back the way they came. He couldn't see any

Tucanans, but he knew they were coming, and he didn't have time to sit around and assure the civilians.

"We're heading to an LZ for a pickup, and we've got pedes on our asses. You can come with us, but that's up to you. Timbol, keep going."

The militiaman seemed in shock that he'd fired on fellow humans, and he hesitated.

Once again, Pax didn't have time to talk the man down. "Veluz," he told the next militiaman. "Take over."

She didn't hesitate, patting Timbol's shoulder, then she pushed past and kept going.

The civilian looked down and spoke to someone. A moment later, four adults, one holding a toddler, jumped up and started sprinting toward them.

"Keep it moving," Pax shouted to his team. "And Tranch, watch the civilians."

He'd told them it was up to them if they wanted to come, but he couldn't really just leave them on their own.

Tranch nodded and moved over to ride herd on them.

Pax reached into his magazine and pulled out his last skeeter. He had to determine where the Tucanans were. He gave a quick set of instructions and launched the little drone before adjusting Pandora's weight and moving off.

The civilians joined the center of their column as the entire group ran through the forest. Pax watched the progress of his drone, which made it 132 meters before it went dark.

Hell.

The drone had been spotted and taken down. How far did that mean the Tucanans were behind them? A hundred and fifty meters? Two hundred?

The pilot reported that he was spiraling in when the first burst of fire raked the humans. Pax turned to see the Tucs spreading out into their assault formation.

The second burst of fire tore into Fuma, and she went down hard. Blood spurted from Mabong's arm as he looked at his fellow militiaman in shock.

Pax had been expecting this, and he'd already decided what to do.

"Take Pandora," he told the young man. "And get everyone to the LZ. It's four hundred meters ahead."

Mabong looked at him in confusion.

"Go!" Pax said, using his best command voice.

He spun away and started firing his Denon. He had to get the Tucanans into their final assault mode. And sure enough, at his first burst, the Tucanans started team rushes, which were almost identical to how Marines and most armies did it. A Tucanan team was three soldiers. Half of the teams gave covering fire while the other half surged forward fifteen or twenty meters before they began to fire.

Pax had no secret weapon that was going to stop the Tucanans, but by getting them to deploy into their team rushes, he was slowing them down. Now he just had to keep alive long enough for them to engage him and not chase down the rest of his team and the civilians.

There was no sense of despair. He'd fought in too many battles and escaped death by millimeters too many times. He's always known he'd fall in battle, just not when. Now he knew.

And surprisingly, it filled him with a sense of pride.

He ran forward while firing a burst of his Denon at the closest rushing team, expending his last AR flechette. He knew he hit two of them, but only one fell to writhe on the ground. The other two hit the deck and started firing back as Pax juked to the left, then back to the right, trying to keep trees between them. But the Tucanan assault formation dispersed the enemy, and it was impossible to keep himself completely covered from all of them. Two rounds hit him, hardening his armor, and another tore through his left upper arm.

He dropped his Denon and raised his Hokker. By charging the Tucanans, he'd closed the distance, and now his handgun was within range with its huge 8 mm rounds. Screaming like a madman, he fired at another team. This time, two went down as the third darted to the side. Pax juked behind a large tree, then reversed his direction back the other way an instant before the air was full of Tucanan Buzzer blades slicing through the air.

Another team was raising their forebodies, and one, two, three, Pax blew them all away. He kept a running count in his mind. That was six down. Add at least two to the mines, another possible three in the initial firefight, and that was eleven.

But that meant there were still at least fifteen or so in the fight. Pax might be good, but no one was that good. All he could do was take out as many as he could before he fell.

He stopped, his back against the base of a tree as he tried to position the enemy in his mind. Tucanans made a soft clicking sound as they ran—the xenobiologists said that the clicking of their segments served a function similar to a bat's echolocation—and he listened, picturing where they were. At least two teams were getting close, and all of their combined fire was narrowing in on him. He could hear the blades smashing into the tree, others zipping past on either side.

But the closer the lead teams got to him, the more the others had to limit their fire or hit their fellow soldiers. He couldn't hear anyone trying to flank him. It looked like they were relying on a frontal assault to bowl him over.

The pilot told him he was landing. Pax acknowledged and looked in the direction his team had taken. There was no one in sight. Hopefully, they were almost at the LZ.

He took a deep breath, knowing this was it. The last few rushes had brought the leading teams almost to the tree. He waited for the soft clicks to stop, and knowing he had a brief moment while the other teams got up and while the lead teams prepared to fire, he spun around from behind the tree and charged.

Pax was surprised that they were so close. But at this range, he couldn't miss. He fired four quick shots, hitting two in the head and one in its weapon-bearing second section. He shifted fire and the first of a torrent of rounds hit him. His armor protected him from the initial few blades, but the STF[2] became more and more vulnerable with each hit.

A round creased his face, and his left arm got hit again.

But it wasn't the massed fire that got him. As he vaulted the one he'd hit in its second section, the soldier shifted its weapon to its third section.

Rookie mistake.

The Tucanans preferred using their second section foot-arms to fire their weapons, but any foot-arm could be used.

Pax realized his mistake while in midair, but he couldn't react quickly enough before the Tuc fired up into his waist.

. . . and Pax's world went dark.

---

2. **STF**: Shear Thickening Fluid. A type of armor that hardened when struck.

PART II

1

Pax's world slowly came into focus, but it took his brain longer to make sense of what he saw.

The lights were low, but the room was a stark white. The only thing marring the ceiling above his head was a single diffused light array. With a groan, he turned his head and finally realized that he was in a bed, a clean white sheet covering his body. A light blue monitor of some sort was on the foot of the bed, the only thing interrupting the featureless room.

Not quite the only thing. As he turned his head the other way, he could see a nightstand beside the bed with some sort of framed certificate on it, but Pax was too disoriented and weak to see what it was.

I'm alive?

Pax had accepted his death when he sent Mabong and the others forward. The extract had been the only one in the area, and humankind was abandoning the planet. But evidently, his life wasn't over. He must have been rescued by someone and received medical attention.

Unless this is . . . he wondered, too tired to actually panic.

But unless heaven was a real place that looked like a sterile hospital room, then he probably wasn't dead and in the afterlife.

And then another thought hit him, and this time panic did start to rise within him despite his lethargy. Rumor had it that some horrible experiments had been done to Tucanan captives while xenobiologists tried to figure out what made them tick. What if this was the Tucs equivalent of an enemy lab?

He struggled to raise himself to his elbows when his eyes focused on the back of the monitor, where it said, "UPP-1030," followed by more numbers and writing, both of which were too small for him to read in his present condition. Unless the Tucanans started buying their lab equipment from human medical companies, it was a safe bet that he wasn't a prisoner of the enemy.

Rising made him dizzy, and he sank back down. His mind seemed to be functioning a little better, but nothing made sense.

Pax had been through eighteen official battles, and he'd escaped relatively unscathed with only two minor injuries. But he'd visited his wounded Marines often enough to know what a Naval Hospital room looked like, and this wasn't it. Not even his four SKIAs who'd been resuscitated had been in something like this.

He could be in some civilian hospital ship, he guessed, but the room didn't feel *alive,* as shipboard spaces felt.

Pax looked to the edge of his bed, hoping to see a call button. But there was nothing, only the framed certificate on the nightstand.

He stared at it for a moment. Maybe there was something there that could explain where he was, but it seemed like too much of an effort to reach over and grab it. Pax was a Marine who'd trained to keep pushing his body as far as it could go, though. He mentally prepared himself, counted down from three, and with a superhuman effort, turned on his side, reached to the nightstand, and grabbed the certificate before falling back.

He lay there for a moment, the frame on his chest while he caught his breath. Now, he knew he wasn't in heaven. Not even the cruelest god would create a heaven where the fit were suddenly invalids.

It took a moment before he was ready to raise the frame so he could read the certificate, then a moment more before his eyes focused enough to see what was there.

The first thing he recognized was the image at the top of the page of a gold Maltese cross with a globe representing Earth superimposed on the center of it and hanging from a brilliantly white ribbon. It was a new award, created when the LoH Navy and Marine Corps were formed, and it was the highest possible military award for valor given by the fledgling government.

Pax had never seen an actual medal in real life, and he brought the certificate closer. But under the image, large letters caught his eye and made him gasp and drop the frame.

He took several deep breaths, then raised it again. His eyes hadn't deceived him. In bold letters, under the image and above what was probably the actual citation, was the inscription:

Sergeant Paxton J. Alejo
League Of Humankind Marine Corps

All of the air left his lungs.
A Cross of Honor? Me?

Pax was a well-decorated Marine. He had two San Marcos Marine Corps Silver Stars, three Bronze Stars with Combat Vs, and a Purple Heart among his many service ribbons. He had an LoH Order of Valor Second Class, and an LoH Order of Valor First Class from after he was transferred. But a Cross of Honor? As far as he knew, there were only a handful of living Navy and Marine Corps holders of the award. They were almost always awarded posthumously.

He really didn't know what to think, and he was in the dark about the details of what had happened after he was shot.

Read the citation, Pax.

Which was easier said than done. His eyes were still blurry, as if someone had applied Vaseline to them. He rubbed them with his right hand and then brought the frame closer. By squinting heavily, he could just make out the smaller print.

THE COUNCIL PRIME of the League of Humanity in the name of the League of Humanity First Council takes pride in presenting the **Cross of Honor** posthumously to

SERGEANT . . .

"WAIT, WHAT?" he said aloud, his voice cracking from disuse.

Pax shook his head, rubbed his eyes again, and looked one more time.

Posthumously.

The word stared him in the face.

"That can't be. It has to be a typo."

A deep feeling of foreboding started to wash over him. They didn't make typos on something like this, so unless this was some warped practical joke, something was very wrong.

He looked around the room again. It had the feel of a hospital, but he'd never seen any ward room so sterile and featureless.

Could it be possible . . . am I really dead? Is this . . .

But no. The framed certificate in his hand was real. Very real. He'd swear to that. He pinched his arm. It felt normal.

Hallucinating?

Pax rarely dreamed, but when he did and could remember them, they tended to be disjointed and all over the place. What he was experiencing now felt different. It felt real.

None of this made any sense.

"Hello?" he croaked, barely above a whisper.

He coughed and tried again, this time a little louder. "Hello? Is anyone there?"

He waited, but the door in the far corner of the room remained closed.

There was more on the certificate than his name, of course. There would be the citation. Maybe that had a clue.

Pax raised the frame again and squinted to be able to read the words. He avoided the "posthumously" at the top and went right to the citation itself.

For conspicuous gallantry and intrepidity at the risk of his life above and beyond the call of duty while serving as a civil contact team leader with Bravo Company, First Commando Battalion, First Marine Force, in connection with combat operations against the Tucana Dwarf Galaxy enemy on the independent planet. Tasked with leading a team of local militiamen to delay the enemy forces while the planet's civilian population was evacuated, Sergeant Alejo led a successful attack on a larger force, which resulted in six enemy casualties, disrupted their movement toward Puerto Princesa and allowed for over two thousand more civilians to evacuate the planet. While enroute to their own evacuation point, an AA-33 antiaircraft weapons system was emplaced where it could pose a danger to the evacuation vehicle. Sergeant Alejo pushed his team to interdict the system. Faced with minimal ordnance, he developed a plan, using what he had available to him, and successfully eliminated the threat despite taking heavy casualties. He ordered his team to move to the evacuation point and picked up a group of civilians along the way. The Tucana Dwarf Galaxy forces gave pursuit and caught up to Sergeant Alejo and his charges. Realizing that they would be overrun, Sergeant Alejo conducted a one-man assault on the enemy forces to give the rest of the humans time to reach the LZ. He personally broke the pursuit and killed six of the enemy before he was killed by enemy fire. His body was subsequently recovered by his devoted militiamen and has been interred at the Cape Town Cemetery of Heroes. By his indomitable courage, inspiring initiative, and selfless devotion to duty, Sergeant Alejo was instrumental in giving the incoming shuttle enough time to board both Boracay militiamen and civilians and get them off the planet before the enemy could stop them. His actions were in keeping with the highest traditions of the League of Humankind Marine Corps. He gallantly gave his life in the service of humanity.

Given under my hand,

Yana C. Kunkle
Council Prime

Pax had heard of out-of-body experiences, but he'd never given them any weight. This is what he was feeling, though. It was as if he were floating above his corporeal self, watching him read the citation. Nothing in his thirty-five years of life prepared him for anything like what he was experiencing.

From all of the evidence, and from what he remembered from the battle, he was dead. Except, dead men don't lie in a hospital bed and read citations of their awards.

Do they?

He placed the frame back on the nightstand, carefully centered, then leaned back in the bed. They couldn't leave him here forever. Sometime, someone was going to have to come into his room and tell him what the hell was going on.

2

IT WAS TWO HOURS, four hours . . . hell, maybe a day later that the door finally opened. Pax's eyesight had cleared up some, but he'd been lying there, his mind relatively blank, as he waited.

A middle-aged man in featureless blue scrubs entered the room. He grunted when he saw Pax was awake, but he didn't say anything and instead went to the monitor and pushed the button on the side several times.

"You're not Navy," Pax said.

The man snorted and said, "No, I'm not."

Pax waited for something more, but the man started quietly talking into a throat mic.

Pax wasn't particularly patient in the best of times, and this wasn't then.

"Can you tell me what the hell is going on?"

The man sighed and gave a quick look around as if someone had snuck into the mostly bare room.

"Look, I don't know much, and even if I did, I'm not supposed to talk to you."

Pax was getting angry, and in a way, that pleased him. It meant he was moving past the lethargy that had dominated him since he woke up.

"Unless those scrubs are part of some big charade, you're medical, and that means you have to be open to my questions on what's wrong with me. That's the law."

"What do you mean?"

"The law. You can't hide medical knowledge from a patient."

The man glanced at the framed citation on the nightstand, then said, "Look, I'd help you out, but all I do is record the numbers."

"Is someone who has a clue going to come and talk to me?"

The man leaned back to the monitor, hit the button on the side four times, then looked at the display.

"Yeah, I think so. Today, for sure."

Pax realized he didn't know what day it was. Or what time it was, for that matter. He was sure he wasn't on a ship, and he'd bet he wasn't on Boracay, so he had to have been under for quite some time.

He realized that he wasn't going to get much more from the nurse-orderly-whatever, so he settled back to watch the guy go about his thing.

It didn't take long. A minute or so later, the man hit the button several times in succession, then stepped back. He looked at Pax for a moment, and it looked like he was going to say something, but he shook his head instead.

He started toward the door but paused in front of it.

Without turning around to face him, the man said, "Good luck," before he keyed open the door and stepped out.

Pax knew that the door was locked, and even had he been at full strength, it probably wouldn't do any good to try and leave. His mind was bouncing around his brain pan like a canary in a cage, and if he let it, he'd probably lose it. He had to draw on his experience. Pax had lain motionless in ambush many times in his career, and while this might not be an ambush against the enemy, he could imagine they were. Paxton Alejo and his problems were shoved to the rear, and Sergeant Paxton Alejo, Marine Raider, emerged. His anxiety faded as he waited.

When the door opened a second time, he just watched as a man in a white lab coat and a woman in a suit carrying what looked to be a real leather briefcase entered. The woman's appearance screamed lawyer, while the lab coat tended to be the uniform of doctors instead of the scrubs of nurses and techs.

Why the hell do I need a lawyer? I haven't done anything wrong.

The lawyer waited until the doctor checked out some readings on the monitor before he nodded to the woman.

"A-S-zero-four-nine-nine-nine, I am Fordyce Dawat, here to explain your current situation."

She glanced at the doctor, who gave the slightest of nods.

"I don't know who you mean," Pax said. "I'm Sergeant Paxton Alejo, LoH Marines."

"Sergeant Alejo was unfortunately killed in action on Boracay almost two months ago. He's interred now at the Cape Town Cemetery of Heroes."

Despite the forced calm, Pax gave a little start. He'd read that in the CoH citation, but to hear her say it made it seem more real.

"Well, I don't know who you buried there, but I'm right here. And I know who I am."

"I can assure you, A-S-zero-four-nine-nine-nine, that Sergeant Alejo is dead."

She reached into her briefcase, pulled out a document, and handed it to him. Pax wasn't too surprised to see that it was a death certificate. His death certificate.

"As I just said, I can assure you that Sergeant Alejo is dead. Both the League of Humanity and the San Marcos government agree with that."

She looked at the doctor again, who nodded one more time.

The lawyer needs his approval before going on? Why?

The canary of his mind was still slamming itself back and forth in its cage, but in the fore, Pax's rational, military mind was trying to make sense. Something told him that while he wanted to explode on the prim lawyer standing at the foot of his bed, he'd better keep control.

He took several breaths, as he would before he fired a long-range sniper shot, to lower his pulse.

"The sergeant's passing was a loss for humanity. He was extremely well qualified to contribute to the war against the Tucanan forces."

Pax narrowed his eyes. *What do they want from me?*

Dawat glanced at the doctor, who hadn't directly interacted with Pax yet, one more time, and once again, she got the go-ahead.

She slightly shifted her feet and squared her shoulders.

Pax had done enough hand-to-hand to realize what that meant.

Here comes the payoff.

"A-S-zero-four-nine-nine-nine, have you heard of the Necromancy?"

The question took him by surprise.

"You mean that thing from fifty years ago?"

She nodded.

What does that have to do with anything?

The Necromancy was a sect that promised eternal life, reanimating the dead . . . all for a cost, of course. A huge cost. The whole thing had proved to be a scam, but not before their compound on Halle Roan had been overrun by the mob and all of the followers killed.

For promising eternal life, they'd all had pretty short lives.

The reaction to even their claim had been intense—so much so that laws had been passed to remove citizenship and protections to any "reanimated person"—even if there never was an actual dead person brought to life.

The law had caused unintended consequences when some zealots demanded that drowning victims who were resuscitated, heart attack victims who were brought back, or SKIA military members who were saved, lost their citizenship and rights as being "against God's plan." The law was amended to differentiate between a simple resuscitation and a reanimation.

Pax was getting an uneasy feeling about this. But he wasn't going to let his imagination run away with him.

"Yes, of course, I've heard of the cult. What does that have to do with me? It was all a scam."

"What if I told you that it wasn't a scam. That the Necromancers had figured out a way to not only reanimate the dead, but to keep all of their memories and knowledge intact?"

"I'd say you were crazy."

His unease grew.

"We'd know by now. That was fifty years ago," he said, his voice not nearly as calm as it was just a few moments prior.

Dawat just shrugged.

"As you know, we're losing all of our skilled military pilots and operators. Every battle takes more of them from us, faster than we can train them up."

"We're killing more of the pedes every day," Pax protested.

"And still more are pouring out of the Tucana Dwarf Galaxy in an unending stream."

Pax didn't reply. She was right, of course.

"So, if there was a way to bring back our most skilled military personnel, don't you think that when humanity's very survival is at stake, we might be willing to look aside and ignore law, not to say the morality, to do that?"

Pax stared at the woman. He didn't like the direction this was heading in, and he started to feel nauseous.

"Sergeant Paxton Alejo was an asset to humanity, and the LoH did not want to lose that."

"You're trying to tell me that the Necromancy was not all bullshit, and you brought me back from the dead."

"We didn't bring you back, A-S-zero-four-nine-nine-nine. You are a non-entity. What we did is bring back Sergeant Alejo's particular skills and knowledge."

Pax understood why the woman kept using the string of numbers. She was trying to dehumanize him, to divorce him from who he was. But he wasn't going to put up with it.

"I'm me, and you know it. Using your logic, I wouldn't be any good to the Corps if I wasn't me."

"I can assure you that you aren't Sergeant Alejo. Technically, you're not anyone. You're not a citizen. You're not anything."

"I'm a citizen of San Marcos!" he said a little too forcibly. "They won't stand for this."

He sat up, unwilling to play the meek, accepting Marine.

She took a quick step back and glanced at the doctor, who shook his head and waved her off. It was only then that Pax really noticed the cable running from the monitor, down the stand, and up and under the sheet that covered his lower body. Of course a monitor would be somehow hooked up to him, but this red cable didn't have a medical feel to it.

Too many fights had ingrained a fine sense of danger detection, and that sense went into high alert. Pax didn't know where he was or what was happening to him, but he was suddenly convinced that if he gave the wrong answer or behaved too aggressively, the doctor would flip a switch, and then he'd be dead in actuality.

Calm down, Pax. Whatever this is, you just need to survive it and fix it later.

He forced a smile onto his face and said, "I'm sure that the Marine Corps and the government of San Marcos know who I am. And if I did die, I was SKIA. You resuscitated me, and so, I am a citizen. That's what the law says."

She shook her head, and with a grim smile, said, "No. The sergeant was not resuscitated. He was declared dead and sent to the ship's morgue."

Pax had figured out where this was going, but it didn't register. How could it?

She reached into her briefcase again and brought out another certificate.

It was a coroner's report. Pax didn't read the entire thing. The cause of death was wounds received in combat that destroyed his lower abdomen, severed his aorta, and ripped into his left lung. Surprisingly, he didn't feel anything as he read it.

And under the detailed description of the damage, was the additional note: "Brain death certified as per MHNT protocols."

"I hope my funeral was done right," he said facetiously.

"Oh, it was. It's not every day that a hero is laid to rest. Your San Marcos governor general came, as did your father."

"I don't have a father."

She looked puzzled and pulled a folder out of her briefcase.

"I have a sperm donor, but no one I'd call a father."

Memories of abuse and abandonment tried to flood him, but he had experience in closing the emotional floodgates.

"He seemed pretty proud of you and distraught at your death."

I thought I wasn't me, so how could he have been distraught at "my" death.

Evidently, despite her attempt to separate Paxton Alejo from whatever his legal situation was now was difficult in normal speech given the vagrancies of Universal.

"Oh, I don't doubt he milked it for all it was worth. Probably tried to raise money, too."

The slightly stricken look on her face told him his biological father had done exactly that. He expected it, but still, even after all these years, it hurt a little.

Pax wanted to change the subject. And he still didn't understand what had happened.

"I . . . if this thing is right," he said, pointing to that statement, "then how did you bring me back?"

"We didn't, A-S-zero—" she started before Pax raised a hand to stop her.

"OK, how did you bring whatever I am back?"

He was afraid that she wasn't going to answer, but after a moment, she relented. "A lot of this is classified, and I'm not an expert in the procedure. But there was a recovery team aboard the ship. Your body was put in stasis to limit cellular degradation, and when you arrived here, a copy was made of your brain so that—"

"Wait, what? It says here my brain was certified dead."

"When you turn off your computer or pad, is all the data lost?" she asked. "When you turn it back on, can you just continue on?"

"Yes. No. I mean, no, the data isn't lost, and yes, you can continue on. But a brain isn't computer memory."

"It isn't? What is thought but data points?"

"Yeah, but a brain is, well . . ." He stopped to try to get his thoughts together. "If what is me is really data points, then how the hell did you, I guess you'd say, *download* them?"

"With the myc—" she started to say, then bit back her words. "I told you I don't know the technical details."

Bullshit. She knows.

"Maybe Doctor Simms can jump in?" she asked, looking to the doctor who frowned and shook his head.

"Well, OK. Suffice it to say that a copy of what made you you was made. And when the damage to your body was repaired, that copy was emplaced. Uploaded, to use your terminology."

It's impossible. You're playing some sort of game with me, but why?

There had to be a way to catch her in the lie.

"If this technology has existed since the Necromancy, then why isn't it being used all the time?" he asked.

"Well, for one thing, the technology hasn't existed. The Necromancy were on the right track. But it needed work. For another thing, the process is extremely difficult and *extremely* expensive. For what was spent on you, the LoH Navy could have bought a new Nyame fighter."

Pax widened his eyes in surprise. From a military standpoint, was a single soldier, no matter how well trained, worth the same as the Navy's top-line fighter?

"The prime reason, though, is that the existence of the tech has to remain secret. If word got out, can you imagine what would happen? Everyone would want—no, demand—the procedure. And it's not only the cost. The process takes some very rare . . . *materials*. Do you know how many people die every day?"

"No. How many?"

She frowned and said, "I don't know the number. A lot. We don't have nearly the resources to reanimate everyone who dies. So, how do we decide who gets the treatment and who doesn't?"

"There are people who have all the money in the galaxy. Tori Hana. If she died, would she be, uh, *reanimated*?" Pax asked, referring to the famous—or infamous—CEO of Hana Enterprises.

"If she did, then she wouldn't be Tori Hana, then, would she? She'd be a non-citizen, without access to any of her empire. That's the law."

This was all so wrong, but he wasn't a lawyer, and he couldn't form a cogent argument against what she was saying. None of this sounded like the full story. And about the rich, all he knew was that in his experience, money could get a person anything.

"So, someone improved on an illegal procedure that was never used and can't be used because it's too expensive and people would riot. Then the government—I assume it's the government?"

She nodded.

"So, the government is using this illegal, secret procedure to bring back soldiers."

"That's it in a nutshell, I guess. But we aren't breaking the law. This operation has been approved by the First Council by a closed proclamation."

"Closed" meant secret.

This was all over his head. Way over. But evidently, he was still part and parcel to something that could go very, very wrong.

"I see a problem with this, though. You implied I've been brought back so we can use my skills in the war. But I'm not me. I mean, I don't feel in condition to fight."

She scoffed. "Your body has been immobile for a long time. Rest assured, your abilities will be practically the same as they were before. You just need to finish your rehab before you join your unit."

The "practically" caught his attention, but that was overridden by the mention of his unit.

"I'm going back to the Commandos?" he asked, excited at the prospect despite everything that had been dropped on him.

"Uh . . . no. You'll be in a special unit, along with others like you."

Pax didn't like the sound of that. "What's special about it," he asked warily.

"I'm not on that side of the program. I can't really say."

For a lawyer, she sure didn't know how to lie. But Pax didn't push her. He'd find out soon enough.

"Exactly what side of the program are you on?" he asked, glancing at the thicker cable that ran from the monitor to under his sheet at the foot of the bed.

"I'm a lawyer . . ."

I figured that much.

". . . and I'm here to make sure you understand the situation from a legal standpoint."

"Which is?"

"I think we've already covered it, but it boils down to the fact that you are no longer legally a human. You are not a citizen, and you don't exist as a sentient being."

He glowered at that, and she added, "Of course, you are sentient. A dog is sentient."

His scowl increased, and she added, "Poor choice of words, but true from a legal sense."

"So, what you're saying is that I have no rights."

She shrugged. "It's the law. I didn't write it."

"But you're sure taking advantage of it."

She had the decency not to protest.

"Your very existence is highly classified. You will make no mention of it at any time. You will become part of a special organization that serves at the pleasure of the Council Prime. And you will forget your friends and family back on San Marcos. There will be no attempt to contact them."

No loss on that last one.

"That's the gist of it. You'll be receiving more details, but we like to brief the reanimees with the basics upon awakening."

"At some point, I'm going to be out of here. What makes you think I'll join this battalion of yours, this battalion of non-people."

He could see her almost look toward the doctor on the monitor, but she managed to control herself.

"Because the enemy hasn't changed? Because of loyalty to humanity?"

"A humanity I'm no longer part of."

"I wouldn't say you're not a part of humanity. Of course, you are. Everything we build, every achievement we make, that's all humanity. You're just not a citizen."

"And no one knows we exist."

"I told you the reason for that. Surely you can understand why it has to be that way."

And he could. If she was right, and the procedure was so expensive, then only the extremely rich could afford it. Once the masses found out, there'd be chaos. But understanding it didn't mean he had to like it.

He turned his head and looked at the nightstand and the certificate again. Was that proof of anything? It would be child's play to print one up as a prop to support whatever they said.

"Is that even real?" he asked.

"Yes, that's authentic. I watched the ceremony at Humanity Hall. Your father was there, too, looking so proud."

I bet he was.

"If you're telling me that I'm not me, then why put that so I can read it? I don't get it."

"It's a little unusual, but Doctor Simms thought it might be a good touch, you know, so that you could see that your death was worth it."

Pax stared at the doctor, whose expression never changed.

"So, what's next? I mean, I can't do much here in this cell," he asked, anxious to bring this meeting to an end.

She gave another wry smile at his use of "cell."

"I think you'll be out soon enough and with the battalion. Someone will come in and explain to you the rest of your rehabilitation schedule. There're some things you'll have to learn about your body and care."

"When will that start?"

"Maybe this afternoon?" she asked, looking at the silent doctor, who nodded. "And with that, do you have any more questions for me?"

About a million of them.

But he just shook his head. She was only a lawyer, there to let him know his legal status, which was basically nothing.

She nodded at the doctor, and they both started to leave before she stopped and faced him.

"I know this is a lot to take in. But despite the legal limbo you're in, the League of Humanity values you, and we're going to take care of you. Don't ever forget that."

Like you take care of tanks and naval vessels. I'm a tool.

But he could see the earnestness on her face, and he thought she meant it.

"I won't forget, ma'am," he said.

It was just easier to say that and get her to leave.

She seemed relieved before she turned and followed the doc out.

Pax lay back in the bed for a good fifteen minutes, trying to sort through his thoughts.

He was alive . . . sort of. Even if not from the legal perspective.

But he was him. Forget the A-S-whatever number, he was Sergeant Paxton Alejo. He was born on San Marcos. He enlisted in the San Marcos Marine Corps and was transferred into the LoH Marines.

But was he? And did he want to keep going as some sort of non-entity. A nobody? He wasn't sure he did.

Without making a conscious decision to do so, Pax sat up and swung his legs over the bed. He was, as he'd surmised, hooked up to the monitor—which wasn't white or even brushed silver as most medical devices were, but oddly pale blue. Several intertwined cables were attached to his ankle.

Pax leaned over, pulled the monitor close, and turned it around so he could see the face.

There were four displays. He recognized the heart monitor, and the other three had that medical look. There was a keypad on the right side, then several touch-screen buttons. On the bottom, though, was a single red, raised button.

Pax was sure he knew what it was for. Push it, and his short life as a non-citizen would be over. He wasn't sure he believed in the afterlife, but push the button, and he'd find out. It was tempting, and he placed his forefinger lightly on it.

One push, and it's over.

The button felt warm, but that could be his imagination. After almost a minute, he pulled his hand back and shoved the monitor away.

He wasn't going to go out like that, because one thing that the lawyer had said rang true in his ears.

No matter that he was being used without a say-so. No matter that he was a non-citizen without any rights. He'd sworn an oath when he enlisted, an oath he'd repeated after each promotion.

I will protect humanity with every fiber of my being and until my dying breath.

WELL, he'd evidently taken his dying breath on Boracay, and that didn't negate that oath. He was still bound by it, and he'd do his best to fulfill that promise to humankind.

3

"And . . . stop," Kelli said.

"I can keep going," Pax said after pulling the breathing tube out of his mouth.

He was huffing like a steam engine, and the tube didn't make breathing easier, especially with his nose clipped shut. Sweat poured down his forehead and into his eyes, stinging them.

"I'm sure you can, Pax. But I've got what I need."

Kelli Than was one of the techs monitoring his rehab. What he appreciated about her was that she treated him like a normal human being. There was no "AS04999." He was just Pax.

He wiped his eyes and then asked, "So, am I alive?"

"Very funny. Why don't you get off that bike and come sit down here?"

Pax yanked off the nose clip, swung his leg over the stationary bike's seat, and plopped himself down on the stool beside her.

She studied the display for a moment, then said, "Looking at these numbers, you're doing well. I think you can probably be out of here in another few days."

Pax raised his eyebrows. He'd woken up nine days ago, and since the lawyer left, the only people he'd seen were the four techs on his rehab team. He was both nervous and excited about meeting others like him.

He still hadn't completely come to grips with his situation, and he wasn't sure that this wasn't some big scam being played on him for reasons unknown, but if he could get together with others, maybe he could figure something out.

"Lung function is within normal ranges, and your cardio readings continue to improve," she said, more to herself than to him. "CR is getting better, as is the KNC range . . ."

Pax understood lung function and cardio, but the techs lost him when they started throwing acronyms around. All he knew was that he was feeling more and more like himself.

Then Kelli uttered the fateful words. "I think we need another session on the Crain. I want to correlate the biosynch readouts."

Pax grimaced. His rehab had been intensive. Most of his time was spent in physical activity—dexterity and balance exercises, strength training, and cardio. But several times a day, he'd been hooked up to the Crain, which administered electrostimulation.

He enjoyed the physical exertion. He'd always liked the gym, and not just for general fitness. Lifting iron was his way of meditating. And he understood the need to get his body back in shape. The dexterity exercises were a little frustrating. Putting washers on a wire, twisting nuts on screws, and fitting shapes in cutouts could drive him insane when his fingers didn't quite do what he wanted them to do, but he understood their purpose.

The Crain stymied him, though. He had no idea why he was being subjected to the medieval torture device.

"When?" he asked, hoping for tomorrow.

"I get off in another hour, so we might as well get it done now."

Of course, it has to be now. Why wouldn't it be? he thought as a sigh escaped him.

Kelli laughed. "Don't be such a big baby. I know it isn't comfortable, but it's necessary."

"Isn't comfortable?" That's an understatement if I've ever heard one.

"Well, if you're going to torture me, let's get it done," he said. "A-12?"

"You know the drill."

They left the bike room and went down the hall to A-12. Inside, the Crain-4004, a meter-and-a-half-tall white instrument, was beside a slightly concave exam table.

"Be gentle," Pax said, patting the Crain before lying face-down on the table.

He waited while Kelli attached the electrodes to his wrists and ankles, then a single electrode to the back of his neck, right on his spine.

"You ready?" she asked as she sat down at the Crain.

"Do your worst."

"Right ankle. Level 1," she said, before adding, "Don't tense up like that. Relax."

Easy for you to say.

But he tried, and she repeated, "Right ankle. Level 1."

A moment later, a shock ran up from his right leg. The leg contracted and jerked. It wasn't exactly painful, but he didn't like it one bit.

"Right ankle. Level 2."

This one was a little closer to pain. Pax had suffered pain a lot as a Marine. It came with the territory. And this was different. But in many ways, it was worse, and he really wanted it to stop.

He didn't understand the purpose. Pax knew it had something to do with his nervous system, but he didn't need electrostimulation to get back into shape. He could go out there and run or bike.

The right ankle went to Level 5, and then she repeated the procedure on the left ankle before moving to the wrists.

The only good thing was that he was never shocked by the electrode on his neck. That might have been worse.

Then it was done, and Kelli said he could remove the pads while she shot the results, in graph form, to the whiteboard on the wall.

"Let's superimpose this with yesterday's," she said.

Kelli had a habit of talking through whatever she was doing, and Pax didn't know if she was telling him or just talking to herself. He quit trying to respond unless it was a direct question posed to him.

But he still looked. There were twenty blue lines on the graph, which he knew represented today, and twenty red lines, which were the ones from yesterday. The red ones didn't climb as high as blue ones, but Pax didn't know if that was a good thing or bad.

"Let's look at this," Kelli said, stepping up to the whiteboard and running a finger along the top blue and the top red line.

"I've got to say, you're doing great. Your myc is assimilating well. Quicker than normal. I'm seeing—" She stepped back to give the whiteboard a calculating look. "—maybe eight percent NTR to C7, ten to the wrist, and, uh . . . fifteen to the ankle?"

Pax made a slight frown.

"Can I ask you something, Kelli?"

She turned around to face him. "Sure, I guess."

"Why do you and the others keep calling my brain 'Mike.'"

She looked at him in confusion until it dawned on her what he was asking. She gave a short, barking laugh, then said, "That's myc. M-Y-C. Not 'Mike,' M-I-K-E. And we aren't calling your *brain* myc."

"Then what the hell are you guys talking about?"

"It's your mycel—" she started before cutting herself off.

"Mycel-what?" he prompted.

"It's not my place to get into that," she said apologetically.

"What's the deal, Kelli? Why all the fucking secrets? This is me, the dead guy, asking. Believe it or not, I'm not in cahoots with the pedes."

She frowned and looked toward the door for a few moments.

"Oh, hell. You'll find out as soon as you hit the battalion."

She took a couple of deep breaths, then asked, "Do you know what mycelium is?"

Pax racked his brain for a moment, then hesitantly offered, "The fungus?"

"Exactly!" she said as she broke out into a huge smile. "Fungus. Well, at least the root-like structures of a fungus. It's a mass of hyphae, which kind of look like threads."

"And that has to do with me just how?"

"Well, you do know that mycelium can store information, right? I mean real information."

Pax didn't know that, but he nodded anyway.

"And that various funguses can alter their DNA during their lifetime?"

Once again, he just nodded.

"Well, we've known for centuries that some organisms can transfer memories via their RNA. It turns out that there are some funguses that can do that, too. And with a little tweaking, we—I mean, first the Necromancers, and then the zombie project at a lab on Graanstaad—managed to create a mycelium that could be implanted into a human brain and then download the information stored there, and then essentially grow into the nervous system and create a parallel, well, control network."

Pax was far beyond shock by now. Heck, his mind had wandered into sorcery and magic to try and explain what had happened to him. But this didn't pass the smell test.

"Are you trying to tell me that my brain's a mushroom now?"

She laughed. "Of course not."

"A mushroom can't control a human brain. It's impossible. They're two different species."

"The Zombie Ant fungus evolved to control a different species, and that's *without* human intervention," she said.

"Zombie Ant?"

"Yeah." She paused a moment to pull up something on her wrist PA. "There it is. *Ophiocordyceps unilateralis*. They attack a certain kind of ant and then control it, making it leave the colony and find a spot suitable to fungal reproduction. That kills the ant in a few days, but the fungus is able to reproduce. So, like I said. If that can happen in nature, then why not with human intervention?"

Pax let that sink in. He shuddered at the thought of mycelian threads taking over his head.

"Do I still have my real brain?"

"I guess. Well, I'm sure of it. Otherwise, the myc wouldn't have been able to absorb your memories."

"I don't like this," he muttered.

"You should. Cellular death and deterioration start with the brain cells first, then the cells in your nerves. Right now, your myc's already stabilized your brain and is sending threads along all of your nervous system, creating alternative neural pathways for signals to travel through your body. That's what the Crain's for. By measuring the amount of time it takes for the signal to reach the spinal cord at C7, I'm monitoring the progression of how it's spreading throughout your body."

"And since my feet are the farthest from my head, it takes them longer to grow that far?"

She nodded.

"But this . . . where . . . I mean, they can just grow this mycelium? So why did that lawyer tell me that it was hard to get the stuff to do a reanimation? Just keep growing more, right?"

"Not so easy, Pax. This myc is very hard to grow and keep pure. Its DNA changes quickly, so that's a fight to keep the strain. And it's not very hardy. It dies easily."

The thought of dead mycelium in his body was even more disconcerting.

Kelli lowered her voice, and almost in a whisper, said, "Some of us think the mortality was engineered on purpose, so, you know, no one was going to make an army of one person. That sounds a little cloney. If you get killed again and haven't been recovered soon enough, most of your myc, at least, probably won't survive, and they'll have to start the process all over from scratch."

Pax just stared at the whiteboard with the graphs on it as if those lines were hiding secrets that could allow all of this to make sense. Instead, he was numb. And it didn't answer a nagging question that had been nibbling at his mind.

"If this was all so difficult and expensive, then why me?"

"What do you mean?" Kelli asked.

"Why me? What did I do to deserve getting reanimated."

"Nothing."

Pax just stared at her for a moment. "Then that goes to my first question. Why me?"

"You were a commando. The pool of potential reanimees all come from the TU Commandos. Spec-ops personnel."

"That's it? Not my Cross of Honor?"

That had been the only thing that made sense to him, but Kelli quickly quashed that.

"Nope. As I understand it, the top brass decided that if they're going to develop the program, they were only going to use the highest trained personnel. You know, to get the biggest bang for the buck. So for now, at least, it's only spec ops. You got reanimated because of your unit, not anything to do with you specifically. Well, that and the fact that you had a recovery team close enough to prep you in time. So, you can say it's because of your unit and luck."

"And if I hadn't been a Commando?"

Kelli shrugged and said, "Then you'd be buried for real somewhere."

Pax let that sink in. He'd been wondering what about him got him reanimated, and it was nothing he'd even considered. He could have been a shitbird—and those did exist even in spec-ops units. But he was in a Commando company.

Check.

There was some sort of what Kelli called a recovery team in the area.

Check.

That's all. It seemed rather capricious to Pax. He'd been swept up in the system without him having any control over it.

"Since we're getting all deep and stuff here, can I ask you something, Pax?"

He snorted and said, "Why the hell not, Kelli?"

"I've never asked any of the others, but some of us have been wondering. Uh . . . can you, you know, feel your myc? Is it like there's someone else inside your brain with you?"

She seemed salaciously eager as she waited for an answer.

Pax scrunched his eyebrows together as he tried to concentrate. Was there anything different? He didn't think so, but what if his myc was really in control, and it was hiding that from him? He was pretty sure that the zombie ant fungus didn't tell the ant it was going to kill it, after all.

If the myc was in control, then there was not much he could do about it, and one thing the Marine Corps had taught him was to ignore what he couldn't affect and concentrate on what he could. And right now, all he could do was get his body back in shape.

"No, I still feel like me. No fungal overlord looking over my shoulder telling me what to do."

From the look on her face, she might have been a little disappointed.

Her PA chimed, and she said, "That's our time. I think you've got Lars now?"

"Yeah. Whoop-fucking-wee."

"Hey, he's not that bad. And I thought you liked the workouts."

Pax did like the workouts, and he really needed one now to get his mind off what he'd just learned. But Lars was the only one of his techs who insisted on using his number instead of Pax. That was enough for Pax to dislike the guy.

"We're scheduled for first thing in the morning," Kelli said as she erased the white board with a press of a button on the Crain.

She had risen and started to leave when she stopped and put her hand on Pax's shoulder. "You won't tell anybody that I told you about the myc, right?"

"No worries. And thank you."

"You would've found out anyway once you got into genpop. I just wanted to make sure you got the real scoop, not whatever is going around in there."

"And I appreciate that, Kelli. Really, I do."

He stared after her as she left. His mind should have been racing with what he'd just learned, but it was mostly blank.

His own PA chimed, and Lars's voice said, "You're late, A-S-zero-four-nine-nine-nine. I'm in the gym now."

"On my way."

But he sat there for a few more moments. What seemed to him to be two weeks ago, he was a sergeant in the Marines, leading civilians in combat. Then he died, but somehow was reanimated. And now, he was some sort of fungus man. That was a lot of transformations in a short amount of time.

"This whole thing is freaky as shit," he said as he hopped off the table and walked out.

4

"Push it, Pax," he gasped.

His lungs were afire, and his legs felt like lead, but he wasn't going to stop.

A hundred meters. Don't let up!

He pulled the last reserves of energy he had and sprinted to the finish. Every step was agony, and he collapsed on the track as he passed Kelli.

"Sixteen forty-two," she said as he lay on the rough surface, his lungs screaming, his chest heaving like bellows.

He managed to push his upper body off the track and look at her. "What? Sixteen forty-two?"

When she nodded, he collapsed back and grimaced.

Sixteen forty-two? I haven't been that slow since I was a private.

Kelli looked at Lars, who said, "He'll continue to improve a little over time, but I think that's close to his potential."

Bullshit, Lars! That's nowhere close to my potential. I broke fifteen last year.

He was dying, but with an intense force of will, he calmed down his breathing and got to his feet.

"You know, you didn't have to do this, Triple Nine," the tech said.

At least the guy wasn't using his entire number, but still, it was dehumanizing.

"You've already been cleared for genpop."

"Yes, I have," Pax said. "But I'm a San Marcos Marine. That doesn't change whether I'm in the LoH Marines or dead."

Lars gave the slightest of eye rolls.

Pax didn't care. He'd done a PFT[1] twice a year, starting in boot camp, and he wasn't going to stop now.

The military services of humanity had as many fitness tests as there were armies. Some were extensive, some were simple. The San Marcos Marines were no different. In fact, they had three. The BPFE—the Basic Physical Fitness Exam—was a six-part fitness test covering strength and cardio. The CRFT—the Combat Readiness Fitness Test—was more practical applications, such as carrying a fellow Marine over a 200-meter timed course.

The PFT was different. It was relatively simple: it was a three-mile run (yes, old-fashioned miles, not kilometers) and timed pull-ups and sit-ups. No one thought it was a comprehensive, accurate evaluation of a Marine's fitness. But thirty-six years ago, General Campos, the commandant at the time, implemented a policy of honoring history by adopting practices from old Marines Corps and naval infantries.

One of those was the US Marine Corps' PFT from the late Twentieth Century. It wasn't as good as the fitness tests being

---

1. **PFT**: Physical Fitness Test.

administered then—which had changed several times since—but it became a tradition that honored those who helped create the Marine mystique and esprit de corps.

Pax hadn't managed 300 points, the max score while in boot camp. But with determination, he became a 300 PFTer as soon as he reached the fleet, and he'd done it every time since then.

Lars might not think he needed to close off his rehab taking the PFT, but he wasn't about to report in to a combat unit without proving to himself, if no one else, that he still had it.

And he did. He'd maxed out of the pull-ups with an easy twenty. To max the sit-ups, he had to do eighty in two minutes. He did them in one minute, forty-eight seconds. It was a little slow for him, but he hadn't pushed himself.

The run had to be done within eighteen minutes for the maximum score. His time was slow for him, but he had to acknowledge that maybe dying and going through rehab might have had something to do with it.

Lars said he wouldn't get much better, but he'd prove the guy wrong. He knew his potential, and he'd regain his form.

It didn't matter, though. He was still a 300 PFTer, and he was ready for the fleet.

Pax shook both techs' hands and said, "Thank you for your help. But I think it's time for me to go join my unit."

5

THE NEWEST MEMBER of the Thirty-first General Maintenance Group—as generic a name as there could be—stared at the door in front of him for a moment as his hand automatically reached down to straighten his gig line[1] before he stopped and smiled at himself. Pax wasn't in Marine alphas, the normal Class A uniform. He wasn't in his bravos, either, the less formal short-sleeved uniform shirt and trousers.

He'd been surprised at his gear issue. Instead of a Marine uniform, he'd been given three sets of blue overalls. They looked like what any mechanic might wear to the job.

After seeing them, he'd questioned the civilian giving him his issue, sure that there'd been a mistake, but the bored-looking clerk assured him the overalls were his new working uniform. Given the

---

1. **Gig Line**: A line that runs down the front seam of a shirt, past the belt, and along the zipper. A gig line should be unbroken, thereby showing that the shirt and trousers are in alignment.

unit title, that made sense, but not for a combat Marine, which he was supposed to be.

The clerk had handed him a route wand, and he'd followed it to an admin office where he checked in, once again to civilians. At least in this office, there'd been a Marine staff sergeant sitting in one of the back alcoves. The SNCO never looked up from his desk, so Pax was never able to catch his eye.

The 31st General Maintenance "Group" was something of a misnomer, in Pax's opinion. From what he'd been told, the group had a full colonel in command, which was normal. But there were the headquarters and only one line battalion, and that battalion only had one company for what were a hundred or so reanimees like himself so far.

A full colonel in overall command of what amounted to a company (minus) of operators. The only thing that might explain it was that whoever was in charge expected there to be a lot more reanimees coming down the pipeline, enough to fully flesh out the group numbers.

Pax spent twenty minutes getting checked in. In most ways, this was like checking into any other unit. The weird part was when he was asked to sign several documents. He started with his normal signature until he realized that the printed "name" was AS04999.

How the hell do I sign a number?

He scribbled something, which seemed to satisfy the clerk.

"Where do I scan my eye?" Pax asked as he looked around for a scanner.

"You don't. You're done here. Go to your quarters and wait for further instructions."

No retinal scan? I've never done anything in my entire life without a scan.

His wand buzzed for his attention. The clerk was still standing there watching, so Pax said, "Have a good day," and left the office. He followed the wand through several corridors, anxious to finally see daylight again.

But he was mistaken. Instead of leaving the building, he walked at least 300 meters through several corridors until he came to BB-21, his new home. A small plaque on the door said, "Staff Quarters 21."

I guess I'm staff, he told himself as he opened the door.

In front of him was what looked to be a common room, about ten meters deep. Three rooms branched off the back wall, and Pax could see bunks in them. There was a sideboard of some kind on the far wall, and a large 2D vid screen dominated the wall to the left. Closed doors flanked the screen.

All of that took a millisecond to register, but Pax's attention was locked on the room's occupants. Three people—two men and a woman—were in their skivvies on the couch in front of the vid screen. Four people were either in skivvies or PT gear and sitting playing a game at a small round table. Several others were either reading or lounging around.

One of the readers was facing the door, and he looked up as Pax came in.

"Dead man walking!" he shouted as he spotted him.

Everyone stopped what they were doing to turn and stare. Pax felt extremely under the gun, and he hesitantly stepped inside.

The reader stood up, walked up to Pax, and stuck out his hand.

"Welcome to the Immortals."

6

"Watch for the assault force, Alejo," Gunnery Sergeant Ezekiel Akai shouted.

"I'm on it," Pax shouted back, before a sneezing fit overcame him, blasting out his left nostril filter.

Damn plugs, he thought as he picked it off the ground and shoved it back in.

All during Pax's rehab, he'd wanted to feel the sun and wind in his face. Now that he had that, he'd really rather be back inside.

Opal-3 was technically habitable by humankind, a Goldilocks planet, which made it very valuable. The problem was that no one wanted to live there. The temperature extremes, the traces of gasses in the air, and the low O2 content made it uncomfortable. Two separate waves of colonization had resulted in the colonists packing up and heading for greener pastures.

The planet could have been fully terraformed, but Tenshueng Industries, the original charter holder, was caught up in multiple court cases involving other planets and went bankrupt. After

Libieri Extraction won the auction eleven years later, they discovered that the initial mineral surveys had been overly optimistic. The deposits were not rich enough to justify the cost of terraforming, and Libieri wasn't in the colonization business.

The planet was left in its natural state with the small, ten thousand-plus workforce living mostly underground.

Ten thousand people was nothing on a planet, which made it very well suited for a secret project. The 31st General Maintenance Group took over an isolated and abandoned station far from anyone else.

But even with simulator training, you couldn't do everything underground. Sometimes, there was no substitute to getting out in the open and maneuvering. Too bad that the Libieri surface equipment wasn't quite up to the abuse that military operations laid on them.

"Damn air's going to give me cancer," Pax said, remembering to breathe in only through the nose plugs before speaking.

His throat was already a little raw from forgetting. He didn't know why they couldn't get full sealed helmets, and he had a feeling it was just to screw with them.

"You're dead. What do you care about cancer?" Corporal Penta "Panda" Mouve asked as the base of fire continued to pepper the target, which was a small shack that had seen more than its fair share of rounds.

It was amazing that it was still standing.

"Even a corpse would rather not rot away from the inside, Panda. Gotta look good, you know," he said as they fired measured shots into the shack.

Pax was in Bravo Team, which was acting as the support element for this exercise. It was a straightforward mission. The shack was a Tucanan hive, where inside a pod of them would be in their semi-comatose sleep cycle.

He'd never actually come across them in their sleep cycle. There were always layers of security surrounding their hives. But whatever the target was supposed to be didn't matter. This was an exercise to test their fire and maneuver coordination. Rehearsing with a simulator was one thing. Doing it with live fire took the pucker factor up several notches.

The assault element would be enveloping the target, coming in from the left side. Pax, who was in the left flank of the line, slowed down his fire slightly as he watched for the lead Marines. The key was to keep the fire on the target as long as possible before shifting away.

There was a sudden cheer from the Marines to his right. Concentrated fire had completely knocked out a supporting wall of the shack, and the entire thing lurched, tilting over a good fifteen degrees.

It was obvious that had been their intent. Whoever operated the range would be pissed, but Marines had a habit of being Marines.

And you could have told me so I could have added my fire.

Pax was readily accepted into the Immortals, as they called themselves, but after only eight days, and despite his previous accomplishments, he didn't get the feeling he was totally one of the crew yet. If they were going to goof off and try to bring down the shack, why hadn't they told him so he could get in on the fun?

"Be professional," Gunny Akai told his team. "No screwing around."

The laughter stopped, but there was an obvious shift to the

right front support. Gunny either didn't notice, or he chose not to say anything.

Probably the latter.

Pax shifted his aim, too. If the team was going to try to take down the shack through firepower alone, then he wanted in on it.

He managed to get in three bursts before it was time. The lead Marines of the assault element appeared, cresting the slope to the left.

"Shifting fire," he shouted, then coughed as he accidentally drew in a little of the harsh air.

It was SOP for him to announce it, but in reality, he needn't have bothered. For all their screwing around, these Marines really were the best of the best, coming from eleven different spec-ops groups. They knew their shit, even if they tended to cowboy it just a bit.

In the real Corps, this kind of exercise would be done with safety officers and extreme control. This time, there was none of that. They were being recorded, which would be dragged out for the debrief, but here, they were on their own.

The support element walked their base of fire ahead of the assaulting Marines. Rounds were hitting meters in front of them. And for their part, they never faltered, trusting their comrades not to shoot them.

When done correctly, this kept extreme pressure on the enemy, not allowing them to show their heads until the assault element was on top of them. Done incorrectly, it could end up with either friendly fire casualties or not enough covering fire so that the enemy was free to engage the assaulting Marines.

This was done correctly, which didn't really surprise Pax. His fellow Marines might be irreverent prima donnas, and being dead, there was something of a devil-may-care attitude, but when it came down to it, they were pros.

The assault element swept through the target. Seeing the lean on the shack, several gave it a few strong kicks, which increased the lean but didn't bring it down, to the supporting element's disappointment.

"Cease fire," Lieutenant Forte, the platoon commander and assault element leader, passed on the exercise net.

"Good job," Gunny Akai told his element. "Now, let's take it back to the barn and some air that we can actually breathe."

7

Pax stared at the mirror. His scalp was sloughing off skin, revealing new, bright pink growth. His head looked like hell, but it itched to no end.

He was told not to scratch, but some orders were just too hard to obey. His hand crept up for barely the slightest of scratches, which then morphed into him pulling on the edge of a piece of dead skin and peeling off a good four-centimeter patch.

"Brains! I want brains," Staff Sergeant Link Kravitz said as he grabbed Pax's shoulders from behind and bared his teeth at his neck.

"You're doing the vampire thing there, you idiot," he said as he shoved the staff sergeant away with a shot to the chest.

Pax wasn't a fan of the whole zombie joking around, but he had to admit that with their scalps and loss of eyebrows, their appearance was beginning to match the term.

Kravitz was nonplussed. He came back to look over Pax's shoulder at their reflections. The staff sergeant evidently had more self-control than Pax did. Link's scalp had larger patches of dead skin, and Pax wanted to do nothing more than reach up and give some of those patches a yank.

Link Kravitz had been a San Marcos Marine before being transferred to the LoH Marines. They'd both been Raiders, but while Pax knew the name, they hadn't really known each other. As the only two SMMC Marines in the platoon, though, they'd gravitated toward each other, and at present, Link was perhaps his closest friend in the Immortals and the one who'd taken Pax under his wing as he adjusted.

The two stared at their reflection for a moment before Link asked, "So, what do you think about our new skullcaps?"

"It means that our masters want to protect their investments."

Link scowled. "That's not what I was asking."

"Well, that's the answer I'm giving, even though Doc Grant says they won't that much to protect us. A shot might not penetrate, but it would create a nasty concussion."

"Maybe it's not supposed to protect us, but our mycs."

Pax shrugged. "Maybe, but I guess that's the same thing. No myc, no coming back."

"But why the rush now? They ran us through like an assembly line."

"It means we're getting closer to go-time. The masters want a return on their investment."

Training had continued at a high pace. All of them were highly skilled operators, but even the best fighters could be defeated if they weren't working as a team, and teamwork was the obvious goal. Even after being absorbed by the LHMC, the various contributing forces mostly remained intact as units despite operating under joint commands. As small as the 31st GMG was, that wasn't possible. They were all working together, no matter their background and way of doing things. Even something as simple as hand and arm signals were different between the Bonderdam SEALs and the Knights of Justice Paladins, for example.

Luckily for Pax, the "base" was the Terran Union Marine Corps, and the SMMC SOP was quite similar to that—no surprise, as the smaller corps was based on the older and larger force.

But for some of the others, even the simplest things had to be relearned. So everything they did was geared toward meshing them as a single unit, and the constant training had an urgent feel to it.

That's why Pax had been surprised when their training schedule had been canceled three days ago, and the Immortals, all 104 of them, had been marched into sickbay.

Three surgibots were waiting for them, and the assembly line began. Each Marine in turn lay down on the table and had their head locked into place, then had a nerve blocker administered. While still conscious, they were essentially scalped, the skin pulled over from their eyebrows all the way to the base of their necks on the back.

A web, they called it, was placed over the skull, and then the skin pulled back on as if donning a mask. And now, three days later, that surface skin was dying.

"It's all normal," the medical tech had told Pax during his checkup that morning. "Your new skin is growing through the web."

Pax wasn't sure how they knew this was "normal" if the procedure was something newly developed, but the tech had said that while this specific procedure might be new, it built upon techniques developed for other medical procedures.

The bottom line was that Pax now had an extra layer of protection against many of the Tucanan weapons—ballistic, energy, and concussive.

Body parts could always be replaced or regrown, but the brain had to remain relatively whole for them to be reanimated. That, and if they could save more of their mycelium, it could extend the time limit for a successful rebirth. When Pax had told Link that their "masters" wanted to protect their investments, he was only being half facetious. There was a lot of truth to the words.

There was also truth in his second statement. He'd been in enough workups to recognize the ops tempo signs. They were going into action soon. He was sure of that.

There were only 104 of them in the unit so far, not including the officers, the sergeant major, and the support staff, all of whom were "freshies," as the Undead called the never-killed personnel.

No matter how effective they were, no matter how elite, they couldn't make a dent in the war as a whole. More zombies were coming down the pipeline, but that wasn't an open faucet. They needed the right candidates who had died under the right conditions and who could be reanimated.

The powers that be needed a proof of concept before more money and effort were spent on what was still an unproven program. And with their new skullcaps, Pax thought that time was coming.

Some of them had already seen very limited and carefully controlled combat while temporarily assigned to other units. Six of the original platoon had even been killed and reanimated again. Link was one of them. But that initial test had been conducting basic infantry tactics as members of regular units. Could they, as individuals, move, fight, and react under enemy fire?

That first test had simply been a dry run. A warm-up. Now, with almost a full company's worth of undead Marines, it was time to see if all the effort was worth it. Pax had been around long enough to understand the command mindset.

They needed that proof of concept. Whatever was coming down the pike at them was not going to be easy.

8

"Damn, I'm glad that's over," Sergeant Olivia "Olive Oil" St. Amons said as she dumped herself on one of the overstuffed chairs someone had scrounged up for the platoon common area. "My throat is raw."

Pax pulled a Nova Cola out of the machine, popped the top to cool it and handed it to her. She took a long, appreciative swig, then handed it back.

"I don't care what everyone else says. You're OK for a jarhead. Maybe some of our Selection Course rubbed off on you."

Technically, they were all Marines, but interservice rivalry had been a part of military service since Babylonian times, and that hadn't changed because they'd all been sent to the LoH Marines. St. Amons had been SAS before the merge, and like most everyone else who hadn't been some sort of Marine, her core loyalty was to the SAS.

It wasn't just non-Marines, Pax knew. He was a San Marcos Marine first, LoH Marine second.

Pax just grunted and took his own swallow, letting the cool pop ease his raw throat. A cold beer would be better, but the company was dry. The official word was that booze would mess up the mycelium, but no one Pax talked to bought that. The general consensus was that it was just one more way of screwing with them, to remind them that they weren't considered full-fledged humans.

They couldn't even make prison hooch. Others had tried, but the command had microdrones patrolling the living spaces and sniffing out any presence of alcohol.

He was surprised they'd even installed the vending machine. The choices of drinks and snacks were limited, but without even a mini-exchange[1]—and money to actually buy something—the two vending machines were better than nothing.

He was getting tired of the bullshit. He understood the up-tempo training, but why the damn nose plugs instead of full enviro helmets? Why no beer? Why no liberty? No exchange where they could shop for the little things in life. He wasn't alone in thinking that the brass was fucking with them, seeing how far the undead could be pushed before they lashed out.

Keep this up, and I can show you how far.

He plopped himself down on the couch beside St. Amons and let out a loud burp. The former SAS soldier grunted, scrunched up her face, and let out an even louder one.

Pax raised his eyebrows. He was impressed. He saluted her with the cola, took another swallow, then handed it back. It was hers now. She'd earned it.

---

1. **Exchange**: a store on a military base. A mini-exchange is military version of a mini-mart.

Link nonchalantly stepped in front of the couch, stretched, and scratched his ass. He subtly caught Pax's eye, who gave him the lightest nod. The staff sergeant's mouth twitched into the tiniest of smiles before he sat next to Pax.

"Nine whole hours before our slavemasters get their hands on us again. What can we possibly do with all that time."

"Shower, eat, shit, sleep," St. Amons said. "Not necessarily in that order."

"No cards?" Pax asked, tilting his head at the table where a game was already being formed. "I thought you love that shit."

"No challenge in that," she said. "It's like taking candy from a lady."

"You mean taking candy from a *baby*," Pax said.

St. Amons scrunched her eyes together in confusion. "Why would I be playing cards with a baby?"

Pax laughed, thinking she was joking, but he cut the laugh short when he realized she was serious.

"I mean, it's taking candy from a baby. That's the saying."

"I think you're wrong," Olivia said, looking at him as if he was an idiot. "That makes no sense."

Pax opened his mouth to argue but then just shut up. He wasn't going to win.

Not that it mattered. None of them actually had money. They weren't citizens, so they weren't paid.

"You don't pay war dogs, do you?" Gunny Akai had asked him when Pax had brought up the subject.

The official excuse was that paying them would leave a paper trail, and after several skimming scandals dealing with dead soldiers still on payrolls, the anti-theft programs that had been developed and installed would catch anything paid to them as they were all listed as KIA.

But gambling had been a time-honored tradition in militaries since the dawn of time, and so the Undead had created their own system of chips, and they were even being exchanged between each other for services or items. Not for Pax, though. He'd been a player when he was a freshie, and a pretty good one, but without real money at stake, the thrill just wasn't there.

Gambling wasn't the only thing they could do in their free time. They had a huge library of books and holos. There were two hobby shops with woodworking, glass, pottery, and metalworking tools. And then there was exercise, something that was almost a religious requirement among operators.

"I'll give you one guess at what our squids are going to do," Link said as he watched Lindersmitz, Carlton, and Amana dump their gear and grab weight belts, gloves, and their hydration bottles.

"Don't need a guess. They live in the gym." St. Amons said. "But first, Amana's got to stop and check himself out."

Which is what the Bonderdam SEAL always did. He walked up to the mirror-screen, adjusted to full length, and did a few light poses.

"You're beautiful, Fridge," Ingot Byeon shouted from where she was sitting with the other card players. "You're getting me all hot and bothered."

Amana didn't stop his posing except to raise his right arm over his head and extend his middle finger.

The three SEALs—two Terran Union and one Bonderdam—were the only former sailors in the platoon, and they were almost wedded at the hip. That wasn't particularly surprising. The various navies had fought tooth and nail to keep their SEALs and other special operators out of the LoH Marine Commando Brigade. They'd won with some of the specifically naval ratings, but the three extant SEAL forces became part of the Undead battalion.

All three were certified studs and excellent warriors, but they seemed to have giant chips on their shoulders, and that made them prickly. Pax had attended BUD/S back on Earth, and he had friends within the teams, but he thought that many SEALs, no matter which Navy they were from, were arrogant bastards who thought they could do no wrong. That wasn't limited to them, of course. The Paladins could be extremely annoying with their holier-than-thou attitude and proselytizing. The Dragons were not shy about proclaiming themselves to be the toughest spec-ops troops in humanity. The Varangians strode around like they were Viking gods. And when you got down to it, Marines weren't known for being humble.

Pax would fight alongside any of his fellow undead, and he was glad to have them at his side. But if a few could get a little comeuppance, then he'd enjoy that.

"Come on, Fridge," Tensing "Ogre" Carlton said. "Let these soft bodies wallow in their slovenly ways."

Amana made a show of flexing his pecs, one after the other, then laughed. He reached down to his weight belt where he'd hung his bottle and raised it to his lips.

The medical team couldn't say whether liquid supplements would be beneficial to the Undead, but since they'd determined that it wouldn't harm the mycs, they'd granted the request to have them supplied.

Amana flipped open the lid, and just before drinking, he looked over to Bycon and mimed kissing her, before he took a long swallow.

He quickly stopped and jerked the bottle away. His eyes got huge before he bellowed loud enough to wake the dead—which was everyone in the room, of course.

Amana threw down the bottle and spun around, as he took a breath before resuming his scream. All eyes swung to him, and all talking stopped.

Carlton took him by the upper arm and tried to ask him what was happening, but he pulled away from her as he looked around in panic before spotting St. Amons, who was still sitting and staring at him with a WTF look on her face.

Amana lunged at her, pushed Pax aside, and grabbed the half-empty bottle of cola. He raised it high and drained it dry before he tossed it to the ground.

In a half-crouch, his mouth wide open, he breathed heavily while sweat started to form on his bright red face. His eyes were like a madman's as he turned to glare at Pax.

"What?" Pax said with a bewildered expression.

But Amana had already moved on. Slowly, with the intensity of a cobra, he turned around until he was facing several of the TU Marines by the holovid, who were in turn staring back at him. One of them, Corporal Wommack, gave a half laugh and pointed at Amana before saying something to the other three.

"You!" Amana screamed. "You fucking jarheads did this?"

"Did what, Sergeant?" Wommack asked.

If anything, the question made him even angrier—if that was possible.

"For the last time, I'm not a fucking sergeant. I am not in the fucking Marine Corpse!"

"Oh, that's pretty good. 'Marine Corpse.' Fitting, too, all things considered," Link told Pax. "You gotta give him credit for that."

And he did. It couldn't have been the first time someone had used "corpse" instead of "corps," but it was the first time Pax had heard it.

He took a step toward the LoH Marine, then Carlton and Lindersmitz grabbed him by the shoulder and pulled him back.

"I'll kill you," Amana screamed, spittle flying out of his mouth.

A drop fell on Pax's arm, and he half-expected it to burn him with the fires of hell, but it was just a glob of spit. He wiped it off on the couch arm.

Amana was struggling like a trapped bobcat as he shifted to an impressive string of obscenities. But his two compadres pulled him to the side and were passing through the door when Lieutenant Forte and Gunny Akai rushed in.

"What the hell is going on?" the gunny asked, looking pointedly at the former TU Marines, who all shrugged their shoulders innocently.

Amana was already out the door when the lieutenant said, "Find out what this shit's about. I'll take care of them."

The gunny waited until the lieutenant was gone before he turned to the four TU Marines and said, "In my office, now."

"We didn't do anything," Sergeant McMurtha protested.

"Now, Mac. Get your posse in my office."

The gunny left, and the four, still protesting among themselves, followed.

The rest of the platoon watched in silence until the four were gone before breaking into a hubbub of conversations.

Pax waited a moment, then without looking at Link, he made a fist. He didn't watch, but a few seconds later, his fellow SMMC alum bumped him back.

It was subtle, but evidently not subtle enough for an SAS trooper.

"You two?" St. Amon asked in an incredulous whisper.

Pax slowly turned his head to her and in his own whisper, said, "You'd be surprised what a little concentrated ghost pepper extract can do to an athletic supplement."

"Ghost pepper? Where the hell did you even get—"

Two sets of eyes bored into her.

She stopped, then after a moment, nodded. "Mucho kudos," she said before she mimed locking her lips and putting the key in her pocket.

Pax turned to Link. They'd been keeping it in for so long, and now they couldn't keep the smiles off their faces.

"Six Ps, buddy," Link said.

Prior Planning Prevents Piss Poor Performance.

"Six Ps."

The San Marcos Marines might be underrepresented in the platoon, but that didn't mean they couldn't have an oversized footprint. They'd keep quiet for now, but at some point, they'd make it known that they'd engineered this two-objective mission.

Not only had they gotten Amana, but through a seemingly innocuous comment Link had made the day before, they'd planted the seed to point the blame to the TU Marines, who thought they were the end-all for the platoon.

You have to love it when a plan comes together.

9

IT HAD BEEN difficult to keep their part in the ghost pepper prank secret. Amana, to give him credit, and after his mouth had cooled down, had admitted it had been a righteous prank. He suspected the TU Marines, and he was going to return the favor when it was least expected, but he knew it had been done within the rules of interservice fuckery. The TU Marines went to full alert, but all of that went to the wayside eighteen days later when the platoon found out why they'd been training so hard. It wasn't just general torture. It was a live mission. They'd be going to Hale's Refuge.

"From the Borstein Range east to the ocean, the pedes are in control. But up here," Captain Snike, the group S-2, said as she pointed to the sand table, "they are massing troops for an expected push through the Viscount Gap."

Tucanan units popped up hovering over their position as Pax shifted in his seat to get a better feel of the terrain.

"If they get through the defenses, that will open up most of the

Plains of Stella, putting the entire continent at risk. And if the continent falls, so will the planet."

The Tuc icons merged to flood through the gap, then spread out over the rest of the sand table, which ended at the ocean.

"What about the Three-Ps?" Colonel Owusu, the group commanding officer asked. "They should be able to block any attempted crossing."

"If it was only this crossing, sir, you'd be right. But the pedes have five other potential crossings."

Five more gaps appeared along the mountain range.

"These three could each handle a major pede force," she said as the three icons flashed. "The other two are not as big and have a smaller roadway, but they could act as subsidiary crossing points.

"J-2[1] believes that Viscount will be the actual target. The San Zhi Zhu CG[2] doesn't agree with that assessment and has spread thirty percent of his forces across all six passes."

"Fucking Three-Ps," Link muttered. "Never trusting anyone else."

Pax grunted. The San Zhi Zhu—the "Three Pillars" in Universal, which formed their nickname of the Three-P's—were effective soldiers, and there were a lot of them. But they had an impression of being prickly and not trusting their allies. Or in this case, the LoH J-2 assessment.

Pax had never worked closely with the Three-Ps. There was one of their Dragons with the Immortals in First Platoon, and he'd worked with them once before on a joint op. They were all good, tough troops. But their command's reputation was not the best.

---

1. **J-2**: The Intel division at the LoH military staff.
2. **CG**: Commanding General

"And the Hale ground forces?" the colonel asked.

"As you know, sir, their planetary army, which was more of a national guard, took significant casualties holding off the pede initial assault, as did the San Zhi Zhu garrison. While their actions might be laudable, the current CG blames the locals for the loss of the garrison, and he's ordered the surviving forces to the rear to act as a reaction force if necessary."

Pax wasn't sure that was a good idea, but then again, he was a sergeant, not a general officer dealing with large, strategic arrows. It just seemed wasteful to keep over 40,000 troops in the rear where they couldn't affect the coming battle.

The San Zhi Zhu troops were certainly better trained and equipped than the Hale's Refuge troops, but there were only 12,000 of them, facing more than 110,000 Tucanan combat warriors.

If the Three-P troops could be emplaced in one of the gaps, then despite the disparity of numbers, Pax thought they could block them. But that would leave open any of the other crossings, and the Tucanans weren't dumb. They weren't going to throw themselves at an impenetrable force when they could take an alternate route over the mountains.

Glad it's you and not me who has to make these decisions.

Pax was confident about his military prowess. Fighting was pretty straightforward, though. You saw the enemy, and you killed them. Sure, the battlefield was fluid. The enemy acted, and you reacted. But everything was right there in front of you.

This big arrow stuff, though, could fry a person's mind. All of the what-ifs had to be considered, and one of the many factors the commanders at that level had to help them was the expected casualty rates. Even for the best missions, a commander had to know that he was going to lose Marines. He was sending them to their deaths.

The decisions facing the Three-P general were tough, but at least he could make them. The invasion of Boracay and Hale's Refuge happened at about the same time. Boracay was lost, with the planet taken over before LoH forces could arrive. The Three-P garrison, as small as it was, along with the much larger planetary army, couldn't stop the enemy from establishing a beachhead, but they slowed them down long enough for the Three-P brigade to arrive.

A stalemate developed, as it often did, and the LoH brain trust was happy to leave it at that instead of committing more troops to try and wrest back complete control. But if the Tucanans were planning a spring offensive, then that meant the enemy was no longer willing to keep the status quo.

The question was what the Immortals were going to do. Only 107 combat Marines—three more had joined over the last twenty-three days—were not enough to make much difference in defending any of the passes. And they weren't set up to be defensive troops.

Frankly speaking, Pax would rather let the planetary army, which had access to armor and heavy weapons, defend a pass than have the Immortals do it. It wasn't a matter of skill, but of bringing the right weapon to the fight. And in this case, the Undead were not the right weapon.

It wasn't until Major Symonds, the S-3, got up to speak that he found out their mission.

The Tucanan Army was surprisingly similar to human armies. It had to be a case of parallel development. If their two militaries were designed to close with and destroy the enemy, then it made sense that both species developed some of the same tactics as the other.

Couple that with the fact that the two species were so similar only compounded the military convergence. They were not overtly similar to the layman, including Pax. One was an advanced ape, and the other was a huge centipede. But from a biological viewpoint, they were almost functional cousins. There could be far more diverse life forms out there, like the enigmatic Mist Clouds that floated around in space. And there were undoubtedly even more that hadn't even been discovered yet.

But there must be certain universal truths with regard to military science. And one thing was certain: interrupt the command and control, and you could limit the other side's effectiveness.

If the Tucanans wanted to remain nimble in picking their crossing point, they needed good comms not subject to human countermeasures. Take that away, and the Three-Pillar CG might have an easier time in holding off the Tucs.

And, as luck would have it, a stealth Navy spy craft had found a major enemy command center. Well, to be more accurate, the spy craft had gathered the data. The numbers crunchers back in the J-2 in the Cape Town headquarters created the actual Intel.

Normally, Tucanan command and control centers were located far from the front lines, or even aboard a ship. And if they were on the planet, then they were surrounded by scores of defensive ranks.

This time, though, the CACC[3], or CP,[4] was relatively close to their front lines. More than that, there was only a battalion-sized force in the area.

---

3. **CACC**: Command and Control Center
4. **CP**: Command Post

Practically unguarded, Major Symonds said.

"Easy for them to say. They're not going to be facing them," Link whispered.

None of their officers, other than the three in the company, would be on the mission with them. That was one of many things that made the Immortals unique. All of their officers were freshies. No zombies.

And it was obvious what that mission was going to be. They were going to go in and take out the enemy CACC.

Pax's heart was beating so hard in excitement that he was afraid it would bounce out of his chest. This was a Raider mission at the core. Pax had been used to the mission creep of the LoH Marines, but for once, his San Marcos training was going to be exploited.

The head shed was giving them a mission that they were actually trained to do.

Elsewhere in the galaxy, pigs were learning to fly.

"Any saved rounds?"[5] First Lieutenant Angela Forte asked.

No one said anything. They'd gone over the mission seemingly a hundred times. And that was after they all attended the initial operations order brief.

Operations orders were normally given to senior staff and officers. But with only 107 operators, Colonel Owusu had brought everyone in to hear it. Pax appreciated the gesture, if nothing else. But it also made sense for everyone to understand the big picture.

---

5. **Any Saved Rounds?**: military speak for "Any questions?"

"Colonel? Do you have anything?" she asked the CO.

"This is no big deal. You're all professionals, the best of the best. So just get it done. I'll be there to see you off, but you've got a lot to do between now and then."

The former SAS colonel stood, so smooth that no one would guess he had two prosthetic legs under his uniform trousers. He lost his legs in a ship explosion, but a quirk in his DNA wouldn't allow for regeneration. Like the Undead, though, he had too much experience to just shuffle him into retirement, so they gave him two fake legs and a desk job where his combat experience should have some benefits.

"Attention on deck," Gunny Akai shouted as the colonel started to leave.

"At ease, and get to work, you reprobates," he said as he exited the briefing room.

Pax hadn't seen the colonel in combat, and he never would. But he thought Colonel Owusu would be the match of any legacy Marine (e.g., someone who was in a Marine Corps or Naval Infantry before transferring into the LoH Marines).

Unlike the lieutenant or Captain Kjellberg, though, the colonel would never see combat with them. Nor would most of the officers in the group.

Pax didn't know why this was the case. Certainly, there were officers within various spec-ops units who were qualified and had been killed. But it was like some of the old black units in various wars of the Nineteenth and Twentieth Centuries on Earth where white officers led them.

The prevailing scuttlebutt was that the LoH leadership didn't completely trust them. And they thought that not putting reanimees in leadership positions could keep an uprising by disgruntled undead from happening.

Quite frankly, Pax would be hurt if that were true, and his gut told him it very well might be. He was just as loyal as anyone else, dead or alive. To put freshies in command over them was a slap in the face.

But all of that was out of his hands. The brass didn't want to know what a sergeant thought about anything.

"If there's nothing else, then let's get going. We've got just over three hours before we jump. Team leaders, I want to see you in my quarters in twenty."

"Get the team ready. The lieutenant wants to inspect at seventeen fifteen," Akai told Link after the platoon commander left.

"When's your inspection? Seventeen hundred?"

"No. No inspection."

Link raised his eyebrows. "No inspection? None?"

"They're all professionals, Link. They can get ready for an op on their own."

"You think they can? Really? What about Wolf? He'd come in naked just to prove his disdain for how we do shit."

Pax grimaced as he listened in. Link might be right. Corporal Ferris "Wolf" Morning Mist was a member of the Apsáalooke people on the strongly independent world of Ashkísshilissuua. Pax hadn't known that any were in the LoH Marines, much less in the Commandos.

He'd heard of the Ghost Walkers, of course. Most people had, although he didn't know what was fact and what was gross exaggeration. From what he'd seen during their training, Wolf was certainly competent. But he had that standoffish demeanor, as if everyone else was beneath him.

And Link was right. The former Ghost Walker just might have big enough balls to show up stark naked, claiming it was his traditional way of going into battle. If it even was, that is. Pax made a mental note to find out more about Ashkísshilissuua and the Apsáalooke Ghost Walkers.

Pax was like every other Marine in history in hating the inspection creep where the troops ended up in formation an hour before the real inspection as every leader in the chain pushed it back fifteen minutes for their own inspection. But sometimes, when you have a Wolf in your unit, he guessed you have to bite the bullet.

That didn't mean he wanted to form up earlier. He watched the gunny to see what his team leader was going to say.

"OK, make that seventeen hundred. And I mean seventeen hundred. Don't you get them fifteen minutes before that."

Link gave the gunny a knowing wink, then shouted, "Bravo Team on me."

Pax didn't like the wink. Evidently, neither did the gunny.

"I'm serious, Link. No inspection before mine. I'm going to check, and I don't want to see anyone forming up before sixteen fifty-nine."

"I got it. I got it."

"I'm serious, Link."

The staff sergeant gave him a thumbs-up, and as he left, the rest of the Marines gathered around Link.

"OK. My inspection goes at sixteen forty."

"I thought the gunny said nothing earlier than his," Byeon said.

Link shrugged. He and Byeon were the same rank, but he was senior and the assistant platoon sergeant.

"He said he was going to check," she said, trying again.

"Which is why we're not doing it here. Hangar C. Sixteen forty. Be there, aloha."

You're a dick, Link, Pax thought, friend or not, as he hurried off before someone else got the great idea to do another inspection at sixteen hundred.

10

"You're good, Sergeant," the civilian rigger said as he slapped Pax's back and moved onto the lieutenant.

Pax didn't like that the rigger was another civilian. He probably had military experience, but that wasn't the same thing as having another Marine check his foil. Any mistake, and he'd have a long fall and a very abrupt stop at the end.

He knew he was being something of a jerk. There was no reason that a civilian couldn't give him his final inspection, but prejudices rarely had any standing. Pax just trusted military personnel more.

"Fifteen minutes until hop," came over the loudspeaker.

There was a shuffling of feet, but not because of nerves. The Immortals were excited. No matter how they arrived in the unit, no matter what they thought of it, all of them were warriors, and they wanted the opportunity to prove themselves.

The rigger gave the lieutenant a thumbs-up, then left the hangar. Everything was done. Now it was just up to the gate team.

At least the six in the team were Navy. They might be in featureless vac suits without patches or insignia, but there wasn't any doubt about them.

The lieutenant left her position and started to walk the line of Marines, asking how they were doing and things like that. This was right out of Leadership 101: act like the concerned commander.

The problem with that was that all of them were seasoned veterans. This wasn't anyone's first rodeo, and in fact, every one of them had more combat experience than she did.

He wasn't quite sure what he thought of her yet. The one thing she had going against her was that she had never died. She wasn't like the rest of them, and that made her an outsider. And the fact that all of the officers were freshies sent a powerful message to the rest of them.

The dead weren't trusted.

Lieutenant Forte had been commissioned directly into the LoH Marines and had seen combat once as an infantry platoon commander. But Pax had sneaked a look at her record, and she'd graduated in the top ten percent in her REC class, so she had to have at least something going for her.

Pax had decided to withhold judgment until he could see her during the op. If she could complete the mission and bring them home, then that was enough. If she couldn't, then it didn't matter what her record at REC was.

The clock ticked down. At ten minutes, the gate team put on their helmets, and four of them picked up their gates, before shuffling to the edge of the hangar.

The atmosphere alarm sounded, and the voice coming over the loudspeaker said, "Seal for vacuum."

"You heard him," Gunny Akai shouted. "Seal them up and give me a verbal acknowledgment."

Pax took one last breath of shipboard air, then put on his helmet and twisted it into place. He started the air, and the pressure sealed the helmet. A moment later, the indicator turned to green as the first Marines started reporting to the gunny. Pax was second to last in the reporting queue, but after him, there was silence.

"You, too, Lieutenant," the gunny said.

"Oh, yeah. Sorry. Sealed."

The gunny reported to the launch officer. Now all they needed was the gate team to do their thing.

At two minutes, the alarm sounded. The hangar curtain was powered up, and then the hangar doors slowly opened. The Marines were staring into space, Opal-3's sun blindingly bright.

A gate could technically be opened on the planet itself, but atmospheres and gravitational pulls were not conducive to their operation. It was safer and took less power to open a gate in the vacuum of space, so that morning, the company had boarded two commercial ships, ostensibly with orders to perform maintenance on a Marine unit on Vaver 4.

One of the first things they'd done after boarding their ship had been to get out of their blue overalls and back into Marine combat utilities. Pax and the others were beginning to feel like Marines again. The next few hours had been their briefings, weapons and ammo draw, getting into their flight suits, and inspections.

And now, as they waited to hop, Pax could almost forget about everything that happened after dying. Muscle and mental memory were kicking in, and it was as if no time had passed at all.

When the timer hit ten seconds, the first gate, this one powered by the ship, shimmered into existence. At zero, the team dove through, carrying the other gates with them.

Personnel gates were much different than the huge shipping gates that made interstellar travel possible. Using enormous amounts of energy, those were massive constructs. The larger the gates, the bigger the ship that could pass through. They were almost always emplaced well outside of systems where stars and planets couldn't stress the large structures, corrupting the programming and linkages.

Unlike the big shipping gates, personnel gates were much smaller, and thereby were more rigid on a square meter basis. But even a slight warping could and sometimes did send the Marines anywhere, so there was a little bit of a pucker factor on each hop.

Compounding the uncertainty was the fact that as a security measure, the Marines were not just hopping from Point A to Point B. The Navy team was setting up a series of five gates, all in a line. Pax and the rest would be shuffled through five locations before emerging high in the atmosphere above Hale's Refuge. If any of those gates were off, then the entire platoon could be lost.

To be fair, the Navy would send through a dummy to ensure a solid tunnel, but accidents still happened.

Pax watched the lights above the open hangar doors. They remained a steady red. One minute passed, then two. The small gates were "set and forget," but it would still take the Navy team time to position them and confirm the link.

At just under three minutes, the red light turned to amber. Another "civilian" deckhand shoved the dummy through. Every Marine held their breath.

And the light turned to green.

"Go, go, go!" Gunny Akai shouted.

Corporal Penta "Panda" Mouve, the former Knights of Justice Paladin, was the lead Marine. With a bloodcurdling shout, he dove through the first gate, with the rest of the platoon on his ass. Two thirds of the way in the rear, Pax pushed against the back of Lance Corporal Nani Vesta, who was directly in front of him.

And then it was his turn. He took a deep breath, then dove through the first gate and into weightlessness, feeling the usual tingle in his very bones.

Pax might be hurtling through five different locations spread around the galaxy, but he couldn't see anything except the soft, soul-sucking gray that surrounded him. The cocoon always gave him the willies, but it was keeping all his body parts connected and working. At any given moment, his head could be in the Perseus Arm while his feet were in the Nona Arm. The cocoon kept his body in one piece.

And then the cocoon was gone, and Pax was falling to the planet far below him. He let out the breath he'd been holding and moved into the age-old freefall position as he triggered his countdown.

This was Pax's fourth edge-of-the-atmosphere jump, nicknamed a "Kittinger" for the Twentieth Century American Colonel Joseph Kittinger, the first man to make a stratospheric space dive and prove it was possible. Like Pax's other three Kittingers, the Overview Effect took his breath away. The system's sun was visible just over the horizon, the planet under them shrouded in darkness 28,000 meters below. Around him, he could see his Marines as they spread out, the sun glinting off their flight suits as they accelerated toward the surface.

They'd never practiced the next maneuver as a unit, but they'd done it enough times in the simulators. By the nature of the amount of time it took them to hop, they were stacked, but not to the same extent they would have been had they jumped from the ramp of an atmospheric craft.

Pax started sliding off to his nine o'clock. At this altitude, the atmosphere was almost nonexistent, so he crabbed slowly. After seventy seconds, he took a quick look around, and seeing no one near, he popped his foil.

The drogue chute went first, slowing him down from terminal velocity so that when the dull black, energy-absorbing wing snapped open, Pax wasn't torn apart inside his flight suit. It was still a pretty hefty jerk before he swung upright beneath the wing. He was slipping just under the rays of the sun, and he caught sight of four of his fellow Marines before they descended into darkness as well.

Hopefully, every one of them had a good foil. And hopefully as well, some forty klicks to the planetary north, the other two platoons were making their own Kitts. There were contingency plans in place so that any single platoon could proceed with the mission, but it would be a lot easier with the entire company in play.

Pax had descended over 9,000 meters in free fall. The next 19,000 would take far longer, almost an hour. He settled in for the descent, and one thing quickly became clear. Inside the semi-rigid flight suit, he was encased in a harness that helped to keep his body from banging around. The deceleration as his foil kicked in had jolted him so that his family jewels were a little out of place with regard to the harness's leg straps, uncomfortably so. He tried to pull on his risers, so he could kick them into a better position, but that was a nonstarter. He was just going to have to gut it out.

The second thing was that the bitter cold was beginning to seep into his flight suit, which wasn't heated. It was heavily insulated, but that was more to keep his body heat from warming up the skin of his suit, which would shine like a torch to any Tucanan temperature-based scanners.

Fifteen minutes into his descent, Pax was feeling cold. Twenty-five minutes, and it was downright uncomfortable. The only good thing about it was that it numbed his compromised balls.

He exhaled heavily, hoping his breath would warm the inside of his flight suit. He didn't know if it actually worked, but the Varangians swore by it.

Pax and the rest of them weren't dopes-on-a-rope. His foil was unpowered to help keep it from being detected. But that meant he had to control it. There were too many factors that could affect his final landing spot, so it was up to him to make the corrections and fly it. He was in darkness, but even with his face shield in NV mode, finding a specific landing spot after twenty-eight vertical and almost fifty cross-terrain klicks was a bridge a little too far. So, like a fighter pilot, he was flying guided by the nav display being projected onto his helmet's face shield.

The platoon emerged from the last gate above human-controlled territory. At seven thousand meters, Pax crossed over the mountain range, clearing some of the peaks by only a klick or so, and into Tucanan occupied land.

He could feel his pulse quicken as he guided his foil down a deep chasm in the north side of the range, hugging the ground the best he could while feeling terribly exposed. The Tucs had to have outposts along the range, and while his foil and flight suit could absorb enemy scans to a large extent, the Tucanans could "see" in darkness almost as well as in daylight. All a patrol had to do was to look up, and they might see him skimming over their heads.

He reached the tree line, which made him feel a little better, but that also meant he couldn't see what might be under the canopy.

Finally, he spotted it—a tall rock formation rising out of the scattered trees like some giant termite mound. That was their rally point. Pax didn't need his display to guide him to his personal LZ a couple hundred meters to the northwest of the RP.

He came down in a circle, looking for an opening, and once spotted, he wheeled like a hawk on a mouse and dove in but pulled up at the last second and came to a soft, stand-up landing.

Pax unlatched his Denon and faced outboard, his senses on high alert, but other than another Marine landing twenty meters away, the forest was silent.

He cracked open his helmet and dropped it to the ground as warm, living air washed over his face, smelling of evergreens and humidity. With three quick movements, he unsealed his flight suit and stepped out as his body began to thaw.

While still facing outboard and scanning the forest for the enemy with his weapon at the ready, he reached down with his left hand and triggered the self-destruct. Immediately, the flight suit, helmet, and foil started decomposing. Within twenty minutes, it would take some sophisticated scanners to tell that they'd ever been there.

The other Marine—Lance Corporal Vesta—walked over to join him, and the two stepped off in the direction of the RP.

They were on the ground in enemy territory—just where a Marine Raider wanted to be.

Undead Marine

PAX SCANNED the forest as the team moved like ghosts through the trees. Positioned on the far-right side of the formation, he was responsible for that flank. Missing something could have serious consequences, so his senses were on full alert as he looked for any enemy sign.

Designated as Bravo Team for the operation, the platoon was in a modified wedge, which put more Marines toward the front. That gave the best security from enemy ahead and gave almost the entire team clear fields of fire. It provided less security to the flanks, and it was harder to control in constrained terrain. Being more vulnerable to the flanks put increased pressure on Pax as he searched for sign of the enemy.

He wasn't the one who found it first. Wolf Morning Mist was on point, and he brought the team to a halt, knelt, and peered forward for a few moments before he reached down and picked something up. He looked at it, then raised his hand exposing three small, round spheres.

Meatballs.

The Tucanans didn't urinate as humans did—liquid was removed from their waste and excreted by small orifices located at each of their segment joints. They had solid waste, though, called *frass* by the xenobiologists, and usually they were disposed of in their version of toilets. But just like Marines on patrol, when you had to go, you had to go. Wolf had spotted some of their feces—"meatballs," in military slang.

Which meant that the team had moved into terrain where the Tucs patrolled. Pax had been watching Wolf. That was a rookie mistake, and he caught himself before his team leader did. He spun back outboard. That was his responsibility, not looking in toward Wolf.

They remained in position for a long minute. Maybe the lieutenant was reporting in to the skipper, but Pax doubted it. They'd expected to come across Tucanan sign, and this was just their turds, so why break comms silence, even for a flash message?

The lieutenant gave Wolf a thumbs-up and signaled the point Marine to continue. They'd known they were in Tuc-controlled territory, but with the actual physical proof Pax could feel the team's energy rise, their warrior readiness building, everyone's senses focused into the trees.

Hale's Refuge was terraformed by the defunct FSD Universal, and the forest had their signature—genmodded conifers at the higher elevations and deciduous at the lower, but the farther from the planned population centers, the more scattered the plantings. This was terraforming on a budget, which was one of the reasons the company was no longer around.

Why that mattered to the Marines was that while the trees around them soared up to fifty meters in the air, it was fairly open down on ground level. That gave them lots of visibility, but not much cover. The Marines wanted to get as close as possible before they were spotted to give any reaction force limited time to counterattack.

They reached the bottom of the slope, and the undergrowth became a little thicker on the valley floor. On the other side, three klicks away, was their target, right at the base of the next line of foothills.

Lieutenant Forte halted them in a laurel thicket and put them into a hasty defense. Now they had to wait. This was supposed to be a coordinated assault made by the entire company. Pax hadn't heard anything over the team net, but he assumed they'd arrived at their assembly area first, so now they'd have to wait until the skipper and Alpha were in position.

Pax was still riding a bit of his warrior high. This was how he liked to enter battle: controlled but with adrenaline flowing just beneath the surface. Extended waiting would dampen that flow, so he hoped they'd step off soon.

It was a foolish hope. An hour passed. Then two. Pax snuck a few glances back at the team leader, but he couldn't tell anything from her posture.

Surely, if Alpha's run into problems, she'd let us know?

After another thirty minutes, Gunny Akai came up at a crouch and knelt beside him.

"You doing OK, Q-B?"

The gunny had been a SagFed Naval Infantry soldier, and he was a Triple Threat, having been to one fewer elite school than Pax. He had twenty-two combat stars, though—far more than Pax. Throw in his rank, and he seemed to enjoy faux deference while referring to Pax's Quad Bod status, although he always said, "Q-B." Even a few of the others had picked that up.

"Just getting antsy, Gunny. Do you know what's taking Alpha?"

"They're on the ground, but the terrain's a little more difficult where they are."

Pax huffed. That was news to him.

In the straight-leg infantry, Pax would be a fire-team leader at the minimum, but probably a squad leader. In that position, he'd be kept more up to date on what was happening.

In spec ops, a sergeant was fairly junior. The platoon had two lance corporals and five corporals, so he wasn't the boot, but still, he was pretty far down on the totem pole.

"Any idea on when they'll reach their assembly area?"

"Maybe another half an hour. Just be patient. You'll pop your dead-kill cherry soon enough."

Pax snorted. It didn't matter how many people or Tucanans he'd killed as a Marine. That slate had been wiped clean when he was killed himself, according to the Immortals's self-imposed rules. Right now, his slate was zero-to-one, with the "one" being him. He was a cherry again.

Gunny patted his shoulder, "Let me go check the next cher—"

They both heard it and froze.

The team hadn't set out sensors for what they'd thought would have been a five-minute stop, nor had the lieutenant sent out drones, which could be picked up by enemy scanners. But they had ears, and there was no mistaking the subdued click of pede segments moving against each other.

Pax was laser-focused to his one o'clock. The laurel thicket was dense, giving them good cover. But it blocked their view as well.

Slowly, the gunny sank to the ground and went prone beside and just behind him. A soft chime sounded in his bonebud. The gunny had pressed the enemy alert.

Pax listened for any change in the sounds that would indicate the Tucanans had picked up the low-powered burst transmission. There was no interruption in the sounds of movement.

The pedes were close, though. Pax saw the top of a shortish Austrian Pine sway as if something had brushed up against it, and a moment later, he caught a glimpse of alien life passing underneath it.

Gunny grabbed his calf, and when Pax looked over at him, his team leader raised the trident he had in his hand a few centimeters.

Duh! Of course.

Pax nodded, laid his Denon on the deck, and slowly pulled his trident out of its thigh holster. The Tucs were maybe thirty meters away and well within the trident's range. And a trident could kill one of them, not just damage a segment.

His heart was pounding as he flipped the switch on the power-pack. He could feel it hum to life. The last time he'd fought the enemy, he'd been killed, and while the excitement he always felt just before combat was there as usual, this time it was tinged with anxiety.

Come on, Pax. You've done this before.

But he'd never been killed before.

He kept watching, and a Tuc came out of a dense copse of laurel twenty meters away.

"Steady," Gunny Akai whispered.

Pax gripped his launcher, his fingers white under the pressure. He quickly counted the segments—nine. It was a soldier, which he'd already known by the Buzzer it was carrying.

But how many more were with it?

The soldier raised itself higher, with four of its segments off the ground, and looked back into the denser brush. It seemed to spot what it wanted, dropped down a segment, and started skirting the heavier brush twenty meters away and roughly parallel to this section of the human line. A moment later, a mule appeared on the other side of the soldier with six segments down, two up. The mules were larger than the soldiers, but Pax would rather face them. They were a little slower to react, and their increased heft didn't seem to give them much of an advantage.

What it did give them was the ability to carry heavier loads, and this one was humping the unmistakable carriage assembly for a BN, as in "Bad News," a deadly crew-served weapon favored by Tucanans to break defensive positions—as in defenders of a pass.

The closest of the passes the S-2 had indicated was almost twenty-three klicks to the north. Pax had no idea where this group was coming from, but he'd bet they were heading there.

He glanced at the gunny after another mule emerged with part of the BN on its back. A Bad News was a pretty high-value target. But the gunny gave him the hand-and-arm signal to freeze, then wait.

Which was the right call. Taking out a BN was a righteous mission, but their mission had a much, much higher priority.

Except, the gods of war were a fickle lot, and the decision was taken out of their hands.

The soldier, which had seemed to be more focused toward the other mules, stopped and raised back up, this time two segments. It slowly turned until its pseudo-eyes were pointed at the Marine line.

"Shit," Gunny Akai whispered. Then, "On my signal, Q-B, take that bastard out."

The pede froze for a long moment as if testing the air. Its right foot-arm started to slowly raise the muzzle of its Buzzer, when Gunny Akai shouted, "Fire!"

Pax brought his right knee up and pushed, raising his weapon as he moved into the kneeling position. He sighted his weapon and launched the trident while a dozen Marines peppered it with flechettes. Two segments were hit just as the soldier opened fire, which jerked the blades high and over the Marines' heads. And then the trident hit home.

It was on automatic, but Pax wasn't taking any chances. He hit the power release, and the current shot down the wire and coursed through the pede's body. Two more segments were lifted off the ground as the enemy's shriek was cut off. The current ceased, and the body curled into their version of a fetal position.

It was dead.

The two Mules might not be as quick as the soldier, and they were burdened by the BN components, but they were still fighters. Almost in unison, they raised their Buzzers and started firing.

Instead of hunkering down and making the Tucanans come to them, though, Gunny Akai shouted, "First Section, assault. Second, envelop right."

With the platoon in a defensive perimeter, it was broken down into quarters, using their direction of movement as the twelve o'clock. The Tucs were moving parallel to the human heading, so only a half—the first section from twelve to three, and second section from three to six, were even obliquely facing the enemy. Those on the other side were masked from firing their weapons.

By ordering the second section into an envelopment, the gunny was freeing at least half of what was now their frontage to supporting fire.

Smart, Pax thought as he slapped in his second trident and got to his feet.

The lieutenant realized what was happening, too. As Pax charged forward, he could hear her shifting the others around to take advantage of the cleared fields of fire.

Pax was half a step behind the rest of the Marines charging the two mules. He was aware of someone to his right spinning around and going down as he readied his trident. But someone else beat him to it. Two someones. The big mule was able to evade the first, but the second one ran true, and a few seconds later, it was deepfried pede.

That left one . . . which of course was BS, he realized. One more in his field of vision. There weren't just three of them wandering around the forest. More started emerging and engaging, including another soldier who appeared barreling around some trees and into the attack.

As the right flank in the previous movement to the assembly area, Pax was now the far-right Marine in the assaulting force. He didn't have a good bead on the soldier, so he slammed the launcher into the holster, raised his Denon, and started shifting right to get a better flanking angle when the base of fire opened up behind him. Flechettes and the heavier fifteen-millimeter rounds of the M-52 Bushmaster started zipping past him, too close for comfort.

He darted back to the left, and that opened up a clear field of fire. Two bursts ripped through the trees to join the other Marines' efforts, but the bastard kept coming. One of its segments seemed wonky, but still the Tucanan soldier advanced, weapon blazing. With a secondary foot-arm, it raised a grenade launcher and fired. A moment later, an explosion boomed to Pax's left. He felt the concussion, but no shrapnel.

This pede was a beast, but even beasts had to die sometime. It staggered under the onslaught, then seemed to collapse in stages. A Marine darted close and systematically put a burst into each section.

The sounds of battle erupted to Pax's right. The enveloping force was engaged.

Here's where it could get tricky. An assault force still in motion. An enveloping force now converging from the right. A base of fire to the rear. Limited visibility.

A recipe for disaster.

Except for the fact that these were elite professionals who'd been working diligently on teamwork. Between their training and the platoon's leaders, they maneuvered like a fine Swiss clock.

Pax was impressed as the gunny swept him up and started giving commands. It was an intricate dance, but a beautiful one.

He brought Pax up on the flank of a mule who was holed up like a badger. It sounded like one, too, with the heavy snarling that the mules favored.

Keeping the trunk of a tree between them, Pax scooted forward, and while the others kept it occupied, it was almost too easy.

Pax fired, and the trident buried itself in the thing's fourth segment. Quick for a mule, it whirled around, both to try and engage him and to try and pull the trident out, but it was too late. The pulse of current reached it, and that was that.

"Target down hard," he shouted back to the gunny.

It was only then that he realized the sounds of fighting had died down.

Was it over?

"First, give me a perimeter," the lieutenant yelled from Pax's right. "Second, sweep the area. And Gunny, give me a head count."

Pax was breathing hard as adrenaline still pulsed through his body. It looked like they'd won the fight and remarkably, unscathed.

"Medic up!" someone shouted, barely visible through the trees.

In the Marines, medics were corpsmen, so whoever called for one had let their old habits take over in the stress of the moment. Medic or corpsman, though, that still meant that not everyone was unscathed, and Pax remembered seeing one Marine going down.

He didn't hear any more calls, though.

"Pax, get on line," Link told him. "We need to sweep the area."

Pax took one more look back at where Doc Grant was working on someone. He couldn't see who that someone was from his vantage point, but whoever it was was sitting up, which was a good sign.

Around him, he could see three dead Tucs. One had the main barrel of the BN still strapped to the harness on its back.

He didn't know how this fight was going to affect their mission, but still, it had been good to get tested and to pass that with flying colors.

Pax dragged the last soldier to the line of Tucanan bodies and dropped it alongside the other soldier. Six Tucs—two soldiers and four mules—had been killed. Pax had been responsible for two of them. No more dead-kill cherry.

He stretched his back as he looked down the line. Three had been tridented, their pill bug roll proof of that. Two had been killed with Denons, and one had been blasted apart by St. Amons on the Bushmaster. Byeon and Wolf were checking the bodies, but were not expected to find anything earth-shattering.

Six Tucanans, only two being soldiers, weren't much of a challenge to a full platoon of spec-ops Marines, but they were still combat troops, and it was hard to argue with success.

The Marines had one WIA. Corporal Wommack had his upper arm sliced open, but Doc Grant had sealed it shut, and Wommack had assured the lieutenant that he was good to go.

The big question was what this fight was going to do to their mission. Their assembly area was a good six klicks from the target, and now the enemy at the command center might know the humans were there. And the last Pax had heard, the skipper and the Alpha Team still hadn't arrived at their assembly area.

"Good shooting there, Q-B," the gunny said as he stepped up beside him.

"I was just at the right spot. Anyone could have done the same."

"Anyone could, but you did."

Pax just stared at the dead pedes for a moment before he said, "Smart move with the enveloping force. That gave the base a clear field of fire so Olive Oil could bring her Bushmaster into play."

The gunny chuckled and asked, "So, I met with your satisfaction? I guess I can sleep well tonight."

Pax felt his face redden, and he stammered out, "I didn't mean it like that, Gunny. I just . . . well, I wouldn't have thought of that."

"You're still a newbie," the gunny said. "You react well, and you don't hesitate. I didn't have to tell you what to do. You're a warrior, no doubt about it. Hell, your Cross attests to how big your balls are. But there's more to being a Marine than being a certified badass."

Pax waited a moment for the gunny to go on, and when he didn't, Pax asked, "What do you mean?"

"Look. You're a sergeant. But in the Immortals, that's like a lance coolie[1] in the rest of the military."

Which Pax was well aware of.

"Right now, you're a weapon. A good one, to be sure. But if you want to be a better Marine, not just a weapon, you've got to start thinking about the total picture. You need to develop a better

---

1. **Lance Coolie**: slang for lance corporal

tactical awareness of what's going on and how everything fits together in relation to everything else. That's what you don't have yet."

Pax frowned and wanted to protest. He'd commanded his militia on Boracay. Same on Uriah two missions prior to that. But he bit his tongue. He may have given orders on Boracay, but as he considered it, he hadn't really done much except to move the squad around and tell them what to do. When the shit hit the fan, he shouldered most of the fighting himself. He didn't fight the squad.

"I'm not sure how I'm supposed to do that."

Gunny Akai put his hand on Pax's shoulder. "I don't think they'll be sending you to SNCO School. So, you'll learn on the job or die."

The gunny was being serious, but that struck Pax as funny.

"You mean again."

It took the gunny a moment, then he laughed. "Yeah. You'll die again."

Nani Vesta jogged up right then and said, "Gunny, the lieutenant wants you."

"I guess she's got our orders," he said, then to Pax, "You'll do fine, Q-B. It just takes practice. Now get back on the perimeter while I find out what's going on."

Pax pondered what the gunny had said as he went back to his position on the defensive line—just because one fight was over didn't mean there weren't other Tucanans in the area. He understood what the gunny said, and it made perfect sense. But how was he supposed to learn all of that? There were too many possibilities in any fight.

Maybe just watching him would be a good start.

He'd barely gotten back to his position when the order was given to form back up for movement.

The primary mission was still on, but the timeline had been cut. They were going to have to move it.

11

THE ORIGINAL OPERATIONS order was for both First and Second Platoons to infiltrate, in unison, as close as possible to the enemy CACC, moving into the assault only when they were discovered—or, best case basis, when they were at their attack position and ready to go. The fight at the assembly area put the kibosh on that, and the company was moving to Plan B, where speed took center stage.

If Intel was correct, then there was only a Tucanan battalion in the area. The Tuc SOP was for a mobile area defense, which gave them flexibility, but spread out their ability to concentrate resources. They could shift their tactics, though, and the humans had to assume that they were aware of the attack and that they'd be collapsing on their CP. The company couldn't defeat an entire Tucanan battalion in a pitched battle. Their only hope to accomplish their mission was probably to beat the bulk of the Tucanans to their command center and take it out before a strong defense could be implemented.

That put speed paramount. They had to move quickly, all while knowing that they could run into Tucs at any time.

Pax was back on the right flank where he had to keep one eye on the formation as they raced through the forest and one eye outbound to spot the enemy.

Wolf was still on point, but now Olivia was on his ass taking care of the navigation and making sure the platoon kept to their avenue of approach. The former Ghostwalker had resisted having her there, assuring the lieutenant that he could navigate and spot the enemy at the same time, but the platoon commander nixed that. When split seconds could be the difference in a meeting engagement, she wanted Wolf's attention solely on spotting the enemy before the enemy spotted them.

In this case, Pax was in full agreement with the lieutenant. It was hard enough for him to keep his position relative to the rest of the platoon while scanning the forest for enemy sign. It would be even more difficult if he had to keep the route displayed in his combat goggles.

Wolf had been nothing but capable in every training exercise, but Pax had a feeling that he might sometimes flash a chip his ass can't swipe.

They were covering ground quickly. Too quickly for a tactical approach, and Pax expected to hear fire at any moment, but to his surprise, they managed to reach their attack position, which was the last covered and concealed position where they could form for the assault.

The platoon was in a heavily vegetated draw that led up to a small access road about four hundred meters ahead and forty meters higher in elevation. The Tucanan's CACC was 170 meters down the road to the right and another thirty meters higher into the mountainside. Once the platoon left their attack position and crossed the Final Coordination Line, they could be spotted by anyone on the road.

Which had been taken into consideration. The platoon was acting as both a fixing force and a base of fire. They would advance until taken under fire, then take whatever cover they could and return fire. Meanwhile, First Platoon would have already climbed higher into the mountainside and would be ready to envelop the command post from the rear.

It was a pretty basic plan and should be somewhat easy to coordinate, but the gods of war had a habit of throwing a wrench into things. They'd already been busy. First was the fight they'd just had. Second was First Platoon's advance. They'd already been held up.

And the longer that Second Platoon hunkered in the draw, the more chance they had of being detected. And the more time the Tucanans had to bring in their security.

"Think First will get in position?" Panda asked Pax.

The two of them were at the edge of the draw, acting as OPs.[1] From their position, they had a narrow view of the access road leading to the enemy CP.

"They'd better. I'm not too enthused about having to do the assault from here. The pedes have the high ground."

"I get nervous waiting. You know, I got killed on Gobbler when our air didn't show up on time."

"What happened?" Pax asked, not taking his eyes off their little section of access road.

A Tuc in walking mode could hug the back of the road and not

---

1. **OP**: Observation Post

be seen, but Pax was confident that he could spot any significant movement.

"I was in a scout team, observing pede movements."

"Kind of like this."

"Well, yeah. But we weren't part of any assault like now."

Paladin scouts were like Marine Deep Recon. They deployed behind enemy lines and gathered intelligence but were not supposed to engage the enemy.

"But the two of us got spotted. We diddihoed out of there with the pedes on our butts. We stayed ahead of them all the way to our extract, but our ride had mechanical problems and had to abort. The Guardian Angel took over, but they were still two minutes out when the fuckers overran us. I got two before I was hit."

Pax risked a quick glance at Panda.

"The pedes overran you? How the hell did you get reanimated?"

"A fast mover cleared the LZ, and the Guardian Angel came in and recovered our bodies. Yada yada yada, and the next thing I know, I'm waking up and being told I was KIA and welcome to the dead."

Pax grunted. Not many of them talked about how they'd been killed. He was curious about the others, but he hadn't wanted to step on any toes by asking. Panda was only the second person to tell him what happened.

"Well, that's not going to be a problem here," he said.

"What do you mean? We're still in pede-controlled territory."

"We don't have any air assets available, so they can't be late."

Panda snorted and choked off a laugh. "Oh, that makes me feel so much better, Sergeant."

"Just doing my duty to keep morale up."

He adjusted his body to relieve his pressure points on the ground.

Panda opening up was a good sign that he was being accepted into the unit. Or maybe it was that he wasn't an Undead virgin anymore. Whatever the reason, it seemed that the universal military tendency to keep the FNGs[2] at arm's length was fading with regard to him.

The sooner the better, and he wanted to keep the openness going.

"What's the story with you and Vesta?" he asked.

"What do you mean?"

"You seem pretty close. And I overheard someone say you two are 'almost a thing.'"

"Who? Wommack? Did she say that?"

It was Corporal Wommack, but Pax didn't want to rat her out.

"I don't know. That was before I knew everyone's name."

"I know it was her. She's just jealous."

He didn't specify who the other corporal was jealous of, and now Pax was genuinely curious.

A rock rolled down the slope and crashed into the trees a hundred meters away. Both Marines froze, but there was no other sound of movement.

After five long minutes of the two searching for any sign of Tucanans, Panda said, "We're just friends."

It took a moment to realize that the corporal was continuing on about Nani Vesta.

"It's not like we can, you know, get intimate or anything like that."

---

2. **FNG**: slang for "Fucking New Guy," used to refer to new joins into the unit.

"Yeah, the doc said that's the last thing that comes back."

Panda turned half his body to look at Pax. "You bought that line of bullshit?"

"What do you mean?"

"Why would fucking be the last thing to recover? Doc Grant says there's no reason. The truth is that they don't want us making little zombies. What a legal quagmire that would be. And that's assuming that with our mycs, we wouldn't have mutant babies."

What?

He had to think about that for a moment. "That makes no sense. They could, you know . . ." he said as he made snipping motions with his right hand.

"Which can be reversed. And they can't cut off our balls because we need the testosterone to fight. They can't remove the ovaries of the girls, either. That's where they get a lot of their testosterone. So, they just give us an implant, and no woodies. No desire, too," he added, sounding dejected.

That seemed too complicated to Pax, and he didn't understand why they'd do it. The baby zombies, sure. But there were easier ways to make sure that didn't happen.

But if it's true . . .

A wave of anger washed over him. It was bad enough that their legal rights had been stripped away, but if they were messing with them like Panda said, that seemed more personal. More despicable.

It seemed like every time Pax started to settle into his new, Undead reality, something else was thrown at him.

This isn't the time to stress about it. Not before a fight.

He promised himself that he'd try to find out after they got back, but still, the niggling thought wouldn't let go, lasting all the way until Link crept up to them.

"First Platoon's stopped. There's a pede bivouac on the north side of the CP, and they're not going to be able to maneuver, so we're switching roles. They're going to fix the pedes, and we're doing the assault."

Reproduction was forgotten as adrenaline coursed through Pax's body.

"Same contingency plan?" he asked.

"Same. We kick off in five minutes. You two stay here until we start to move, then fall into your position. Got it?"

"Got it," Pax said.

Link slid back down to the rest of the platoon.

Pax looked at Panda and said, "Playtime's over. Now we earn our salary."

"We're not getting paid."

"OK, then we just get to kick pede ass."

"Now you're talking my language."

IT WAS ACTUALLY eleven minutes later when the fusillade of fire erupted several hundred meters to the north.

The Tucanans reacted quickly, returning fire within seconds. The heavier, unmistakable whump of two BNs quickly joined the Tuc response.

"Shit. I hope our guys have got cover," Link said.

It was probably too much to hope for that the Tucanans would be limited to small arms. As light as the Marines' body armor was, it was still reasonably effective against the Tucanan's Buzzers and Ballistas. The BN, however, was a different story. The big chemical rounds could damage most armored vehicles and would make short shrift of any Marine hit.

"That's it. Let's go," the lieutenant said.

Immediately, the lead team started up the draw, followed a few seconds later by the rest of the platoon.

The draw severely constrained their formation, concentrating them far too closely together. A few indirect rounds could wreak havoc among them, so the key was to move as quickly as possible to limit their time in a danger zone.

But the draw still gave them cover as they climbed to the access road. Visual concealment, that was. A Marine unit would have filled such an obvious avenue of approach with sensors. The Tucanans made less use of ground sensors—their many foot-arms could detect vibrations in the ground quite well, and that seemed to give them somewhat of a sense of complacency—but they didn't totally ignore them.

As Pax pushed forward through the brush, he kept listening for the firefight to shift and for them to start receiving incoming fire. But amazingly, the lead team made it to the top, right at the edge of the access road.

Staff Sergeant Justice Bethel halted the platoon, which was spread out for thirty meters down the draw. The access road, with visibility of almost sixty meters to the right and forty to the left, was a danger area that they had to cross, need for speed or not. A single Ballista in position could decimate the platoon. Bethel was on his belly just shy of the road, and he pulled out his snake-eye to get a visual down its length.

"Outboard, Pax," Link said.

Pax dutifully shifted his attention to the flank. He couldn't help but glance back as Bethel looked through the optical device, though. He immediately spun around to signal the lieutenant: "three Tucs," a "crew-served weapon," "approaching," and "thirty-five meters."

Evidently, the enemy had detected them, at least enough to find out what was there.

The lieutenant signaled back to engage, then signaled for everyone else to get ready.

"Get ready to rush straight up," Link told the element. "Flank the suckers."

They were supposed to cross the road in a column, which would leave them in position to assault across to the CP, but with enemy on the road itself, Link had taken it upon himself to alter the plan to meet the threat.

The element was about four or five meters below the edge of the road. Pax couldn't see the enemy, but he could just pick up the soft click of pede foot-arms. He wiped the palm of his hand against his chest, then gripped the stock of his Denon.

At the apex of the draw, Wolf and Olivia had switched to their tridents, while Bethel and Wommack had their Denons. As one, they rose and fired.

"Now!" Link shouted.

Pax shoved with his leg as he scrambled up the slope, his feet slipping as he went. It took ten seconds to reach the road, and by then, it was already over. Fifteen meters away, two of the Tucs were in their death curl, tridents still impaling them. Another was feebly moving one set of foot-arms, the "fingers" aimlessly opening and shutting. A Ballista was in a heap on the ground.

Behind them, the platoon was crossing the road and climbing up the other side.

"Panda, burn the Ballista. Pax, finish off that pede," Link ordered. "And quickly."

Pax stepped up to the wounded Tucanan. Six segments were dead, leaving the primary alive. The segment was leaking clear, yellow-tinted "blood," and one of the foot-arms was blown off about eight centimeters from the joint.

Behind him, a flare burst into life as Mouve dropped his mini-magna incendiary grenade on the Ballista, creating harsh shadows around the enemy soldier as it tried to push its first segment upright with its one working foot-arm.

The thing wasn't going to survive much longer, and Pax hesitated. This was the part of the war that he hated. He was reluctant to just kill an enemy when it obviously wasn't a threat, but that was the way it was.

"Fulling potto," it hissed in Universal as Pax stood over it. "I'll kill you."

No one knew why the Tucs thought "fulling" was a general curse word, nor why they called humans "pottos," which were a slow-moving primate from Western Africa on Earth.

"Fulling pede, you aren't doing anything. You lost," Pax said as he reached for his lance.

"Now, Pax. Or are you going to bore it to death?" Link shouted.

Pax had no problem killing Tucanans in combat, but this was nothing to be proud of. It had to be done, though, and now. He closed the flap over the lance, realizing he needed to be quick. Instead of the lance, he raised his Denon and aimed at the anterior third of the surviving section. The Tucanan reached for the muzzle as Pax pulled the trigger.

At this range, the hypervelocity dart blasted through both the armor applique and the shell beneath. Yellowish blood spurted, spattering Pax and covering his combat goggles.

"Shit!" he said as he tried to wipe them clean.

The goggles had a hyperstatic exterior lens which repelled most dirt, but pede blood was nasty, sticky stuff, and Pax was smearing it more than anything else. The glare from Mouve's grenade only made things worse.

"Move, Pax," Link said.

Hell.

He dropped the goggles around his neck. He was going to have to go without them.

The staff sergeant had already started to move off to join the rest of the platoon, but he'd stopped and was waiting for him. Pax gave him a thumbs-up and began to jog.

They joined the column of Marines crossing the road, falling in behind as they made their way up the slope. The battle to the north was raging, but for the moment, they were still in the clear. That wouldn't last. The Tucanans had to know they were there.

The first rounds impacted the road moments after Mouve, who was now Tail End Charlie, stepped off it. Shrapnel peppered the branches. More rounds hit the draw.

Too late, pedes.

Pax missed the first few words coming over his bonebuds, something he'd always had a problem with. Being transmitted through his temporal bones was a little different than normal hearing, and even after all these years, sometimes he had to realize what was happening and concentrate on what was being said.

". . . as fast as we can," the lieutenant was saying.

With their presence compromised, there was no use keeping to radio silence. It probably wouldn't last. The Tucs had decent enough jamming capabilities. The platoon comms AI would keep running countermeasures, but the end result always favored the jammers.

The platoon forged ahead, past a particularly steep section, until it leveled out onto a shelf. They were now slightly above the enemy CP and two hundred meters away.

The lieutenant gave the order, and the platoon essentially conducted a right face. They were now in their assault formation as they started to move.

She'd wanted something a little more intricate than a simple flanking movement, but the captain had insisted that she keep it simple. They'd originally been tasked to be the supporting element, after all.

Given the terrain, Pax was happy it was more basic. As the right flank, his team was on the downhill side, where the slope was steeper. So, they had to crab along the slope, providing cover while keeping on line. And when they did initiate contact, he wasn't sure they could support and be supported by the rest of the platoon.

Indirect fire rounds started landing closer to the platoon, but the Tucanans seemed more to be trying to seek them out. Pax couldn't believe that there weren't sensors or that the enemy weren't sending out drones to locate them. Yes, he could hear they were heavily engaged with First Platoon, but they had to realize their vulnerability to the south and west.

It was too good to last. Somehow, they spotted the Marines and reacted—just not in the way Pax would have expected. Instead of using indirect fire, instead of setting up a defense, the Tucanans sent a platoon of mall cops—six-segmented, smaller versions of the soldiers who normally protected rear area installations and depots.

They can't think that this is really the rear area, can they? Pax wondered as the platoon net came alive while the Marines engaged.

Pax had never seen a mall cop in real life, and craned his head to spot them, but he couldn't see the enemy. He expected Link to maneuver them around so that they could contribute, but he kept them in place.

Good thing, too.

A minute later, Mouve passed, "Contact, right!"

The team dropped to a crouch, Pax using a fallen branch for cover. Going to their belly was the SOP, but the slope made that impractical. He peered through the branches, but it took a moment before Pax spotted movement coming up the slope while using the trees for cover.

"They're trying to flank us," Link passed. "Hold your position until I give the order."

Pax shifted toward the oncoming Tucanans, then hunkered down and tried to melt into the earth. Behind him, the sounds of battle raged, but his focus was on the Tucs climbing toward them.

They were hard to see at no-mast, every segment on the ground, but he thought they might be mall cops, too. They flowed like an evil, animated carpet as they closed the distance.

"Tridents and hoppers," Link ordered.

Something exploded in back of Pax, and two pieces of either wood or shrapnel pinged off his shoulder and leg, but he ignored it. He had to trust the rest of the platoon to do their job.

He reached into his thigh pack, pulled out a hopper, and set the grenade to two meters—just right for Tucanans at no-mast.

It looked like there were six or seven of them. Their movement through the trees and brush made it hard to tell.

"Steady," Link passed. "Wait for my signal."

Suddenly, one of them popped up to half-mast as if it had spotted them.

"Now!"

Pax rose to one knee and threw his hopper, then fired the trident just as the Tucanans started firing. The trident shaft grazed a tree trunk, which sent it ricocheting off to the right. The hopper hit the ground and detonated. The warhead shot two meters straight into the air, then it detonated, sending down a cone of tiny, explosive-tipped darts. If the tiny dart hit anything hard, the tip would be the third detonation as it burned into the body.

Tucanan bodies were hard. At least four darts took out two segments of the nearest Tuc, and another dart burned into one just behind the first.

All of that barely registered as Pax raised his Denon and fired. In less than ten seconds, it was over. The other hoppers had torn through the enemy, and two tridents had hit home.

The team stopped firing, but only for a moment. Panda nailed one of the wounded when it tried to recover its Buzzer with a still-working foot-arm. Three more were twitching, not making any offensive moves.

"Down," Link ordered.

Tucanans were known to send mall cops or mules forward while soldiers held back to engage humans, who then exposed themselves.

Pax went back down to his crouch. The firing above him was becoming more and more human.

A few moments later, the lieutenant ordered the platoon to cease fire, and that was followed by a "Clean the field. You've got one minute."

Which was a too-polite euphemism for making sure no

Tucanan was able to come at them from the rear after they went on. The enemy wasn't above playing possum when it suited them.

Looking out at the six Tucs, though, Pax thought none of them would be mobile anytime soon.

"Panda, Pax. Go to it. You've got thirty seconds."

SOP was to send two Marines forward to "clean." One to do the coup de grâce, with the other to cover them.

Panda had often said that he loved being the executioner, so Pax wasn't surprised when he pulled his lance out of the case and released the flexible blade, which unrolled to its sixty-centimeter length. Pax was fine with that, too. He'd cover the corporal.

The closest pede was a trident hit. No need to do anything to that. The next was badly injured, but two of its segments were showing signs of movement.

"Quick clean, Panda. We don't have time."

The corporal nodded, placed the tip of the blade at the juncture of the first segment and the head nodule, and like an ancient matador, slid the blade in before giving it a seesaw motion.

A full clean was to do that between every segment. They didn't have time for that. But if they severed the nodule, a Tuc was essentially blind.

Good enough for government work.

The lieutenant was already giving the order to resume their assault by the time Panda dispatched the third Tucanan that still showed signs of life. Pax hurried back to his position when he saw that Link was sitting on the ground.

"You OK?"

The staff sergeant winced and turned to where Pax could see the blood leaking from his body armor's elbow joint.

"Took a hit, but I'm OK," he said as he struggled to his feet, his left arm dangling. "Let's go."

"You're left-handed."

The staff sergeant scowled and hoisted his Denon with his right. "This baby doesn't care which hand I use to send rounds downrange."

There was no time to argue—and really no recourse. They were outnumbered behind enemy lines. Unless Pax wanted to carry his friend, Link was going to have to get out on his own two feet. And if he could fire his weapon, then he could be an asset to the mission.

The platoon was already moving.

"Watch for kneecappers," the lieutenant passed. "First ran into them."

"Of course, they'd use them here," Link said as he staggered forward.

Kneecappers were an infantryman's bane. When the war with the Tucanans started, the small mines were designed to send out a circle of death made from a linked set of thin expanding bars, but at a height of about twenty centimeters. Against another Tucanan, if it detonated within about five meters, the bars would cut right through multiple sections, separating the bottom half from the top and slicing foot-arms in two. This design was indicative that they were created to use against fellow Tucs.

Against humans, the bars took off legs at the knee, cutting through body armor with ease. After five meters, the bars detached from each other and became less effective, but under that and the legs were gone.

Within a year, though, the kneecappers had been adjusted to detonate at 120 centimeters, which meant the cutting bars hit humans in the torso. But while they no longer detonated at knee-level, the name stuck.

They were difficult to detect and reportedly caused twelve percent of human infantry casualties.

As operators, the spec-ops community didn't run into the kneecappers often, but this close to the human lines, it made sense that the Tucanans would employ them around their CP.

The company moved into the assault, closing the distance as rapidly as possible. Pax kept expecting the enemy to open fire, but there was no sign of them. And that was in and of itself worrisome. This was a CACC, and for the centralized Tucanans, it was more important than a human CP would be.

Why was there no security? Was Intel even right about the CP being there?? It looked like this entire operation might have been for naught until a volley of fire hit the left side platoon.

Pax had never felt relief about receiving fire until now. Maybe the CP really was there.

It wasn't particularly effective fire, mostly Dingers and mini-Buzzers, which the Marines' body armor deflected. Both weapons were common among mall cops.

The platoon started team rushes, with four-person teams rushing ten or fifteen meters, hitting the deck, and providing supporting fire for the next team. The platoon had practiced this hundreds of times, and it was second nature to them. They quickly closed the distance to the CP entrance.

Until the Pilum team opened up.

A Pilum was a powerful, 23 mm automatic weapon that fired a larger version of the Tucanan Buzzer ammunition. The round could disable lightly armored vehicles, so it had no problem with a Marine's body armor.

With two of the Pilums, the Tucs could lay down an impenetrable curtain of death. It seemed as if the enemy wasn't leaving their CP completely undefended.

Every Marine in the platoon hit the deck and took whatever cover they could as the big Pilums filled the air over their prone bodies.

Link's team was still on the downhill side of their advance, so Pax couldn't see the gun positions, but he could sure see the storm of leaves and branches falling to the ground.

"Get ready," Link said. "We may have to take out those damn guns."

The platoon had done many exercises taking out weapons positions, and they knew what to do. But in every exercise, they'd been assessed casualties, sometimes heavy ones. But if the four of them were in defilade, then they could theoretically maneuver closer before launching an assault from the flank.

The problem was that the Tucanans knew that as well, and they probably had something in place to greet them as they maneuvered forward.

The expected order never came, though. The lieutenant had a different plan. One of her drones had gotten a quick look at the intervening ground between them and the entrance to the CP, and on the downhill side, it looked clear all the way. There could be mines and booby traps, but there didn't look to be any Tucanans.

Link took the call, then told the others, "The mission's on our heads. The lieutenant and the rest are going to keep the pedes occupied. We're getting Wolf, then we're moving around to try and ram a Saber down into the objective."

Pax was thrilled. The entire mission was down to them. It was the proverbial chance at glory.

Abject failure, too. But Pax violently shoved that thought away. He wasn't going to entertain the possibility that they wouldn't succeed.

Wolf crawled down the slope, sending a mini-avalanche of debris as he came. His smile was so big, Pax didn't see how his face didn't crack in two.

The corporal stopped beside Link, patted the Saber slung on his back, and said, "Let's nail us a pede CP."

The five of them started crawling farther down the hill. Link was struggling, and Pax gave him a wary eye, but gravity helped make it easier on him. They stopped short of the access road—the Tucs would have eyes on it—and turned toward the CP.

They had only made it about forty meters when Link stopped them at the underside of a large boulder that jutted from the mountainside. He motioned Pax closer.

His face was ashen, and he said, "I don't think I can go any farther. You've got to take over."

He fell back against the rock and slid to a sitting position. His breaths were shallow and quick.

"What does the lieutenant say?" Pax asked, concerned for his friend.

"She says nothing," Link said, then paused for a moment before continuing. "She gave us the mission. That hasn't changed. Only now, you're leading it. I'll just rest here for a bit."

Pax didn't know what to say. Link looked horrible, but he was right. The mission hadn't changed.

"Let me check with the L-T."

"Bullshit, Pax. We've got the mission, and you need to step up."

He hesitated for only a few seconds until he remembered the gunny telling him he needed more experience. Maybe this was one of those times. And Link was right. They still had the mission to accomplish.

"OK. I've got it. You wait here, and we'll come back for you when we're done. And I'll get Doc Grant to come fix you up."

"Don't forget me," Link said with a laugh that turned into a cough.

Pax patted his friend on the shoulder, then motioned for Nani, who was on point, to step off again. There were some questioning looks, but no one said anything.

The depleted team started forward. Pax took one last look back at Link—his friend had his Denon across his knees as he watched down the hill—before turning to the front.

He'd worry about Link later. Right now, he had a job to do.

The sounds of the fight were steady, but not overwhelming. But that made sense to him from a tactical standpoint. The Tucs, with their dug in Ballistas and Pilums, were in a good position. And all they had to do was delay the platoon until other Tucanan units could arrive. Why risk an escalation that could get more of them killed?

And as for the lieutenant, she'd already decided to let Pax and the others make the strike. If the rest of the platoon could fix the Tucanans in place, then that would give Corporal Morning Mist his best chance of success.

And if Wolf failed? Then it would be on to Plan B, which would result in more Marine casualties.

Let's make sure we don't fail, then, he told himself as they hurried closer to the CP.

The trees opened up ahead. The area in front of the entrance was cleared, and a wide approach led up from the access road. Pax was just about to bring the team to a halt when Nani opened fire with her Denon. She bolted forward a few steps and fired again.

That was it. The Tucs knew they were there.

"Now!" he shouted as he surged to join Nani. He caught a glimpse of a wounded mall cop on the ground as another was dragging itself to the entrance, which was a two-meter-high, three-meter-wide hole cut into the rock. There was a two-meter overhang at the top of the opening—Pax couldn't tell if it was natural or Tucanan-made, but that's probably why Intel had such a hard time detecting it. Various spikes that were the Tuc's versions of antennas sprouted from the rock face, and a dish was about ninety meters higher. Two more mall cops were firing from out of the entrance, the Mini-Buzzer blades cutting into the trees.

He wasn't sure why the Tucanans had only four mall cops guarding the entrance, but he wasn't going to complain.

Pax took cover behind one of those trees, while Panda and Nani were behind two others. One blade zinged off Pax's shoulder as he leaned around the tree to engage the enemy.

"Wolf!"

But the corporal was already unlimbering his Saber. Preparing the weapon was a three-step process, and it couldn't be rushed. But the missile powered up, and Wolf looked ahead.

They were about ten meters from where the trees ended, and then it was another thirty-five or forty meters from the entrance.

"I can't fire from here," he said. "I need a clearer shot."

He had started to low-crawl forward when they found out that the Tucanans weren't relying on the four mall cops for security. With a heart-dropping bud-bud-bud, a concealed Pilum started firing from inside the entrance.

What had been splinters breaking free from the Mini-Buzzers

now became trees exploding into pieces. Pax dropped to the ground a split second before the tree he'd been taking cover behind was blasted in half, right at shoulder level. He was peppered with chunks of wood and got scored right where his body armor stopped and under the back of his helmet.

Shit!

He ignored the pain and tried to look ahead, but his visibility was limited while his face was in the dirt. The two pedes inside the entrance had quit firing. Why bother when a Pilum was spitting out violent intent? All they had to do was keep low and not get hit.

Alongside him, Nani and Panda were kissing the dirt, too. Just one of those Pilum rounds would be enough to take them out, and with so much damage that Pax didn't think reanimation would be possible. Not even myc could survive a hit to the head. There wouldn't even *be* a head to try and salvage.

Pax twisted around to ask Wolf if he thought he could take the shot, but the corporal was already rapidly low-crawling to their left.

It was obvious that he wanted to try and flank the entrance. The Pilum team had limited fields of fire, seeing as how it was inside the opening. If Wolf could get out of that cone of destruction, he could get closer.

But the same restriction applied to him. The Saber was an amazing weapon. With both an armor-piercing warhead—designed to penetrate bunkers or reinforced doors—and the main thermobaric warhead, it could take out a wide variety of targets, but the missile had limited maneuverability. Wolf had to have a direct shot into the entrance to send it on its way. From the flank, he wouldn't have an effective strike, and most of the main warhead's energy would just splash across the mountainside.

And now, why the two mall cops hunkered down at the

entrance became clear. They were there to keep anyone like Wolf from getting a clear shot.

"Wolf!"

The corporal looked back.

"Give me the signal when you're ready. We'll cover you."

Wolf gave him a thumbs-up and resumed his advance.

"Nani, Panda. Wolf's going to try and get a shot. But we need to cover him from the mall cops. And don't forget the two wounded pedes. They can still fire their weapons."

He shifted his position slightly so he could watch Wolf, making sure that he didn't expose himself. The Pilum couldn't quite depress far enough to hit the three prone Marines, but it was close. Get a little careless, and Pax would pay the price.

They'd have to expose themselves to cover Wolf, but that was unavoidable.

With the loud bud-bud-bud of the heavy weapon, Pax almost didn't notice that the amount of small arms fire around the platoon had diminished. One of the two Pilums there was still firing, and the Dinger and Mini-Buzzer fire were less. Which could mean that some of the mall cops facing the platoon were breaking off to reinforce the entrance. If that was the case, the team was in trouble.

"Hurry, Wolf," he passed on the team net. "I think we've got company coming."

He lost sight of the corporal, and it wasn't as if he was going to stand to see him again. He was just going to have to wait until he got the signal.

Thirty seconds passed. Then another.

If the mall cops were coming, there was almost no time left.

"Wolf, we—"

"I'm ready. On five," he passed on the team net.

Pax pulled up a knee. Beside him, Panda was stirring.

"One . . . two . . . three . . . four . . . FIVE!"

On Wolf's count, Pax stood and shot at the entrance, hitting one of the Tucs there. Around him, the Pilum was still firing, chewing up more of the forest. Wolf darted in from the left, his helmet off. In one smooth move, he went to one knee, swung the missile to his shoulder, and fired.

He turned to bolt back to safety as the missile ran true and into the entrance.

Pax held his breath. The missile was extremely effective. It could even defeat one ninety-degree bend—both the penetrating and thermobaric warheads were directional. (Two turns would negate the armor-piercing warhead, though.)

One of the Tucanans in the entrance raised its body to half-mast, almost as if it was trying to physically catch the missile, and that exposed its underside. Pax reacted automatically, firing a burst at it the moment the missile struck somewhere inside the entrance.

There was the sharp crack of the armor-piercing warhead, followed almost immediately by the lower boom of the thermobaric detonation. That was directional, but a wave of heat still rolled back and out the entrance.

The pede Pax had hit was already falling down when that shock wave helped it to the ground.

Pax shifted to try and take out the other one when a secondary explosion sounded deep within the mountain.

Dust seemed to jump up from the entire mountainside, and then a volcano of fire shot out of the entrance, followed by a wave of heat that made Pax turn his head away before it blistered the unprotected skin on his face. He weathered the storm for a good ten seconds before he turned back.

Flames were still reaching out of the cave entrance. The two wounded pedes were now corpses in the open area, their bodies afire. There was no sign of the two that had been inside. And twenty meters away—

"Wolf!" Pax shouted.

A blackened body, wisps of smoke rising from its back, was face-first on the ground. Pax had started to rush forward when the body lifted its head, a huge smile almost splitting his face in two. His white teeth were almost blinding against the scorched head.

Wolf put his two hands together, fingertips touching, then mouthed, "Boom!" as he separated his hands, miming the explosion. He got to his feet and ran unsteadily to join Pax and Mouve.

"Holy-shit, Wolf. That was epic," Panda said in awe.

"No big deal."

Pax snorted. It was a big deal. That was one of the most amazing things he'd seen. He'd wondered if Wolf was all talk, but he'd walked the walk.

"You OK?" he asked, noting what looked like burn marks around the back of his head, and he could smell the burnt hair and flesh.

"Never been better."

"I need a BDA now!"[3] the lieutenant passed on the net.

Pax looked back at the entrance. A few flames seemed to be sticking to the walls both deep inside the tunnel and in patches on the ground, and smoke was now the main sign of damage. But he couldn't see very far in, and he was about to report back to the platoon commander that they probably needed another missile when there was a sharp crack from deep inside the entrance,

---

3. **BDA**: Battle Damage Assessment, or Bomb Damage Assessment

followed by more in rapid succession as if someone had lit a string of Chinese New Year firecrackers.

There was a roar, and Pax caught a glimpse of the roof of the tunnel collapsing in a wave, starting from the back and working forward until a cloud of dust obscured his sight. At the entrance, the entire mountainside, going back twenty or twenty-five meters, caved in on itself.

"What the hell was that?" the lieutenant asked.

"I don't know if the Saber reached the CP, but if it didn't, no pede's getting out of there anytime soon. The entrance's gone. Collapsed."

"Roger that. Understood," she passed as another volley of artillery rounds hit the platoon.

The mission might have been achieved, but the Marines were not out of the woods yet. The Tucanans weren't just going to quit if their CP was knocked out. If anything, they'd be seeking revenge.

"What's happening?" Panda asked.

"I think she's reporting to the skipper."

He turned to Wolf to tell him good job but stopped. "Um, Wolf. I think your hair's still on fire."

Not that the former Ghost Walker had much hair to begin with, but a wisp of smoke rising from behind his head seemed to be getting bigger.

Wolf reached behind his head and swiped a few times. "Did I get it?"

"I can't see if you're facing me. Turn your ass around."

Wolf complied, and Pax could see strips of burned skin hanging free. But whatever was smoking seemed to be put out.

"You got it, but your head's still all sorts of fucked up," Panda said with a hoot.

Wolf shrugged as if it didn't matter.

"Keep an eye on the entrance. I don't think anything can make it through, but you never know," he told the other two.

Wolf raised a singed eyebrow as if to say, "Something's getting through that?"

Pax just pointed, and a few seconds later, the lieutenant came back on the net.

"Stay in place, Sergeant Alejo. The skipper wants me to do a BDA."

"What, he doesn't trust my judgment?" Pax snapped, then immediately regretted his tone, if not the words.

"It's not that. He just wants my take," she said.

Because he wants a freshie officer to confirm what the dumb Undead grunt says.

"I'm on my way."

"Roger that, ma'am."

He turned to the other three and rolled his eyes. "The skipper wants the lieutenant to confirm that BDA."

"Typical freshie-shit," Wolf said.

There was another surge of enemy fire from the Tucanans facing the platoon, and almost immediately, an even greater return fire from the Marines. Never in a million years would Pax have thought they could get even a local superiority of numbers, but sometimes the gods of war smiled on the undeserving.

But there was no denying that the company was badly outnumbered, and time was running out while the captain sent a lieutenant to confirm what Pax had reported.

"What now for us?" Nani asked.

"Probably wait for the lieutenant. But let me check with Link."

He opened a channel to the staff sergeant, but there wasn't an answer.

"Link, you still dead?" Pax passed.

"Yeah, still dead," Link said in a quiet voice.

He sounds pretty bad.

"Really, are you OK?"

"Still breathing," he responded, then coughed.

"Um . . ."

Pax wasn't sure if he should push it, but he decided to just report.

"Wolf nailed the CP, and the secondary explosions brought down the entire entrance. If the pedes aren't dead, they're not going anywhere for a while."

"So, mission accomplished. I knew you'd get it done."

"But the skipper, he doesn't trust me, I guess. He's sending Forte over to confirm what I passed. Can't trust an Undead, of course."

There was a grunt, and then Link said, "I don't know if that's an Undead thing or officer thing."

This time it was Pax who grunted. Like most of the others, his us-versus-them was more in the line of Undead-versus-freshies, but the officer-enlisted gap went back a long, long time. Maybe it was that instead.

"Could be either, but no matter what, we're wasting time. The pedes aren't going to be just giving up because their CP was knocked out, you know. But anyway, I wanted to know what we should do now? Do you want us back there?"

An explosion, followed by Marine fire, accented his question.

"No. Stay put until the L-T gets there. See if she needs you."

"Roger that. You . . . you sure you're OK?"

"I'm sure."

"Because with all due respect, you sound like shit. Has Doc Grant seen you?"

"They're still mopping up the mall cops. He'll get to me soon enough."

"OK, I guess. But make sure he checks you out. We've still got to walk out of here."

"Don't remind me," Link said with a soft laugh before cutting the connection.

"He wants us to stay here and wait for the L-T," he told the others.

"How is he?" Panda asked.

"He says he's OK, but he sounds like shit."

"We're gonna haf' to help him back," Panda said. "I don't think he can keep up unless we do."

"We'll do what it takes. Now, let's get in defensive mode. This fight might be almost over, but sure as shit, more pedes are rushing to join the party."

The four Marines faced outboard. A little more than a hundred meters around the CP, the rest of the platoon was mopping up the mall cops, who, from the sounds of it, were down to just a few but were not giving up. Five hundred meters to the northwest, First Platoon was still lightly engaged. And between them, right at the objective, the four of them were the calm in the middle of a hurricane. It was surreal.

Pax didn't know where the lieutenant had been, but it took her almost eight minutes to get to them, four minutes after the last of the firing petered out. She came up from the downhill side, accompanied by two Marines.

The lieutenant gave Pax an apologetic shrug as she stood alongside him, glanced at what had been the entrance to the CP for barely a second, then passed to who Pax assumed to be the captain, "Just like Sergeant Alejo said, the CP is out of commission."

Pax raised his eyebrows at not just being given the credit, but in the way she said it. If he didn't know better, he'd say the platoon commander was scolding the company commander.

He watched her as she received the response, and a moment later, she opened the platoon net.

"That's it. We're moving out. Gunny, get a head count and be ready in two minutes."

She gave another look at the entrance, longer this time. "Hell, that's a lot of damage. One Saber did that?"

"One Saber, L-T. Corporal Morning Mist laid it right down the middle of the tunnel, and it must have set off some ammo or something."

"Storing ammo in a CP? Idiots." She turned to Wolf and said, "Good job. I can't wait to see the recording." She made a double take and stepped closer to the still smoldering Marine.

"Are you OK?"

"Still de . . . I'm OK, ma'am. Combat ready."

The Undead Marines had started to use "Still dead" for "I'm OK," but that was only amongst themselves and not freshies.

"You need Doc Grant to check you."

"After we get out of here, ma'am. I'm good to go."

She frowned, then told Pax, "Wait here. We'll pick you up as we pass through."

She signaled the other two Marines to cut straight across toward the platoon when Pax said, "We've got to go pick up Staff Sergeant Kravitz."

She looked around as if noticing for the first time that he wasn't there. "Staff Sergeant Kravitz? Where is he?"

"He took a round in the upper arm, and I don't think he's doing too well."

"Shit, why wasn't I told that? And why isn't that showing up on my battlebot?" Before Pax could answer, she asked, "Where is he?"

Pax pointed and said, "About sixty meters."

"OK, lead on. I'll get Doc Grant to give him the once-over before we step off."

She motioned for them to step off and fell in behind. Her two Marines, Grace and Toba, took up rear security.

Gunny Akai was passing word on the platoon net, but Pax tuned him out. He wanted to get Link attended to quickly and before they had to step off. Every minute they spent here was another minute that the Tucanan soldiers had to reach them.

They reached the rock, and Pax rushed around. "You still dead . . . Shit!"

Link was sitting on the ground, back against the rock. Blood had seeped out from his shoulder joint and run down his side.

A lot of blood.

His head lolled to the side, and his Denon had fallen from his limp right hand. His helmet was off and beside him.

Pax leaped forward and took a knee beside him when he saw the biolink flashing a slow red.

"Link!"

He tapped the biolink as if that could shut off the alert. It remained maddeningly red.

"Is he . . ." Panda started to ask as he came around Pax, but he stopped when he saw the light.

"He was just shot in the arm," he said in confusion.

The lieutenant stepped up beside Pax. When she saw the red light, she slapped the side of her helmet as if wondering why Link was not registering as KIA.

"It's been at least five minutes now. Jab him," she ordered. "Then prepare him. You need to have him ready by the time we come back through here."

Pax didn't quite understand why they needed to wait five minutes after someone died to inject the zombie juice. It had something to do with giving the mycelium enough time to encapsulate, but wouldn't that make the process more difficult?

It wasn't his call, though.

"We're taking him back, right?" Nani asked.

"Damn right we are. Now, get him ready."

She patted Pax on the shoulder as she, Grace, and Toba passed them.

Pax was already kneeling by Link's body, so he wiped the blood away from Link's left thigh and grabbed the injector from the holster there.

"Let's see if this damn thing works," he said, more prayer than statement.

He twisted the charging cap twice to the right, then once to the left. "Right or left?" he asked the others.

Link's head and neck were untouched, so their options were open. But as far as they knew, no one had used an injector before. They'd only been issued three weeks before the mission.

"Doesn't matter," Nani said. "Either carotid works. That's what the guy giving us the brief said."

Pax nodded and pushed the nozzle up into the left side of Link's throat, right under the mandible.

"Make sure the angle's steep enough," Wolf said. "It needs to get into the brain."

Pax raised the angle just a bit, took a deep breath, and squeezed the trigger.

The blast surprised him, and he almost dropped the injector. They'd been given dummies in training, nothing live.

Link's head slammed back against the rock under the force of the blast, then bounced forward again, making Pax lose contact with the injector. But the thing was just a shell now, empty.

"Did it work?" Panda asked.

Pax took a quick look up Link's nose. The force of the injection looked like it had blasted through the nasal cavity. Beyond the mess, though, a gel was oozing out like a gray nosebleed.

"We've got the gel at the nose, at least. I don't know if it's working."

The gel was a bioengineered stabilizing agent, designed to protect both Link's myc, which should still have Link's memories stored if it was still alive, and his brain, which was dead. Without the mycelium, the brain began to deteriorate in minutes, and unless the KIA was hooked up to a life-support system, like Pax was when he was killed, it was beyond redemption in four or five hours, depending on environmental conditions. With the quickly nicknamed "zombie juice," that could supposedly be stretched to twelve to fourteen hours. And the myc could be kept alive for up to three days, according to their brief.

All this was theoretical, as far as Pax was concerned. But he hoped that this time, the R&D folks were right.

Up the slope, Pax could hear the platoon form up for the retrograde/exfiltration.

"Quick, get him ready."

This was something they knew how to do. Spec-ops operators often were far behind enemy lines and without ready air assets to extract them. If someone couldn't walk, they had to be carried. But limp bodies were extremely difficult to lift and carry. So, every operator carried a simple, but ingenious harness that essentially packaged the human body for transport. It bound the extremities and stiffened the body while providing numerous straps, including shoulder straps so a body could be "worn" like a backpack.

Link was stripped of all his armor except for his helmet, which, despite him having the same skullcap as the rest of them, they had put back on him for added protection. The staff sergeant was tall, so his legs were ratcheted up, knees tilted outboard. That brought his center of gravity back, which would make it a little harder on whoever was carrying him, but it was probably the best option.

They got him trussed, and Pax considered the four of them. Wolf was a stud, but the skin was burnt and hanging from his neck and the back of his head. He may look like it didn't bother him, but Pax knew he was suffering.

Nani could do it, but she was the smallest of the four. That left Panda and him. He was about to take Link, but Gunny Akai's words from before surfaced. He had to learn to lead instead of just doing.

"Panda. You've got him first."

"Got it."

They helped hoist Link's body to the corporal's back just as the first of the platoon started past them.

"You've got Link?" Staff Sergeant Byeon asked.

Pax gave her a thumbs-up.

"If you need help, we've got a lot of strong backs here."

"Will do," Pax said as he motioned his team to fall in behind the lead element.

It was time to get out of here and back to human-held territory. The only question was if the Tucanans were going to let them go.

12

THE TUCANANS WERE NOT JUST LETTING them go. As the platoon started moving out, one of the lieutenant's drones picked up a large force of soldiers coming down the access road. They were a little more than two klicks away and moving quickly. The drone only transmitted a few images before the enemy knocked it out.

That was enough, though. The platoon knew the pursuit was on.

And it wasn't just those behind them. First Platoon was still engaged with the original force that had stopped their advance. They could break contact, but that would leave Second exposed.

Hopefully, the lieutenant was on the hook with the captain figuring out what to do, and quickly. The sounds of their fight were getting closer, and time to create a plan was getting short. Carrying Link and with Wolf burned, the lieutenant had shifted his team from the right flank to the middle of the formation. That didn't mean they could relax. Pax positioned himself beside Panda and scanned the heights for Tuc snipers. One of them positioned in the trees could be bad news if the lead team missed it.

The sounds of firing were getting too close for comfort, and Pax wondered if they were just going to wander into the Tucanan's position. But finally, the lieutenant brought them to a halt just short of a small ridge that angled off to the left—which was also uncomfortable given the soldiers coming up their ass.

"Take a knee and listen up. In sixty seconds, the skipper's got an incoming fire mission, and he's also going to open up with everything he's got," the lieutenant passed. "That should create a gap that we can exploit if we react quickly enough. First, I want you in a wedge. The second the arty hits, head right at them. Everyone else, just get on their asses. Do not stop no matter what."

Pax and Panda exchanged glances. What the lieutenant ordered was tactically sound but fiendishly difficult to pull off. Leave too early, and they'd be hit by friendly fire. Go too slowly, and the Tucanans would recover and hit them from the flanks as they tried to break through.

Something like this took coordination and rehearsal. Yet here, the lieutenant had given them a ten-second frag, and that was it. In half a minute, they were going to have to put that frag into effect.

"Are you OK with Link?" Pax asked Panda.

"I'm good to go," the corporal said as he jerked the straps to seat them better.

They were about to sprint, and he wouldn't want Link's body to be bouncing around too much. The tighter the harness, the better.

"Ten seconds," the lieutenant passed. "Get ready!"

There was more rustling, like racehorses at the gate, ready to go. Ten seconds passed. Then fifteen. Pax glanced over to the lieutenant when the world just twenty meters in front of them erupted in flames.

"Go!" the lieutenant shouted as debris rained down on them.

The lead element didn't hesitate but rushed forward into the maelstrom. One oft-told adage was that for danger close, the arty had to be landing on the leading friendly forces. Pax had never experienced that before and frankly thought it was just one of those sayings. But he saw Staff Sergeant Byeon jerk to the side after being hit by shrapnel before she regained her feet and started forward again.

A total of eight rounds impacted across about a forty-meter frontage. Pax half-expected another barrage, but it was the familiar reports of First Platoon's arsenal of weapons that sounded like children's toys in comparison.

These children's toys had a bite, though. Pax just hoped his company mates knew exactly where Second Platoon was breaking through.

Debris was still floating down when Pax reached the impact area. The dystopian landscape was destroyed. Trees were toppled, and dust was suspended in the air. Pax didn't see how anything could have survived the onslaught, but ahead of him, one of the Marines—it looked like Kildeer—fired his Denon at something to his left as he ran.

Pax kept one eye on Panda, who was having problems with his footing among the pummeled ground, and one eye searching for signs of the enemy. They were devilishly hard to completely kill, and he couldn't assume they had a clear shot forward.

He had to jump over a two-section chunk of Tucanan, and several steps farther, a badly damaged Tuc, with several foot-arms weakly moving, was on its back across a shattered tree trunk.

Pax didn't slow down to finish it off. There was no time. He grabbed Panda by the shoulder and helped him up a little rise, their feet trying to gain purchase in the pulverized soil. They reached the top just as a flurry of fire opened up. Ahead, Byeon's team had taken their knee and were firing at an unseen target.

Whoever it was, they were firing back.

"Keep moving," the lieutenant was shouting.

She stopped just short of Byeon, turned back, and motioned for the rest of the platoon to hurry. Something hit the side of her helmet, knocking off a chunk, and she almost went down.

"Keep moving," she repeated as she straightened back up, one hand reaching to the side of her helmet.

Pax moved to the other side of Panda, getting between the corporal and whoever was firing at Byeon's team. He tried to spot the enemy as he reached them, but while a buzzer round zipped harmlessly past, he didn't see any of them.

And then they were running downhill into the forested gully that separated First Platoon, who was on the far rise, and the enemy forces on the near side. The trees here had escaped the damage at the breach position, and they gave them a degree of cover, but that also meant the Tucanans could be lying in wait.

The lieutenant moved them into a wedge to give them more security, but it wasn't Tucanans that they ran into. A team from First Platoon met them to act as guides to get them through the mines the platoon had set up.

It looked like the mines had been a good idea. As they climbed the rise to the platoon's position, they passed the remains of at least fifteen pedes from a failed assault. Several had been tridented, but the others showed signs that they'd been first stopped, then given the coup de grâce.

First Platoon increased the intensity of the outgoing fire as the new lead team reached their position. Quickly, Second Platoon completed the passage of lines, which then gave First the chance to break contact.

The company was united, but it wasn't out of danger. They had seventeen klicks and a mountain range to scale before they'd be back in human territory, all while being outnumbered.

This was where they were going to see what they were made of.

BROKEN BRANCHES and leaves rained down on them. Pax grunted under Link's weight as he tried to swivel around to see if anyone had been hit. It looked like everyone was moving.

The Tucanans were still after them. Right after the platoon married up with First, they'd started receiving indirect fire, and far more accurate than the previous incoming. Without the trees overhead affecting the detonation height, there would probably be more KIA. As it was, several Marines had been hit, but all were still mobile.

It wasn't just the artillery, and it wasn't just the soldiers who'd rushed to intercept them. The officers had sent up a steady stream of their dwindling number of drones, and before each was knocked out, they'd spotted two different groups of Tucs soldiers as well as the group of mule and mall cops closing in on them. And in this terrain—high canopy with limited undergrowth—the Tucanans could make better time on their sixteen legs than humans could do on two.

And as close as they were now, they could hit the Marines with Pilum and mortar fire, which were depleting the company's shielding and body armor. Pretty soon, those enemy weapons would be racking up casualties.

"Where's our arty?" Pax mumbled.

Panda heard him and asked, "You need me to take him back again?"

The corporal had carried Link for almost twenty minutes before Pax had taken over.

"No. I was just wondering about our arty."

"Not for another two klicks at least."

"I know. Just bitching 'cause there's not much else I can do at the moment."

He swung a leg over a fallen tree trunk, dragged his butt across, then finished stepping over.

The Three-P arty was well out of range, and the militia arty was petrified by the Tucanans' far more reactive indirect fire batteries. The captain had requested that they displace closer to the boundary between the two forces to give them cover, and the militia CG had flatly denied the request.

The support they'd gotten to breach the Tucanan line had come from a single battery that had displaced forward, fired a single salvo, and then immediately retreated, fearful of counter-battery fire. But now, all of the planetary artillery wanted to stay out of range of the Tucanan batteries, and in their present position, they couldn't reach the pursuing pedes. So, before they could do any good, the Tucanans had to advance another two klicks or so.

Which put the Marines in a tough position. They wanted the arty to suppress the pursuing enemy and get the Pilums and mortars off their asses, which meant they had to get closer. But by getting closer, they'd be able to engage with their small arms and close-in weapons systems.

The company was retreating on two axes parallel to each other. First Platoon was on the left, Second on the right. This wasn't SOP[1] for an exfiltration, but it offered some degree of security while avoiding bunching up as the company strove for speed. It also gave the company commander more flexibility should the Tucanans catch up.

Pax shifted the harness's shoulder straps. The dead man's harness made it much easier to lug Link, but no matter how you packaged it, a human body was not the easiest burden for another human to carry.

A flurry of Ballista fire reached Pax from the far left before it cut off. He forged ahead, listening to his comms, but they remained quiet. The burst of fire had lasted only for five or six seconds.

Maybe it was a skeeter.

Or maybe First had been hit by a scout team. Or maybe . . .

Pax grunted. He hated not knowing what was going on. But his world had shrunk to Link's body on his back and putting one foot in front of the other. And right now, that was getting tough. Hale's Refuge had only an eighteen percent O2 level to begin with, and they were at altitude. Add to that, they were climbing even higher and not on a nice, smooth road. The closest pass was held by the Tucanans, so they were marching overland, and the going was rough. But up ahead, another 600 meters in elevation and who knew how many steps, they'd move into human-held territory. That was what was keeping Pax moving.

A loud explosion of a Tucanan artillery shell reverberated from

---

1. **SOP**: Standard Operating Procedure

the slope ahead, followed a moment later by a sharp crack, and then voices shouting out, "Take cover!"

Pax paused and looked ahead through the scraggly trees, when his heart fell.

"Fuck!" he shouted as he turned and ran sideways for all he was worth. All around him, Marines were scrambling for safety.

The rockslide bounded down the hill, crushing the trees as if they were blades of grass. Some of the smaller boulders slid to a stop, but the larger ones kept coming, bouncing through where Pax and the others had just been.

The closest boulder had passed not ten meters from him, but the danger was past. At least for the moment. He bent his head to try and get a better view. Small rocks were rolling down the slope, which looked extremely unstable. They wouldn't be climbing up that.

"Give me a head count," the lieutenant passed. "Did anyone get swept away? And keep moving. We don't have time to stop."

Pax took several deep breaths, then started climbing around the debris field, waiting for his spot to report in.

"Did the bastards plan that?" Nani asked as she came alongside him.

"Smart if they did. They could've wiped out a bunch of us. Or it could've been just more harassment fire, trying to slow us down."

"That scared the shit outta me," Nani said. "I ain't gonna lie."

"You and me both, Nan."

More rounds were peppering the mountainside as they continued to climb, but none started another avalanche. Despite the near miss, Pax wasn't overly concerned about the indirect fire. The constant specter of the Tucanan infantry closing the gap monopolized his attention. If they caught up with the company, the Marines would have to circle up and hope for the best. But dollars to donuts, if that happened, the Three-P CG wouldn't be sending in the cavalry.

They just had to keep up the pace. He'd turned around a few times as they climbed in altitude, and he'd caught several glimpses of the Tucs below. They were firing a few Dant missiles at them, but the Marines who were carrying the Hornets to knock them down were spaced well to protect the rest. The *fft-fft-fft* of the Hornets as they fired mini-rockets to intercept the Dants was music to his ears.

Once they closed to about four hundred meters, they'd start firing their BNs, and that was when things were going to get hairy.

Pax might have been more concerned with the enemy infantry, but he still flinched at the whistle of a shell passing directly overhead. He wasn't the only one. It only took a moment, though, to realize the shells were coming from human-controlled territory.

"It's about fucking time," he said.

Beside him, Nani and Panda high-fived. Now, maybe they could put a damper to the Dant launcher that had been harassing them. He began to think that they might actually get out of this in one piece. Up for four klicks over the shoulder ahead and then the next slope, and they'd cross into human-held territory.

He took a moment to look down the slope to where a cloud of dust was rising from the trees. Hopefully, a few of the Tucanans might be on their way to Tuc heaven. But even if the arty only slowed down the pursuit, then that was a win as well.

The key was to keep enough distance between them and the pursuing Tucanans so that the friendly arty could engage them before the slopes up ahead put the enemy in too much defilade for the arty to hit them. He wasn't sure how far the militia's artillery could chase the Tucanans, but anything was better than now.

They reached the shoulder, which was a welcome respite. Pax straightened up, then stretched out his legs. The rounds flying overhead, while not numerous, were music to his ears. Not even the incoming arty from the Tucanans could dampen his spirit. One more climb, and they'd be in human territory.

The Tucs *could* chase them past the boundary, and Pax almost hoped they would. They'd be sitting ducks for the militia's heavy direct fire weapons.

They quickly crossed the shoulder, which, while welcomed, made the enemy indirect fire more effective. The air bursts could cover more area, and one of the Marines in First Platoon was killed and another wounded. Tucanan mortars couldn't compare with human artillery, but it still had a bite.

They reached the far side of the shoulder and started up the final slope. Pax leaned forward into the mountainside to adjust his center of balance. It helped, but not much.

"Do you want me to take him?" Wolf asked.

Pax was tempted, but while the corporal was moving easily, his burnt exposed skin was sloughing off. Most of Wolf's skin had been protected by his armor, but enough hadn't been, and carrying Link could only damage the skin that might be able to heal.

"We're almost into friendly territory. I can manage it a little farther."

He was grateful, though, to reach the top of the slope. His feet were barking. In death, Pax wasn't in quite as good shape as he'd been before he was killed, but constant exercise had gotten him close. Carrying almost a hundred kg of Link, though, along with his normal gear, had pushed him approaching his limit.

He didn't care. Another klick, and they should reach the militia forward lines.

His comms lit up.

"Militia-Forty-Three, this is Lima-Hotel-Twenty. Our lead platoon is about to conduct our passage of lines," Captain Kjellberg passed to the net, but keying in the entire company so they could hear.

"Roger that, Lima-Hotel-Twenty. And welcome back."

Ahead of him, the lead elements surged forward. All they had to do was go down into a small depression with a mountain pond in the middle, then up the other side and into the trees where the militia were dug in. There was a feeling of elation that they'd made it, and relatively in one piece. As a sergeant, Pax wasn't privy to the situation in First Platoon other than the one KIA, but as far as he knew, while there were several WIA in Second, Link was the only KIA.

Those were pretty good results for an operation inside enemy-held territory. Better than they'd had any right to expect.

"Hang on, Link," he told his dead friend. "We'll get you out of here so they can bring you back one more time."

The scrub trees in front of the platoon gave way to the grass of the meadow, but that slowed the Marines down a bit as their feet sunk into the marshy soil. No one cared. They could slog through it.

Pax, with Link's extra weight, sunk in a little more than the rest. He had to struggle to pull each foot free.

Step, yank. Step, yank.

And then, he was stuck. Maybe his toe was under some sort of root. He strained, jerking back on the foot, but that only drove his left foot deeper.

"Shit!"

"You OK?" Nani Vesta asked.

"I think I'm stuck. Can you give me a hand?"

Much lighter than Pax, she was able to step up to his right side.

"What do you want me to do?"

"I think my foot's stuck. Can you feel around and see what it is?"

Nani had Link's Denon strapped across her back. She slung her own weapon and started to kneel to the right and just behind Pax's stuck foot.

"Give me Link," Panda said as he made his way to them.

"Yeah. Just a sec."

The first shot took Pax by surprise. But his reflexes were honed by years of combat. He was already hitting the deck as the lead Marines started shouting "Take cover."

But with his foot stuck and Link on his back, he couldn't go down. Nani stood to try to help him, when the round hit her in the chest. There was a muffled explosion as she was shoved violently to the side.

In the same instance, Pax was pushed forward. His leg strained as he fell, with pain lancing through it until the mud released its grip and he went face first onto the sloppy ground.

"Nani!" Panda shouted as Pax hit Link's quick release.

"Cease fire!" and "We're humans!" filled the net, and after a moment, the firing stopped.

Pax had been hit, but at the moment, he was running on adrenaline, and he didn't feel anything except his leg. He immediately pushed off to Nani, and he knew things were bad. The body armor around her torso bulged outward, and blood was coming out of her mouth and eyes.

He pushed her on her back just as Panda reached her.

"Nan! Nan!" the corporal said as he shook her.

But Lance Corporal Nani Vesta was gone.

Pax had recognized the distinctive report of a Buffalo. The weapon had been designed with the Tucanans in mind. It fired a relatively slow-moving round, almost more of a grenade, that was designed to impact, then detonate a breaching force to pierce the enemy's armor and shell, before a secondary detonation sent both a shock wave and thirty-four wickedly effective darts into the soft tissue inside.

It wasn't always effective in getting to that soft tissue, but when it did, it destroyed that section and sometimes the adjoining sections as well as the darts ricocheted off the insides of the Tucanans' shells.

Only in this case, one of the rounds had managed to get past Nani's body armor, and once past, the darts were just as effective as against pede flesh.

After they were fired, rounds didn't care who they hit. Flesh was flesh.

Panda was shouting and shaking Nani, sending blood splattering from her face and coating the inside of her goggles.

"She's gone," Pax shouted as he pulled the corporal's hands away. " We'll jab her. They'll reanimate her."

That seemed to sink in. His expression changed from horror to determination as he pulled the injector from Nani's thigh holster.

Pax stood and looked up the slope. Marines were getting back up, and in the far tree line, so were Hale militia.

The net was alive with chatter, until the lieutenant cut in. "Anyone hurt?"

No one else seemed to be down. The Buffalo fired a slow

round, and it was possible to avoid it in the right conditions. But with Pax stuck in the mud and Nani trying to help, they'd been caught in a precarious position.

"Lance Corporal Vesta is KIA," he reported.

"Shit! Those fucking weekend warriors were told we were coming through! What the hell happened?" the lieutenant passed, then added, "Jab Vesta."

"We're on it," Pax responded. "Just two more minutes."

He looked to the tree line, his anger growing into a white-hot flame. Friendly fire was a fact of war, but he'd heard the skipper let the militia know they were coming. And what the hell? They were in the open. How could the idiots think they were Tucanans?

Pax wasn't the only one who was angry. The lead Marines had started forward again with nasty intent. The militia realized that, too. They turned and ran, which started a rush from the platoon until the skipper came over the net.

"Second Platoon. Hold your position! Do not advance. I'm in contact with the local company CP, and we're coming forward. Until then, do not move, and do not engage!"

The lieutenant immediately repeated the command.

Pax couldn't turn off the anger that quickly. It was one thing to lose a buddy fighting the enemy, or even by friendly, danger-close arty, but this was just a travesty. It should never happen.

He forced himself to turn away from the sight of the last militiamen disappearing into the trees.

"Did you jab Nani?" he asked as he realized he'd lost track of the time.

"I think I got it right," Panda said. "But I'm gonna kill me some militia dogs as soon as I get the chance."

He wasn't going to do that—at least Pax thought it was just

bluster—so he let the corporal rant on. As the adrenaline started to fade, he gave himself a quick-once over. He'd been hit with the shrapnel when the round exploded on Nani's armor. Most of the detonation was aimed inward, but there was always secondary shrapnel that peppered the immediate area. It wasn't as powerful, and after checking, he confirmed that nothing had penetrated. His leg still hurt, but he was fine.

Better get Link.

He stepped over to the body, and it was immediately clear that Link had been hit again. The dead man's harness had several tears, and one strap was completely severed. His lower jaw was a mess, with blood oozing onto the mud. His right arm, which had been the closest to Nani, was shredded. And there was a gash in the side of his chest.

Pax's heart instinctively gave a little lurch until he reminded himself that Link was already dead. He'd had his helmet on, so the brain hadn't taken more damage. The new injuries might extend his recovery after being reanimated, but it shouldn't make much of a difference in the long run.

"Sorry about that, Link. But it is what it is."

Wolf, Panda, and Pax got Nani into her harness, placed her by Link, then sat and waited. After about five minutes, the lieutenant came back to check on them.

"What's going on now?" Pax asked her.

"The skipper's in comms with the local area company CP. They say they never got the word about us from higher headquarters, so he's dealing directly with the boots on the ground here."

"That's a bullshit excuse," Panda said. He'd been quietly—and sometimes not so quietly—seething. "It don't matter none that they didn't get the word. We're not fucking pedes. And they can see us."

The lieutenant frowned. "They said they thought we were quizzies."

"What the hell? There's no report of quizzies on the planet."

"Quizzies," or Quislings, were rumored humans who were fighting with the Tucanans against the rest of humanity. As far as Pax knew, that's all it was: rumors.

"We're in different uniforms from them," Wolf said quietly. "Different weapons. They've probably never seen LoH troops before. And we're coming at them from pede territory."

Panda turned on Wolf and snapped. "So, you think they were justified?"

Wolf didn't seem bothered by the vitriol in Panda's voice.

"I'm not saying they were justified, only that it's possible they did think we were quizzies."

"Look at Nan and tell me that," Panda grumbled.

But Pax had to admit Wolf had a point. If he put himself in their position, he could see how they might get confused. A different uniform coming at them unannounced after hearing what sounded like a huge artillery duel? They'd probably have been on edge.

They still should have realized who they were, or at least challenged them before opening fire, but it could have been a stupid, yet honest mistake.

At least no permanent harm done. Nani had a long haul ahead of her, and Link's would be more difficult now, but they were the Immortals, after all. No harm, no foul.

They stayed in position for three more hours while the skipper burned up the comms making arrangements for the militia CG to evacuate the area directly in front of them. That was probably a good idea.

Pax kept waiting for the Tucanans to hit them with their arty. They had to know the company was there. But for whatever reason, the Marines were left alone.

When the order was given to move out, the company passed through an abandoned section in the line. Another two klicks farther, two Condor transports were waiting for them despite them being originally told there were no available assets.

"Probably an apology for firing on us," Wolf said.

Pax thought he was right. They quickly boarded the Condor, which flew nap-of-the-earth for forty minutes before rising to altitude. Another hour, and they were landing at an out-of-the-way auxiliary naval base for a quick ride off the planet and transfer to a Bonderdam corvette where Link, Nani, and the three SKIAs from First Platoon were put into life vats where their tissues would be kept alive at best or in a state of stasis at worst for the duration of the voyage back to Opal-3.

For the rest of them, it was time to unwind and maybe pat themselves on the back. They'd been given a risky, almost impossible mission. The Tucanans had cooperated by some bonehead decisions, but the fact was that the mission had been accomplished.

You couldn't ask more of that from them.

13

THE FIVE TRANSPORT chambers were lined up in the hangar, ready to go. The bodies inside would be in almost the same condition as they were when they were placed in the stasis vats aboard the ship.

Three of the wounded were standing by. Most of the wounded were in various stages of healing and would accompany the rest of the company down to the surface, but the ship's surgeon wanted these three to have priority.

Sergeant Teri Brandt was in a lift chair. She'd managed to make the trek from the objective under her own power, but the surgeon had decided to perform the surgery on her leg during the voyage, and now she had to stay off her feet.

The alarm sounded, and a red light by the hangar door started revolving, casting the beam across the breadth of the space.

"Stand by for hangar opening," came the announcement.

Pax felt a little flutter in his stomach. Across the galaxy, hundreds of thousands of ships were plying space, and hangar doors were opening to accept cargo and shuttles, all without a problem.

He knew his nerves were irrational, but there wasn't much he could do about it. He just kept his face as neutral as possible so others weren't aware of his phobia.

The big hangar doors cracked open and slowly rose. Pax held his breath, as he always did, refusing to let it out until he was sure the ship's atmosphere didn't rush out in a blast.

With the door opening, Pax could see the black of space, pincushioned by a swath of stars. This didn't bother him, at least. Others couldn't take the vastness, but for him, once he knew the curtain was keeping the air inside and the vacuum of space outside, he was fine.

Pax wished he could see Opal-3, but it would be on the other side of the ship. They'd be down on it soon enough, though.

"Stand by for curtain passage," the person on the 3MC[1] passed.

The shuttle slipped into view a few minutes later. It slowly approached as it lined up to enter the hangar. Pax could see the pilot through the vision ports, but she was superfluous. The craft was AI-piloted, as were almost all shuttles, but laws that had been in place for centuries required a human pilot on board at all times.

Pax couldn't recall an instance where a pilot actually had to take control of a surface-to-ship-craft, but the law was the law.

A run-of-the-mill shuttle took about seventy minutes to make a trip from the surface of an Earth-normal planet to a ship in orbit. However, the last 500 meters could take ten minutes. Once again,

---

1. **3MC**: Term for the shipboard announcement system for the hangar deck.

an AI pilot could cover that much quicker, but laws and tradition limited the closing speed.

The company stood in formation as they watched the shuttle edge closer. Finally, the voice on the loudspeaker said, "Commence curtain passage." The tractor beams took over and brought the shuttle in through the curtain and put it down on Pad A-2.

The back ramp started to lower, and Captain Kjellberg shouted, "Company . . . atten-HUT!"

Every Marine came to attention. Even Brandt stood up, her right leg in a regen chamber.

Colonel Owusu slowly made his way down the ramp. Instead of marching up to the captain, though, he turned sharply to the right and up to the five transport chambers, motioning Brandt to sit down as he approached.

He stood over the chambers, head down for twenty or thirty seconds before he motioned to crewmen who were standing in a line against the near bulkhead. The crew sprang into action, raising each capsule and quickly floating them up the ramp and into the shuttle. He then said something to the three WIA, and they glanced back at Captain Kjellberg before they hesitantly, and with the help of the corpsmen standing by, followed the SKIA into the shuttle. The corpsmen came back out, and the ramp rose. Then, to Pax's surprise, the colonel gave the signal, and the ship's tractors lifted the shuttle and sent it out through the curtain.

The company had been standing at attention all of that time, but there were a few glances out of the corner of the Marines' eyes at each other as they watched.

The colonel waited until the shuttle was under its own power before he turned and started toward the formation.

Pax appreciated the gesture, even if it wasn't really necessary.

They weren't dead-dead, after all. They were SKIA. All five would be evaluated for reanimation. And whether they left now or after the company's gear and personnel had been loaded really didn't make a difference to them.

But it was a signal. No matter their legal status, the colonel was there for them.

Their commanding officer marched up to the captain, who shouted, "Alpha Company, reporting back from their mission."

"Put your company at ease, Captain."

"Company, at EASE!"

The colonel swept his gaze across the formation.

"I wanted to come up here personally to congratulate you on a successful mission," he said. "Make no doubt about it, this was a test. You were given a difficult job that many thought you'd fail at. And if you somehow succeeded, you'd suffer massive casualties. Instead, your professionalism and military prowess proved the doubters wrong."

Pax knew that a good part of their success was due to the inexplicable choices made by the Tucanan command, but still, the company had performed well. They'd been flexible, ready to react to the situation, and when they did engage, it was with deadly intent.

"I'm proud of you, and it's an honor to be your commanding officer. I mean that from the bottom of my heart."

Pax always took anything an officer said with a grain of salt, especially when he hadn't served under fire with one. But something told him that the colonel was being sincere. And that gave him a warm feeling.

"We've still got our after-action reports, and every one of you are getting interviewed. Be honest in those. Give us the good, the bad, and the ugly. But that isn't happening now. Captain Kjellberg, when we get back to the Opal, I want the weapons back in the armory and the gear stowed. But as soon as that's done, I'm granting a seventy-two."

There was an audible intake of breath from the company. Seventy-two hours of free time?

It wasn't as if they had anywhere to go, but the most free time while awake they'd had since Pax joined the unit, at least, had probably been a few hours. Training had been full-bore. The idea of just doing nothing suddenly sounded amazingly good.

With the company still at ease, the colonel stepped up to First Platoon and started shaking hands. Captain Kjellberg looked unsure what to do. After a moment's hesitation, he hurried after the colonel, but he didn't call them to attention. Almost as if under group mind control, the Marines came to a position of "modified at ease," which was a relaxed parade rest, arms crossed behind the back.

"A seventy-two?" Panda whispered to Pax. "Will wonders never cease?"

Pax shushed him, but he felt the same.

The commanding officer shook the hands of First Platoon's first rank, stopping with a quiet word with most of them. Then, instead of going to the second rank, he moved over to Second Platoon.

Pax straightened his back a bit, as did the Marines on either side of him. Slowly, the CO made his way down the rank until he hit Wolf. The corporal had already received treatment for his burns. Several patches were still covered with artificial skin, which protected against infection and temperature loss, but some of the new skin was already growing, shiny and pink.

"Corporal Morning Mist, I know what you did. That's what we expect in the Immortals, but still, you made yourself proud. You made me proud."

Pax winced. He had no issues with the colonel, but for him, a freshie, to use the Undeads' name for themselves, seemed wrong, somehow.

"Thank you, sir."

"I'm trying to press the issue on awards. And if I do get permission to start recommending them, you're at the top of the list."

Pax had his eyes locked straight ahead, but he frowned.

What's the issue with awards? Why would he need permission? Wouldn't we be eligible for all LoH military awards like anyone else?

"Just doing my job, sir."

"I know, son, but—"

Whatever the colonel was going to say when the loudspeaker blared, "Standby for curtain passage." A Navy chief stepped out toward the formation, shouting, "Clear the hangar deck."

Pax hadn't noticed the next shuttle approaching.

"Company, atten-HUT!" the captain shouted, then almost immediately, "Fall out and get back behind the yellow line."

The Marines hurriedly backed up as the chief watched them with eagle eyes to make sure everyone was clear.

The shuttle was tractored in and came to a landing. A moment later, the ramp lowered.

"Gunny Akai, can I have your working party?" the chief asked.

If the ship had docked at the station, all of this would be automated and so much easier. But the powers that be wanted a manual transfer. The accepted excuse was that they still didn't want people to see the company.

Or "be contaminated by the Undead," as Panda insisted.

Pax didn't care much, but this meant there was a lot more work in getting both gear and personnel down to the surface. The Navy crew on a corvette wasn't as used to making planetary descents, so the Marines were asked to supplement the manpower.

This was one working party, however, that no one minded. Especially now, with a seventy-two in front of them.

"You heard the chief," the gunny shouted. "Working party one and two, hop to it. The faster we get this done, the quicker we start our libbo."

It was amazing at how quickly Marines could get something done when properly motivated.

14

ALL EYES SWIVELED as the lieutenant came into the room and silently watched her as she made her way to the front. She looked pensive, and Pax feared the worst.

They were all officially on their seventy-two, but everyone was hanging out to wait for the word.

"I just spoke with the doc." She paused, sniffed deeply, and said, "Staff Sergeant Kravitz looks good. She doesn't see any major roadblocks with him. We're looking at four to six months for him to get back to us. The three from First Platoon look good, too."

And . . . ?

Pax was relieved to hear about Link, but he wasn't the only one in the platoon who'd been killed and prepped for reanimation.

She pursed her lips and in a quieter voice, said, "They're not going to attempt to reanimate Lance Corporal Vesta."

There was an immediate protest from the platoon.

"Her brain was almost untouched," Panda Mouve protested as he stood up. He rapped on his own head as if to emphasize the armor skull caps they'd all received. "And we gave her the zombie juice, just like we were supposed to!"

"It wasn't that," the lieutenant said. "Her myc was in good shape. But the rest of her was too badly damaged. There wasn't anything to work with."

"You mean they didn't want to waste the resources," Panda said, his voice full of venom. "You know that!"

"At ease, Corporal Mouve," the lieutenant snapped back. "I don't know any such thing. Lance Corporal Vesta suffered too much damage to her body. There really wasn't much left for the docs to work with."

Pax didn't know what to make of that. He'd seen some pretty messed up people who managed to survive even before he was killed. One of his fellow recruits from boot camp had lost half of his body, from his hips down, and they'd managed to regrow everything he'd lost. It took a couple of years, and he'd been discharged, but he'd come back to their five-year reunion.

The underlying consensus was that the brass wouldn't waste overly many resources on someone who was too badly hurt—and that's a big reason they were kept in the limbo of not being legally recognized people.

But another train of thought was that they'd already spent so much time, money, and resources on them that they'd go that extra mile to keep them fighting.

Both theories made sense, and Pax wasn't sure which way he was leaning. But if they weren't going to try and reanimate Vesta, then that had an impact.

"They're going to preserve her myc, but for now, that's about it."

"Fat lot of good that's gonna do for her if she ain't got no body," Panda said, and then when the lieutenant's eyes flashed, added a belated, "Ma'am."

"Look, I know you're all close given your . . . unique circumstances. But shit happens in war. Folks die."

Panda started to argue before Byeon pulled him back down to his seat. Good thing. Pax had no idea how their officers would discipline any of them. No one had really broken any serious regulations, at least as long as he'd been with the Immortals. What were they going to do? Give them brig time, which would just be keeping them out of combat?

He imagined that they'd be given a little more leeway, just as elite forces always seemed to receive. But all someone needed to do was back one of the officers into a corner, and they'd feel like they had to take action to restore their authority.

Gunny Akai must have realized the same thing, because in a droll voice, he said, "Yes, ma'am. Marines die. We know that better than anyone else. Ask Staff Sergeant Kravitz. That's his third time."

The anger faded from the lieutenant's face, and several of the Marines softly laughed.

Panda was still upset, but Byeon was whispering something in his ear, her hand gripped tightly on his shoulder.

"Well, uh . . . yeah," the lieutenant said. "I just wanted to get that word to you. You're still on your seventy-two, so you're free until Tuesday morning formation at zero-seven. I'll try to have a schedule for the next two weeks before then."

She hesitated for a moment as if she was going to say something, but finally, it was just, "Gunny, you've got the platoon," before she spun on her heel and left.

"Bitch," Panda muttered once the hatch closed behind her.

Pax wasn't sure he agreed with that. All she was doing was passing the word.

The real question in his mind was whether Vesta could have been reanimated again or not.

"What do you think about Nani Vesta?" Olivia asked Pax as she plopped down at the foot of his rack. "Was Panda right this afternoon?"

Pax lowered his pad while suppressing a sigh. Maybe the seventy-two wasn't such a great thing. They'd exhausted much of the recreation opportunities at the camp, and the civilian communities were off limits. But there were always books he hadn't read yet, and he'd started reading to take his mind off of the meeting with the lieutenant counting on elves, dwarves, and dragons to help him escape. Unfortunately, as non-persons, they evidently didn't rate private quarters, instead being assigned to six-person rooms.

He was tempted to simply say he didn't know and hope she'd leave him alone, but he liked Olivia, and she was obviously troubled.

"He wasn't right in attacking the lieutenant. It wasn't her call. She was just the messenger, and I think she was getting pissed at him. Good thing Byeon was there."

Byeon leaned her head over the edge of the rack above Pax's. "Did I hear my name being taken in vain?"

"I was just saying that it was a good thing you were there calming down Panda. I think the lieutenant was about to lower the boom."

She hooked her arms over the edge of her bunk, then did a

somersault thing to flip over and land on her feet before she gave Pax a shove on his shoulders and sat down by his head.

"He and Nani were kind of a thing, and you know those Paladins. Everything's a crusade."

Pax grunted and shifted over to give her more room. He hadn't known about Panda and Lani before the operation and had only found out during it. And as Terri had told him, their sex drives would be the last to recover—if they ever did. So maybe Byeon was referring to a friendship more than a romance.

But she was right about the Paladins. The Knights of Justice were a religious order in service of the Church of Reformation, and they would fight to the end for a cause they thought was right.

To be honest, Pax was not alone in thinking they could be rather arrogant and condescending to nonbelievers, but he couldn't fault the Paladins for their military prowess.

"Crusade or not, Panda's got to keep control of himself," Pax said. "I don't know what the officers would do if someone goes off the plantation, but we don't have any rights . . ."

Olivia's eyes got huge, and she asked, "You don't think they'd, like, *delaminate*—"

"No, nothing like that."

But that was what had just hit him. He shouldn't be passing that, though, *especially* if there was any truth to it.

"But there's other things they can do to make our lives miserable if they got it into their heads to do so."

"You still haven't answered my question, Pax. What about Nani?"

He'd been hoping she'd forgotten that. It was something he didn't want to think about.

"I think Wolf might be on the right track. They've spent a lot of money and resources on us. And the myc is rare, right? Are they going to waste that? I mean, they spend time fixing up wounded Marines, right? That can't be much of a cost compared with us."

"Wounded Marines are people. We aren't," Byeon said.

Pax shrugged. "From a legal standpoint. But we're still weapons. They'll fix a tank or fighter that's been blown to hell. Why would we be any different?"

"Maybe," Olivia said. "But it seems like they shoulda tried, you know?"

"The lieutenant said her myc was OK. So, they tried to save that," Byeon pointed out. "Did you catch that?"

"Don't know what for," Pax said. "Research? I mean, you can't stick a brain on some robot body. That's pure science fiction."

"Why not?" Olivia asked. "Colonel Owusu's an iceberg, right? Both his legs are prosthetic. That kinda makes him an iceberg."

"I think you mean cyborg, Olivia. And they've had prosthetics since pirates were given a hook for a hand and a pegleg to walk on. A brain's a little different."

Olivia laughed and hit her forehead with the palm of her hand. "Duh! Yeah, a little."

"You're probably right about the research, Pax. Dissect it and see if being inside of Nani changed it any," Byeon said.

For the thousandth time, Pax tried to sense his myc, and for the thousandth time, he got nothing. The idea of a fungus inside his brain was still a little creepy to him, but what Byeon just said was interesting. What if his mycelium was creeped out being inside a human? Was that a possibility? And how more so if it was changing by its convergence with him.

"So, what you're saying is that you think there really was nothing they could do with Nani?" Olivia asked.

Pax wasn't sure, but he was leaning that way, so he nodded.

"And you?" she asked Byeon.

"It is what it is," the staff sergeant answered. "So it doesn't matter what I think about it."

Which was a pretty pragmatic way to look at it.

Olivia thought about it for a moment, then said, "I guess you're right." She sighed. "I guess I'm overthinking it. You know, much ado out of a molehill. But thanks for listening."

She stood up and wandered out of the sleeping area.

Byeon stood, bent her arms over the edge of her rack, then did a reverse kip thing that would be at home in a circus to pull herself back into her bunk. Pax watched the bottom of her mattress shift as she settled into place before he turned his pad back on to his novel.

Dragons and dwarves would be much better companions for him tonight.

15

Lance Corporal Nani Vesta had been the first of the Immortals to come to the end of her journey and not be reanimated. And no one had thought of what to do after that. The staff was of the opinion that she'd already had a funeral back on Mars, her home planet, so another one wasn't appropriate from both a legal and moral standpoint.

How they brought up "moral" was beyond Pax.

The rest of the reanimees weren't going to accept that. They may be legally dead, but they were in a new, untried situation, one from which Nani had passed. So, they were going to celebrate her passing.

The freshies steered clear of the reanimees' living area, which was where they had their own "Funeral 2.0."

All of the different providing forces had their own traditions, and they created a hybrid ceremony to mark her passing. But she'd been a Terran Union Marine Corps Gold Beret, so Funeral 2.0 leaned heavily upon their ceremony.

Like the San Marcos Marines, the TUMC used a roll call that went back to the UK Royal Marines of the Nineteenth Century. So the entire company, minus the officers, formed up in the gym.

Gunny Akai was the senior Immortal, so it was up to him to call the roll.

"Alejo, Paxton."

"Here, Gunnery Sergeant," Pax said in a strong voice.

"Anderson, Wanita."

"Here," the former SAS commando responded.

"Azel, Nicco."

"Here, Gunnery Sergeant."

"Baden, Hans . . ."

One by one, the gunny went through the roster until he got to the Ks.

"Kravitz, Lincoln."

"Excused for medical reasons," Staff Sergeant Byeon responded.

"Kravtiz, Lincoln. Excused," the gunny said before continuing.

"Krull, Anna."

"Here."

The roll call continued. As it got into the Ts, Pax could feel the tension rise.

The gunny moved on.

"Van Mejor, Lupo."

"Here, Gunny."

"Wang, Ming."

"Here."

Wang, Zu."

"Here, Gunny."

The gunny paused just for a second, then in a stentorian voice, said, "West, Nani."

There was no answer.

"Vesta, Nani."

Pax felt a lump form in his throat.

"Vesta, Nani."

Gunny Akai paused again before saying, "Vesta, Nani. Killed in Action, March Twenty-first, Sixteen Fifty-three, PD[1]."

And there it was. Every Marine was well aware that Nani was dead, this time for good, but somehow, hearing it in formation made it seem more real.

The roll call wasn't over, though. The gunny had to finish it.

And finally, he said, "Yoshino, Jesus."

"Here, Gunnery Sergeant Akai."

The senior enlisted raised his eyes to the formation for the first time since he started and announced, "Alpha Company, all present or accounted for."

He took a step back and nodded at Doc Grant, who had been a Terran Union corpsman, and Panda Mouve, who'd been close to Nani. They brought up a hologram of her. It was a short loop of her leaning against a table and laughing.

A bagpipe filled the space. This was the real thing, not a recording, and a contribution from the TU SEALs. The mournful notes playing "Amazing Grace" seemed appropriate to Pax, and he was glad that was part of the ceremony.

Several of her friends spoke a few words. Panda started to but broke down. Wolf Morning Mist didn't speak but placed a small

---

1. **PD**: Post Diaspora, meaning after humanity first left the home system.

leather pouch at the base of the holostand. Food for the journey to the afterlife.

And finally, as the Knights of Justice did, the entire company filed past the hologram.

"Rest in Peace, Marine," Pax whispered as he stood in front of her holo.

He hadn't known her long, but he didn't have to. She was a comrade in arms, and that was all that mattered.

16

Nani's ceremony didn't kill the anger among the Undead, but it had calmed things down a bit.

Pax had spent the next two days of their seventy-two aimlessly. Mostly reading, but he'd tried a few games of Six to a Dozen to break the pattern, where Olivia took his shirt.

Something was missing, and he was getting antsy as he tried to figure out what it was.

Not even the woodshop was helping. Pax wasn't some woodworking genius. But he was getting the hang of it, and he found the process soothing. There was something about hand sanding a vase that calmed the soul. And Undead or not, he knew he had a soul.

He was proud of his advancing skill, and more than proud of the simple willow bowl he made and that was now in a place of honor on the shelf alongside his rack. It was speed-grown wood, of course, so the grain wasn't as fine as real wood. He thought it was beautiful just the same.

But this was the second time he'd come into the shop and

stared at the tools, but not started a new project. He just wasn't in the mood.

He stood there over the lathe, trying to convince himself to pick something to make, but the mental energy wasn't there. Instead, he wandered over to the metal station where Staff Sergeant Byeon was at the screen beside the mill.

Pax never worked metal. It wasn't "alive" like wood was, so it seemed rather sterile to him. But looking over her shoulder, he watched Tonya work on an image of a female troll, maneuvering the arms and legs until she was satisfied, then adjusting the troll's expression.

He was frankly mesmerized as she played with the image, and when she was finally satisfied, she saved it to the control.

She'd been concentrating so hard that it was only then when she realized Pax had been standing there.

"Fuck, Pax. You scared the shit out of me. What the hell are you doing?"

"Just watching, Staff Sergeant. That's pretty cool. I didn't know you were so good at that stuff."

She sniffed. "It isn't hard. The program does most of the work. Here, watch this."

Byeon went to the shelf and removed a container, then poured what looked like ball bearings from it into an opening on the mill where a red light was flashing. When the light turned green, the staff sergeant quit pouring, returned the container, then sat back at the console.

"Here we go."

She pushed the button, and the mill came to life. A ghost image appeared on the screen, an image that slowly filled from the feet up, forming a fleshed out—or metaled out—figure.

The console dinged, and Byeon opened the sliding door, reached in, and pulled out the green metal troll.

She gave it a cursory glance, then satisfied, handed to Pax.

If he considered metal dead, that went out the window. The troll was exquisite, if you liked trolls. And Pax read fantasy, so yes, he liked him well enough.

"Pretty cool," he said, and he meant it. "And you just made the image, then it made this? How? Printing?"

"No. Casting."

"Casting? But it's not hot!"

"Magic, Pax," Byeon said with a laugh. "How about it? Do you want to make something?"

"Me? Oh, no . . ." he started, before something hit him.

It may not have been the biggest thing on his mind, but it was one of many that had been bothering him.

"Yeah. Maybe I would. Can you help me?"

"Grab a chair, young apprentice."

Pax pulled one up, then stared at the screen.

"What do you want to make?"

That was the question. He hadn't even begun to think about that. Several thoughts fluttered against each other, but nothing stuck.

"Any day, now. Chow's in only five hours."

"Sorry. It's just . . . I'm not sure what would be appropriate."

"Appropriate? I'm making damn trolls. Whatever you want's appropriate."

And then it came to him.

"I want a zombie."

"A zombie."

"Yep."

"OK, a zombie," Byeon said with a shake of the head. "Who am I to judge?"

She spoke into the mic and said, "Zombie samples."

Hundreds of zombie images filled the screen.

"See anything you like?"

There were too many, and Pax scanned image after image, rejecting one after the other while Byeon bemusedly watched. Finally, after what seemed to be ages, he saw it.

"This one."

"You're sure."

"Yeah, this one."

She pulled the image to the center of the screen and banished the rest to zombie purgatory.

The zombie image was cartoonish, mouth gaping open with teeth bared, one eye falling out, and arms raised over its head. Clothes and flesh hung loose, and the right arm was skeletal.

"OK, how do you want to change it?"

"I don't. It's perfect."

"You're an easy date, Pax."

"But can you do it in bronze? No. Gold. Yeah, gold."

She entered the command, and this image switched to gold.

"No other colors?"

"No," Pax said with conviction. "This is just right."

"Right. How big do you want it to be?"

"Seven centimeters?"

"Seven it is. Full figure?"

"No. It needs to be flat. With a little eyelet on the back so it can hang."

She raised her eyebrows but entered his request without saying a word until, "Well, go get yourself the stock. Second shelf. It's recommending Number Twos."

Pax found the correct container and poured the ball bearings in. Then he sat in eager anticipation as Byeon checked everything, then pointed at the button on the screen.

"It's your zombie."

Pax pushed it and the mill hummed to life. His figure was flat and smaller than her troll, so it only took about ten seconds before the console dinged. Pax eagerly opened the door and pulled out the zombie.

"It's perfect!"

"And what are you going to do with it? It's not going to stand on a shelf," Byeon asked.

Pax looked around the shop until he spied the brown couch someone had dragged in and stuck in the far corner.

"That's what you're going to help me with, Staff Sergeant."

PAX AND BYEON stood by the door to the galley, watching the Marines troop in for chow.

"Were you waiting for me?" Olivia asked as she approached.

More often than not, the two ate together with a couple of the others.

"No. You go in. I'll try and find you later."

If she looked a little hurt, Pax didn't notice. He was too giddy with anticipation.

The two Marines delayed until everyone was inside and mostly seated while they waited for the chow line to open.

"Ready?" Byeon asked.

"Ready."

"Detail, atten . . . HUT!" she hissed, then "Forwaaard, HARCH!"

With her leading, they marched in single file into the galley, then to the far side.

A few people noticed, but no one said anything as Byeon said, "Detail, HALT! Right, FACE!"

There were a few desultory claps as the two faced the company.

Byeon waited a few moments, then raised her voice. "Company! Atten . . . HUT!"

A few of the junior Marines started to stand, but most of the company just turned to the two while ignoring the command.

"I said, company, atten . . . HUT, you reprobates!"

"Staff Sergeant Byeon, what the hell are you doing?" Gunny Akai asked.

"That means you, too, Gunnery Sergeant Akai. All of you, atten-fucking-HUT!"

The gunny stared at her for a few long seconds, before he sighed and said, "OK, I'll bite."

He slowly got to his feet, and the rest of the company, in fits and starts, came to what was a relaxed position of semi-attention.

"Corporal Morning Mist, front and center, HARCH."

There were some chuckles, and Ogre Carlton gave Wolf a shove in the back.

The corporal was scowling. Pax could tell he was suspicious by the way he was looking furtively around as if to plan out an escape route.

"Center yourself on Sergeant Alejo."

Pax could see confused looks spread through the galley. Ogre gave Wolf another shove, and the corporal reluctantly marched forward until he was in front of Pax, who struggled to keep his face frozen.

There were a few murmurs from the other Marines until Byeon shouted, "You're at the position of attention. Zip your yaps."

Pax waited until the talk died down.

"Adjutant, read the citation."

Wolf's eyebrows scrunched together in confusion, but he held his position of attention.

The Secret Society of Undead takes pleasure in presenting the Zombie of Valor, Second Class, to Corporal Ferris Morning Mist, Undead Marines, for service as set forth in the following citation:

As a member of Alpha Company of the Immortals, Corporal Morning Mist distinguished himself in action against the enemy on April 16, 1653 PD, on the planet Hale's Refuge. With his platoon pinned down by the bastard pedes, he was part of a four-person team tasked with completing the entire company's mission. Typical that it all lands on the head of the junior Marines, but that's the way of the galaxy. The four-person team maneuvered to the entrance of the pede stronghold, but the bastards had mall cops, no biggie, and a damned Pilum to suggest the team leave them alone. But Marines are hardheaded, Wolf especially. Instead of taking the suggestion, Wolf stripped half naked, sauntered out into the line of Pilum fire, and sent a missile up the stronghold's asshole, giving it a Saber enema. Which, as nasty as the pedes are, was too much for them to take, and their entire CP was destroyed. Corporal Morning Mist's assault enabled the company to get the hell out of Dodge, their mission completed. His actions reflected courage, determination, and a complete disdain for authority, and were in keeping with the finest traditions of the Immortals and the Undead service.

Given under my hand,
Dead N. Rotten
King of the Undead.

THE COMPANY HAD LISTENED QUIETLY for a few moments before the laughter started. When Staff Sergeant Byeon finished, they erupted into roars of approval.

"At ease, at ease!" the staff sergeant shouted.

It took a bit of time before it was quiet enough for Pax to speak.

"I was with Wolf, and I swear this is all true. And when Colonel Owusu spoke to him, he apologized that he couldn't get the medal he deserved, because, well, you know. Undead."

There was a chorus of boos, and Pax had to raise a hand to quiet them down.

"That's bullshit, and we all know it. But when you get down to it, we don't need no freakin' medals!"

This time there were cheers, and Pax had to wait again.

"But, on the other hand, medals are cool. They're sexy, and they could get you laid if that was still possible."

More boos mixed with laughter.

"Wolf might not get a medal from the overlords, but who wants one of those nasty things? It's medals from those who love you that matter, and Wolf, we love you."

Wolf had remained at attention during Pax's little speech, and when Pax looked at him, he was surprised to see the corporal's eyes glistening.

The cynical, distancing Ghostwalker? Crying?

"And so, without further adieu . . ."

Pax removed the zombie from his pocket, then held it up for the company to see. The brown couch had sacrificed a patch for the ribbon, and Byeon had created a pin.

The company went wild, cheering and hooting. Pax brought it back down and pinned it to Wolf's chest.

"You deserve it, Wolf."

"Thank you, Pax. Or should I say, 'Dead N. Rotten'?" he said as he lifted the medal from his chest so he could see it.

"I'm sorry it isn't the real thing, but—" Pax started before Wolf cut him off.

"No! It *is* the real thing, more than you can realize. And I'll treasure this for the rest of my Undead days."

17

"Hey! You still dead?" Pax asked as he entered the room.

Link was in a regular hospital bed. A portable heart machine was on a stand next to him with two tubes, filled with blood, running into his chest. His right arm was still encased in a vacuum chamber, as was his torso.

Pax didn't look at the small chamber perched on the nightstand next to the bed. He'd seen it during his first visit, and it gave him the willies. Why Link wanted it there was a mystery to him.

"Deader than a doornail, and about as good as can be expected," Link said. "Just got my jaw unwired yesterday. Now, if my damn gut can hurry up, I can eat me some real food."

"How long will that take?"

Link shrugged. "Damned if I know. The docs here aren't going out on a limb on anything."

Pax frankly thought Link was doing much better than he should be. Nine days ago, he was certifiably dead. Six days later, he woke, his body damaged but reanimated, and his memories restored.

Now, his broken jaw had its surgically emplaced organic splint, and Link could at least talk, unlike during Pax's first visit. The splint was slowly breaking down and being absorbed as his mandible knitted and healed.

It had taken Pax four weeks to awaken from death, and here was his friend, bitching about food after only nine days.

He still had a way to go. The round had entered through his left shoulder joint in the armor, hit his scapula, and ricocheted down to his gut, nicking the abdominal aorta. That's what had killed him—he'd bled out. The doctor who examined him said that it had been a miracle that he'd made it to the objective, given the amount of blood he'd lost.

That one round might have killed him, but the second blast, the one that killed Nani, had done more damage to his dead body. With his armor being removed so they could carry him, the blast had broken his jaw, shattered his right arm, and most seriously, punctured his heart. Pax had been surprised when he heard how extensive the damage was. Both lungs and his gut had been pretty torn up as well, and he'd had extensive surgery to repair some of the most severe damage. Now, barring complications, it was up to the millions of nanos roaming his body and doing their thing.

"How about your, uh . . . ?" he asked, tilting his head at the chamber beside the bed, unwilling to even look at it.

"This baby?" Link asked as he reached over to grab it and pull it into his chest.

Now Pax had to look at that Frankenstein monstrosity. The chamber was clear, and suspended in the fluid was Link's mangled heart.

"Look at this!" Link said, clearly excited. "You can see where part of the substrate's already being covered by tissue."

Pax's stomach was queasy as he gave it a quick glance. "Wow," he said without much emotion.

As a combat Marine, Pax had seen horrendously damaged bodies, bodies torn apart by the horrors of war. But somehow, seeing Link in the bed, cradling his heart in a small chamber, made him nauseous.

"This grow-juice," Link said, giving the chamber a little shake, "is speeding up the process. Another two weeks, they'll slam it back into my chest, give it a jolt, and it'll start ticking. And I can get rid of these tubes."

He gave the heart machine's tubes a dismissive flick. Pax wanted to tell him to be more careful, but he knew it wouldn't do any good. A guy who convinces the doctors to put his heart on the nightstand beside him instead of keeping it in some lab was not someone who was too concerned about the process.

Maybe because this was his third reanimation. Getting killed three times might have that effect.

Link became more serious and returned his heart to its place. "How was Nani's ceremony?"

"Emotional," Pax said. "We gave her a good send-off."

"Wish I coulda been there," Link said.

"You came close to being a guest of honor at the ceremony, Link."

"Hell, my first death was worse," he said. "This is nothing."

"Uh . . . in case you haven't noticed, your heart's in a jar beside your bed, and your gut was shredded."

"Shit. Like I said. Nothing."

"What do they have you doing?" Pax asked, wanting to change the subject.

"Not much. They'll come in and help me walk a few steps, but I think they're afraid my intestines are going to fall out on the deck like some anaconda. I gather the real rehab won't start until my gut's firmly back in place and my right leg's out of the splint."

"And your heart machine? Don't you need that?"

"This thing's portable. It's got wheels on the bottom," he said as he slapped the case of the machine.

"Just take it easy. Don't rush things. Remember what happened to Tinkerbell?"

"Tinker-who?"

"Tinkerbell. Remey Murfton. Sergeant, one each."

"Who's that?"

"Oh, come on. Tinkerbell. He was in your company. Tore his right pec and triceps when you guys went to Fordham's Reef."

Link shook his head.

"Thought he could tough it out in the gym too early and tore them both again doing the bench? I know you remember him."

"Yeah, Fordham's Reef. But I don't really remember him."

Pax laughed as he reached over and rapped lightly on the top of Link's head. "You sure you didn't get this scrambled?"

Link frowned and pushed Pax's hand away.

"My head's fine. I just don't remember him. I was already a SNCO when we hit the Reef, and he was probably in another team."

"OK, just joking. No matter. What I meant was that he rushed back into the gym and ended up going back and having to start his rehab all over again. If you need the time, take it."

"I'll take my time, don't worry. I can use a bit of a vacation."

"Yeah, on the lovely Opal. Such a great vacation spot."

"Hey, I heard about Wolf getting his medal. Was that really your idea?"

"Yeah, but Byeon helped a lot. And it was her idea to have the ceremony in the chow hall."

"What did you call it? A 'Zombie of Valor?'"

"Second class."

Link chuckled. "You're OK, Pax."

"Are you two decent?" Gunny Akai shouted at the door, then came in with his hands dramatically over his eyes as if afraid to see what they might be doing.

"The good sergeant already serviced me," Link said.

"Eat me, Link," Pax said.

"No, I'm the staff sergeant. You're the sergeant. It goes the other way around."

Pax would have given him a hard shot to the arm if this friend wasn't so messed up.

The gunny removed his hands from his eyes.

"I heard you could talk, so I figured I'd come down and see for myself. I know how much that must have tortured you, not being able to speak."

"Hell, *me* talk a lot, Gunny? You're the one with the tongue long enough for ten rows of teeth."

"That's what she said," the gunny answered with a laugh.

Pax tried to come up with something to throw in, but the rapid fire trash talk was out of his league.

The gunny got serious for a moment and looked around at the medical equipment in the room.

"Did they give you any timeline yet?"

"Maybe a couple of months," Link said.

"They told the lieutenant about six months. Just do what they tell you, and don't push it."

"I know. Quad Bod here already gave me that lecture. Pretty uppity for a sergeant, if you ask me."

He tried to shift his body and winced. Link might be putting up a good face, but he'd been hurt pretty badly.

"Any ops on the horizon?" he asked as if he was ready to get back in the saddle.

"Nothing to share now. But you won't be going anywhere for a while." The gunny paused, and in a quieter voice said, "No more hero stuff, Link. You've only got five more lives left, you know."

"Can't help it much," Link said. "'Sides, like you said, I've still got five more."

What?

"Um . . . five more lives?" Pax asked.

Gunny looked at him like he was an idiot. "You know, nine lives?"

Pax was confused for a moment before it sank in.

"Oh, like a cat. Nine lives."

Gunny looked at Link with another "Who is this fool?" look before saying, "Yeah. Like a cat."

Pax admired the gunny, but he wasn't too happy at being treated like the village idiot. So, he didn't understand the gunny's reference. Big deal. It wasn't as if there was a direct connection between feline folklore and Link being in the hospital.

He suddenly felt uncomfortable. Rank structure was somewhat loose in the Immortals, even more so than in the Raiders or other elite forces. But a SNCO was still a SNCO, and Pax wasn't in that club. He and Link might have that San Marcos connection, but it seemed that wasn't as strong as old military habits.

"I've got to be getting back. If you need anything, just give me a call," he told Link.

"OK. Sure will. And thanks for coming."

Pax wasn't sure if he should shake hands or something, and he stood there for a moment, now feeling more embarrassed. Finally, he just spun on his heel and walked out.

As soon as he turned down the corridor, he could hear the two SNCOs laughing.

18

"What the hell's wrong with that idiot?" Byeon, who was the acting team leader until Link returned to full duty.

"That idiot" was Lance Corporal Hastings "Bozo" Lymon, formerly of the Royal Charter Marines.

"I'd slit his throat and be done with it, but they'd just bring him back," Wolf said.

Pax gave the corporal a sidewise glance. He didn't think Wolf was serious, but if anyone would do something like that, he'd put money on the former Ghost Walker.

"How the fuck was he ever a commando?" Byeon said. "I don't know if he can be trusted to get his boots on the right feet."

"He was connected, Staff Sergeant. You know that," Pax said.

Hastings had made it through REC, so he had to have had some degree of military prowess. But if you looked up "dumb as a rock" in the dictionary, you'd see his goofy smiling face.

REC and the other courses tested the mind as well as body.

You had to be in shape, and Hastings was that, but you couldn't be a dummy and make it through.

Unless you had a lot of help.

Hastings came from an influential family with royal ties as well as military history. His uncle was the commandant of the RCMC. And that made a difference, even in this day and age. Pax had gone through REC long before Hastings had, so he didn't know exactly what happened, but the fact he'd arrived with the nickname "Bozo" was a pretty good indication that the journey hadn't been smooth. Nor was the fact that he'd been killed in his first action as a commando, where rumor had it that he'd screwed up.

What had surprised the rest of them was that Hastings had been reanimated. Sure, he'd been in the right kind of unit, and there'd been a recovery team with them, and that's all it usually took. But a royal, even a fringe one who was no longer a citizen, seemed like a liability to the program. Pax would have thought they'd bury him with full military honors and leave him in the grave.

Instead, he was an Immortal and Pax's headache.

"Connected or not, you've got to show something to get through training, even REC," the acting team leader said.

Pax was used to Byeon's opinion of REC. She's been a Hangul Black Beret, and like all of them, she thought their Geomeun Beremo was the most difficult course across the breadth of humanity's militaries. Pax didn't know about that. They did have the highest mortality rate of any school, although he questioned if that was because of poor leadership within the course rather than because it was so tough.

She pointed at Pax. "He's your bitch. I want him welded to your hip, understand that?"

He nodded while his heart deflated.

"No more fucking screw-ups from him. This is embarrassing, and I'm not going to put up with it. You with me?"

"I've got it, *Hasa*," he said, using her old Hangul Army rank, hoping it would calm her down and get her off of his ass.

For many of them, they'd been some type of Marines before being absorbed into the LOH Marines, and the ranks and militarese had stayed true after they'd been killed. Most former non-Marine types, though, resented the Marine culture. While the former Black Berets, SAS, SEALs, and other groups technically became LoH Marines, they'd been operating within their old units, and so they'd never bothered to use their new official ranks until now in the Immortals.

In the Immortals, since they were mixed, using the various other service ranks didn't work. But Pax was not above using whatever he could to manage his seniors.

She snorted and said, "You wish we were in the Black Berets. Now go take care of your imbecile shadow."

Pax took that as a dismissal, so he spun around and stalked up to where Bozo was waiting.

"You do know that you're not supposed to shoot one of us, much less three, right?" he asked.

"Sorry. I didn't see them, and they were the ones moving in front of me."

"Damn it, Bozo! We're covering them as the advance. Of course, they're going to be maneuvering."

There was a flash of defiance in the lance corporal's eyes. "Come on, Q-B. How am I to know—"

"That's 'Sergeant,' not 'Q-B.'"

As he'd found out earlier, there were times when the laid-back attitude in the unit wasn't appropriate.

"Look over there. Do you see Sergeant St. Albans, Corporal Mouve, and Doc Grant?"

"Yes, Sergeant," Bozo said.

"You killed them. Dead. We're going back to restart the exercise, and this time, try not to do that again."

"It's just training," Bozo said. "They're not really dead. I mean, no more dead than any of us."

Pax grabbed the lance corporal by the collar and shook him. "You're an embarrassment to REC, Bozo. We don't kill our fellow Marines, whether that's in training or in combat."

He gave the lance corporal a push as he let go.

"Even if I did for real, they'd just bring them back," Bozo muttered, barely loud enough for Pax to hear.

"A cat only has nine lives, Bozo," Pax said.

The lance corporal looked confused and asked, "What?"

"A cat . . . oh, forget it. Just don't kill anyone else today. Got it?"

"Got it, Sergeant."

"OK. Let's go. We're forming up for another run at this."

He stood there for a moment as Hastings turned to go back to the range starting line.

This guy's going to be an anchor around my neck. Thanks, Byeon.

With a sigh, he followed the lance corporal back to the start line for another go at trying to do this right.

19

Olivia caught Pax's eye as he came in and tilted her head toward the back of the space at Juric Rutledge. The other sergeant was leaning back in an old ratty chair someone had scrounged up, eyes closed.

"What's the matter with him?" Pax whispered.

"His kid's bornday."

Pax was used to Olivia's somewhat interesting choice of words by now, but it took him a minute to realize what she was saying.

"Shit."

Rutledge had been married and had two kids when he was killed, and being unable to contact them had been heavy on his mind. His picpod had been taken when he'd been killed and sent to his family along with his other personal possessions, so he didn't even have an image of them, but he had his memories, and he'd shared a lot of those with the other sergeants. It was obvious to the rest of them that Rutledge was having difficulty coming to terms with his new existence.

"I'd better go talk to see if he's OK," Pax said.

"I tried to, but he wasn't listening. Maybe you'll have better luck."

He gave her a pat on the shoulder as he walked past to their fellow sergeant, crossed the room, and flopped down on the even rattier chair next to Rutledge.

"You think we're going to get our mission soon, Rut?" he asked.

The rumor mill was spinning full speed that something was coming down the pike, but no one was keeping the lower ranks informed.

Sergeant Rutledge didn't answer. One finger was tapping his knee as if keeping the beat with a song. Pax couldn't see an entertainment pod, but that could be back in his locker, for all he knew.

Pax was tempted to just leave Rutledge alone, but he knew he should make a stronger effort. He reached out and shook the other sergeant's knee.

"You OK, Rut?"

Rutledge opened one eye to stare at Pax, but then he closed it. A single tear rolled down his cheek.

"Hey, Rut. It's OK."

Rutledge sniffed, then said, "I miss them, Pax. I really miss them."

"I know you do. This sucks, but you've got to move past it."

"You don't understand. These are my kids. My flesh and blood. And it's Tanner's fourth birthday." He paused to sniff again and drag his forearm across his nose. "They think I'm *dead*!"

Well, you are, kinda sorta. At least legally.

He didn't say that, though.

"That sucks, yeah. Big time. But that'd be true even if you weren't xeroxed," he said, using the slang term for getting reanimated that was becoming more popular. "At least now, you're still in the fight, trying to help save humankind."

He almost winced at his own words.

Boy, that was sure lame.

And Rutledge didn't take it well.

"You don't understand," he almost shouted as he sat up straight. "You don't have kids. And you never will."

Pax blanched at the onslaught.

"No, I don't," he said quietly. "And I never will."

Rutledge's mouth dropped open, and he said, "I . . . I'm so sorry, Pax. I didn't mean to, uh . . . You've got your people, of course. You miss them."

Not really. There's no one I've left behind. But that was a low blow about children.

Pax didn't give a whit about his father nor his cousins, and he'd lost his mother years ago. But while he'd not actively thought about having kids of his own—his childhood wasn't something he'd wish on any child—the sudden realization that the matter had been taken out of his hands suddenly hit him hard.

Sorrow turned to concern, and Rutledge said, "Look, I'm sorry. I'm just thinking of Tanner and his birthday."

Pax was still a little angry, but he'd walked over to cheer his fellow sergeant up, not to get in an argument.

"That's normal," he said, his voice gruff. "You miss him. You miss all of them. But you've got to push forward, or you're going to kill yourself."

"I know. It's just so hard—"

The door opened, and Corporal Morning Mist stuck his head in. "The skipper's calling a meeting. All hands."

"What's up?" Olivia asked.

"I don't know for sure, but I think we've got a mission."

"Notice who isn't here?" Pax asked Olivia.

She gave a quick look around the briefing room. "First Platoon. What gives?"

"Is this really a warning order or just another exercise?"

When the word came out for the meeting, the Marines had assumed they'd be getting the rumored mission. But First Platoon wasn't there, so that put a damper on the speculation.

Trying to guess what was going on was a waste of time. They'd find out soon enough, but human nature was to try and figure out what was happening.

"Attention on deck!" someone shouted from the back of the room.

Pax joined the others in coming to attention as the colonel, Major Symonds, and Captain Kjellberg entered the room and marched to the front. The colonel and captain took seats in the front row, while the S-3 took a position in front of the assembled platoon.

"I'm sure you've all heard rumors about Dentemon," the major said.

Olivia nudged Pax's side with her elbow.

"Told you," she whispered.

Pax just frowned. He wasn't going to give her the satisfaction of admitting she'd been right.

"And in this case, the rumors are true. The battalion remains in Condition 1-Alpha for a potential deployment to the planet. However, that does not include Second Platoon."

That took the Marines by surprise, and there was a low murmur as that sunk in.

"At ease, Marines," Gunny Akai said.

"First Platoon will be the sole unit to respond to the situation on Dentemon should the call come in."

What? We're not good enough?

But what the major said next was even more surprising.

"You are being given a different mission. On Lemon's Hold."

Lemon's Hold?

The name was vaguely familiar to Pax, but he couldn't quite recall much of it. It was in the Tannaman Quadrant, which was not in the San Marcos Marines' area of responsibility. He thought it was one of the many contested worlds, where the Tucanan invasion and advance across the planet had been halted, but the powers that be were afraid to risk or were unable to organize a full-out counteroffensive for fear of the scorched-earth tactics the Tucanans often employed in such situations.

Just listen, and you'll find out soon enough.

"As some of you know, Lemon's Hold was invaded by the pedes a year and a half ago. The initial assault took control of about a third of the landmass before the Hangul Republic Army was able to reinforce the Lemon's Hold guard and stop the advance. Since then, the situation has been at a stalemate with minor skirmishes along the front lines."

Which was the case in more than a few worlds. Pax was a Marine, and he wanted to throw every enemy fighter off human soil, but for reasons way above his pay grade, the brass seemed willing to accept these stalemates. On some of these planets, life was almost normal in the human-controlled territory, with interstellar commerce continuing, even if at a reduced level.

Unless the decision had been made to initiate a major counteroffensive, Pax didn't know why the Immortals—well, a single platoon of them—would be given a task there.

He was about to find out.

"This morning, a VIP was conducting a mission over pede-held territory when his Petrel was shot down."

"What the hell was a VIP doing flying over the pedes?" Pax whispered to Olivia.

If Lemon's Hold was a stalemated planet, then what did the VIP think they were doing? And if they were shot down, what did that have to do with the platoon? High-ranking military and civilian VIPs had been killed in the war often enough, so what was one more?

"No one knows why he went on this mission, but this particular VIP is in Intel, and he has extensive knowledge that we do not wish to fall into enemy hands."

Oh, there it is.

"We believe the VIP was killed when his Petrel was shot down."

"Better hope the pedes don't have mycs to pull everything he knows," Panda said.

"However, a distress call was picked up by the planetary guard. That could have been automatic, but we have to consider the possibility that the VIP is alive and behind enemy lines. He knows too much, and we cannot let him fall under pede control."

Pax winced. The pedes were experts in extracting knowledge from captured humans. What they would do to a human . . . well, Pax wouldn't wish that on his worst enemy.

"There are several courses of action under consideration, and a rescue is one of those. That's where Second Platoon comes in. In approximately two hours, you will be embarked aboard a still yet to be determined vessel and put in position to react should you get the mission. Or any other mission, for that matter."

You mean a kill mission, Pax thought with disgust.

"I don't need to say it, but whether this happens or not, you need to assume you'll get the mission. Captain Kjellberg and I'll be working on the mission details, which will be sent to you en route. And it will be up to Lieutenant Forte and Gunny Akai to get you prepared and ready to go."

He let his gaze sweep across the room.

"I'm not taking questions now. You'll get the ops order soon enough. Colonel?"

Colonel Owusu stood and faced the Marines.

"We don't know if anyone will pull the trigger on this rescue or not. But I trust you to answer the call if it comes to that. And I know you'll get it done."

"Ooh-rah!" most of the Marines in the platoon shouted.

It wasn't as loud as it usually was. The uncertainty in the situation probably affected that.

The platoon came to attention as the colonel and major exited the conference room. Captain Kjellberg waited until they went through the door.

"Gunny, if you can get the platoon ready with Assault Pack Bravo?" he ordered. "And lieutenant, if you'll come with me?"

"Team leaders," the gunny said as the two officers left.

Pax and Olivia exchanged looks. "So, you were wrong," he said.

"Eat me," she responded automatically, then followed that with, "Is this goat rope gonna go?"

"I sure the hell don't know."

The warning order hardly qualified as such. Nothing in it told them anything about the situation or what they might actually do. And they'll be embarking on a mission without any more information, it looked like.

Situation normal, in some ways.

They could be making a trip to the Tannaman Quadrant for nothing. But they had to go with the mindset that they'll be conducting a rescue op, whether it happened or not.

Anything else could be a recipe for failure.

20

Pax felt everyone's eyes on him as he followed the others to pick up their luggage. This was his first time in "civilized" company since being killed, and he thought each civilian knew what they were and would be after them with pitchforks and blazing torches.

Most of the people rushing back and forth didn't seem to notice the platoon, all who were in their blue overalls with the "Romero Industries" patch on the shoulder. They were just another contracted workforce coming to the planet. With a large portion of the population conscripted into the planetary guard to man the lines, work teams were common. Not even forty meters away, a group of about a hundred of them in matching orange "Nuester Corp" windbreakers were milling around.

A child screamed, and Pax wheeled about as a four- or five-year-old girl ran past them into the waiting arms of a man in a business short jacket. The man swept her up and enveloped her in a hug as she kissed his cheek.

Pax was emotionally torn. He was both excited to see

normalcy, while at the same time, he was nervous being out among freshies.

Lemon's Hold might be partially occupied by the Tucanans, but here in Waterton, things seemed normal. It didn't look like a planet at war. If he squinted his eyes, he might be back on San Marcos.

But it had been driven into his head that as an Undead human, he was an animated anathema, and that "real" people would not tolerate them. Captain Lakmal, the staff officer who'd come with them, had driven that point home yet one more time as soon as they boarded the shuttle to go down to the surface.

There had even been whispered conversations among themselves about what they'd do if the people attacked them. Some swore to fight back, but others, including Pax, said they'd let the people kill them. They weren't going to fight fellow humans. Besides, they'd just get xeroxed again.

No one knew just how the people were supposed to recognize them. It wasn't as if they were the zombies of books and holovids with flesh falling off of them as they staggered around looking for brains.

A woman walked past the group, a small brown and white dog in her arms. Pax wondered if the dog could tell, and as he stared at it, his nerves on full alert, the dog caught his eyes and wagged its tail.

So much for that trope.

The main terminal was a large, open area under a high dome. Shops were along the periphery.

Olivia nudged him. "Oh, my god. A Cinny Star!"

Pax turned away from the dog and looked to where Olivia was pointing. As soon as he saw the small booth with a line of about twenty people in front, his mouth started watering. He could almost smell the aroma of the freshly baked stars wafting across the terminal.

His nervousness had been fading, and the bakery took over. He hadn't had a Super Star, the largest of the Cinnamon Star offerings, for a couple of years, but the memory of the gooey, cinnamony star-shaped buns was suddenly overcoming him.

Is that my myc making the memory stronger?

"Think we could snag one?" she asked. "I could use something that actually tastes good for a change. The shit we've been eating isn't fit for human constipation."

He almost snorted at her choice of words, but his body had taken over, and his mouth was watering. He wanted one of the gooey buns more than anything, but he was also a realist.

"We don't have any money. How are you going to pay for it?"

"By doing whatever anyone wanted," she said wistfully.

It wasn't just the Cinnamon Star. He scanned the lines of shops. Golden Mountain. Bomburger. Fleck's. White Castle. And more that he didn't recognize. Between the training, then with their two operations, it had been easy to subsume himself in the mission. Now, seeing a vibrant civilian setting, he was hit with what they were all missing. It was like a mule kicked him in the gut.

It sounded like he wasn't the only one. The group was murmuring among themselves, so much so that the gunny had to say, "Steady. Remember where you are."

They waited for another five minutes before Captain Lakmal said something to the lieutenant who then told them, "OK, our luggage is ready. Mr. Akai"—it grated on Pax's ear to hear a Marine gunnery sergeant called "Mister"—"if you can get the shift to B-12, we can load up and get out of here."

"Mister" or "Gunny," Akai took over and moved the platoon to the luggage carousels and to the last one in line. Their bags—uniform blue duffels with the Romero Industries logo imprinted on the sides—were already emerging. It didn't take long for the Marines to remove them and start carrying them out to the nondescript hover waiting for them.

Captain Lakmal gave a few quiet instructions to the lieutenant, then stepped back.

"What? That freshie was just along to babysit us this far?" Panda said.

Several Marines quickly hushed him. They'd been warned not to use military terminology. "Freshie" wasn't exactly military, per se, but everyone knew it wasn't allowed.

Pax threw the last bag into the hover bed where Rutledge stacked it.

"That's it," Pax told the gunny.

"OK, load 'er up."

With a sigh, Pax clambered aboard, followed by the rest. He'd been hoping for a bus where he could see out, but he should have expected this. With the hover's cargo bed covered, they wouldn't be able to see out, and the locals wouldn't be able to see in.

Within a minute, they were all crammed into the back, and a few moments later, the hover took off.

Through the opening in the back, Pax saw Captain Lakmal silently watching them as they drove away.

"THEY DID WHAT?" Staff Sergeant Byeon asked in shock.

The entire platoon had their eyes locked on Corporal Carlton, who'd just returned from a four-hour stint as the duty NCO.

"They carpeted the whole fucking area. Banshees," he said, his voice hushed. "Right where our VIP was supposed to be."

"Holy hell," Panda said. "They'll kill a light bird[1] to make sure he don't get rounded up by the pedes? That's some heavy shit."

The Marines exchanged silent looks with each other. They knew by now that their "VIP" was a Marine Intel lieutenant colonel out of LoH Marine Headquarters back at Cape Town on Earth. They weren't told why he was out here on Lemon's Hold or why he'd been in a Petrel flying over enemy-held territory.

They'd received three different contingency operations orders during the transit, and one after arriving at their temporary camp, but it looked like someone had decided that enough was enough and issued the order to take out the lieutenant colonel.

No one was sure that he was even alive, but intermittent signals from his SAR[2] beacon meant he could be. They didn't have an absolute lock on his position, though.

"I guess that cancels our mission," Wolf said matter-of-factly. "It'll be back to the big Opal for us."

Pax nodded. If they finally got a position on the officer, and they fired a full salvo of Banshee antipersonnel missiles, then a Marine in a flight suit wouldn't have stood a chance.

It was just shocking that the powers that be would resort to that. And it was a lieutenant colonel, to boot. Back in Cape Town at the Puzzle Palace, a light bird might be nothing, but to grunts in the field, an O-5 was just a half-step below god.

---

1. **Light bird**: slang for a lieutenant colonel
2. **SAR**: Search and Rescue

"Don't be too sure about that, Wolf. We might have to send somebody out there to confirm the kill," Doc Grant said.

That sounded so wrong to Pax, but he knew the corpsman was right. If they were going to ice a high-ranking officer, then they wouldn't hesitate to send a team in to get a BDA.

"And if this missile strike pisses off the pedes?" Pax asked. "What then?"

No one answered.

The situation on Lemon's Hold had been static for four months. At some point, either the Tucanans would probably attempt a major reinforcement to take the entire planet, or the humans would start an operation to throw the enemy off. But as on other stalemated planets, until then, not much was being done. There were no rules in this war, but both sides seemed to accept a semi-cease-fire. Which was why commercial shipping could still come in to several spaceports far from the front lines, and the Tucanans could bring in small vessels unmolested.

Pax thought this was madness. They were at war, not playing patty-cake. Blockade the bastards and starve them out, if nothing else. But when that had been done early in the war, the Tucanans had reacted by scouring three planets, wiping out all life, human and Tucanan alike.

Until the human forces had enough naval forces in the system, they could not risk a scouring. And until that time, the stalemate would be observed. The missile barrage, however, might have broken that unofficial agreement.

"What does the gunny say?" Olivia asked.

"He's there with the L-T, trying to get some sort of orders."

"So, I guess we wait," Byeon said. "I suggest trying to catch some Zs."

Pax leaned back against his duffle, but sleep wasn't coming. He'd known that a kill mission was a possibility, but he'd figured that had just been thrown out there. It couldn't be a real choice. It looked like that decision had been made. Whatever the officer knew was too important to be in Tucanan hands.

"That's some shit, right?" Olivia said as she stretched out beside him.

"I didn't think it would come to that."

"And if they're gonna do that to a lieutenant-fucking-colonel, what'll they do with us? They don't even think we're human."

Damn it, Liv. Thanks for the reminder. Now, I'll never get to sleep.

21

Olivia nudged Pax's foot, waking him. He groaned and turned over. The hard cement floor of the dilapidated supply shed they were using as housing did nothing for his tired body.

"Leave me alone," he said before the rustling around him caught his attention.

He opened his eyes to see the lieutenant and gunny moving to the center of the shed. His brain fuzz immediately vanished as he sat up.

"We going home?" Wolf asked.

The lieutenant waited until she had everyone's attention before she said, "I've been in contact with Colonel Owusu. Our VIP is still alive."

Pax raised his eyebrows and exchanged glances with Olivia. Either the Lemon's Hold Guard were poor shots or the VIP hadn't been where he was reported to be.

"He has also. . . I'm not quite sure how to put this."

"The lieutenant colonel has said he intends to remain among

the living, and that he's now protected from more 'inadvertent barrages,' is how he put it," Gunny Akai interjected.

"Well, right. That about sums it up," the platoon commander said. "So . . ."

She touched her wrist, and a 3D map holo materialized in the center of the shed.

"The VIP is located somewhere in this grid square."

A box appeared, bordered in red. It was about a klick and a half by a klick and a half and encompassed some rough terrain.

"We can't narrow it down any more than this."

That didn't make sense to Pax. With any tracker, the location was down to half a meter at most.

"To further complicate matters, there is significant pede activity in the area."

"They know the VIP is there," Olivia whispered, pronouncing V-I-P as "vip."

"The command has decided that we need to go in and get him, so we'll be going with Plan C."

"Rescue or kill mission?" Byeon asked the question on everyone's mind.

"Rescue, if possible."

So, get him out if we can, but kill him if he's going to be captured.

Pax was not happy about that possibility. He wasn't even sure he could pull the trigger if it came to that.

"There are some changes, though. There's already been some pushback because of the Banshee mission."

That caught Pax's attention. Pushback? That might mean that the top brass didn't know about the Banshee salvo. Maybe someone lower on the chain took the initiative?

"So, this is going to be a minimal footprint. We are not going in full strength. The mission will be conducted with three two-person teams."

There was an immediate murmur in response. Plan C had the entire platoon infiltrating in and covering the search area in a grid pattern.

Three teams? To find some officer in the middle of a bunch of pedes?

"The three teams will depart in two hours. This is going to take some quick adjusting, so I'm going to name the teams now. You six need to huddle up with the gunny and me to work this out. The rest of you, well, I've got nothing. Just stand by. Things could change in a heartbeat."

She paused a moment, then said, "Gunny, if you can announce the teams?"

"First Team. Ogre and Lindy."

That made sense. For as much as everyone was a Marine now, the two former Terran SEALs were both extremely capable and worked well together.

"Second Team. Staff Sergeant Bethel and Nugget."

That wasn't as logical, but as a staff sergeant, Bethel had lots of experience, and Corporal Derion "Bambi" Kildeer, with her small size, could move like a ghost through most any terrain.

Pax glanced at Byeon, who was puffing up her chest. If Bethel, as the First Section leader was going, then she'd probably be leading the third team to go out.

Maybe I'll go with her?

He turned back to the gunny in eager anticipation. He hadn't been with the Immortals as long as most of them, but he thought he'd proven himself.

"Third Team. Wolf . . ."

Pax's face fell. Wolf was good, but he thought he would have been a better choice.

". . . and Q.B."

It took him a moment to realize that was him. No one else regularly called him that.

When it sank in, his eyes widened in surprise. He quickly glanced at Byeon, who couldn't hide her disappointment.

Olivia patted him on the back.

"OK," the lieutenant said. "If those six Marines can join the gunny and me in the CP? The rest of you, carry on."

The gunny motioned to them, and Pax followed Wolf out the door. He was surprised that he'd been picked, but he was determined to prove to the lieutenant that it was the right choice.

"Go," Pax said.

Wolf stood and nonchalantly walked across the road. Pax expected a shot to ring out, but his teammate made it unscathed to a thicket on the other side.

Now it was his turn. He stood, brushed off his front, and patted his right front pocket before he followed Wolf. He'd never felt more exposed in his life.

He was sure that he looked like what he was—a Marine pretending to be a civilian. But he wasn't challenged, and no buzzer rounds reached out to cut him down.

He reached and joined Wolf on the other side as his heart threatened to burst out of his chest.

"I hope we don't have too many of those," Wolf said.

"You and me both."

The two Marines were in basic tech overalls. There were hundreds of thousands of humans, at the very least, who were trapped under Tucanan control. Unless the hostilities intensified, those humans should be somewhat safe. The enemy didn't wholesale slaughter humans in most cases.

The going theory was, in part, that it was because the Tucanans wanted to keep the infrastructure going, and they didn't have the pedepower to do all of that themselves. So technicians, in particular, were kept on the job.

By infiltrating in civilian overalls and mostly unarmed, the hope was that the six of them could escape capture or death if they were spotted.

They were only mostly unarmed. Each had a multitool—and if one of the tools was a large, wicked combat blade, well, that was just one of fifteen perfectly mundane tools. Their other weapon was a high-speed, low-drag handgun, made of paper, of all things.

It didn't look like a real weapon. But the lieutenant assured them that it would work. They only had six rounds, but if the Tucanans took interest in them, then with a few quick twists, the handgun would come apart into pieces that weren't obviously weapon components. And best of all, it wouldn't be picked up by normal scanners.

Pax didn't like being in civilian clothes, but this wasn't the first time he'd done that. As a lance corporal on the mission on Baramoor, they'd used civilian clothes to assemble unnoticed. In every one of the human conflicts over the last centuries, that was against all of the rules of war. But the Tucs didn't sign treaties with humans, so all bets were off with them.

"Let's move off," Pax said. "I want to be in our AO before dark."

Wolf nodded and stepped off into the forest. He was obviously on full alert, and he moved through the undergrowth with barely a sign that he was there, yet if a Tucanan did spot him, he looked like he was just on a casual stroll.

Pax had to admit that the corporal's warcraft was impressive, which was why he'd been picked for the mission. What he didn't know was why the lieutenant and gunny had selected him.

This wasn't false modesty. Pax knew he was a good Marine, and he didn't need his Cross of Honor to prove that. But being on a two-person team trying to find a downed lieutenant colonel took a different skillset.

He was proud that he'd been selected, but that was colored with the fear of failure. He had to prove to both leaders that they'd made the right choice.

Pax tried to follow Wolf as silently as the corporal was moving, but it was impossible. He stepped on hidden twigs that snapped, or brushed by undergrowth that swished against his overalls.

I guess that's why they call them Ghost Walkers.

The day was getting warmer, and down on the forest floor, there wasn't a breeze to help cool them off. And drive away the humidity. Sweat dripped into Pax's eyes and down along his back. He reached up with his forearm to wipe his brow when Wolf suddenly stopped, then sunk to the ground.

Pax followed.

"Pedes," he signaled with his hands. "Fifty meters. Five/six."

Pax's eyes were still burning from the sweat, but he tried to peer forward. He couldn't see anything, but he was going to trust the corporal.

Wolf signaled "Interrogative."

Pax reached into his pocket and pulled out an innocuous-looking music library. The little piece of gear actually had over 5,000 songs that could be transmitted to his bonebud. But with a twist of the top while pulling out at the same time, and it converted to a tiny battle comp.

It was still in passive mode. To transmit would require a much more determined manipulation. But in passive mode, it could receive, and several spysats, which were in geosynchronous orbit above human-held territory and keeping an eye on the closest 200-klick-deep of enemy-held territory, were broadcasting.

The data they were gathering might be a little more focused on the area where the missing VIP was, but hopefully, not enough more to alert the Tucanans that there were Marines in the area looking for him.

The Tucanans had to know that the humans knew where the officer went down. The Banshee strike was a little obvious. But Pax had hoped they'd figure that after the Banshee strike, the target was dead, and call off their search.

If they had stopped searching, then who was ahead of them?

Pax pulled up the latest update. He could see where the two of them were located, but there wasn't any indication of enemy forces nearby.

He used his hand-and-arm-signal for "Activity?"

Wolf shook his head and shrugged with his arms horizontal and palms displayed. He didn't know.

Then he indicated that they were moving from left to right, using his hands to indicate the direction.

Pax checked the time. They were still nine klicks away from their search area, and darkness would fall in four hours. That was very doable, even if they stayed in place for a while.

Every minute they delayed gave the Tucanans another minute

to find the lieutenant colonel first, but they weren't going to do anyone any good if they were caught. He didn't want to risk running into the Tucs, so he signaled Wolf to hold in place.

They both edged themselves into a dense thicket alongside them and settled in to wait.

The planet's sun started to pierce the dark forest floor. Mist hovered just a meter high—Pax knew it would burn off within minutes, adding more humidity to the already saturated air.

After dodging four more groups of Tucs, the two had made it to their AO before dark. But while daylight favored humans, the dark was the friend of the Tucanans. Pax had wanted to start checking their list of potential locations for their target, but with the amount of Tucanans moving about the area, he'd made the tough decision to stay put until morning.

All he could do was hope that the lieutenant colonel could avoid capture one more night.

He nudged Wolf's foot. The corporal awoke with a start, then nodded that he was ready. Pax pulled out a combat bar, and Wolf followed suit.

The standard LRSB[1] didn't taste bad, but neither did it taste good. There was a slightly cloying aftertaste that hinted at raisins, but a single bar provided all of the necessary calories and nutrients needed to sustain a Marine for twenty-four hours. It didn't satisfy hunger, but it would keep them going.

"Where first?" Wolf signaled.

---

1. **LRSB**: Long Range Sustenance Bar. A calorie packed combat ration.

Neither one of them had spoken aloud since crossing into Tucanan territory. Wolf, as a Ghost Walker, still made a few departures from Marine hand-and-arm signals, but that hadn't caused any problems. Most military hand-and-arm signals were readily understood within context.

Pax showed him his battle comp. The first objective was under a sheer rock wall about 140 meters from their present position. The big battle AIs listed it as the third most likely place a human could hide in the two Marines' AO without being discovered. He didn't know if he really bought that. A person on the run isn't necessarily evaluating every location before deciding where to hunker down. They might be in a state of panic at worst, merely stressed and wanting to get out of sight at best. So, they'd tend to take the first hidey-hole they came across.

Wolf studied the position for a few moments, looked up to get his bearings, then stood and started to move out of their position. It shouldn't be hard to navigate to the spot, but if he had problems, then Pax was there with the battle comp, which relied on tiny internal gyros as well as satellites to determine exactly where they were. Both systems were passive, so the Tucanans shouldn't be able to pick them up.

At least from the battle comp. The Tucs had a wide array of sensors that could alert on the two of them.

They headed slightly uphill, and within sixty meters, they spotted the rock face, which rose to ninety meters at its highest point. But that wasn't where they'd be looking. The two followed the face for about thirty-five meters to where a slab had fallen probably centuries before, and a huge conifer had grown sideways around the slab before heading upward.

Pax took the lead and slowly advanced toward a small hollow, then stopped, his hand on the handgun in his pocket. There were the unmistakable signs of Tucanan foot-arms in the soil at the base of the face.

He turned to Wolf to point at the tracks, but the corporal had already spotted them as well. He took a deep breath, edged around the tree, and looked into the hollow formed by tree, slab, and cliff face.

Somebody had been there. Certainly the Tucanans, but there was also a clear human footprint in the very back of the recess. A Marine lieutenant colonel? Pax couldn't tell. The human print could have been there for a long time.

Or a single night.

One thing was for certain. There was no one there now.

Pax pulled up the next target. It was only fifty meters away, but above the rock face. The two had to move back to the beginning of the cliff, move uphill, and climb.

He didn't have much hope for this location. It was at the edge of the Banshee strike. And if their VIP had been killed by the missile, then who had sent the message?

Nope . . .

Then he suddenly wondered if it was all a trap. What if the strike had killed the officer, and the Tucanans had sent the message to lure in rescuers? No one would be fooled by a pede talking, but they had the tech to simulate human voices.

He stopped his climb for a moment, and Wolf turned around with a questioning look on his face.

Pax was about to ask him what he thought about the possibility of this being a trap, but then he mentally waved it off. That was stretching things. And if they had captured the VIP or knew he was dead, then what was all the Tucanan activity in the area? It sure seemed like they were looking for something.

He gave Wolf the signal for "negative" and motioned for him to continue. He didn't think they were walking into a trap, but that didn't mean he wasn't going to be cautious.

They quickly saw signs of the missile strike. Unlike in the lower-lying areas where the trees were much larger, up on the rocky hillside, the trees were smaller and not as uniform—mostly genmodded Piñon Pines, according to their brief.

These smaller trees had been devastated by the detonation—*detonations*. This was bigger than what could have been made by a single Banshee—the trees coming apart into so much kindling and eliminating cover. The two Marines stopped short of the cleared area and pulled out the lens from their multitools which enabled them to glass the chewed-up ground.

There was plenty of Tucanan sign. Pax counted fourteen of their discarded water bulbs littering the area—undamaged water bulbs, so the pedes had searched the area after the strike.

They didn't see any sign of the lieutenant colonel until Pax was about to call it when he spotted something out of place about twenty-five meters ahead of their position.

He pointed it out to Wolf, who studied it for a moment before signaling, "retrieve, interrogative."

Pax couldn't quite see what it was, and he was hesitant to send one of them into the open, but he thought the risk was worth it. The day was getting hotter, and the Tucanans liked to hole up in the heat when they could.

He nodded, and Wolf signed he would get it. Pax covered the corporal who darted out, retrieved the object, and ran back to their position.

Wolf handed the object to Pax, who looked at it for a few moments before recognizing it. He was holding the bottom third of a standard human-made military pouch . . . just like the ones that carried search and rescue beacons.

This wasn't a coincidence. It was possible that this tattered case fragment came from somewhere else, but Pax was sure that this was their target's.

The fact that the case was a damaged portion was not a good omen. But according to their brief, the VIP had sent his blunt message after the missile strike. So, he must have survived the barrage.

Pax gave the area one last look-over, then signaled to Wolf that they needed to move on. He was reasonably confident that their VIP had been in the area, but the burning question was where he was now.

And if he's even alive.

The two Marines were at the edge of their AO. On the other side of the high ground was Staff Sergeant Bethel's and Corporal Kildeer's AO. For all Pax knew, if the lieutenant colonel might have crossed over into their area, and he and Wolf were just chasing a ghost.

But they couldn't consider that possibility. They had to conduct themselves as if the officer was in their AO.

The Combat AI had plotted their route to cover the most likely hidey-holes in the shortest amount of time. But humans had a habit of not complying with the suggested courses of action, as determined by an AI. So, as the two descended back into the lower ground, they had to not only watch for Tucanans, but for any sign of their target. Leaving Wolf to focus on the enemy, Pax's head was on a swivel as he thought about where he might hole up if he had to remain undiscovered. He stopped Wolf two times to investigate what he thought were likely spots, but both turned up empty.

And then it was Wolf's turn to stop them.

He signaled enemy ahead, and the two melted into the underbrush.

"Twenty. Forty meters. Stationary," he signed.

The two were coming down the side of a steep hillside. According to his battle comp, the area flattened out where the Tucanans would be.

"Activity?" he asked.

Wolf shook his head.

Pax had to find out. He signaled Wolf to cover their rear, then he got on his belly and low-crawled forward about ten meters until he could see down the faint game trail they'd been following and he could see the pedes.

There were more than twenty. Most were huddled against the mountainside at their backs and in the shade. A good fifteen were pill-bugging it, the same as when they were fried, but without the rigidness of death.

Tucanans could function in the dark or light equally as well, but they were not fond of heat. So to see them bivouacking during the heat of the day wasn't uncommon. That was good, in a way. If this large, platoon-sized group was in their bivy, then they wouldn't be moving around in the area, possibly giving the two Marines a freer rein.

And if it came to a fight, the sleeping soldiers had removed a good portion of their body armor. Tucanans breathed through the spiracles throughout their exoskeletons. Their armor was designed to allow for the movement of air, but it was a commonly held belief that armor made breathing more difficult, and so they'd remove it whenever possible.

But, just like Marines, they weren't all sleeping. Pax could see at least half a dozen manning defensive positions. Most were oriented downhill, but they weren't stupid. They'd have a full defensive perimeter.

Pax studied the high ground. It was dotted with the mini-Piñons with little underbrush. The ground itself was loose rock, probably sloughed off during seasonal repetitions of cold and heat. If he and Wolf tried to go around them from above, they'd surely be spotted, and Pax wasn't confident that their civilian overalls would pass scrutiny, given the circumstances.

No, they'd have to go down where soft soil replaced the rocks and the larger trees gave them more cover.

He started to edge back, when a thought hit him. Staying low, he pulled out his battle comp again and studied their route.

He didn't *have* to get past the Tuc bivy. By heading straight down into the wash and up the other side, they could cut across to the eighth target position, then work their way back.

A Marine was supposed to be able to adjust on the fly as the situation demanded. So, that was what he was going to do.

Pax showed Wolf what he wanted. They'd back up another fifty meters, then cut across. The change should only add about two hours, and they should be able to hit all of their targets before sundown the next day.

After that, things were up in the air. They'd meet up with the other two teams at the RP and get their new orders. Hopefully, though, someone would have the package, and they'd get the hell out of Dodge.

The two Marines carefully retraced their path until they were around the bend and could deviate. As they were descending, Pax slipped on a bit of loose rock, which sent it tumbling down into the ravine. Wolf gave him the stink eye, and they froze for a couple of minutes, but there wasn't any sign that the Tucanans heard it—Tucs "heard" vibrations through their shells, and they could detect those for quite a way when the intervening distance was direct and uncluttered. Around obstacles and through obstructions, they needed the mechanical repeaters they had, usually attached to their third segments.

Pax was the rear man of the two, and he was on edge, continually turning around to scan the forest. It wasn't until they crested the opposite side of the ravine that he started to relax. He used his battle comp to get another bearing, and they started the movement to Position Eight, which was rated at the ninth most probable position.

There was more pede sign as they approached the jumble of rocks where the lieutenant colonel might have taken refuge, which heightened Pax's dismissal of it as a valid hiding place. The xenobiologists had long ago determined that the Tucanans had evolved from a burrowing creature. Pax didn't know if that was true. What he did know was that when fighting the enemy in rocky, jumbled terrain, the pedes could move quicker and more assuredly than humans. Maybe it was their multiple segments and foot-arms, or maybe it was evolutionary. All he knew was how it affected fighting. And if their target had decided to hide among boulders, well, that was the Tucanans' sweet spot.

But it had to be checked. They skirted a small marshy area. Pax could just see some of the outlying boulders ahead through the trees when Wolf stopped and froze.

Pax froze as well, but he slowly edged his hand toward the

pocket holding his paper handgun. He didn't see any sign of movement, though. No pedes, nothing. Not even the birds that had been flitting through the trees just minutes before.

He slowly turned his head to Wolf to find out what he'd detected. The corporal was locked onto a tangled pile of brush a few meters to the right. When the corporal removed his weapon, Pax followed suit.

The brush didn't look big enough to conceal a pede, even a smaller scout. But assuming that it couldn't hide one was a good way to get killed again—this time, maybe for good. They were a long way from a medical facility, after all.

"Come out," Wolf hissed. "We're LoH Marines."

What?

Pax had been the one looking for signs of the lieutenant colonel, but it was Wolf who alerted on the brush. If there was a human in there, that didn't mean it was their target. But they had to check it out.

Pax automatically moved to the side, making a triangle between the two Marines and the brush.

"LoH Marines," Pax repeated, his throat cracking from disuse.

There wasn't a response, but as he stared, things suddenly came into focus. There was definitely a person there. Pax could see the back of a dirt-covered leg, and then what looked like a shoulder.

Pax pointed to a branch while he kept his weapon trained on the figure. Wolf carefully reached for the end of the branch and pulled it free . . .

. . . revealing a dried-mud-caked body. Dark blood stained the figure's right side. Only the brown eyes surrounded by too-white sclera broke the washed-out colors.

"Lieutenant Colonel Sampsel, I presume?" Pax asked.

He'd thought of the line as soon as he'd learned of the mission, never really thinking he'd get a chance to use it.

The officer didn't seem to appreciate the humor or history.

Like a creature coming to life, he opened his mouth and said, "Before you kill me, please know that I have vital information that has to get back to Headquarters."

Pax's mouth dropped open, and he half-lowered his weapon. "What?"

"It should be pretty clear what I just said. Before you kill me, you need to know that I have vital information that has to get back to the head shed. I'd appreciate it if you'd inform your command what I just told you."

Pax and Wolf exchanged confused looks. They'd arrived to rescue the officer, and he's going on about killing him?

"I'll make that a direct order if it makes any difference."

"What . . . Why do you think we're here to kill you?"

The lieutenant colonel rolled his eyes, then raised his right arm, exposing more of where the dried mud had absorbed his blood. He winced in pain, but kept his side exposed.

"That wasn't us, sir," Wolf said. "We're here to rescue you."

Pax saw the slightest glimmer of hope in the officer's eyes, but then they shifted to the weapons in their hands.

"Lieutenant Colonel Sampsel, I'm Sergeant Paxton Alejo, LoH Marines," Pax said as he pocketed the handgun. "This is Corporal Ferris Morning Mist. We're here to get you back to friendly lines. I assume you want to be rescued, sir?"

The officer stared hard at Pax for a moment before he sighed, shook his head slightly, and said, "I guess I don't have much of a choice. Keep in mind what I said, though. I really do have some vital information."

Pax held out a hand, which the lieutenant colonel took, then helped the man to his feet. The officer groaned but was able to stand.

"Are you OK? Do you need a medbot?"

"I've already taken the injections, son. I'll manage."

Wolf handed the officer a set of overalls that matched theirs. It was his size, of course, as were the boots that followed.

Lieutenant Colonel Sampsel had caked on mud to help camouflage him, but now it was a hard, dry shell. He needed the two enlisted Marines to help strip off his uniform. On top of that, muddy uniform and blood had mixed, making a nasty scab that had to be pulled away.

The VIP looked terrible, but Pax didn't have any answers for that. It was just going to have to do. He gave the officer one last look, then said, "I need to report in, and then we'll get on our way."

The lieutenant colonel put out a hand and stopped Pax. "Is there a locator function on that thing?"

"Well, yes, sir."

"Are you sure you want to do that?"

"What do you mean?"

"I had a locator on my SAR beacon. They bombed the hell out of it."

Wolf pulled out the partial case. "This, sir?"

"Looks like mine," he said with a nod.

"If you don't mind, sir, this thing was out in the middle of a Banshee strike. How the hell did you survive?" Wolf asked.

"Banshees? That's what they were?" he asked. "I didn't have it on me. I suspected what might happen, so I reported in, then moved away from the beacon. Not far enough, I guess," he added, pointing with his left hand to his bloody side.

"So, how did you call back after that?" Pax asked.

"I never go anywhere without two of anything," he said, patting his left cargo pocket. It's turned off now, but if you send your message, command will know where we are.

Pax hadn't really considered that. He looked at Wolf, and he could see the distrust in the younger Marine's eyes.

But why would they go through all the trouble to send us out only to kill the officer?

They missed once. Maybe they want us to pinpoint him, he answered himself.

His thoughts drifted to Nani Vesta, and he almost returned his battle comp to his pocket. He knew that no matter how difficult and expensive it was to reanimate them, they weren't indispensable, and he was far from sure that the command wouldn't sacrifice them for the greater good.

But there were four more Marines out there, and the longer they were, the greater the chance that they'd be compromised. That's what decided the matter. He keyed in the message that they had the package and were heading back to the RP.

One quick pulse, and the coded burst message went out to the other two teams and the rest of the platoon. It was low-frequency, quick, and low-powered—enough to get the job done, but hopefully too weak to be picked up by the Tucanans.

"Done," he told the others. "Let's move."

Pax didn't *think* he'd just called for fire on their heads, but why hang out there?

"Wait," Lieutenant Colonel Sampsel hissed.

He was bent over, hands on his knees as he gasped for air.

Pax resisted rolling his eyes. Yes, the officer was Intel and not a grunt, much less spec ops. Yes, he was older than the two enlisted Marines. Yes, he was wounded.

But he was still a Marine, and the gash in his side was somewhat superficial. Additionally, he'd had three days for his nanobots to start the healing process. He should be in better shape than this.

Pax stepped up and whispered, "Hand-and-arm signals, sir. We're still in bad guy territory."

After their first conversation, Pax had told him that they were going to have to rely on the signals to communicate. But the lieutenant colonel kept forgetting. The philosophy was that every Marine was a rifleman, no matter their MOS.[2] So even an intel lieutenant colonel would have been taught them.

The officer nodded, weakly waved a hand, and whispered, "Right. Just let me catch my breath first."

What the hell did I just say?

Wolf was watching them, and Pax gave a little shrug of the shoulders. There wasn't much they could do. The lieutenant colonel was the purpose of the mission, and other than carrying the man, they were limited by his ability to keep up.

With his mind on endurance, he gave Wolf the once-over. The corporal looked fine, but being on point was mentally draining. It was probably time Pax took over.

---

2. **MOS**: Military Occupational Specialty

He signaled the switch, and Wolf nodded and moved past both the lieutenant colonel and him to take up Tail End Charlie.

Pax took one of his high-caloric civilian meal tubes out of his pocket and handed it to their charge.

Putting his mouth up against the man's ear, he whispered, "Eat this. Then we've got to get moving. We've got four klicks to the RP, and if we don't make it by sundown, we're going to have to hunker up for the night.

None of them had NVDs. Pax was confident that he and Wolf could move through the night without a problem, but if the lieutenant colonel was having this much of a problem now, then Pax couldn't have him stumbling along in the dark.

The officer remembered to use the signal to acknowledge. Pax let him down the tube of "Blueberry Parfait," which was a fair approximation of how it tasted, then gave him another two minutes before he signaled the other two to move out.

Some Marines loved point. Others hated the stress. Pax was one of the former. Being on point gave him a thrill, and he felt more alive than nothing else other than possibly the feeling actual combat gave him. Every sense seemed heightened, and he almost felt invincible.

Which was not good. He was vulnerable, and intellectually, he realized that. But he still felt that he could kick Tucanan ass.

Mindful of their package, he kept the pace slow as they wended their way down the ravine that should eventually take them to their RP. A small trickle of water made its way along the very bottom, but stripped and broken branches littering the ravine were evidence that gully washers sometimes gushed through.

The debris and rocks made their progress more difficult, but Tucanans were like humans in many ways. They liked the easy path, so when the team was given their route to the RP, the lieutenant had selected this both to give them cover and hopefully lessen the chance of running into any pedes.

The downside of using the wash was that if they were spotted, the Tucanans could ambush them from the high ground. The ravine would become a killing ground.

All the more reason for Pax to spot them before they spotted the humans.

The ravine took a sharp bend to the left, which had caused a pileup of flood debris. The three Marines had to hug the far-left side, climbing partway up the walls to get past a tangle of wood. That left a short, meter-and-a-half jump back down to the bottom. Pax wasn't sure how well the lieutenant colonel would take that, so he made the jump down himself so he would be between Wolf and him, and then they could maybe lower the officer.

As soon as his feet hit the dirt, his peripheral vision caught movement. Before he registered what it was, he was wheeling around while drawing his paper handgun.

His warrior brain, trained by too many combat operations, made a mental snapshot of what he saw. The nearest Tucanan, just twenty meters away, was at quarter-mast, its Buzzer covering the other one who was down flat, half of its body inside the tangle of flood debris. Another Buzzer was leaning against a branch next to it.

The upright pede jerked at Pax's surprise landing. The scout twisted around and started to move to half-mast while swinging the big weapon around.

Pax was quicker, and he didn't hesitate. He double-tapped his handgun—or at least he tried to. The first round fired, impacting on the second section, the one holding the Buzzer. The second shot tore the handgun apart, the barrel breaking off and shooting up and to the left.

Pax tossed the useless weapon away and drew his multitool blade as he dived to the left, away from the muzzle swinging toward him. But the swing had stopped. The paper handgun may have broken apart, but there was nothing wrong with the 11 mm round. It cracked through the pede's shell with a burst of flesh and yellow blood. The enemy scout dropped the Buzzer from nerveless foot-arms but then almost immediately bent over to try and pick it up with its first section foot-arms.

He wasn't going to give it that opportunity, not if he could help it. Pax reversed his movement and sprang for the pede, intent on severing the head and blinding it. But two, three, four more rounds hit the length of the body, sending it into a writhing mass of agony.

Wolf had entered the fray.

And the second scout was attempting to join the fight as well. It was quickly backing up through the debris, and from his angle, Pax didn't think Wolf had a shot.

He didn't consciously make a decision to attack, any more than someone thinks about catching the glass that's rolling off the table. He was already moving forward, so by planting his right foot, he was able to redirect his motion and launch himself onto the second scout.

The Tuc convulsed as Pax landed on it, and foot-arms tried to reach behind to pull him off. Pax grabbed the base of a foot-arm, right where it emerged from the body, and then plunged the multitool blade between the second and third section.

This wasn't the thin coup-de-grâce blade. The multitool bade was serrated and twice as thick. It hung up for a moment before plunging deep.

"Die, potto," the scout shouted as it instinctively tried to raise its upper body, only to have it get caught in the tangled branches.

It started writhing, though, as if trying to buck him off. Pax's legs swung from the back, but he still had a grip on the foot-arm. With that anchoring him, he yanked free his blade, then struck down again, this time on the middle of the next section.

Easier said than done. The tip skittered off the flexible armor sheath, across its shell, and then back into the wound he'd already made.

The scout didn't like that at all, and it reverted to screeching in Tucanan. One of the good foot-arms flailed wildly and caught Pax across the face and almost knocking him free.

With an effort, the Tucanan managed to get enough foot-arms working to pull its body back, freeing its trapped upper third. The thing raised the upper two sections and twisted around, those foot-arms—with the tips opening into fingers—reaching for him.

Pax slashed at one, breaking it more than cutting, when another shot rang out, and the first section was hit, knocking the two sections back.

He who hesitates in bare knuckle combat is lost.

Pax was in full warrior mode, acting instead of thinking. He lunged forward again, and this time, his knife went between the second and third sections. With a twist, he severed the connection between them.

A Tucanan's sections could act independently, but they were more deadly in coordination. And with another shot, Wolf took out the thing's head. It was now blind. Pax was still in close to berserker fury, but the corporal pulled him off the still flailing—and still dangerous—body.

Pax almost fought Wolf in his berserker-fueled intent to rend the enemy apart, but his rational side managed to take control, and he took a couple of deep breaths.

The first Tucanan was down, but it looked like two sections were still alive, even if only barely. More of the second one was alive, but the foot-arm motions were aimless.

"You look like shit," Wolf said. "Are you OK?"

It was only then that Pax realized he was covered with pede gunk. And he stunk. Tucanan innards were slightly toxic to humans. It probably wouldn't kill them, but it could sure make them uncomfortable. He'd gotten a few drops on him on Hale's Refuge while administering a coup de grâce, but this was something different.

And he didn't like it. Already, his eyes were burning.

"This stuff is nasty," he said as he tried to wipe some of it off.

"There's some water over there. Not much, but try and clean yourself," Lieutenant Colonel Sampsel said from the high ground Pax had jumped from.

For a moment, Pax wondered why he hadn't joined in the fight, and he felt a tiny flicker of anger. But then he realized the officer was in pretty bad shape. Wolf had vaulted down just like Pax had, but that might have been beyond the lieutenant colonel's abilities. And the entire thing had probably taken less than thirty seconds.

Besides, the man was right.

"Go ahead, Pax. I'll take care of these," Wolf said as he took out his own multitool.

Pax shuffled over to the tiny rivulet. His knee hurt, and thought his face might be swelling, but all told, it could have been worse.

Behind him, Wolf finished off the two scouts while he did his best to remove as much pede off him as he could, using a stick, mud, and sand to help. It wasn't great, but it was better than nothing.

"Uh . . . Sergeant? I think it might be a good idea to move on," the officer said after a few minutes. "Who knows how far the sounds of your shots carried."

Pax looked around. The ravine walls would have blocked much of the reports, sending whatever did escape straight up. But some would have carried.

He didn't particularly like to be corrected by anyone, much less officers, and even more less by non-infantry, but the lieutenant colonel was right. They had to move.

He signaled Wolf to take point but then went over and picked up his destroyed handgun. He didn't even know where the barrel was. It looked like what someone might expect a paper handgun to look like if it was destroyed—like shredded cardboard.

"Stupid piece of shit," he muttered as he reared his hand back to toss the trash away.

"Keep it, Sergeant," the officer said. "We don't want to leave anything behind that the pedes can analyze, and our R&D will want to figure out what happened to that."

Shit, that's twice he's corrected me. What the hell am I doing?

Pax knew very well to leave no sign. But with his adrenaline still coursing through his body and his disgust at the worthless piece of crap, he'd let his emotions get a hold of him.

"Roger that, sir," he said as he put the weapon in his pocket.

"And if someone can help me, I can get down and join you. I don't think I'm up for jumping like you two."

"I got you, sir," Wolf said.

He climbed back up, then helped the lieutenant colonel make his way down to the bottom of the ravine.

Pax tried to extend his senses, listening for any sign of Tucanans. Now that the lieutenant colonel had mentioned it, he was concerned other Tucs had heard the fight and would come to investigate. He wanted to be long gone from here if they did.

Within two minutes, they were ready. Pax gave the order to move out.

His face was beginning to burn, and his eyes were watering. But Pax felt pretty damn good. He'd fought a Tuc hand-to-hand and come out on top. Sure, it had been partially trapped by the debris, but still, that was a good resume stuffer. He couldn't wait to get back to the rest of the platoon and do a little humblebragging.

If we get back. There's still a long way to go.

He'd feel a lot better when they reached the RP and linked up with the other two teams, but he wasn't going to relax until they were in the rear and their package was sent on his way.

22

"I want to thank you two," Lieutenant Colonel Sampsel said, shaking Pax and Wolf's hands.

"Just doing our job, sir."

"Just doing your job saved my life, and I'm kinda partial to that, you know. And about that other thing. Sorry for accusing you of wanting to kill me back there."

"They did try to ghost you, sir," Wolf said. "The Banshees and all of that."

"Still, you've got my gratitude. If there's ever anything I can do for you, just reach out, OK?"

Pax didn't know how to respond. Sergeants did not "reach out" to lieutenant colonels.

"Uh, sure, sir. We will."

"Colonel?" Lieutenant Forte interrupted. "It's time. The drone's inbound."

"Well . . . once again, thanks. And now I'm about to get slingshotted, something I never thought I'd ever say." He turned to the lieutenant and said, "Lead on."

Their VIP followed her to the opening in the trees that was acting as a pickup point. He'd been rode hard and put up wet, as Pax's grandfather—the only person in his family who ever treated him with any degree of love—used to say.

Pax had to give the man credit. He hadn't thought the officer was going to make those last few klicks, but with what had to be a ton of perseverance, he'd made the RP on his own two feet, where, to Pax's surprise, the rest of the platoon had displaced to. It hadn't been in the original plans, but Pax had been relieved to see them and the gunny's team. Staff Sergeant Bethel and Kildeer hadn't arrived yet, though.

Upon reaching the RP, the lieutenant colonel had immediately collapsed, but two hours and several jolts of magic nanos from Doc Grant later, he was mobile again.

But he was hardly in good shape. The man hobbled after the platoon commander, each step in obvious pain. It wasn't just his beat-up body, though. The V-harness was a god-awful contraption that forced the human body into an unnatural posture, with the straps digging into it and the neck and back support limiting movement.

Pax watched the lieutenant colonel penguin-walk away, and while he could think of at least a hundred reasons not to, he called out, "Make sure your jewels are positioned just right, Colonel. You'll regret it if they're not."

The lieutenant spun around, her eyes huge, while Pax added, "With all due respect, of course, sir."

The lieutenant colonel turned and gave a short laugh and a thumbs-up. "Thanks for the warning, Sergeant Alejo. I'll keep that in mind."

He turned back to hobble after the lieutenant, who gave the I'll-see-you-later look, before leading their package away.

"Holy fuck, Pax," Olivia said with a laugh.

"What? I was just giving him some advice as someone who's been in that situation before."

Both Wolf and Olivia looked at him in surprise.

"You've been slingshotted?" Olivia asked.

"Once. On Justinia. And during the insert on Hale's Refuge, for that matter."

"And were your balls 'positioned just right'?" she asked.

"No. That's why I wanted to warn the poor guy. He's been through enough."

"Well, no harm, no foul, now that you're an Undead. No use for them here," she said.

The memory of extract on Justinia was something he'd tried to push out of his mind. Two minutes of searing pain. Much worse than the Hale insert.

"You're saying you rode the slingshot," Wolf asked.

"That's what I just said."

"No way no how. Just leave me on the ground and be done with it," Wolf said with a visible shudder.

"Wait a minute. If you had a gazillion pedes chasing your skinny ass, you wouldn't ride the slingshot?" Olivia asked.

"Nope. Not never."

"Uh, 'not never' is a double negative. That means you might."

"I'll make it a triple negative if that's what you want. No. Nope. Never."

Pax was somewhat surprised. Corporal Morning Mist, former AGW Ghost Walker, was a super soldier. To find out he was afraid of a slingshot wasn't something he expected. And that made this super soldier a little more relatable.

The three Marines watched the two freshie officers reach the designated EZ where Fridge Amana waited to give the lieutenant colonel one more brief. The slingshot had been developed for the Bonderdam SEALs, so Amana got the nod to explain it.

Who couldn't nod was the lieutenant colonel. The neck brace prevented it. But even this far away, Pax could see him listening with rapt—and probably anxious—attention.

Then it was time. Fridge released the small chameleon skin balloon, which rose, pulling the retrieval cable behind. Pax watched it until the skin made it too difficult to spot. Fridge and the lieutenant stepped back, and all eyes craned skyward.

No one saw it until the last moment—it was stealthy, after all. The recon drone, all three meters of it, appeared just over the treeline.

It looked like most other drones, with a minimal rack on the underside and a small catch V protruding from the nose. There were hundreds of these drones patrolling up and down the lines, taking care to remain just on the human side of the lines. Drones that crossed the boundary had a habit of getting shot down.

The lieutenant had said that this one had been patrolling for nine hours already in hopes that it would be used.

The drone was aimed at the balloon, hopefully to catch the retrieval line in the V. Pax probably wasn't alone in holding his breath.

It was a good catch. One moment, Lieutenant Colonel Sampsel was standing in the high grass. The next moment, he shot into the air as if fired by a cannon.

There was a collective gasp. Within seconds, their VIP was out of sight.

"Like I said, no, nope, never," Wolf muttered.

The drone was fairly slow flying, unlike the Condor that had jerked Pax to safety when he'd been slingshotted. Even so, Pax didn't think any human could take an uncushioned jolt if they'd simply been snatched with a static line. But the retrieval line had a certain amount of give, and the retrieval frame had a hydraulic system to absorb some of the shock.

It hadn't felt like it to Pax when he was extracted. It had felt like his guts were being forced out of his asshole by the force. But the engineers had taken everything into account: aircraft speed, body weight, planetary gravity, weather, the specifications of the V-harness, everything, to calculate just how quickly they could retrieve the person without killing them.

Pax had survived, and he trusted that the lieutenant colonel would, too. He just wasn't sure that it was necessary. They were inside human-held ground. They could have trucked him or flown him back via normal aircraft.

Evidently, though, the command wanted him back now, and they didn't want to risk any normal personnel transport. Just as the planetary Guard battery had fired into Tucanan territory, the enemy might and probably would do the same for what they considered a high-value target.

So the battered officer would fly, strapped to the bottom of the drone, back to wherever.

I hope he took my advice on his balls.

"Find them," Pax said as Olivia passed by.

She gave him a quick thumbs-up.

Staff Sergeant Bethel and Bambi Kildeer still hadn't returned by what was now seven hours after Lieutenant Colonel Sampsel had been slingshotted out of the RP. Nor had they triggered the locator on their battle comps. On orders directly from their secret command center in Cape Town, Lieutenant Forte had broadcast a position query.

The always cynical Panda had wondered aloud whether that was so a rescue could be attempted or if it was so a waiting battery could hit the spot.

The Immortals' very existence was still top secret, and the brass couldn't help but be concerned that the Tucanans might capture the two Marines and discover what had been done to them.

Despite that, Pax didn't think that their overlords would eliminate the two.

Mostly.

It didn't matter. Bethel didn't respond. No one knew if that was because he chose not to or if he couldn't.

In the end, the order came down. They were to send out two patrols to work their way through Bethel and Kildeer's list of targets. One patrol would start at Target Nine, their final objective, and one would start at Target One.

These weren't snoop and poop patrols. They were going in ready for combat, should it come to that. And if they found that the two Marines had been captured, the patrols were to attempt a forced rescue.

With two patrols going out, the remaining personnel were not enough to form a full defensive perimeter around the RP, so Pax was out as an OP, an observation post, thirty meters deep into the forest. Staff Sergeant Byeon led her patrol right past him as they headed into pede country.

Pax felt abandoned. It didn't make any sense, he knew. He'd just been one of six to try and recover Lieutenant Colonel Sampsel, but now he felt like a little kid looking through the fence as the bigger kids played. He watched until Ogre Carlton, the Tail End Charlie, disappeared into the trees.

Now it was a waiting game for those in the RP. Without contact, the patrols should meet in another seven or eight hours and head back, hopefully with the two missing Marines. Call it ten hours.

Pax settled in to wait.

Gunny Akai checked his position after an hour.

"Think they'll find them?" Pax asked.

"The Light only knows."

"But if you were a betting man, Gunny, where would you place the bet?"

"Staff Sergeant Bethel's a good Marine, Q-B. He'd reach out if they were still alive."

"So, you don't think they're alive?"

The gunny shrugged. "Stranger things have happened."

Alone on the OP, Pax's mind had been wandering. He finally realized that this whole Immortal stuff wasn't really accurate. Sure, if everything worked right, they could keep getting xeroxed. But sometimes, things went wrong, like with Nani Vesta. Or now, with Bethel and Kildeer.

If they kept getting thrown into the worst and most dangerous situations, the Grim Reaper was going to catch up to them, mycelia or not.

Take the missing team. Even if they were found by the patrol

KIA, too much time had passed for the zombie juice to be effective. Unless . . .

And here's where his imagination had tried to come up with some way that the two could be reanimated.

"Let me ask you a question, Gunny."

"Go ahead."

"I've been thinking. Say Staff Sergeant Bethel and Corporal Kildeer, they get in a firefight. One gets killed, and the other's pretty messed up. The pedes, they leave them alone."

That last part wasn't much of a stretch. While humans administered the coup de grâce to eliminate each Tucanan section, the Tucs usually ignored dying humans.

"So, the one who's still alive, he administers the injector."

"OK," the gunny said. "That's one of them. But who administers the zombie juice to the other?"

"That's what I'm getting at. What if he does it to himself?"

Pax mimed taking the injector and jabbing his neck with it.

"That would probably kill him," the gunny said. "You've been through the briefs. That's why we have to be so careful with the injectors."

"But he's dying anyway. Would the zombie juice work then, though?"

Gunny Akai grunted. "I guess it would. But . . . well, I don't know but what." His eyebrows scrunched together as he considered the question. "Surely, someone must have considered that."

"But then why didn't they brief us?"

"Hell, Q-B. You ask some tough questions. That's a good one, though. I'm going to have to ask when we get back."

Pax frowned. He was hoping the gunny would assure him that

injecting yourself would work. But at least he hadn't shut Pax down. That was something.

"Don't get yourself too worked up over this," the gunny said. "Keep your mind clear. You've got a job to do."

He patted Pax on the shoulder and moved off to check on the next OP. But not getting worked up was easier said than done sometimes. Add in the fact that he'd been awake for fifty-three hours—well short of the drug-aided combat maximum of sixty-five hours—the time could still mess with a mind. He tried to focus on spotting anything in the forest before him, but his thoughts kept drifting to what it really meant to be Undead.

Even after he was relieved and able to try and get some sleep, his mind was racing. Finally, though, he drifted off to sleep, only to be awakened by the patrols' return.

He hurried over to find out what had happened, but it wasn't good news. There hadn't been any sign of the two Marines. It was as if they'd been swallowed by some portal to another dimension.

Pax grabbed a combat ration, and using that as a prop, he hung around on the periphery while trying to listen in as the lieutenant and gunny discussed what was next. He wasn't the only one. Most of the patrols were hanging around, trying to be inconspicuous. Olivia and Doc Grant came up to stand beside him.

With Doc there, Pax almost asked him about self-administering the zombie juice, but he was too distracted by trying to listen in to the platoon's two leaders.

The lieutenant, who'd led one of the two patrols, must have already reported in, because she held up a hand to stop the gunny while using the other to cover her left ear.

It shouldn't make things any better with her bonebud, but it was a habit some people had a hard time breaking.

No one tried to pretend they weren't listening in anymore. All eyes were locked onto the platoon commander, who kept nodding but saying nothing.

Finally, she said, "I understand. We're on it."

She nodded a couple more times to what the person on the other end of the comms was saying, then her intensity faded, she sighed, and her body seemed to slightly deflate. It took a few more moments before she realized that most of the platoon was staring at her, waiting for the word.

"We've got our orders, and they're coming from the very top."

So, not the colonel.

No one knew exactly what the "very top" was, other than the fact that their overlords occupied a nondescript and mundanely designated office at HQMC in Cape Town. Knowledge of the Undead's existence was very limited, they knew. But who was in charge? How far up the chain were decisions made?

All of that was unknown.

From the look on the lieutenant's face, whatever their orders were wouldn't be good.

We're going back in until we find them.

Pax knew it would be risky. Olivia had told him the Tucanans were swarming the area, and they'd almost been spotted twice. But that was the only answer. Marines didn't leave Marines behind.

"Make sure you have your zombie juice," he whispered to the other two. "This could get hot."

The lieutenant stood silent for a long moment before she said, "We're getting pulled back. And no one else is coming forward."

What the . . .

There was dead silence for a few seconds as if no one believed what they'd just heard. Then, there was a collective protest.

The lieutenant just absorbed it for a few moments before the gunny shouted, "At ease. We're still within hearing of the pedes."

In the back of his mind, Pax noted that the gunny wanted them to quiet down because of the enemy, not because they shouldn't protest orders. But he filed that away. Right now, he was angry.

Yes, he knew that Bethel and Kildeer were most likely dead. But as long as there was a chance that they were alive or could still be reanimated . . .

It was commonly believed that Marines never left anyone behind. It was the same with most militaries. Pax had just thought the oft-used phrase a few moments ago. But in reality, that wasn't the case. There were millions, if not tens or hundreds of millions of MIAs, the "Missing in Action," soldiers and Marines who were lost in combat and never recovered. And that didn't even include the larger number of sailors whose ships had been lost with all hands aboard.

Pax knew all of this from an intellectual perspective. But this was emotional. There were only a few more than a hundred Immortals, and for their overlords to just dismiss two of them was a little hard to take.

Kildeer and Bethel had been in a limited area, one that should be possible to search, even if that were only with drones. Let them locate the two Marines. And if they were dead, it was possible that at least one had been administered his zombie juice. Then, a quick, small recovery team could be launched despite the increased numbers of Tucanans.

It didn't seem right that when there was a potential for reanimation that all measures weren't exhausted.

The lieutenant let the wave of protests wash across her longer than Pax would have imagined she would.

Finally, she said, "That's our orders," with a surprising amount of venom.

That silenced some of the protests. It was as if everyone had been blaming her, and now they realized that this was out of her hands.

"There's a truck on its way—ETA in two and a half hours. We *will* be on that truck when it leaves."

"But what about Nugget and Staff Sergeant Bethel?" Panda asked.

"That's not up to us. Command . . ."

Whereas the Undead tended to refer to their unseen and unnamed commanders as their "overlords," the freshies normally just used the generic "command."

". . . considers our two platoon mates as combat losses."

There was another combined hiss. "Combat losses" could mean anything, but it was generally used with regard to equipment.

Pax was surprised that the lieutenant would repeat that. She had to know the connotation.

"Until then, I want a hundred percent security. We're not going to be surprised if the pedes decided to repay our own excursion into their area. Gunny, can I see you and Sergeant Tömörbaatar?"

That shut down the protests. Sergeant Ki "Mongol" Tömörbaatar was their drone wrangler. Everyone in the platoon could control the more common drones, but Mongol had been a school-trained TU Marine Gold Beret before coming into the LoH Marines. If the lieutenant wanted her, then it didn't look like she was giving up on their two MIAs.

"Staff Sergeant Byeon, get everyone placed in our perimeter," the gunny said before he motioned for Mongol to join him.

It was a very slow-moving group that started to move to their positions. Pax kept looking back as the lieutenant spoke to the wrangler.

Mongol listened, then nodded and removed a small black case from her backpack.

Pax didn't need Olivia's elbow to the ribs to know the significance of that. They all did. And to a Marine, they all stopped to watch.

As the wrangler, Sergeant Tömörbaatar didn't physically carry all of the drones in the platoon. Those were spread out among the Marines. But she did keep some of the specialized drones, including the "zoo."

Inside that black case were about twenty drones that, to the naked eye, looked like common insects: dragonflies, beetles, bees, and such. These were technical marvels, and they came with a commensurately steep price. And aside from their remarkable appearance, they were also both quite stealthy and shielded from emissions. Depending on how much flying they did as opposed to crawling, they could remain on station for eight to ten days.

The zoo drones were normally sent ahead of Marines to detect enemy activity. That way, they could be recovered as the Marines moved in. Losing a Z-Drone, even in combat, was a serious matter and required a detailed report explaining how it had been necessary. More than a few lieutenants and captains had their careers cut short due to losses that were not deemed necessary.

Everyone watched as Mongol entered her instructions. About a minute later, the different drones rose out of the case and flew toward the Tucanans. Pax didn't know what their instructions were, but he could guess. They'd spread out in a search pattern and cover every square meter of that team's AO. If they spotted anything, they'd send a message and relay the information. And if nothing was spotted, they'd expand the search until they ran out of power.

With the platoon leaving the planet, they wouldn't recover the drones.

Gunny put his commiserating hand on the lieutenant's shoulder and said something to her. Pax couldn't hear, and he wasn't a lip-reading expert, but he was pretty sure he said, "You did the right thing."

Then, the gunny looked up and seemingly noticed the watching Marines, all of whom immediately bolted into motion.

Two and a half hours later, the platoon was loading the truck. The Z-drones hadn't spotted anything yet, but they'd keep looking long after the platoon was off the planet and heading home.

23

"I'd die to be out there," Doc Grant said as they stood on the table to be able to see out the small window to the city beyond the spaceport.

"You did die, Doc, and look where that got you," Pax said.

He understood the sentiment, though. He'd been thinking much the same thing.

The platoon had been parked for the last two days in the same empty hangar at the edge of the spaceport, far away from the terminals and other buildings. The hangar had a few small windows, and after hearing explosions, several of the Marines had grabbed a table and dragged it under one of them.

Pax had jumped up on the table, but instead of Tucanans attacking the city, he saw fireworks and motioned for others to join him.

Out beyond the fence was a festival of sorts, one with an intensity that filled the air with energy. The Tucanans were only 220 klicks away, and the looming threat hanging over the population's head needed an outlet.

The fireworks lasted a good twenty minutes, a laugh in the face of an actual bombardment. But the lights stayed bright, and they could see the top of a Ferris wheel above the nearby buildings. Depending on the wind, they could hear the music, and once, a wave of festival food aromas wafted past.

Some of the Undead hadn't seen civilization of sorts for almost two years. There'd been the terminal on the way into the planet, but that had been a hurried military movement. Out there, people would be enjoying themselves, eating junk food, going on rides, and mingling while raising a middle finger to the Tucanans and the war.

Pax wanted to be with them almost more than he could stand. Just an evening. He needed to feel part of humanity.

Olivia companionably leaned up against him. "I used to love festivals. We had a Greek one, over at the Orthodox Church every year, and oh, the black lava was to die for."

Pax frowned. "Black lava?"

"Yeah. The Greek dessert? You've never had it?"

"Oh, you mean baklava. Yes, I've had it."

She laughed and said, "They call it black lava."

It isn't even black.

But he'd learned that it wasn't worth arguing. Besides, he thought her little Oliviaisms were kind of cute.

Then he focused on the rest of her statement.

"Are you Greek Orthodox? You're from New Leeds."

"Uh, Earth to Pax. We're not all limeys. We let others on the planet."

He rolled his eyes. Of course, people from all over the galaxy moved somewhat as they pleased. On his own world of San Marcos, there was one of the largest Mennonite communities in all of humanity.

"Hey, how about letting someone else take a look," Fridge Amana asked.

Pax turned and looked down. There were about ten Marines waiting. The table was big enough to hold about five or six standing on it.

"Shall we?" he asked the others.

Doc sighed and said, "If we must."

They jumped down while the others scrambled up for a look at humanity in its natural environment.

"Think they'll fry her ass?" Doc Grant asked, pointing across the hangar floor.

Lieutenant Forte was sitting against the far wall, her head back, her eyes closed. The zoo drones were still out there doing their thing. The gunny told them that after reporting what she'd done, first Captain Lakmal, who had met the truck as they arrived, in person, and then the battalion S-4 over the comms, had come down on her head and demanded she recall them. But 220 klicks were a long way to go for a tiny dragonfly drone, and neither one of the captains authorized some sort of transport to go retrieve them.

This was one case where having orders to keep a low profile might have helped out.

None of the Z-drones had detected anything yet, but there was still hope.

Pax hoped that the platoon commander wouldn't be punished. She was a freshie, but she was *their* freshie, and she was turning out to be OK.

"They probably will. Those little bugs are worth a mint," Olivia said.

"That was real righteous of her, you know," Pax said after a moment's hesitation.

There was this thing about offering praise for an officer among some Marines, much less now when one was a freshie. Pax didn't want to get a rep as a brown-noser.

"She did it for us," Doc said. "Not for you or me, but for us Immortals. She doesn't treat us like we're non-human tools."

"She's good people," Olivia said. "For a freshie officer, I mean."

Yeah, I know what you mean.

No one added anything else. Probably embarrassed for saying nice things about a lieutenant. But it felt good to know he wasn't alone in his opinions.

"What now? Wanna play Six to a Dozen?" Doc asked.

Pax looked behind him. Seven Marines were standing on the table, just able to see out the window. Four more were waiting their turn.

"Look at Rut," Olivia said. "He's about drooling looking at freshies having fun."

Rutledge was shifting his weight back and forth with his hands in a death grip on the windowsill. He looked like a puppy at the door waiting for its human to come home.

Pax chuckled at the sight, then said, "I think I'm going back in line to take another look at people being normal. Maybe we'll get one more sniff of popcorn."

"Everybody up," Gunny Akai said.

Pax opened his eyes and groaned. It felt like he'd just fallen asleep a few seconds ago.

Then he jerked upright and asked, "Did the drones find them?"

The gunny shook his head and said, "We're leaving."

"Off planet or back to the RP?" Doc Grant asked.

"Off planet."

Marines exchanged glances with each other but didn't say anything. They'd known this was coming, but as long as they were stashed in this abandoned building, there'd been hope. They'd talked about how Bethel and Kildeer would be found, and how the overlords would authorize a mission.

Pax didn't really believe it, but on one level, it made sense. They couldn't want an Undead, even a body, to fall into Tucanan hands, right?

Now, that pipe dream was gone. They were returning to the Opal. If the Z-drones eventually found something, then it wouldn't be the platoon who reacted. And judging from what they'd seen from the Three-Zs and the planetary Guard, none of them had confidence that anything could be done.

With a sigh, Byeon stood up.

"You heard him. Get your shit together. And clean this pigsty up."

They really didn't have much to pack up, and "pigsty" might be a reach. Still, it was surprising at how much trash could be generated in two days even without much to start with.

The military gear was already crated and ready to go. Pax stuffed his belongings in his seabag, then joined the rest in a police call[1] for trash. Within ten minutes, the platoon was ready to go. So, of course, it was almost three hours before their transport arrived.

Undead or freshie, some things never changed.

They loaded the bus and left the spaceport grounds—the bus wasn't going to be allowed to cross the tarmac to the terminal and had to make its way around the perimeter. That route took them past one side of the festival.

"Looks like *they* could use the police call," Panda said.

What had seemed like a wonderful dream the night before now looked like a dystopian disaster. Trash was blowing everywhere in the morning sun despite several autojans that were moving up and down the venue attempting to clean up. A single vendor was opening up his food stand.

"Reality sucks," Pax said.

The bus made its way around the spaceport and eventually reached the front. But they didn't stop at the main terminal.

"There go my Cinny Stars," Olivia said.

"You don't have any money to buy one," Doc said.

"But I could smell them. That's free."

The bus let them off at a small, private terminal, the kind the rich and famous used so as not to be rubbing elbows with the unwashed masses. And it was pretty nice inside, with plush chairs and numerous holoscreens.

There was even a full bar, which was locked, to their disappointment. They still weren't allowed alcohol, but Pax didn't think that would have stopped very many of them. The regular food and

---

1. **Police Call**: military terminology for cleaning up trash and debris

drink vending machines were working, and everyone mobbed them, oohing and aahing over the choices.

Some foods, such as chiles were on their verboten list, but the lieutenant wasn't saying anything, and when the gunny dialed up a jerk chicken, that opened the floodgates.

"If my myc doesn't like spicy, screw it," Pax muttered as he pulled a bowl of vindaloo out of the dispenser. "This is for me."

He gave it a sniff, and his eyes started to water. A huge smile spread across his face. He took his meal and plopped down beside Olivia and Doc on a couch in front of a large holoscreen.

"Barbarians versus the Qs?" Doc asked.

Like almost everyone on San Marcos, Pax was a football fan, and Real Lago de Oro was his team. He had no idea who the Barbarians or the Qs were, but he really didn't care.

Doc pulled up the game. It was Slamball. Anything was better than nothing, so Pax settled in and took a big bite of his vindaloo, which he'd dialed at a Spice Level 4, just short of the max SL 5.

It was . . . *amazing*. He'd forgotten how intense foods could be. And if he might have felt a little twitch inside his head, well, that was probably his imagination.

He took a second bite, and then waving his spoon around like a pointer, he said, "They can send us into incredible odds. They can xerox us. But they won't let us have a little fire in our food."

Olivia just grunted, her mouth full of buffalo wings and face smeared with the sauce.

Pax settled in to watch the match. Slamball might not be the "beautiful game," but there was a lot of action and a lot of violence. Good Marine stuff.

"You know, if this is how they want to keep us away from all the freshies, I'm on board," Doc said.

"You and me both."

But as with everything military, all good things come to an end. Captain Lakmal—who'd probably been on per diem in some four-star hotel all this time—entered the terminal.

"That's it, Marines. Vacation's over. The ship's ready for you, so we'll move to the gate and into the shuttle. Once on the ship, we'll head directly to our berthing area." He paused to good-naturedly let the groans die out. "I don't have to remind you that you're not to mix with the other passengers.

"Lieutenant Forte, there's a transporter outside the door. Please get the pallets loaded, then troop everyone to the gate. We're already cleared for security."

That elicited a laugh from several of the Marines. They might be officially cleared, but no one had actually run any checks. And they were combat Marines.

They might not be able to smuggle an artillery piece past the general security in the terminal, but they had stealth capabilities. The paper handguns, for example, could almost assuredly get past the terminal-wide scanners.

And Marines had a habit of keeping whatever they could when returning from combat.

That wasn't their worry, though. The platoon quickly loaded the pallets, then the gunny marched them into the main terminal—which was after security—and to the people mover that would take them under under the tarmac to Gates 90-99.

"Grab a seat," the gunny told them.

This was as close as they were going to get to the freshies. Pax watched the people at the other gates, all going about their daily business. None of them seemed to be paying attention to what looked like just one more work crew in their blue overalls.

It still seemed surreal. This was normal life, but on a planet where a third was occupied by the Tucanans, and who knew how many of their fellow citizens had been killed? If the Tucs wanted to, they could easily knock down all of the shuttles taking people to and from the ships in orbit. Yet, by some perverse and unwritten policies by both sides, that probably wasn't going to happen.

Six minutes after they were seated, they were given their five-minute warning. Some of the civilian passengers had already gotten in line—even for a relatively short flight up to their ship, they had to make sure they got a good seat and could find room in the carry-on bins.

"Everybody up," Gunny said. "Give me a head count."

The phrasing and how the Marines each counted off might seem a little military to any passenger who might have served, but no one seemed to notice.

The count went until Staff Sergeant Byeon said, "Thirty-four."

Everyone started to move to the line for the shuttle when the gunny said, "OK, which one of you bozos didn't sound off? Again. Head count."

This time, as everyone counted off, the rest paid attention to see who the idiot who missed their count was. And once again, Byeon was at thirty-four.

"What's the problem, Gu . . . uh, Mr, Akai?" Captain Lakmal asked.

"The count's at thirty-four. With me, that's thirty-five, and with Ms. Forte, that's thirty-six. We're supposed to be at thirty-seven."

"I'm here, too."

"I'm not counting you, sir."

"And with the two . . ."

"Already taken into consideration."

Pax was confused. They'd been sitting in three ranks of seats and were now standing in front of them. No one had skipped their count as it made its way down one rank and up the next.

He tried to figure out what went wrong, when a thought hit him, and he did a quick scan of the faces.

Shit. I knew it.

"It's Rut!" he said aloud.

Gunny Akai looked at him, then to the rest of the platoon.

"He's right," the lieutenant said. "It's Rutledge."

"Check the head," he told Pax.

Pax rushed to comply, but he knew he wouldn't find the man. And he didn't. He reported back to the gunny, who had put everyone back in their seats while the captain and lieutenant huddled together to figure out what to do next.

Sergeant Rutledge, the man who'd been so upset to miss his son's birthday, the man who'd been staring longingly at the festival the night before, had gone UA.[2]

He'd run.

"Most of all, remember, you're not here. No one should give you a second glance," Captain Lakmal said.

The man was worried. What had been a nice boondoggle for him had turned into a potentially career-ending disaster.

Pax didn't care. Lakmal was a self-serving freshie. But he did care about Rutledge. His fellow sergeant was in deep shit, and they had to pull him out.

---

2. **UA**: Unauthorized Absence

The only good thing was that the captain hadn't reported Rutledge going UA yet. He probably thought if they could recover the sergeant quickly, he had a chance of making this all go away.

He was also deluding himself. When he'd pulled the platoon from the terminal, that alerted the battalion that something was wrong. And unless he could come up with an innocuous explanation, then his ass was still grass, even if they got Rutledge back.

It was possible that the battalion could keep it from the overlords, but Pax had a feeling that as easygoing as the colonel seemed to be, Lakmal would be thrown under the bus in a heartbeat if this wasn't quickly nipped in the bud.

With few options, Lakmal had decided on two courses of action. The first was to report Rutledge as a suicide threat to the police but leaving out most of the details and sticking to the working party playacting.

Olivia had gasped when they were told that, wondering if the suicide possibility was real. Pax didn't buy it. Rutledge didn't bug out to kill himself. He was going to try and go home.

He also didn't think that the police would put this on a high priority. If he were a Waterton cop, he'd assume that Rutledge was in some alley, sleeping off an epic drunk.

That left the second option, and this one surprised Pax. Captain Lakmal probably realized that the cops wouldn't be too much help, unless Rutledge got himself arrested, and then, if he started talking, all of them would be in a heap of trouble. So, he decided that they'd be proactive in searching for their lost Marine.

He ordered that the platoon break down into two-person teams, each to cover either an assigned sector or transportation hub. As soon as that word was passed, there was a rush as Marines paired up. Olivia had grabbed him a second before Doc asked.

The captain and the lieutenant would remain at the spaceport, both to have a central location and to search for Rutledge there. Pax guessed that the sergeant could still be there, but the man had no money, and he wanted to get home. The only way Pax could figure out how that could happen would be to get to one of the alternate commercial spaceports and hook up with a tramp crew. Some of those bordered on—or went over—the line on legality, and they might not care as long as they had a warm body.

He was surprised that the captain didn't mention something to that regard, but when he started assigning search sectors, Pax volunteered Olivia and him to take Unday Station, one of the smaller spaceports in the city.

"You think he's gonna try and get off planet there?" Olivia whispered.

"There or one of the others. He wants to go home."

They were all in their blue overalls, which the captain thought would make them too conspicuous, so he bought thirty-seven t-shirts from one of the spaceport gift shops, the kind that businessmen and women bought on their way off planet when they hadn't gotten presents for their kids.

Some of them were very touristy, probably from before the invasion. At least Pax got one with the cartoon image of a Guardsman stomping on a Tucanan soldier and the caption, "Stomp the Pedes!"

"I'm keeping this," he told Olivia.

One of the last things before leaving was a surprise, and a little unsettling. The captain had retrieved their gear before they returned to their empty hangar. He told them to file by and issued each team a paper handgun.

Pax didn't know what they were supposed to do with them, and he was afraid to ask. He wasn't going to use it on one of the locals, and certainly, he wasn't going to use it on Rutledge.

If they were caught with the weapon, well, they did have their military IDs—fake names, of course, but real IDs. That should keep them out of trouble, but local cops wouldn't like armed military in civilian clothes poking around their city.

The captain went on for a few more moments, ran a comms check, and then it was time. The platoon filed out of the building, passed through the gate, and were out in the real world.

"Good luck," Doc, whose partner was Mongol Tömörbaatar, said before they split up. "Let's bring him back."

Pax and Olivia broke off to the right and made their way to the magtram. They each had credit wands, paid for by the captain and lieutenant. They were only charged to twenty credits each, but that was enough to get them to and from their destinations.

Eight other teams headed to the same stop. They ignored each other, but with their blue overalls and tourist t-shirts, Pax thought they sort of stuck out like a sore thumb.

But no one approached them, and no accusations were thrown at them. They boarded without incident and were on their way.

Unday Station was on the other side of the city, an hour and twenty-minute ride away. The two settled in for the ride, trying to act like any other passenger.

Pax had wanted to see Waterton, but not under these circumstances. Still, they were just sitting there, so he stared out the window as they passed. And while the main spaceport had looked in good shape, that wasn't the case everywhere. The worst was a five-block area that had been destroyed in the invasion. The streets had been cleared of debris, but it didn't look like anything had been done to the rubble that had once been buildings.

And in the streets, hovers and pedestrians made their way to and fro as if the destruction wasn't even there.

As a Marine, Pax had seen lots of devastation. He'd caused some of it himself. But it was in and out. He'd never been on any planet after the fact. To see the people just accepting it was a little surreal, and it hit home why the festival was held, even with the enemy still on the planet a couple hundred klicks away.

Not all of the city was in rubble. Most of it, in fact, looked untouched. Unless you knew better, it would be easy to assume that Lemon's Hold was just one more planet going through life without a care.

One by one, the other teams disembarked. Pax knew they weren't supposed to acknowledge each other, but he mouthed, "Good luck" to each team as they got off.

He didn't give them much hope, though. This had been a big city before the invasion, and now, with the influx of refugees, it was even more populous. Just wandering around looking for Rutledge was the proverbial searching for a needle in the haystack.

No, the only ones with a real chance of finding him would be the three teams heading to the commercial spaceports or the two going to the refugee camps on the edges of the city.

And if Rutledge had already managed to get out of the city? Well, then they were screwed.

"Next stop, Unday Station. This is the last stop on the Purple Line. All passengers must disembark now," came over the speakers.

Olivia nudged him with her elbow and whispered, "Let's hope he's here. For his sake."

This wasn't Jennifer Harrington Spaceport Station, with the bright lights and mosaics of Lemon's Hold destinations on the walls. There was no doubt that this was an industrial area, and a slightly seedy one at that. Most of the people getting on and off the magtram here were in work clothes, to include overalls, and Pax wondered if their t-shirts were really necessary. There were far more crewsuits, which would be expected. Business suits were few and far between.

The security cams lining the halls were far more obvious than the discreet ones at Harrington. Pax tried to walk normally as they passed them. He didn't think he'd be in any database that was being actively flagged, but still, this whole cloak-and-dagger stuff the captain had them on had him on edge.

The cams did get him wondering how long it would be until the overlords got wind of what was happening, if they didn't already know. Once that happened, the security AIs would be alerted to Rutledge. And then, their wayward Marine would be quickly swept up if he was still on the planet.

"So, we'd better find you before then, Rut," he said under his breath.

"Did you say something?" Olivia asked.

"No, nothing."

She scowled at his answer but then asked, "What now? We haven't really talked about it."

"Let's just get a feel for the place first."

The captain had given them a printout of the station, but a facility map could only indicate so much. Pax wanted to see the ebb and flow of personnel and patterns in the movement.

The two followed the crush of commuters to the terminal where people started splitting off to their destinations. Many headed to the food court to stand in line for coffee or meals before their shift started. That seemed like as good a destination as anywhere, so the two Marines headed in that direction.

"Look, another Cinny Star," Olivia said.

Most of the food vendors were local with few of the galaxy-wide chains, but the ubiquitous Cinnamon Star was probably in every port in human space. And business was good. The line was probably twenty-five deep.

They didn't have a lot of credits on their wands, but there was probably enough to get something to eat and drink. Not now, though. They had other priorities.

"Maybe later. We're here for Rut."

Olivia sighed, but she didn't argue.

They split up, one going right while the other went left as they made the circuit. Pax checked each line but spent more time scanning the seats in the middle. The two met at the far side of the court, and Pax didn't need her slight shake of the head to know they'd struck out.

That would have been too easy.

"We'll come back later, but let's cover more ground."

For the next hour, they wandered the main terminal, but to no avail. Finally, as they stood on the observation deck watching the ground shuttles picking people up at the gates, Olivia said, "I don't think he's in the terminal, unless he's already down there. And we can't go there without going through security."

At her "security," Pax was very aware of the handgun in his pocket.

"So, the hiring hall?" he asked.

She nodded, and the two made their way to the main entrance, then they hiked over a klick to a two-story, Smith-frame building. There had been some obvious repairs to part of the roof and front wall. Pax didn't know if that was Tucanan damage or just the normal wear and tear, though Smith-frames were known for their durability if not their comfort.

"OK, look like you're looking for a berth," he told Olivia.

"Oh, I'd love one. No joke."

He gave her a sidewise glance.

Is she serious? Or is she just being Liv?

They entered the building to a low buzz of activity. Like most Smiths, the center was open, with booths and tables along both the ground floor and the second-floor walkway. Someone standing in the center had a direct line of sight to each booth.

Pax was somewhat surprised at the number of what he assumed to be crew in the building. He couldn't get over the fact that even with the planet partially occupied, commerce continued, seemingly unabated.

He mentioned that to Olivia, who said, "Don't forget. Crew coming in or out get a hazardous duty bump."

"Really? And how do you know that?"

"I keep my nose to the ground," she said, tapping it with a forefinger.

"You mean your ear," Pax automatically started to say, then let it go.

It wasn't worth the effort. Instead, he took a moment to scan the hall.

Most of the center of the ground floor was occupied by the bigger names, both transports and cruise liners. Their displays were larger and in better shape, all promising rewarding work with great benefits. Pax recognized most of the names. There weren't that many people seeing what those companies had to offer.

Surrounding them were companies with smaller but still professional-looking displays. There were more people interested in those. That confused Pax for a moment until he figured out that the big guys must be well-known entities for professional spacers. Maybe these smaller companies were not as well known, and those looking for work wanted to check them out.

On the periphery of the first floor, the booths were down to desks with maybe a banner or two. And then, on the second floor, were what Pax assumed to be the employers of last resort, the lowest of the lows of space commerce.

Pax pointed up there, and Olivia said, "Got it."

The elevator wasn't working, so the two made their way up the stairs. They could split up like they did in the food court at the main terminal and cover more ground, but this floor looked sketchy. He was confident that he could take care of himself if anything went astray, but he didn't really want any attention. Maybe the two of them together would fare better.

When he suggested that to Olivia, she readily agreed.

"Right or left?"

She pointed to the left, and they started along the walkway.

They'd only passed two booths—and "booths" was being generous—when the woman behind the third desk asked, "You looking for work?"

"Maybe. It depends on the perks," Pax said.

Is that how spacers talk? "Perks?"

He probably should have figured out what to say before they started. They needed to look like they belonged.

"Perks? You're in the wrong area," she said, tilting her head down to the first floor. "I don't suppose you've got your certs, either?"

Pax's warrior senses perked up at her "either."

"Why do you ask that?"

She didn't answer but said, "Your company must be a shit place to work. Is it a line or labor company?"

Pax frowned and asked, "What do you mean?"

The woman pointed at his butt. "Your company patch. The 'Romero Industries' on the back pocket."

Both Pax and Olivia automatically reached back to the pocket where a fictitious patch for their fictitious company had been placed on the pocket for verisimilitude.

"One of your buddies was here earlier. He didn't have any spacer certs, though."

It was as if lightning struck him. Beside, him Olivia stiffened.

"When was he here?" he asked, fighting to keep his voice calm.

"A couple of hours ago. Tall, slender dude. Looking nervous. Hey," she said, lowering her voice. "I don't know if you're breaking a work contract or not, but throwing on a t-shirt when you're still wearing your company overalls doesn't do the trick. If they want to track you down, the security will find you in a pede minute. And the cops here? They're very friendly to the corporates, not to labor, if you know what I mean."

"He was here?" Olivia asked, ignoring the advice. "This morning?"

"Yeah, like I said."

"Did you hire him?" Pax asked.

The woman snorted. "Also like I said, he didn't have his certs. Some of the others," she said while indicating the other hiring desks with a flick of her wrist, "they don't care about that. Of course," she said, going down to almost a whisper, "with a little payment, anything's possible."

Pax didn't know if the woman was asking for a bribe, right after implying that she'd only offer positions to those with one of the spacer certifications. But Rutledge had no money, so he wouldn't have been able to offer her anything.

"Uh . . . I think we'd like to stick with our friend," he said.

The woman shrugged, now seemingly disinterested. She went back to her screen where a holovid was playing. It was as if they weren't there.

Pax pulled Olivia aside.

"That's him," she said.

"Has to be. I'm calling it in."

He pulled the throat mic out of a pocket and applied it to the base of his neck. "Connect to Razor," he subvocalized.

No one should be able to break into military comms, but Captain Lakmal was more than a little paranoid, and he insisted that they use a code name, even just while activating the circuit.

"What do you have?" came over almost immediately.

"Our . . . friend was here. Asking for a job."

"Are you sure?"

Pax could hear the excitement in the captain's voice.

"Ninety-nine percent sure."

There was a pause, then, "I'm pulling some of the others to your pos. Keep looking, though. We don't want him heading off to a new job."

"Roger that."

Olivia looked at him, her eyebrows raised in a question.

"He's sending more teams here, but we're supposed to keep looking."

They took one more sweep of the hiring hall but came up empty.

"Back to the terminal? Check out the gates?" Olivia asked.

They couldn't actually go to the gates, but at least a dozen would be in view of the observation platform, so that was as good an idea as any. They headed back.

The Greater Waterton Spaceport, which included Jennifer Harrington, Unday Station, and two more, was the third largest spaceport on the planet and the second largest still in human-controlled territory—and the closest to the Tucanans. Logic might seem that traffic would be far lighter than normal, given the war-footing. But it sure seemed to Pax that the place was bustling.

There were reports that some of the businesses were relocating farther away from the enemy, but that should be more of an issue for ground and air transport, not space. And the increase in military traffic should be limited to the military base outside of the city. Looking around, though, Pax had to assume that commerce was alive and well on the planet. Without the anti-missile batteries, and the repaired damage to the terminal, it would be easy to forget that the planet was in a, though temporarily quiet, fight for its very survival.

They entered the terminal and made their way to the lift. Unday Station was the city's first spaceport, used for both passenger and commercial lifts. Now, with Jennifer Harrington shouldering most of the load, it was strictly commercial, but it had been designed with passengers in mind. Hence, the observation deck, a glassed-in platform overlooking two-thirds of the gates and the tarmac beyond.

Unlike the more modern terminals, where passengers were whisked underground to their shuttle, goods were taken by autoloaders from the warehouses, but crew and deadheads—slang for passengers who paid less for a berth with the crew—were taken by electric trams from their gate to their shuttle.

If Rutledge got a contract, he'd have to go through one of the gates. The problem was that Gates 11-18 were not visible from the observation deck. Neither one of the two Marines could figure out how to get eyes on those gates no matter how hard they wracked their brains.

"We just gotta hope he's going out from one of these," Olivia said.

But there wasn't any sign of him by the time Ogre and Lindersmitz arrived.

"You sure he's here?" Ogre asked as he looked down at the gates.

"I'm sure he *was* here," Pax said. "No telling now."

"Is that him?" Lindersmitz asked suddenly.

"Where, Lindy?" Pax asked.

"Over there. Gate 9. The guy who's not in those maroon jumpsuits."

The other three swiveled to look. There was a man slouched in a chair among the maroon crowd. No one seemed to be talking to him, just like people tended to do with newbies.

But after a moment's study, Olivia said, "No. Too thin. He's as skinny as a beanbag."

"I think you're right," Lindersmitz said with a sigh. "I was hoping it would be that easy."

"If he is there, what do we do? We're not cleared," Ogre said.

"That would be up to Captain Lakmal," Pax replied. "He'd probably call the cops for help. Make up some excuse on why we're in civvies instead of uniforms."

He rubbed his eyes, and Ogre asked, "You want us to spell you? Let you go check out, like, the chow hall or something?"

Pax looked to Olivia who said, "I could use a break."

"We already searched the food court, but that was a while ago. He might have returned."

The two teams switched, and Pax and Olivia made their way back.

"I gotta get something," Olivia said as she flashed her credit wand. "I'm famished."

Pax was pretty hungry, too, and the wand was burning a hole in his pocket, but he said, "Let's make a circuit, first. We don't want Rut spotting us first and making him rabbit."

It didn't take long, and ten minutes later, Olivia was ordering a döner kebab. He'd thought she'd get a Cinnamon Star, but with limited funds, it looked like she wanted something a little more substantial.

There were a lot of choices, but after a moment, Pax just went the easy way and ordered the same thing.

They took their kebabs and stood in the corner, observing the food court while they ate their meal.

"You notice who's eating here?" he asked through a mouthful of the meat.

"What do you mean?"

"Look. Lots of station workers. But not too many spacers."

She looked around. Most of the people were dressed in a variety of clothing. Work clothes and uniforms, primarily, although there was a group of about twenty in their company windbreakers—probably an incoming or outgoing off-planet work team whose company was shipping them on the cheap. What there wasn't was a lot of spacer jumpsuits.

"You're right. That's weird."

"Hey," Pax said to a passing guy in a security uniform with a food tray in his hands. "Where do the spacers eat?"

The man seemed surprised at the question, but he said, "At the spacer lounge."

Once again, Pax's heart gave a little jump, and he felt something akin to what he experienced before going into combat.

"Where's that?"

The man pointed with one hand out the door and to the right. "Near the hiring hall. But you can't eat there. Not that you should want to. Bunch of drunken assholes, all of them."

He left them, and the two Marines wolfed down their döners.

Pax licked his fingers clean, wiped them on the hem of his t-shirt, and said, "Let's go."

They hurried out of the terminal and headed to the hiring hall again. Just on the near side was another building with jumpsuited spacers coming in and out. A sign was beside the door with the words, "Spacer Lounge sponsored by FOS, Hall 29878" and the Fraternal Order of Spacers' eye and star emblem.

"How'd we miss that?" Pax asked.

The two hesitated. They weren't in jumpsuits. But no one stopped them as they entered.

Inside the door and to the right was the food line. Another sign said you had to have your spacer card to eat. The two Marines weren't there to eat, so they slipped past the line and checked out the tables.

No Rutledge.

There was a rec room with two pool tables, six gaming stations, and a large shelf with hundreds of ratty looking books—physical books, not normal electronic.

Pax had always heard that spacers had some sort of fetish for physical books, and now he guessed that might be true.

There was a door in the back of the room with a sign saying

"Quiet Space" on the jamb. Pax and Olivia made their way to it and looked in. The lights were low, but they could see a couple of dozen fully reclining chairs, most with bodies in them.

It took a moment for their eyes to adjust, and suddenly Olivia grabbed his upper arm.

"There!" she hissed.

He followed her finger, and in the last chair to the left, was a familiar figure.

Rutledge wasn't in a jumpsuit, but he had a cloth folder, the kind barebones operations might give their crew. And if the empty food wrapper by the little table alongside the chair was any indication, their fellow Marine had made it through the line and been fed.

Sergeant Rutledge, Undead and LoH Marine, had managed to sign onto a crew.

Olivia had started to enter the room when Pax grabbed her and pulled her back.

"Wait. Let me get Ogre and Lindy. Rut's fast. If he gets past us, he's gone. And I don't think these spacers are going to just let us haul him off if we do stop him."

She gave Rutledge a long look, then nodded.

"Keep an eye on him," Pax said before stepping back.

He slapped his mini-mic on his throat and connected with the two former SEALs. "Ogre, we've got him. But I think we need you two here if we're going to bring him back. He's in the spacer lounge, the one-story building before the hiring hall. Three hundred meters to the left out the terminal entrance."

"Damn! Good job. We're on our way now."

He then connected with Captain Lakmal.

"Tell me you've got good news, Alejo."

"We've found him, sir. He's here at the Unday Station spacers' lounge."

"Oh, by the saints, thank you. What's his status?"

"He's asleep right now. Sergeant St. Amons has eyes on him. Sergeant Amana and Corporal Lindersmitz are on their way."

"What's the . . . are there other spacers with him?"

It's a spacer lounge. What do you think?

But he said, "The place is packed. That's why we wanted Amana and Lindersmitz before we grab him."

There was a pause, then, "Wait until Knopf and Bartok get there before you do anything. And I'm sending a van, civilian-type. Put him in it."

"Roger that, sir."

"And whatever you do, don't let him get away. We've got to bring him back to Opal-3 with us."

"I understand, sir."

"And keep me informed."

The connection was cut, and Pax could imagine the captain nervously pacing the floor in the hangar as he wondered if his career was over. Lieutenant Forte, too.

No, not Forte. She's probably calmer.

He told Olivia what was happening, and they tried to both keep an eye on the sleeping Rutledge while looking innocent. Amana and Lindersmitz joined them, and eighteen minutes later, Knopf and Bartok arrived.

Pax wasn't senior. Lily Bartok was, but in cop terms, this was his and Olivia's collar, and the captain was going through Pax. So he took over.

"There're a lot of spacers here, so we've got to be a little discreet. But knowing Rut, he's going to dash. Lily, you and Blue, I want you on the door here. If he does rabbit and gets past the four of us, you do what you can to stop him."

"Got it."

"The four of us, we need to surround him. Let's see if we can convince him to come without a struggle. But this is Rut. He might agree, then bolt. So, keep your guard up."

"This really sucks, you know?" Ogre said. "He's one of us."

"No argument from me," Pax said. "But it has to be done. Are we ready?"

The other five nodded. "Then let's go."

With two of them on the door, the four went through. One of the pool players gave them a sustained stare, but he didn't say anything.

Pax was glad Rutledge was in the last chair in the line. The four of them surrounded the chair, then Pax nudged Rutledge's foot.

The UA Marine opened his eyes, then sat upright as he recognized them.

"Uh, hey, Liv. Guys." he said, failing in his attempt to sound nonchalant.

"Man, Rut. What have you done?" Pax said, keeping his voice low so the other sleeping spacers wouldn't wake. "We've got to take you back with us."

"No! I mean, no you don't. I'm sorry about leaving you all, but I've got to get home."

"That's not going to happen."

"My kids! My son and daughter think I'm dead!"

"We know. And that sucks. But you were killed."

I can't believe I'm using that argument.

"But we're friends. You know me. Can't you say you haven't found me? In three hours, I'll be off planet."

"And then what?" Pax asked. "Do you think they're going to let you get to your family? Even if you somehow make it to New Aberdeen, they won't let you get anywhere near them."

"You've got to let me try, Pax."

"Do you really want to do that? I'm not saying the overlords will do anything to your family, but they've already mourned you. You show up and somehow reach them against the odds, and then you're yanked away again? It's like dying twice."

"Shut the hell up over there," one of the spacers said before rolling over in the chair, his back to them.

"Come on, Rut. Let's go."

"Liv?" Rutledge said in a plaintive voice.

"You've got to come, Rut."

The Marine deflated. He sat there for a long moment, then with a sigh, swung his legs over the edge of the chair.

"It's the right decision, Rut. But I am sorry. Not that it makes any difference, I know."

Rutledge stood, defeated and dejected. Pax turned to where Bartok and Knopf were waiting when Rutledge came to life, snatching his spacer folder and bolting past Pax, giving him a hard shot to the chest.

Pax tried to grab him, but he was too slow.

Fast or not, Bartok and Knopf filled the door, and when Rutledge crashed into them, they took him to the ground. The other four were quickly there, and they yanked him to his feet with Lindersmitz twisting one of Rutledge's arms behind him.

"Hey, what's going on?" the pool player shouted as he stepped closer, not coincidentally blocking their way out. Several other spacers joined him with looks of concern on their faces.

"Nothing that pertains to you," Lily Bartok said, stepping forward to meet the pool player, Ogre at her side.

The spacer took in the work folder on the ground at Rutledge's feet. "Are you OK, brother?"

"Think of your kids," Pax whispered. "The overlords."

It was a cheap shot, and it made Pax feel dirty.

For a moment, it looked like Rutledge was going to shout for help, but then something changed his mind. It might have been Pax's comment about the kids. It might have been that he didn't want anyone to get hurt.

Whatever the reason, he said, "No problem, brother. I, uh . . . I owe these guys some money, and it looks like they want it before I go off planet."

The pool player stared at Rutledge for a moment, then shifted his gaze to the other six Marines. Pax could see his mind racing as he tried to decide what to do. And Pax could recognize leadership, and he knew whatever this guy decided, the others would follow.

Finally, he grunted and told Rutledge, "Spacing to get out of a debt makes us all look bad. You get these guys paid, huh?"

"I will."

"And once he does, he's good with you?"

"He'll be off planet and on his way by evening," Pax said.

The man nodded, then stepped to the side.

Pax nodded back, one leader to another, and the seven Marines made their way to the entrance and down the steps to where a black van was already waiting with five large civilian men in dark gray trousers and shirt standing at the doors.

"That must have cost our freshies a farm and an egg," Olivia said. "I didn't know captains made that much."

"That Rutledge?" one of them asked in a deep gravelly voice

that had to have been practiced in front of a mirror a thousand times to get it right.

Pax nodded, and the man pointed to the sliding door on the side.

"Just keep your head up," Pax whispered to Rutledge. "It'll be OK."

"Fat chance of that," Rutledge said.

They escorted him to the van, and he stepped inside.

But when the other Marines tried to follow, the civilian said, "Just Rutledge."

"No. He's with us. Or we're with him."

"We've got our orders."

Pax looked at the others, then at the civilians. They were huge, but there were six spec-ops Marines here. He was pretty confident that they could prevail, if it came to that. But that would cause a scene, and already, there were people, mostly spacers, who were taking an interest in what was taking place.

Even the pool player was standing in the doorway watching.

"Wait one," he said as he slapped the mic on his neck.

The civilian leader crooked a half-smile and waited as if he didn't have a care in the world.

"Captain Lakmal, we've got Rutledge in the van you sent, but the civilians won't let us on," he said after connecting.

"Good to hear," the captain said. "Really good to hear. We might survive this fiasco after all. And don't worry about the van. That was part of the deal."

What deal?

"You just get your asses back. I'm recalling everyone, and Lieutenant Forte is turning our transport back on."

"But—" Pax started to protest.

"That's an order, Sergeant. You leave Sergeant Rutledge to them."

Pax's mouth gaped open a few times, but nothing came out. Finally, he said, "Aye-aye, sir."

It wasn't as if he had any choice.

He took a step back and motioned for the civilians to proceed. Without changing expression, the leader hit the side of the van, and the door started sliding to a close.

"Wait!" Lily said as she moved to grab the door.

"Orders, Lily," Pax said, then just before the door snicked to a close, he shouted, "We'll see you back at the spaceport, Rut!"

"What the hell was that?" Ogre asked.

"That was the captain."

The civilian gave Pax a mocking half-bow before he stepped into the passenger seat. A moment later the van lifted off the pavement, rotated around, and took off. The six Marines watched it until it disappeared out the gate.

"That's all sorts of fucked up," Knopf said.

"What are they going to do to him?" Lily asked. "You don't think . . .?"

Pax didn't know what to think except that he didn't like what happened, not one bit. It was bad enough to play cop and track a fellow Undead down, but then to hand him off to some civilian security types? That wasn't how it was done.

Marines took care of Marines, for good *and* bad.

He was having huge second thoughts as guilt lay heaving on his shoulders.

"What now?" Ogre asked.

"The captain said make our way back. The L-T's trying to hook us up again with a ride."

"Fuck it," Ogre said as he started to walk to the gate.

Pax turned around. The pool player was still standing at the door, cue in hand. Pax averted his eyes in shame.

It was a quiet group of Marines that walked back.

They were just about even with the terminal entrance, where they'd turn right and out the gate, when Olivia said, "The magtram costs two and a half."

"We've got it," Pax said.

"I know. We've still got eleven and a half."

"Your point being?"

Pax's shame had taken a turn toward anger, and he wasn't in the mood for arithmetic.

"We're not going to get extra credit for bringing back funds to the captain's bank account. And as shitty as I feel right now, I say screw him. There's a Cinny Star in there," she said, pointing into the terminal.

"A Cinny Star?" Ogre said, jerking up his head.

"Yeah. A Cinny Star."

Ogre looked at Lindersmitz and said, "We've got sixteen and a half left."

"I . . . uh . . ." Pax started.

He was angry at what had transpired. They all were. But now they were talking about damn Cinnamon Star?

But Ogre was already moving, heading into the terminal with Lindersmitz on his tail. A moment later, Lily and Knopf followed.

"Well?" Olivia asked.

"Ah, hell. Like you said, no extra credit."

He wasn't going to get any himself, but when he was standing with the others, the smell of hot cinnamon stars filling his nose, he gave in and ordered two Super Stars.

Pax was still angry. He was still upset. But the two large buns would just about zero out his credit wand after paying for the magtram ride back, and depleting the captain's bank account had its own allure. It was one way, albeit a childish one, to get back at the man.

It was almost an act of violence to bite into the hot, gooey mess, but he couldn't help calming down as the shock of cinnamon filled his senses.

No one could stay angry after eating a cinnamon star.

24

The ride back to Opal-3 was uneventful. Captain Lakmal had a mini-meltdown about the empty credit wands. And it wasn't just the six at Unday Station. At least half of the Marines had depleted their wands, and the others were regretting their lost opportunity. But the captain couldn't say much, knowing he was on thin ice, and he might need them to defend his actions.

The colonel didn't come up to their ship this time, and that put a little panic in the captain's eyes. Pax didn't know if what Rutledge had done was a death knell for the officer, and he really didn't care. The guy was just another freshie and kind of a jerk. He hoped the shit wouldn't splash on Lieutenant Forte, though. But with officers, you never knew how things would fall out.

Rutledge was kept isolated, and all questions posed to the captain were ignored. It wasn't until they loaded the shuttle for the trip down to the surface that they saw him again.

Pax tried to catch his eyes so he could mouth, "I'm sorry," but

Rutledge kept his eyes on the deck. He looked resigned to his fate as Corporal Wommack escorted him to the back of the shuttle.

A few Marines had criticized the six for bringing Rutledge back—Wolf and Panda being the most critical. But even those two knew they hadn't had much of a choice. It's one thing to say they should have taken a stand. It's another to defy orders, especially when that wouldn't have mattered in the long run.

What Pax had told Rutledge about the overlords not letting him reach his family was true. Even if the sergeant had boarded a ship as a spacer, everyone knew where he was headed. He would have been swept up if he made it as far as New Aberdeen.

No one exactly knew what the authorities would do for a serious infraction such as disobeying orders, and Pax was not anxious to be the guinea pig. Unfortunately for Rutledge, he was going to be the test case.

Four civilian guards met the shuttle to escort Rutledge away, which in itself was a slap in the face. It should have been Marine MPs.

It was just one more piece of evidence that no matter what they did, the Undead weren't "real" Marines.

Rutledge tried to put on a brave face, turning at the hatch to wave to the rest, but they could all see he was broken.

After he was gone, Gunny Akai said, "That's it. Let's debark. Staff Sergeant Byeon, form a ten-person working party on the pallets. I want to be on our way in twenty minutes."

Typical SNCO tactic. Keep us busy to get our mind off some shit.

But maybe it was better to keep active, so he volunteered for the working party, lining up with the others.

"Welcome back to the Opal," Olivia said as they stepped off the shuttle.

"Holy shit! Look who's back!" Pax said as he entered the platoon office.

"Vacation's over," Link said. "I'm back to crack the whip."

Pax rushed forward and pounded the staff sergeant on the back.

"Easy there, young stud. I'm still an invalid."

Pax jumped back, a look of horror on his face. "I didn't mean . . . I thought, since you're here . . ."

Link laughed and said, "You are so fucking gullible, Pax. Yeah, I'm officially combat capable. I'm fine."

"You sure? I mean—"

"I'm fine. I just like yanking your chain."

Link looked beyond Pax. "Liv."

"Staff Sergeant."

Pax knew that Olivia wasn't fond of Link, and that feeling was probably mutual. He didn't understand why, so he mostly ignored it.

"How was your recovery? I mean, I thought it was supposed to be six months."

Link shrugged. "So I heal fast."

Pax frowned, and the staff sergeant added, "It's no big deal. I got xeroxed, and my myc did its fungus thing. They sewed up my body, gave me lots of protein and shit, and here I am. You didn't think I was going to let you go off and have all the fun without me, did you?"

Pax and Olivia grimaced, and Link said, "Yeah, I heard about that. It sucks. First Bethel and Kildeer. Then fucking Rutledge. Sorry you all had to go track him down like that."

"Do you know what they're gonna do to him?" Olivia asked.

Link shook his head. "They're not coming to me for my take on it. All I can say is that I wouldn't want to be in his shoes, given how paranoid the freshies are about our very existence."

"You don't think they'll, uh . . ." Pax said before he made a quick slashing motion with his hand across his throat.

He couldn't even voice the words, as if just saying them might will them into being.

"Hey, they've spent a lot of money and effort on us. He's too valuable to just shitcan him."

"Do you really believe that?" Pax asked.

"Sure. Why not?"

He doesn't sound sure.

Byeon stepped into the office, and her eyes lit up. "Link! You don't know how glad I am to see your sorry ass back."

Link laughed and said, "Not so fun being the gunny's POG,[1] right?"

"That's putting it lightly," she said as she strode up to give him a back-pounding hug.

"You didn't complain when she walloped you," Pax said.

"SNCO privilege," Link said, giving Pax a wink.

Pax was only half-surprised at the evident joy Byeon was showing. When she'd taken over the team, she'd been gung-ho and ready to rock and roll. Then she realized that a lot of her responsibilities became all the admin and mundane work the gunny threw at her.

Almost all spec ops-types were alphas who wanted to be in charge, but that was in combat, not being bogged down by all the

---

1. **POG**: also "pogue." Someone not in a direct combat specialty.

details necessary to run the military. That took a different mindset, one Byeon didn't have—Pax either, for that matter.

With Link back, those responsibilities would slide to him again, and she could focus on combat and training for combat.

"So what's next, Assistant Platoon Sergeant?" she asked him. "Any good scoop?"

"What's next is the fifty-three new Undead in the company."

"Fifty-three?" Pax asked.

"That's what I said. Fifty-three of them."

"How many more of us are they going to make?" Olivia asked.

Link shrugged, and Pax said, "The original Immortals, you know, the ones in Persia, there were ten thousand of them. And each time someone got killed, there was another waiting in line to join, so there were always exactly the ten thousand."

Three sets of eyes turned to him, and Byeon asked, "So, what are you? Sergeant History?"

Pax's face reddened, and he said, "I'm not dumb. And I can look things up. Since we're calling ourselves the Immortals, I thought I should see who we were naming ourselves after."

"So, you're saying we're gonna be ten k?" Olivia asked. "That'll be when pigs die. You really think that'll ever happen?"

"Ten thousand? No. Geez. I just thought you'd be interested."

"We'd be packed like wolverines in a pan," Olivia said, elbowing Link. "Could you imagine it?"

"What's the organization?" Byeon asked Link, ignoring Olivia.

"The newbies are in a training platoon now, but with Second back, the company's getting reorganized. We'll be up to three platoons and a headquarters."

Pax ran the numbers. With 105—no, 102 with Kildeer and Bethel gone and Rutledge. . . whatever was going to happen with him. With 102 Marines and corpsmen, add the 53, that made 155, which was a lot for three platoons. Unless . . .

"First Platoon. How did they do?" he asked, dreading to hear the answer.

"First?" Link asked. "They didn't do anything. They never left the Opal. Their contingency kind of evaporated."

There was a rush of relief, but then that raised his initial concern. "Those will be three pretty big platoons."

"We're spec-ops. The platoons—hell, even the company—those are mostly for admin. We fight in teams or even sections," Link said.

"We just deployed to Lemon's Hold in a platoon," Olivia said.

Link made a dismissive sniff, then said, "And from what we were told, you sent three teams out to recover your VIP. Like I said, teams."

Pax couldn't find fault in what Link had just said, but he didn't have to like it. He liked things a certain way, so he understood where he was in the grand scheme of things. He liked being surrounded by people he knew and had worked with.

He *hadn't* liked the transfer from the San Marcos Marines to the LoH Marines, even though there wasn't that much of a difference. He hadn't liked the change to the Immortals, and not just because of the whole Undead thing going on.

And now, just as he was getting comfortable with the Marines in his platoon, more changes were being thrown at them.

But he'd learned a long time ago not to stress over the things he had no ability to change. If they were going to have oversized platoons, so be it. It really wouldn't affect his duties.

He'd help train up the newbies and be ready for their next mission.

Because that's what Marines did.

25

"Well, shit. This is where you ended up?"

Pax stopped, closed his eyes, and sighed. Being killed had come with a lot of baggage, but there had been a few bennies. One being never having to hear a certain voice again.

"I don't friggin' believe this," he said, not turning around. "Are you stalking me, even in death?"

There was a low chuckle, then, "I wonder if I can get a refund. I didn't know they were scraping the bottom of the barrel for this unit."

"Liv, please tell me that I'm hallucinating, and there's no one behind me."

Olivia looked at Pax like he was crazy, then turned to see who was there.

"There's a Marine standing there looking at you."

"Red hair? Looks like Satan?"

"Red hair. Who is she?" Then, to the Marine, "Who are you?"

Pax turned around. A buzz cut with a shallow Mohawk. Broad, square shoulders. Wasp waist. Thighs like a weightlifter.

"That, Liv, is Sergeant Tonya Donnabháin. Former TU Marine. Former LoH Marine. Current bitch."

The sergeant gave him a sardonic grin, and Pax asked, "How the hell did you get here?"

"Probably the same way you did, Quad Bod. I got myself killed. Woke up here."

Pax just stared at her as he asked the gods of war why he was being punished.

"You got killed," he finally said.

"On Parsous. I forgot to duck."

Pax had heard about the fight on Parsous, but he hadn't known his old unit had been there. Evidently, the fighting had been intense, with both sides striving for a complete annihilation of the other. No Lemon's Hold situation there.

"You're looking pretty hale yourself for being dead," Tonya said. "And I know you died. I had to stand in formation for a damn hour at your Cross of Honor ceremony. Tears were shed. Paxton Alejo. Great guy. Blah, blah, blah."

Pax gave a wry chuckle. "That must have killed you."

"No, a pede soldier killed me."

"What's going on here?" Olivia asked.

"Tonya was in my last unit. Good fighter, I'll grant her that, but I've never seen such a self-centered, backstabbing ladder climber in my life. And now she's in my death, too."

"Me? That's the pot calling the kettle black. Remember Kilgore?"

"That wasn't true, and you know it."

"So you say," she said with a harumph.

"Are you two, just, you know, yanking each other's train?" Olivia asked.

"Yanking each other's *train*?"

"Don't worry about it. Liv talks like that." Then to Olivia, "No, we're not. I honestly don't like her, and she doesn't like me."

"At least we can agree with that," Tonya said.

"And now you're an Immortal," Pax said. "Lucky me. Please tell me you're not in Second Platoon."

"None of us have been assigned yet."

"We can hope. Come on, Liv. Let's go."

"Good to see you, too, Quad Bod," Tonya shouted at their retreating backs.

"What was that all about, Pax?" Olivia asked once they were out of hearing.

"Like I said, she's a bitch."

"That's . . . that's not like you, Pax. You don't badmouth people," she said in a disapproving tone.

"Sorry, but you don't know her. Tonya's a good one to have in combat, I'll grant you that. Real good. Me and her, on Kilgore, we got into the shit, and when Nibbles—that was Greg Abbot—when he went down, it was just the two of us, and we got Nibbles out with about twenty pedes on our asses."

"Kilgore. She said something about you there."

"Yeah. She keeps saying I tried to take all the credit for saving Nibbles, and she's mad I got a Bronze Star out of it."

"Did you? I mean take the credit?"

He gave Olivia a hard stare.

Why is she questioning me?

"No! At least, I don't think so. I got it because I was the one who carried him. Tonya covered us. Probably kept us all alive, yeah. But I can't help who command wants to send up for a medal."

"If she kept you alive, then don't you owe her?"

"Geez, Liv. Give it a rest. Tonya's good in a fight, but the problem is everything's combat for her. Even back in garrison. It's her against everyone, and she has to come out on top. And it's not just me who doesn't like her. Everyone hates her, and she's never had a friend. I just hope to God she's not assigned to Second."

They walked in silence for a moment, and Pax said, "You'll see, Liv. I'm not making anything up."

The two of them reached the gym when Olivia said, "I think I've changed my mind. I don't feel like a workout now."

"But we just . . ."

He could see that she was upset, and he didn't quite know why. But he knew enough not to push it.

"See you at chow?"

"Uh, sure," she said. "Have a good workout."

Pax stared at her as she walked away.

Damn it, Tonya. Even dead, you're making my afterlife difficult.

. . . thirty-one . . . thirty-two . . . uuhh!

Pax pushed the barbell back onto the lower hooks and sat up.

"Come on, Pax. What the hell's the matter with you?" he muttered.

Before he was killed, he'd been able to make thirty-six reps of a hundred kilos on the bench. Not every time he tried, but he'd always been able to get at least thirty-four reps. Since he'd been reanimated, the most he'd done was thirty-four, and that was only once.

He knew dying had to have taken a toll on his body, but it had been eight months. Certainly, he had to be back in shape now.

He turned around and smacked the plates on the left side of the barbell—but he wasn't sure if he was mad at the weights or Tonya . . . or Olivia.

Maybe all three.

Twenty-eight thousand LoH Marine spec-ops troops. Twenty-eight thousand. And she gets xeroxed? What did I do to deserve this?

He sat there brooding for a few minutes while he waited for his body to neutralize the lactic acid in his arms and chest.

"Just deal with it. You know she's good in combat. Take that and avoid her back in the rear," he told himself before slamming his back on the bench.

He grabbed the bar, and with a shout, started the set. This time he was going to beat the bar into submission. Thirty-six or die trying.

. . . twenty-nine . . . thirty . . . and his arms started to give out.

He wasn't going to quit. He arched his back, straining, when two hands appeared over his head.

"Push it, Marine!"

With another shout—and a little help from his spotter—he made it up, then once more before his arms gave out.

"I didn't see you come in, Gunny."

"Crappy situational awareness, Q-B. That'll get you killed . . . again."

Pax gave a rueful laugh and said, "I guess so. I was just a little riled up, and maybe that took me out of it."

"Riled up? Anything I should know?"

For a moment Pax considered telling him about his history with Tonya, but then he realized that would be out of line. Whatever happened, it was up to him to deal with it.

"No, nothing important."

"Actually, it's good I saw you here. I've got an answer to your question."

"My question?"

"Yes. You know, about injecting the zombie juice while you're still alive."

It still took Pax a moment before he remembered. He'd completely forgotten about that musing. It wasn't as if he'd actually asked the gunny to find out. He'd just been spitballing.

"Ah, OK."

"Well, it seems the answer is they don't know."

Pax chuckled. "They sure don't know a hell of a lot, do they?"

"It's all pretty new. But what the doc said is that the concern is how a fully conscious myc would react to the injection. It might shock them into cell death."

"Fully conscious?"

Pax was taken aback by the phrasing. He'd considered his myc as something akin to an organic thumb drive. Let it record the information, then when it was needed, download it. But if the doctor said "fully conscious," did that mean it had a mind of its own?

The thought made him queasy, and for the thousandth time, he tried to search his mind for any sign of the myc. Once again, there was nothing.

"Ah, they don't know for sure. It's something about the force, too, when the injector goes off."

Pax nodded. He remembered how hard Link's head had jerked back when he injected him.

"Like I said, this is all new ground. But it's about to be OBE," the gunny continued.

"What do you mean?"

"For all their science smarts, they never considered the practical field aspects of the process. Like the injector. It should be inert."

"So it won't be as easily picked up by pede scanners."

"Right. And what they didn't think about until you mentioned it was what to do if everyone gets killed. Who injects the last one?"

"What? How could that never have come up?"

"Like I said, none of them have field experience. They're not even military."

That's unbelievable.

"But it turns out that not everyone was oblivious, and there are plans for an autoinjector that I guess we'll all wear. But with your question, they realized the importance, so it's getting off the back burner and given a higher priority.

"You should have seen them. They were like little kids on Christmas morning as excited as they were when they all started discussing the injector. Before I left, they said we might have them in a month. So, the question isn't about if you can get the juice while you're alive because as soon as you die, the injector is going to do it automatically. Pretty cool, right?"

Pax had just been idly wondering more than anything else, but if they were going to get these things in a month, then that was important. Maybe some lives that would have been lost might be saved.

"Yeah, cool. Are all of the freshie grunts going to get them, too?"

"That, I doubt. The zombie juice isn't easy to make from what I hear, but the big thing is that it would sort of let the cat out of the bag. For now, the recovery teams with freshie spec op units will have the regular injectors, and they don't even know what they're actually doing, you know."

The gunny patted him on the shoulder. "They might have already thought about it, but your question is what goosed them to make it a higher priority. Good job. Now are you going to just sit there like a frog on a log, or are you going to let an old man show you how to lift some iron?"

"I'm already spent, but I figure I've got enough left to make you regret that challenge."

The gunny laughed. "Then how about you getting your tired ass up and let me set the bar. Most reps at a hundred kilos?"

"You're on, Gunny. Prepare to get your butt kicked."

26

"Do they know it's us?" Pax asked.

The gunny shrugged. "Doubtful. Right now, it's being treated as some kooky conspiracy theory. The government's media reaction team's probably working overtime to tamp things down."

"Which government? LoH? The national ones?" Panda asked.

"Does it really matter?" the gunny asked. "They're all experts at this kind of thing. Hell, probably half of all those who post social media platforms are bots."

Gunny Akai, who was by now the de facto leader of the Immortals, had called an ad hoc meeting of all of them, but in the gym—which gave it a decidedly unofficial tilt.

A rumor had started to appear on the undernet, mostly, but even a few mainstream media-promulgators had picked it up. It concerned "zombies" being made for the military. And conspiracies being what they were, some of them attributed this to nefarious purposes, such as taking control of humanity.

The problem was that some conspiracies were real, or at least based on fact. And "zombies" was cutting it a little too close to home.

"Would it be a bad thing?" Staff Sergeant Byeon asked. "I mean, if the public knew what they did to us, it could help our situation."

"Can it, Innie," the gunny said a little too sharply.

He looked around the gym and lowered his voice. "This does affect us. There's concern that maybe one of us is a leak. That's why we're all going in for interviews. And that's why I wanted you all in here so I could give you a heads up."

The staff sergeant's eyes widened, and she protested, "It wasn't me!"

"No one's accusing you. Yet."

Pax blanched at the "yet."

"But it's probably better if you didn't express that opinion when you go in for your interview."

"But Gunny," Olivia said. "We're cut off from the outside world. We don't have even normal calling slots available to us. And we're on this motherforsaken planet where even if there was a city near, we wouldn't be allowed libbo. If it was anyone here, it's gotta be the freshies."

"Which is why all of the civilian support staff will be going through a lot more detailed interrogation, the Light help them. But they're not going to leave a stone unturned, so we're on the suspect list ourselves. And from what I've been told, expect to be pulled in starting this evening."

"And training tomorrow? We're scheduled to be on Range 107 at zero eight hundred," Staff Sergeant Lannie Neirmeyer, one of the SNCOs from First Platoon, asked. "If they're going to interrogate all of us, there's no way they'll finish by morning."

Gunny Jesus Yupanqui, First Platoon's senior enlisted and Gunny Akai's counterpart, said, "Range is canceled. You're right in that this is going to take a while. The lieutenant's going to try and find a time to reschedule."

Gunny Akai took a moment to scan the room as if trying to make eye contact with as many of them as possible, before he said, "This isn't anything to be concerned about, at least as far as the interview. Just be honest. Don't let them rattle you, and things will work out fine."

He paused for a second, as if considering what he was about to say. "That's as far as anyone accusing us of leaking anything. About any long-term effects if, in fact, the zombies really are us, well, we'll cross that bridge when we come to that."

"Yeah. That's when they'll quietly liquidate us," Wolf Morning Mist muttered.

Pax turned to give the corporal a long stare. He didn't think he'd ever met anyone as cynical as Wolf, but could there be any truth to what he just said?

Olivia heard him, too, and she whispered in Pax's ear, "You don't think they'd do that, do you?"

They were in the back of the group, up against the wall, and Pax made a small flick of his wrist to indicate the rest of the Marines.

"They've invested a lot of money and effort to make us. I don't think they'll shitcan the project because some freshies are screaming zombies."

"Yeah, you're probably right."

Except he wasn't nearly so positive. He was sure all of them were the basis of the rumors, and while he wasn't as cynical as

Morning Mist, he was pretty sure that the LoH wouldn't hesitate even a millisecond if they thought the Immortals were a liability.

"You're up," Olivia told Pax as she tapped the bottom of his boot.

He'd fallen asleep while waiting. He rubbed his eyes and swung his feet off his rack and onto the floor.

The interviews continued through the night and well into the day. The more senior Marines, starting with Captain Kjellberg and the two freshie lieutenants, were taken before the junior. And now, at fifteen thirty-five, they'd finally gotten down to Pax.

Everyone had been restricted to their racks while they waited—probably to keep them from gathering and coming up with a story. Even head calls had to be done one at a time, and there'd been no food.

"How'd it go?" he asked.

Olivia shook her head, but Pax didn't know if that meant it had gone poorly or if she'd been told not to discuss it.

"You're in B-4."

He tried to read into her eyes, but he couldn't tell what she felt right now.

Better not keep them waiting.

Pax stood and left berthing, aware of several sets of eyes locked on him.

B-4 was in the B corridor—no surprise—one of six small classrooms.

A civilian guard/traffic cop was standing at a desk near B-1, and he scanned Pax in and said, "B-4."

"Right."

Pax walked briskly to the door, telling himself he had nothing to be afraid of, so he should just march right in. But he hesitated at the door. He knew he hadn't let anyone know about the Immortals. But Wolf's cynicism was based on facts. Humanity was in an existential war, and he was just one minute part of that. If the powers that be needed a scapegoat, they'd create one in a heartbeat.

And so, what if that was him?

They're not going to pick you, Paxton Alejo.

Still, as he pushed open the door, he had butterflies in his stomach. . . which faded somewhat as he took in the middle-aged, librarian-looking woman sitting on the other side of a table.

This is my interrogator?

The woman gave Pax the slightest of smiles and indicated that he take the single seat across the table from her.

He sat down while she studied the pad in front of her. A bit of that anxiety returned as the time ticked on without her saying anything or even looking at him.

Finally, she raised her head and asked, "A-S-zero-four-nine-nine-nine, do you appreciate being reanimated?"

Just like that. No introduction. No breaking the ice. The use of his official number and not his name. Her voice wasn't particularly stern, but Pax thought he could detect a force of will.

Maybe this isn't going to be as easy as I thought it was.

"Ma'am?"

Her neutral expression didn't change, but there was still the steel in her voice as she said, "You were killed. You were reanimated. Do you appreciate what was done to you?"

"I'm . . ."

Pax hadn't expected the question, and to be honest, he hadn't really thought of it. Not seriously, at least. In fact, he generally avoided any such conversation among his fellow Immortals.

He thought this interview was to ferret out anyone who might have leaked details of the program, not to find out if Pax was a happy camper being given a second shot at life. Or reanimated death, from a legal standpoint.

"I'm . . . grateful, yes," he said after resetting himself.

She didn't seem to react to his answer, but moved on to the next question. "Is reanimating the dead a valuable tool in the war against the Tucanans?"

Pax stared at her for a moment, wondering where this was going and what he needed to say. But his delay as he pondered his reply started to feel uncomfortable, and he had a sudden mini panic attack as he realized silence could sound suspicious.

"Yes, it is," he blurted out.

"Even when there is a lack of the rights afforded *freshies*," she said, using their nicknames of the living humans as if it was no big deal.

His face reddened at her usage, but he wanted to shout that the lack of rights was criminal. But he was on guard.

"This is war. We have to do what we can to save the human race."

That response elicited a tiny tick in her right eyelid, but Pax didn't know what that signified.

The woman continued with her next question, and then the next. For the next ten minutes, all of them centered on Pax's opinion of his situation, his degree of resentment at being isolated from the rest of humanity both on Opal-3 and in the camp, of his lack of choice at being part of the program.

Nothing seemed to be directly related to any leak except for a single question, which was asked in almost an afterthought.

"You were just on Lemon's Hold. At any time during that deployment, did you speak to anyone about the program."

"No, ma'am. And I was never alone. There was always someone with me."

Her expression never changed at his response. Her seeming disinterest could mean that they already knew the answer somehow, or maybe this was part of some interrogation technique, to lull the subject.

The questions veered back to his general mental state and opinions of the program, and Pax thought things were winding down. He started to relax.

Until . . .

"Do you know a Gregory Alejo of Lago de Oro, San Marcos?" she asked, almost as if in passing.

Pax's heart fell, and he suddenly became more wary, as if he was on patrol approaching a potential ambush.

"Yes."

"He's your father, correct?"

"Biological father. I have no contact with him."

She sniffed, the first time she seemed to break into a human reaction. "No contact?"

"Not for years. Not since he wanted to borrow some money."

She looked back down at her pad and stared at it. As the silence lengthened, Pax realized she was doing that on purpose as part of her technique. But even knowing that, it worked. He was getting more nervous as he wondered what Greg had done now.

"Do you know that on Our Tribe, your father had posted sixty-three times about how the LoH has created a division of zombie soldiers?"

There it was. She'd lulled him with softball questions as to his attitude, then hit him with the right uppercut.

Pax's mouth dropped open as he struggled to regain a semblance of control, all while she coolly observed his reaction.

"I don't know anything about what Greg posts or not. But he's always been a conspiracy nut."

"And this is the first time you've heard of this?"

"Of course, it is. How could I have known? We are cut off from social media here, and Our Tribe . . ." he said, a little anger replacing his anxiety. " Sheesh! They're all wackos there. You know that. I'm sure you guys monitor them."

Pax didn't even know who this woman was, but he was also confident that "you guys" was appropriate.

"If you had a means to communicate with your father, would you detail the program to him?"

Pax couldn't see any obvious scanners in the room, but he wasn't naïve. He knew they were there, measuring all sorts of biometrics to determine how honest he was being.

"Look, Ms. Whoever-you-are. What you're doing with us Immortals is criminal."

Another eye tic.

"You're breaking just about every constitution and declaration of rights, no matter whatever legal mumbo-jumbo you can dredge up. But like I said, this is war, and sometimes in a war, bad things have to be done.

"I swore an oath to the people of San Marcos when I enlisted in the Corps. And then that became to all humanity when I was absorbed into the LoH Marines. That oath didn't change just because I was killed. And if serving in the Immortals is how I can best perform my duty as a *human being*, then I don't have a problem with that."

He was breathing hard, and he was sweating, which he knew the scanners would detect. He knew he should just stop, but months of suppressed resentment bubbled to the surface.

"How you're going about it is wrong. There's no reason to keep us hidden away. There's no reason to take away our rights. But it is what it is, and I'm not going to break my oath.

"And I'm not going to contact that piece of crap whose only relationship to me was the sperm that fertilized my mom's egg. So, if you think I did, then arrest me. If not, then let's stop this interrogation."

She just stared at him, her face still maddeningly expressionless. For a moment, Pax thought she'd dismiss him, but she couldn't let this end on his terms.

"Do you think the Cross of Honor awarded to your precursor will protect you if you go over the line?"

Pax flinched because that was exactly what he'd been thinking. And she saw the flinch, of course. She made a "I thought so" smile.

"I was awarded it. Not some 'precursor,'" Pax snapped.

"Really? That person is dead and buried at Cape Town."

"I don't know what body you have in that grave, if there even is one. But I'm here, and I have the DNA to prove it if necessary."

Her smile got bigger. "That's so cute. You don't think records can be replaced?"

Of course, they could. Pax didn't know who this woman was or who she worked for. But it didn't matter. LoH. San Marcos. Whatever. Any government could switch DNA records. It would be child's play to them.

Anger warred with a sudden feeling of helplessness. Among the Immortals, there was an underlying belief that their situation was bound to improve, and maybe a mini scandal like this was the first step in getting their rights restored. But looking at the confident woman sitting across the table from him, he knew that was a pipe dream. The LoH held all the cards, and the immortals were pawns. No, even pawns had some rights. They were tools.

Pax knew that with one lunge, he could kill the smirking woman. Maybe they'd reanimate her and let her see what it was like. But as tempting as that might sound, he knew it would be the recipe for disaster with no good outcome.

He took a deep breath and said, "I'm sure you've tracked down all of Greg's communications and know it couldn't have been me. He's just spouting off the latest conspiracy theory. So, once again, are we done here?"

She made a show of looking at her pad again and then asked, "If the existence of this program became public knowledge, what do you think would be the result?"

"I don't have a fucking clue," he said, glowering at her.

She went on for another five minutes, but there were no more specific questions relating to a leak. Pax got the feeling that she'd already made up her opinion on whether he was involved, but that she had to keep going to remain in control.

Finally, she told him they were done . . . for now.

"You are not to discuss this interview with anyone else. Is that clear?"

"Yes, ma'am. Don't talk about it. Got it."

"You may go, and please tell Corporal Ferris Morning Mist to meet me here in this room."

Pax stood. "Sure you don't need a head break or something?" he asked, knowing he was being reckless.

To his surprise, she gave a—not a smile, but close to one—and said, "I'm fine. Just send in Corporal Morning Mist."

Pax spun around and left the room, only to lean back against the bulkhead as soon as the door hissed to a close.

Stupid. Why'd I let my temper get the best of me?

He knew this wasn't over, and not just on the supposed leak. Everything he'd said had been recorded and would be gone over by psychs, who built his profile. He'd stressed that he'd do his duty to humanity. But what about the rest?

Did Nani Vesta ever say something that made her suspect? Could that be a reason she wasn't reanimated after Hale's Refuge?

This was too much for him to absorb at the moment.

With a sigh, he pushed off the bulkhead and went to let Wolf know it was his turn in the breach.

27

"Whatcha watching?" Olivia said in a little girl's voice as she hopped over the back of the couch and plopped down beside Pax.

"The news. Be quiet."

"What's the news, Daddy? The news. What's that? Can I watch with you? Can I?"

Pax rolled his eyes and said, "Come on, Liv. This is important."

Reverting to her normal voice, she said, "Nothing's important. They might have given us the holovid, but they aren't going to stream us anything good."

"They are now. This is the LoH Military Network News."

During the interviews, a lot of the Marines had taken the opportunity to point out that they had no way to leak their existence to anyone. They were completely isolated from anything going out or coming in. And it may have been a coincidence, but four days later, they'd gotten the holovid displays. Then, in dribs and drabs, different feeds were added. While LHMN had been one of the first feeds, LHMN News—LHMNN—had just started that morning. It was the only news feed they were getting.

Olivia only then really looked at the screen. A military journalist in full battle gear was reporting from a camp. Nine bodies, covered with tarps, were lined up on the ground behind him. The chyron on the bottom said, "Attack on San Zhi Zhu Outpost, Lemon's Hold."

"Hey, is that—"

"Yeah. Lemon's Hold," Pax told her.

". . . reporting from somewhere in the frontier, Lemon's Hold."

The feed switched to the LHMNN sector studio in Oosterdam where the talking head—in this case, a Navy chief petty officer, said, "This is only the latest in a series of small, isolated attacks inside of human-controlled territory, all with similar results. Authorities are examining the sites to see if there is any connection between them."

The chief signed off, and the feed switched to a show a cheery civilian giving tips on how to prepare a family for a PCS[1] move.

That sure didn't pertain to them, so Olivia asked, "What was that all about?"

"Some Three-Z Dragon camp got overrun, and they don't know who did it. Or at least the reporter didn't say."

"They just set up camp in occupied territory, and they thought the bastards wouldn't notice?"

"That's the thing, Liv. It was inside the lines. From the looks of it, they were using it as a base for recon operations on the other side. But the camp itself was on our side."

"So, they hit something, and the pedes chased them back."

---

1. **PCS**: Permanent Change of Station

"That's the other thing. There's no sign of who hit them. No major movements were picked up."

"Weird. A condomdrum. No sign?"

The Tucanans were not particularly stealthy, relying on numbers and force to achieve their objectives. Yet the orbital scanners hadn't picked up any major pede movements, and visibility over the camp had been blocked off somehow during the attack.

"It looks like this isn't the first time something like this has happened. And if LHMNN is saying it, then it's probably bigger than that. This isn't a public feed, but still, it isn't a classified feed, either."

Pax wondered if the civilian news networks were reporting the incident as well. The war was huge with hundreds of millions of people in uniform, so what were nine mysterious deaths out in the galactic boonies?

They'd probably gotten the feed because Lemon's Hold was in their sector. Still, Pax was somewhat surprised that they'd received such an unvarnished report. The main LHMN broadcasts were mostly intended to provide entertainment to isolated sailors, Marines, and soldiers with sports, movies, and series. The news division, LHMNN, feeds were heavily feel-good stories—military personnel serving the public, victories against the Tucanans, high medals awarded, units coming home after long deployments. The feeds rarely showed battle losses.

Pax didn't like mysteries in battle. That was a good way to get yourself killed. And not knowing who or what had killed the Dragon team was bothersome.

"Maybe some guardsmen came in and surprised them," Pax said.

"Why would they do that? The Three-Zs are there to help."

"You know them. They can be rather arrogant SOBs."

But he agreed with what she said. That didn't sound like something they'd do.

"Maybe I can get some more from battalion," Pax said.

"Hey, the news is over," Wommack called over.

Pax tossed him the remote, and the screen was immediately switched to a live feed from a concert. He and Olivia gave up the couch.

"I'm glad they finally gave in and got us the feeds, but maybe they could have sprung for a couple more receivers?" Olivia said.

"Just be glad they gave us these two. Third Platoon doesn't even have one."

Pax walked over to the locker and pulled out two colas. He popped the tops, waited for the cans to frost over, and handed one to Olivia.

He took a long swallow of the fizzy drink—thank goodness their science minders hadn't determined that carbonation would screw up their mycs—then casually said, "I saw you with Tonya this morning."

Sergeant Donnabháin, to Pax's dismay, was going to be assigned to Second Platoon after the end of Third's training cycle. She wouldn't be in his and Olivia's team, but anywhere in the platoon was too close, as far as he was concerned.

"Yeah? And . . ."

"Just be careful, Liv. She's trouble."

"Look, Pax. I know you don't like her, but she's OK. And maybe your feud should have ended when you both, you know, got killed?"

"That sounds good and all, but you don't know her."

"And maybe you don't want to know her."

Pax took another swallow, considered what he was about to say, then decided to dive right in.

"She's just being friendly with you to get back at me."

Olivia's eyes got big, and she put her cola down on the table.

"Pretty big ego there, Pax. You know, not everything here's about you. Maybe she just likes me. That's possible, you know. I am likable."

"Of course, you a—"

But Olivia had already spun around and was walking out of the platoon lounge.

Shit, Pax, you idiot. Every time you bring up Tonya, Liv gets mad. Maybe just avoid the subject?

He stared at her barely touched cola. Sweat beads had condensed on the can, forming drops that started to flow down the sides.

With a sigh, he picked it up, and with colas in each hand, he walked over to join the Marines watching the concert.

28

"CLICK, CLICK, CLICK," Pax said as he crept along the gully.

"What the hell are you doing?" Wolf asked.

"We're the pedes, right?" Pax said. "So we should sound like them."

Wolf rolled his eyes, then looked back to Olivia with a "Can you believe this guy?" expression on his face.

Olivia just ignored the both of them. She was the patrol leader for the exercise, and her mind was on the hill ahead, where Third Platoon would be settling in for the night.

The company had been in the field for eleven days as Third Platoon was reaching the end of their training cycle. Three more days, and the company would be reorganized.

There was a general degree of relief. The new joins had needed the training to be integrated into the unit, but that meant real training for First and Second Platoons had been limited. It would be nice to get back to normal.

Of course, that meant Pax had three more days until Tonya

was officially a member of the platoon, but there was always a bit of grit in every smoothly working machine.

Field training on Opal-3 was far from comfortable, but at least they had better quality face masks. They weren't constantly breathing in the air. Still, everyone wanted to get back to camp, and even if not warranted, some ill will was aimed at Third Platoon.

By mutual platoon sergeant agreements, night actions over the last five days had stopped, but evidently, Gunny Akai was not above the fray. That afternoon, he'd tasked Olivia with setting up a little reminder that war doesn't end when the sun goes down.

Olivia had jumped at the opportunity. Pax was there to support her, even if he might have been going into this with a less-than-serious demeanor. He couldn't help it. If they were supposed to be pedes, then they should act the part.

The patrol leader brought her Marines to a halt at the attack position. Pax followed her as they crawled up the slight bluff so they could see the platoon's camp. The night had cooled significantly, and small fires were scattered about the camp, little beckoning lights.

"Their eyes won't be able to see in the dark," Pax said.

"See if you can spot the security." Olivia said as she glassed the platoon.

Pax took his time searching the area.

"I only see one," he finally said. "Over by the trail. And they're facing inboard."

"That's what I've got, too. So I think we stick to the plan."

The two slid down to the waiting pede-Marines.

"We're on," she told them. "They've got fires going, so try not to look directly at those."

"Fires?" Wolf said derisively. "FNGs."

Olivia gave the order to move out, and Pax, on point, led the patrol toward the back side of the hill. His adrenaline started to flow. It might not be a real battle, but that didn't matter. His competitive hunter instincts were in full flower as they crept through the low brush, taking advantage of every gram of cover.

Laughter rolled across them. Third Platoon was in good spirits. All the better for the pede-Marines.

It took almost an hour to get into position, all the while Pax expecting to be spotted. He and Olivia had only seen one Marine on security, but while they didn't look to be operating on a tactical basis, there could be security that escaped being seen.

Finally, the patrol of eight Marines was hugging the hillside, forty meters from the platoon. Several small fires created flickering shadows where they were crouched. The low murmur of voices, overlaid by someone snoring loudly, reached them.

Olivia gave the signal to check their weapons.

Pax glanced at his "Buzzer." The A-10 trainer was a simple barrel and pistol grip that could simulate a huge variety of personal weapons, to include the Buzzer. An onboard computer would mimic the characteristics, and based on those and the aiming point, the Training AI would assess hits and effectiveness.

It was a high-tech version of children running around saying, "Bang, you're dead!"

Neither of the moons was out, but the stars were in their usual stunning display, providing more than enough light for them to see each other. Olivia asked for a thumbs-up from everyone, and once she got it, she counted down with one hand from five. As she lowered the last finger, she dropped her hand and shouted "Go!"

The eight Marines jumped to their feet and rushed forward as they fired their weapons.

"Die, potto scum!" Pax screamed as he fired at the Marines who jumped up in alarm and scrambled for their weapons.

He hit one of them—it looked like that SAS staff sergeant—who stopped and slammed his fist into the ground in anger as his hit indicator went off.

It was a madhouse as the patrol swept through the Third Platoon, dropping Marines right and left. Pax was laughing like a madman, killing four of them before his own hit indicator went off.

He sat down in place while the remainder of the platoon rallied. Olivia was the last one to fall, and Pax could see the glint of excitement in her eyes, reflecting from the fires.

"You bastards," Staff Sergeant Inkoma snarled at Pax. "We're not supposed to be tactical."

"The pedes don't follow no stinkin' rules," Pax said, to which there was no acceptable response.

Olivia gathered her dead pedes, who high-fived each other under the glare from the Third Platoon Marines.

"Tell Gunny Akai that him and me, we're having a talk. I know this was his doing," Staff Sergeant Oreon, the platoon sergeant, told Olivia.

"Will do," she said cheerfully. Then to her patrol, "Let's get out of here."

As they started to file out, Pax spotted Tonya, who was looking at him stone-faced. Using his forefinger and thumb, he mimed shooting at her.

She used a finger back at him, but it wasn't the forefinger.

Yes, it had been a most excellent way to spend an evening.

29

"And finally, I have some bad news to report," Chief Petty Officer Tilda Jeng said.

Her news hour, given six days a week at nineteen-hundred local time, had become a must-see if the Marines weren't training. LHMNN was still their only news feed, but her best-friend persona and cute, bobbed hair look with way more makeup than was usually allowed in uniform had a lot to do with her popularity among the platoon.

Many of the men and more than a few of the women had a crush on her—platonic, of course, as none of them had a sex drive.

"What now?" Olivia asked.

"The planet Kuama in the Third Sector has been declared lost to the Tucanans. We at LHMNN offer our deepest sympathies to those who have lost relatives or friends there."

"Shit," Blue Knopf said. "That's three in the last two weeks."

"That doesn't mean there's a major offensive," Fridge Amana

said. "Sometimes, things just come in bunches. Janaria, that was six months in coming. And it should have fallen months ago."

Pax scowled. Janaria was another sore spot with him. The planet had never been heavily populated. The weather was too extreme, the gravity too strong to make it a target for large-scale colonization. But there was mineral wealth, and when there's money to be made, humans will put up with a lot. There had been over 300,000 people on the planet, mostly employees of the four corporations with operations there. Among those 300,000 were about 24,000 security personnel.

The Tucana Dwarf Galaxy had a very low metal content when compared to other galaxies, so it was a good bet that the Tucanan home world didn't have much in the way of mineral wealth. That would jive with the fact that the Tucs often targeted metal-rich planets in human space, and so security tended to be relatively heavy on other such planets.

And the enemy had done it again, landing on the planet in force, surprising the small naval presence in the system.

Pax was of the belief that humans had to oppose every Tucanan land grab. They had to throw the enemy off every planet they invaded. Planets like Lemon's Hold, where everyone seemed OK with a stalemate, drove him insane. But even worse was a case like Janaria, where the powers that be decided to essentially cede the planet. They didn't think it worth the expenditure in lives and time to take it back, so they abandoned the people there, hoping the Tucanans would let refugees leave.

Sometimes, the Tucs did. This time, they did not, shooting down hundreds of shuttles and destroying three liners that were waiting to evacuate. And whether that was the deciding factor, the 24,000-person security force decided to fight.

Those poor, brave souls managed to hold off the vastly larger invading force for six months before the last of them were overrun. As Pax would tell anyone who listened to him, if the Marines had sent a task force to the planet, they could have saved it and 300,000 fellow humans.

Pax was just a sergeant, and he was no scholar of strategy, but he firmly believed that the military's sole purpose was to kill Tucs while saving humans.

He almost responded to Fridge with a comment to that effect, but he knew that while many agreed with him, they were tired of hearing it.

"Isn't Bordelay, over in First, from Kuama?" Doc asked.

"Was it Kuama, or was it Kante?" Mongol asked.

"I think Kuama."

"We should find out," Olivia said. "He's gonna be torn up if it's true."

Chief Tilda, as everyone was calling her, signed off, and the LHMNN Sports Hour came on. Pax stretched and contemplated hitting the rack early. The platoon had a zero-five formation to be followed by a five-day exercise, and sleep might be in short supply.

"I think I'm calling it. You guys play without me," he told Wolf.

"Ah, come on, Sergeant! We need a fourth."

"Get Mongol. He's probably up for a game. I need some sleep."

"You can sleep when you're dead."

"Uh . . . in case you didn't notice, I *am* dead," Pax said as he stood.

He didn't get far, though, before Wommack grabbed him. "The lieutenant wants you."

"What the hell for? It's twenty hundred."

"No idea. I'm just the messenger."

"A kiss-ass, you mean."

"I can't help it if she keeps grabbing me," the corporal protested.

There was more than a little truth in that, Pax knew. Wommack and Lance Corporal Kaleetha Morgan, as junior Marines, often got yanked as sort of platoon clerks or runners. In the fleet, there'd be privates and PFCs[1] for that kind of duty, but in the Immortals, they were junior.

"OK, is she in the platoon office?"

Wommack nodded.

With a sigh, Pax made his way out of berthing and into the company headquarters. To his surprise, Sergeant Bordelay had the duty. He almost asked him if he was from Kuama, but he bit his tongue. If he was, then he shouldn't learn about what happened from him.

He made his way to the platoon offices, but instead of going directly to Second Platoon's office, he knocked on First Platoon's hatch.

"Enter."

Pax pushed his way in. Gunny Yupanqui was deep into his datasheets, and he looked surprised to see Pax.

"What do you want, Alejo."

"Is uh . . . Bordelay. Is he from Kuama?"

"Yeah. Why?"

"It was just declared lost. Saw it on Chief Tilda's broadcast."

"Ah, shit. It was only a matter of time, but still . . ." the gunny said, rubbing a hand across his eyes. "Thanks."

---

1. **PFC**: Private First Class. E2. The second lowest enlisted rank.

Pax nodded then slipped out of the office. A moment later, he was rapping on Second Platoon's hatch.

"Come in!"

The lieutenant and the platoon sergeant were having a conversation, but when Pax came in, the lieutenant said, "Gunny, can you give us the office?"

"Sure thing, ma'am."

Pax could see that the gunny was puzzled, which meant that for whatever reason the lieutenant wanted to see him, the platoon commander didn't know about it.

Which could be good or very, very bad.

Pax stifled a gulp as the gunny left the office and closed the hatch behind him.

"Take a seat, Sergeant."

He sat in the chair the gunny had just vacated. Despite himself, he only took a few inches of it and sat at attention.

"I should ask you how you're doing and all of that, but frankly, I'm just too tired, and I'm going to get right to the point. What's the deal with you and Sergeant Donnabháin?"

"Ma'am?"

Pax sure hadn't expected that.

"Donnabháin. Sergeant, one each. What's the deal between you?"

"There's no deal, ma'am."

She sighed and pulled up a screen on her pad.

"On March eighth of last year, you were both reprimanded for fighting."

"What? That was unofficial. Not on my records," he said, his voice rising.

Lieutenant Forte raised her eyebrows and then stared at him, waiting.

"It wasn't—sometimes, emotions are high, ma'am. Words are said."

She gave a little huff. "On June first of last year, the two of you were accusing each other of . . . wait, let me read it. You two accused each other of spreading rumors."

Pax didn't respond.

"A half an hour ago, the colonel came into my office. The colonel never comes into my office. Do you want to know why he came now?"

Pax wasn't sure how to answer that, but the lieutenant went on without waiting for him.

"He wanted to know how the two of you were doing. So, I'm asking you now, why? And why did he interject himself to assign Sergeant Donnabháin to the platoon? I don't like it when colonels reach down and play puppet master with my platoon, and I don't know why."

"I don't know, ma'am. He's a colonel," he said as if that answered everything.

There was another knock on the door, and the lieutenant shouted, "Stand by until I say so."

Then she said, "I don't know what is going on here, but if there is anything going on in my platoon, I need to know now."

"Ma'am, Sergeant Donnabháin is an excellent combat Marine, and I can tell you in all honesty that I have no problem with her in that capacity."

Please just accept that.

She wasn't going to leave it there, though. "But not in garrison," she said.

He wasn't going to confirm that, but she knew.

"Sergeant Alejo, are you a member of the CMA?" Then she quickly added, more to herself than to him, "Of course not. I've got your records here."

Pax didn't know where this was going. What did the Combat Marine Association have to do with anything?

"How much do you know about them?"

"Uh, not much. The local post used to have cookouts for us when I was in my infantry battalion. But mostly, they're a bunch of old farts who get together to drink and tell war stories."

"They're a lot more than that, Sergeant. They work hard to make sure the laws protect veterans. You owe many of your rights to them."

"I'm an Undead. I don't have any rights," he snapped, unable to stop himself.

She gave a short, wry laugh and said, "Point taken, Sergeant. But still, they do good things. More pertinent to you right now is that the colonel is a member. So am I, for that matter.

"And there's something they say before every meeting that I think explains the CO's personal interest. Before each meeting, we have a ritual. We say, 'Do not let petty jealousies or trivial personalities influence our deliberations.'"

Now Pax saw where this was going.

"I didn't realize the colonel got down this deep into the weeds, but he knows about your past history with Sergeant Donnabháin. And he knows that can be a cancer that slowly rots away at the unit. It doesn't matter if you really think she's a good combat Marine, that cancer will spread. It's my bet that he wants to see if you two can kiss and make up."

"And if we don't?"

Once again, Pax spoke before thinking.

And once again, the lieutenant didn't seem to take offense.

"I honestly don't know. Maybe I . . ."

She stopped short of voicing that thought, but Pax could guess. After Lemon's Hold, Captain Lakmal disappeared. The lieutenant stayed, but she was probably on thin ice. Maybe she was the one being tested by seeing how she could handle the situation.

And that put a different spin on things. Pax didn't like Tonya, and he never would. He'd love it if she were transferred to another platoon. Another company, if there was one, would be better. And, if he was honest with himself, he could accept administrative black marks.

What were they going to do with him? He was Undead, after all. The lieutenant, however, she was vulnerable. She already knew too much, so if she was shitcanned, she'd be shipped off to some isolated, do-nothing post. Her career would be over.

"Ma'am, you tell the colonel the next time he asks that Sergeant Donnabháin and me, we're fine."

"But will that be a true statement?"

He paused for a few moments while he ran that through his mind before saying, "Yes, ma'am. It'll be true."

She let that sink in for a few long moments, then said, "Very well. You're dismissed. Go get some sleep. We've got an early reveille."

Pax stood and came to attention, then turned and left the office. He wasn't surprised to see Tonya waiting in the passage. She was surprised to see him, though.

"What's this about?" she asked.

It wasn't up to him to tell her, so he just said, "The lieutenant's waiting."

She gave him a calculating glance before the lieutenant called out, "Sergeant Donnabháin, come on in."

Tonya passed by him, so close that he had to shift his body slightly so they wouldn't bang into each other.

He didn't say anything.

This might be harder than I thought.

Because he was going to make good on his promise. As far as he was concerned, his feud with her was over. Hopefully, she'd be on the same wavelength.

And now it's time for the rack. I can still get seven hours sleep.

He was almost happy as he bounced down the corridor. Just before he exited the building, Gunny Akai shouted, "Q-B!"

Pax came to a stop. "Gunny?"

"You've got the duty. Sergeant Bordelay got pulled off, and I need to get someone else, and you're it."

"But I'm hitting the rack."

"Not now, you're not. Grab the duty belt and take your position."

Pax just had the duty a week ago, and he wouldn't be due for another month. But orders were orders.

He tried not to sigh as he picked up the white duty belt that Bordelay had left at the station, then settled in for a long four hours of boredom.

30

"I can't believe it. Two weeks to get ready?" Pax whispered. "There's gotta be some catch."

"The catch is that there's more time for them to fuck with us. You watch," Link said. "You'll end up wishing that this was an immediate call out."

Pax knew his friend was right. Admin types like to . . . well, *admin*. Instead of using their deployment SOPs and prepacked gear, the staff was going to massage their equipment lists, and if the past was any indication, as soon as the company thought they were ready, that list was going to be changed. And again. And probably again.

The command staff was designed to be able to expand into a full regiment with three battalions. Whether they'd ever have enough Undead to man those numbers was unknown. But those freshies in the command felt like they needed to make their mark, and with only one company so far, the Immortals would be the subject of their meddling. They wouldn't be able to keep their hands off the Marines.

And to make matters worse, this wasn't your normal mission with a set SOP and off-the-shelf operations order. That just gave them more opportunity to get their fingers in the pie.

Their target was Volante, once invaded, but now a planet at the center of the fight. During the Tucanan invasion, the planetary Guard, along with quick reaction from the Navy, had managed to throw back the initial Tucanan force before the Marines had even arrived in system.

But a planet is a big body, and the Tucanans were persistent vermin. No one knew how many had survived the main battles, but they were out there, skulking around.

Smaller communities had coalesced around the industrial heartland, and defenses were strengthened, but large areas—mostly where the native vegetation and animal life were still predominant—had been abandoned.

The Guard made well-promoted forays into the "outback," on "pede hunts," but the reality was that as long as the Tucanan survivors didn't make a nuisance of themselves, there weren't major efforts to bring them to bay.

But now, it looked like that was what was happening on Lemon's Hold and a few other planets, small military outposts were getting hit. Three had been attacked on Volante, with a loss of all hands.

Comms during the attacks had been spotty, not revealing much. And at one location, there had been definite Dragonfly sign—Dragonflies being a native carnivore. But while not much was known yet, the pattern matched what had been happening on at least five other planets.

So, the company's overlords decided that a good mission would be to try and find out what was happening. The three line platoons were being deployed as bait to help determine what was going on.

This was a Warning Order, not their actual Operations Order. The intent was to let the Marines know what was coming and to give them enough information to start to prepare. Two weeks in advance was a luxury, but looking at briefs, briefs, and more briefs, inspections, inspections, and more inspections, Link had a good point. It probably would be less of a pain to just leave now.

The Warning Order finished, but instead of being dismissed, Colonel Owusu moved to the front.

"Before you break up to start your preparations, I wanted to have a word with you. Look, we don't know if all of these incidents are connected. What's happening on Volante could very well be isolated. But I want each and every one of you to take this seriously. The Volante Guard are not amateur hour, so if something took them out, that same thing is a threat to you, too."

There were several chuckles at that, including Pax's. Hubris wasn't lacking among spec-ops troops, and that didn't change after being killed.

"STOP LAUGHING," the colonel shouted in rage.

A couple of laughs were cut off, and the room fell into an immediate silence.

The CO stared at the gathered company and staff, sweeping the entire room.

What the . . .

"Yeah, you are all *operators*," he said with scorn. "The best of the best. Killing machines."

He stopped again for a moment. Pax could see him try to regain control, and that confused him. What had they done wrong?

They were the best of the best, after all. That was the whole reason they'd been reanimated.

"All of you are skilled. Yeah, that's true, and we've been spending the last year and a half training you up even more. But all of you—every single one of you—is here only because you were killed. By pedes. Dead."

He took several deep breaths. "You are not invincible. Staff Sergeant Kravtiz, I see you sitting there."

Beside Pax, Link squirmed. "You lead the pack. You've been killed three times. And what about Lance Corporal Vesta. Do you see her sitting here beside you?"

Link wasn't the only one squirming now.

"I told you the Volante Guard aren't amateurs. They held off a pede invasion, by God. And if three of their outposts were wiped out, whatever's doing it is a threat to you, too. Got that?"

You could have heard a pin drop in the auditorium.

It looked like the colonel was going to continue along that vein, but he said, "You all better get that attitude checked and get your head in the game," before he abruptly cut off, pulled back from the podium, and started to leave.

The sergeant major belatedly jumped up to follow him while shouting, "Attention on deck!"

Pax jumped to his feet and locked his body, his eyes straight ahead. He watched in his peripheral vision as the colonel stalked out.

No one said a word even after the door swung to close behind the commanding officer until finally, Captain Kjellberg, in a subdued voice, said, "Carry on."

"I HOPE WE'RE READY," Pax said as he dropped his civilian duffle bag along with the others in the line.

After two weeks that seemed like two months, the company was finally ready to embark. Junior enlisted normally complained about being kept in the dark, but the last two weeks had been overload, and there were more than a few sighs of relief as they started to form up in the quad.

"It's not like these are boots, Pax," Link said. "You've just got FNGitis."

There was a lot of truth to what the team leader had just said. All of the new Undead were skilled operators, and they knew their way around a military operation. He'd seen that in training. But there was more to fighting than individual skill.

"No, I don't. But we really haven't worked together yet, and Josiah was a slinger."

"You worry too much. She'll come around, and just maybe she can be an asset? Did you think of that?"

"Of course, she can. But she's got no infantry experience."

PFC Rachel Josiah was one of three Knights of Justice snipers, or "David's Slings," who'd joined the Immortals while the platoon was on Lemon's Hold. The three had died together in an equipment malfunction that ended up gassing them while they were preparing to support a Paladin operation. They weren't Paladins, so they weren't special ops troops.

Pax didn't know if that was a signal that the makeup of the Undead was expanding, and he didn't have a problem with having the PFC's skill in the team. But Knights of Justice snipers were identified early in recruit training, yanked aside, and given intensive sniper training before being assigned to a two-person team to be floaters, or knights without a specific unit. The teams usually operated alone.

So, not only were they not operators, but they'd never served in regular infantry units. Yet now, PFC Josiah was an integrated member of the team, like all the others, who just happened to be skilled with her H-33 David's Sling rifle.

"And that's why you're going to keep an eye on her, right?" Link said.

"Yeah. First Bozo and now Josiah," he muttered.

Link put an arm around his shoulders, "I couldn't think of a better man to do it."

Pax shrugged off the arm. He has a sneaking suspicion that he'd been tasked to babysit Josiah because Link was his friend and he wouldn't argue. It wasn't as if he'd done such a bang-up job with Lymon, who, until Josiah had shown up, was the weakest member of the team.

Well, at least Josiah can shoot.

She'd proven that during training by performing an amazing display at the range.

"Where's Lindy?" Link asked as he craned his head around.

"Last I saw, he was still screwing with his seabag," Pax said.

"Go light a fire under his ass, OK? The gunny's going to be here any minute."

Pax sighed. The lieutenant had Wommack to be her gopher. The gunny had Link. And somehow, Link now had Pax.

He returned to berthing to find the former SEAL in the middle of the lounge, his gear strewn about the deck.

"Hell, Lindy. Get that shit packed. Everyone's mustered except for you."

Lindersmitz scowled. "If we gotta use civilian gear, can't they give us something decent, like High Country? I can't fit all of this in."

High Country Trek was one of the companies that sprang into being during the camping and hiking trend of twenty years ago. The Tucanan invasion put a damper on the activities, so they'd gravitated by producing high-end and innovative gear.

"We're supposed to be a corporate workforce, so you think they're going to spring for that kind of gear? Just cram that stuff inside."

Pax picked up a tube of cream that had rolled halfway across the lounge and handed it to Lindersmitz, who shoved it into the duffle bag. For all the junior Marine's bitching, it really wasn't that bad of a bag. Unzipped and expanded, it could be used as a dresser of sorts. That's what Pax did with his between deployments.

He helped Lindersmitz stuff everything in, then the two got back to the Quad less than a minute before the gunny arrived.

They'd had a junk on the bunk inspection that morning. Despite that, Pax still expected the gunny to conduct another one. But, miracle of miracles, once Link told him all hands were present and accounted for, he let it go at that and just wandered through the platoon, making small talk with the Marines.

"Maybe he hates doing the inspections as much as we hate getting inspected," Olivia said when Pax gave thanks that they had escaped the evolution.

Olivia, while a kickass Marine, could seem like an airhead with her malapropisms, mixed idioms, and generally weird way of speaking, but Pax often had to wonder if that hid a keen intellect. He'd never really considered inspections from the inspector point of view, but now that she mentioned it, he thought she could be right.

The palletized gear was already on the lowboys, ready to go. It was a typical loadout. Pax had been hoping that they'd have the new autoinjectors, but even with supposed off-the-shelf components, those were evidently still a long way off.

They were as ready as they were ever going to be, and when the buses showed up, the colonel and the sergeant major came out of the CP to watch. It was like a herd of wildebeests back at Kruger Terran Park watching the lions lounging under a baobab tree. The Marines were the herd animals, the ones watching and nervously waiting. The colonel . . .

The CO hadn't been around much since dressing down the company. But his words had an effect. There had been a little less boasting and a little more attention paid during the operations order.

The colonel didn't mingle with the Marines, however. Pax didn't know if that was a good thing or a bad thing. But then it didn't matter. The buses rolled in, and the Marines were loaded. Twenty minutes later, after one more head count inside the buses, they were on their way to Volante.

31

"I'm going to miss this good chow," Panda said as he plopped his tray on the table.

"Wait. Mr. Cynical, actually saying something is good?" Wolf asked.

Panda shrugged and sat down. "I'm just saying the grub's decent here."

"Well, eat up," Pax said. "This is the last hot chow we're getting for a while. We leave at zero dark thirty."

"He's right about the food, though. Who would've thought the Volante Guard would have good chow halls?" Olivia asked.

"Or that we'd be eating here," Pax said.

How their presence would be explained had been a matter of intense discussion among the command and the overlords. They couldn't go in as contractors as those would not be out sitting in the bush. And they couldn't present themselves as a contingent for the fictitious 31st General Maintenance Group. They wouldn't be in the bush, either, without a unit to support.

That left it down to being a Guard or a Marine unit. The problem with trying to look like a Guard unit was twofold. First, they'd have to explain the reasoning to the actual Volante Guard, and second, the Marines didn't know enough about the Guard to pass as Guardsmen.

So, it had to be LoH Marines. But why would Marines be sent to a planet that was technically secure? The final decision was elegant, Pax thought. They were impersonating a Surveillance Company.

Surveillance Companies were not part of a division. They were a force asset out of J-2, Intelligence. As such, they were out of the local command, and much of what they did was highly classified, so others expected a veil of secrecy about what they were doing.

A Marine surveillance company might raise some eyebrows, but no one would ask questions. And while they might be Intel, they had a bite to them. They had the weapons and training to defend themselves.

And with a quirk going back millennia, snipers were part of the Intel side of the Corps, so having David's Sling sniper rifles would be par for an LoH company, which made the three former Knights of Justice Marines very happy.

For Pax, the best part had been just landing at the Guard spaceport as Marines, in Marine uniforms. He hadn't realized how much he hated the blue civilian overalls. They'd spent two days at Camp Testerlin, which had taken some heavy damage during the invasion, but in a show of planetary resolve, had been built up in record time and to a much better condition than it had been before the fight.

"What time do we turn into pumpkins?" Panda asked Pax.

"Kravitz wants us back at twenty-one forty-five."

"So, twenty-two hundred."

"Twenty-one forty-five," Pax repeated.

"Still, time enough for the E-Club?" Panda said, looking at the others for their reaction.

"Still can't drink," Pax said.

Besides the fact that it could screw up their mycs, they didn't have any money. A few of the platoon tried to keep the credit wands Captain Lakmal had given them, but wherever the officer had gotten to, he'd had access enough to cancel them.

"But there's pool, gaddy, and they've got that 3D holojector."

Olivia shrugged, and everyone else kept at their food.

"And there'll be babes there. Or hunks if that's your pleasure."

"You're into freshies now?" Doc asked.

"Sure. I used to be one, you know."

"Shit, Panda. You couldn't do anything even if you somehow managed to get one of them to talk to you."

"I don't need to do anything. I just enjoy the looking."

"I'm in," Olivia said.

"You are?" Pax asked, surprised.

"What else are we going to do? Sit around our barracks? And I can use a little eye candy, too, before I'm stuck with your sorry asses out in the jungle."

That pretty much decided it. The six Marines and Doc hurried with their chow now that they had a destination, then walked to the large, impressive building.

"Welcome to the Sorenson Enlisted Club," a live attendant said as they entered the open, airy space. "My name is Leila. Would you like a tour of the facility?"

They exchanged glances before saying, "Sure."

"The Sorenson Enlisted Club was named for Private First Class Elijah Sorenson, who was posthumously awarded the Honor Nova, First Class, during the Tucanan Invasion."

She pointed to a plaque near the entrance. Pax made a mental point to come back to read the account.

"It was finished eighteen months ago, and it's the premier club on the planet." Her voice lowered a few decibels. "I'd like to think it's one of the premier clubs in the galaxy."

Pax didn't know about that, but it had to be up there from what he could see.

"It's a combined enlisted club, but as you'll see, while SNCOs might come by, the patronage is mostly non-rates and NCOs."

She led them into the club proper, and it was pretty impressive. There were the prerequisite drink and snack bars, but the drink bar could put many civilian bars to shame, and to call the restaurant a "snack bar" was rather an understatement. There were three game rooms. The largest had the pool and gaddy tables. One almost as large had immersion cubicles and game consoles, and then there was one for board games and cards.

Pax was surprised at the quiet room, with lay-flat loungers. Six Guardsmen were asleep inside. But the crème de la crème was the holojector with theater seats surrounding it.

"That's a Sanzu VJ-8001," their guide said proudly. "The only one on Volante."

A dozen Guardsmen were watching what looked to be a reality show, with emphasis on the "reality." There was none of the translucence that cheaper projectors had. It was as close to reality as Pax had ever seen—almost as if the contestants were right there over the base.

The rest of the club consisted of a few meeting rooms, a commercial comms center, and a library. All of the place was impressive.

Their tour ended up in the bar, where Leila asked them to take a seat. Pax wanted to check out the holojector, but he couldn't just bug out. They sat down, and Leila said she'd be right back.

"How about that 'jector," Doc said. "Top shelf."

"They sure treat their enlisted well here. Better than we got in the SEALs," Fridge said.

"Or our LoH Marines," Pax added.

He didn't compare it to his love, the San Marcos Marines, because he didn't want to admit that this place put those to shame.

"I guess when you hold off the pedes, the people appreciate that."

"At a cost," Olivia reminded them.

Casualties during the battle had run high, over seventy percent.

"They earned this place," Pax said.

Leila came back with two pitchers of beer and placed them on the table.

"Uh, we can't—" Doc started to say before Pax kneed him in the thigh.

"We can't accept this," Pax said. "Regulations, you know."

"Fillfoodle," Leila said. "This isn't an official government facility. This was built by the citizens of Volante. And the beer, along with a restaurant credit of twenty knocks apiece, has been paid by the patrons."

It was only then that Pax looked around the seating area. All of the Guardsmen were looking at them, and when the Marines looked back, the patrons all raised their glasses and toasted them.

"So, you don't have to drink, and you don't have to eat, but do you want to insult your hosts?" Leila said with a laugh.

"Did you say a food credit?" Fridge asked.

He'd come to the Immortals with the nickname, and his appetite proved the accuracy of it.

"Twenty knocks apiece. That's like twenty-four universal credits. And I think you'll find the food up to Marine standards. Now, I've got to get back to my desk, so please, enjoy. It's the least we can do for you coming here to help us."

"That's a little awkward," Olivia said as they gave little waves back to the Guardsmen. "The Marines never arrived for the fight."

"But we're here now, right?" Fridge said as he activated the menu. "Look, they've got Pasta Francine here. I love that stuff."

He tapped in the order, and a moment later, everyone else started looking at the menu. They might have just left the chow hall, but anyone who's ever been in the military knew never to turn down food before an operation.

Pax had eaten seconds in the chow hall, but the Ostrich Burger intrigued him. He knew it wasn't really ostrich. It would be fabricated like anything else, but there was a real cook back there in the kitchen to grill it.

"What about the beer?" Panda asked.

"What about it? We can't drink it," Doc reminded him.

"They're looking at us. Should we at least pretend?"

They turned to look at Pax.

"I guess that wouldn't hurt."

They made a show of pouring out some beer. The heady smell of hops made Pax's mouth water, but that was as far as it was going to go. The food came, and it was as good as the promise. Pax's Ostrich Burger may or may not have tasted like real ostrich, but it was sure delicious. And he had enough left over to get some desert. The Key Lime Pie was extremely tempting.

But that was going to have to wait. That Sanzu was calling his name.

"That's it for me. I'm hitting the 'jector. Anyone else coming with me?" he asked as he keyed the table to open the trash chute and tossed his plate inside.

Everyone else joined him until Panda asked, "What about the beer?"

Pax looked around. The Guardsmen were back to their own business and not staring at the Marines.

The beer was in self-cooling steins, condensation dripping down the sides. Those were reusable.

"Dump the beer in the trash, and we'll return the steins."

Panda picked up the stein near him and sniffed it. "Screw it," he said, lifting it to his lips.

"Stop," Doc said. "You know that can damage our mycs."

"Hell, Doc. I breathed that nasty air on Clovis-Four, and if that didn't kill my myc, then nothing will."

That was before Pax's time as an Immortal, but he'd heard all about it. That's where Link was rekilled for the first time.

Panda still hadn't swallowed, though, and he looked over the stein at Pax, waiting for him to object.

Pax knew he should, and he could feel everyone's eyes on him. He knew what the right thing to do was, but . . .

I'm not going to be the bad guy here.

"Your funeral, Panda."

It looked like Doc was going to object again, but he held back, and with a slight smile, Panda closed his eyes and took a sip. A bigger smile crept over his face.

What didn't happen was his eyes bulging out. No myc came out his nose. He didn't start choking.

"How do you feel?" Olivia asked breathlessly.

"Like I'm taking another sip."

"Me, too," Fridge said as he took one of the other steins.

In the Marines, a person was liable for any damage done to government property while drunk. That included their own persons. If they did screw up their mycs by breaking orders, then they'd be in a world of trouble.

He could still stop it. Panda was still undead and presumably combat capable. But for how long?

Pax reached out and took the stein from Fridge with the intention of pouring the contents down the chute.

Something held his hand, though. Maybe it was Panda's statement about the air on Clovis-Four. Maybe because he'd never been too convinced that the myc, if it was some amazing life-form, would self-destruct if a little alcohol touched it. Or maybe, he just wanted a chance to shoot the proverbial middle finger at the overlords.

Instead of dumping it, his hands made a detour of their own volition to his mouth. Olivia actually gasped.

The aroma filled his senses, and as far as he could tell, that didn't bother his myc in the slightest.

Before he knew it, he took a swallow, and the cool effervescence flowed down his throat in an exquisite wave.

He closed his eyes, trying to feel if something was off. His throat was tingling, but that was all. Like always, he couldn't sense his myc.

He opened his eyes to see that everyone was staring at him, including Panda.

"Still dead," he said.

"Good enough for me," Doc said, grabbing one of the other steins.

"Don't get drunk," was all Pax had to say.

No one actually got to the holojector that evening.

"Still dead?" Olivia asked him as he got out of the rack at zero four hundred.

"Still dead."

He actually felt pretty darn good, all things considered.

It had been a pretty good night. Some of the Guardsmen had recharged their two pitchers, then came over to join them. They'd had an enjoyable evening getting to know their hosts and exchanging war stories. Some of the stories had even been true.

Mostly.

While a couple of the Guardsmen had been three sheets to the wind, none of the Marines had gotten drunk. Pax had limited himself to three-quarters of a stein. While he hadn't keeled over dead again, he didn't want to push his luck.

In retrospect, drinking had been a bad idea. The scientists seemed to think booze could hurt their mycs, and there probably was a reason for that. The eight of them had risked their health, and for what? A couple of sips of beer? And while they all seemed to have survived the alcohol, what if the effects took time to manifest?

With none of them drunk, and after spraying their throats with the mini-containers of Breath Alive the E-club staff had so conveniently placed by the exit, they'd been able to get back to bed-check without anyone being the wiser. They'd all sworn the others to secrecy, so hopefully, it would never get out.

Still, Pax felt good. It wasn't just the beer or the food. It was the fact that the Guardsmen seemed to generally like them. For a few hours, Pax had felt like part of the human race again instead of a rightsless piece of military gear.

It was a nice interlude.

Link pounded on the hatch, shouting, "Everybody up. Formation in twenty."

Now it was back to reality.

Pax kicked the base of Doc's rack. "Up and at 'em."

The corpsman gave a groan, and suddenly, Pax was concerned. But Doc sat up and rubbed his eyes. He was just too-early-morning grumpy, not from any effects of the beer.

He turned to make sure Wolf, the last of their four-person cube, was up, but the rack was empty. With a guilty start, Pax jumped to his feet, hoping that the stein and a half of beer the corporal had drunk hadn't caught up with him.

But the hatch opened, and Wolf strode in, towel wrapped around his waist and a toothsonic dangling from his mouth.

"If you're gonna shower, better get to it. Kravtiz's saying formation in twenty minutes."

"You make me sick, Wolf," Doc said.

"And I had the showers all to myself. So there."

"And I had more sleep. So there back to you."

"You can sleep when you're dead."

Doc nodded. "Ha-fucking-ha."

Pax poked his head out the hatch. This deck had communal showers: four water and four sonic stalls. Already, other members of the platoon were lining up.

"Looks like showering's out. Let's just get ready."

Wolf punched Doc in the shoulder. "Now I'll have to smell your ass all the way to our CP."

"Eat me, Wolf."

Pax ignored the bickering. The two friends were constantly at it. But in something like seven hours, they'd be in their position. The back and forth would cease as the mission began.

32

ONE GOOD THING about acting like a surveillance company was that to pull it off, they had to have high-end surveillance gear. So, as the platoon set in, the second order of business was to set up the gear, which should give them ample warning if something was heading their way.

Most of them were sure that if something did come for them, it would be the Tucanans taking the bait. No one gave the local fauna much consideration, despite the dragonfly sign at one of the overrun camps.

Pax placed another tiny nib on the rubbery skin of a Volante tree. Alone, the nib wasn't much and almost impossible to detect. But together with a quorum of them, they created a field that would detect anything that entered it.

The brain of the CCM-2032 was a small, innocuous-looking box with limited AI capability that learned from what disturbed the field and would send the results back to the camp.

The physics was well beyond Pax's understanding. All he knew was that if they'd set this up correctly, then anything from the size of a hummingbird and on up would be detected if it entered the field.

"I've emplaced the last nib," he passed to Link.

"Roger that. Powering up."

Pax stared at the nib, but as expected, there was no sign that it was active. The nibs themselves had no power. That came from the control box.

"Looks like it's working. Wait a sec. Let me eliminate the humans." A moment later, he passed, "Yep. You just disappeared. Bring it back in."

Pax signaled Wolf and Panda, who'd been providing security. He stepped back, and his foot slipped in a patch of the whitish slime that dotted the ground. He came close to landing on his ass, but he kept his balance.

"Watch out for the cum," Panda said.

Or course, Marines were going to give the stuff a nickname, and a perverted one was always better than an innocuous one.

Olivia, Ogre, and Lindy were waiting for them up the next ridge, and together, the six headed back to the camp. They were about two klicks away. As they marched, Pax tried to take in as much of the terrain as possible. They had accurate topos, of course, but it was always best to be as familiar with an area as possible.

Sergeant Danit, his first squad leader when he was in the infantry, had told him that when in the defense, plan out an assault upon the position. Chances are, someone planning an actual assault would use that plan, too.

Link met them as they came into camp. "Take a break. Let me

check with Byeon to see where we are with emplacing our sensor network."

The six marched to the center and dropped down on an area of cleared dirt.

Olivia grabbed a stick to try and scrape some of the white goop from her boots and legs. The stick was a little too pliable and wasn't very effective as a scraper.

"I don't know why they don't finish the terraforming here. This place is half-raked," she said.

"They did," Wolf said. "We can breathe, right?"

"You know what I mean."

"Lots of effort and cost if they don't need it," Pax said.

Volante was a little strange, though. The atmosphere had always been life-sustainable for humans. The terraforming had been to adjust it to make it a little more comfortable.

With abundant geothermal power and minerals, the planet had become a hotbed of manufacturing, but localized to the mountain ranges where the power could most easily be tapped. Entire valleys were stripped of native life and replaced with Earth vegetation, both forests and crops. Where power was more costly to recover, the land was left fallow. And after the invasion, smaller communities were abandoned.

The communities left were protected from the planet trying to reclaim land by erecting huge repeller domes, some stretching along valleys for two hundred kilometers.

But nature has a fierce drive for life, and the native flora always managed to get through the fields. To combat them, the Volantites used armies of small drones to sniff out and snip native plants in the bud.

When the three platoons made their very-much-in-the-open move out into the bush, as the people called it, they encountered a buffer area just outside the repeller field, where native and Earth life coexisted in a slow-moving battle for supremacy. The farther out they marched, the more the native life gained the upper hand. Here, at the position they'd been assigned, it was mostly native, with only a few hardy jatropha and tamarack scrabbling for a toehold.

Pax would really rather be in an Earth zone. The native life wasn't green like an Earth forest, but rather tended to the dark purples and blues, although washed out. His first impression was that the vegetation had a fungus-like appearance, but maybe because of his myc, he was more attuned to fungus.

Maybe there was a similarity to the black wood ear fungus of Asian cooking, but there weren't mushrooms sprouting everywhere.

The place stunk, too, like something rotting. And then there was the snot-like goop, the "cum" as Panda called it. Pax wished he'd use another term as the image kept intruding into his mind.

One of the local bugs flew in and landed on Pax's bent knee. He absentmindedly flicked it off with his forefinger.

It was easy to ignore most of the mobile life as bugs, even though he knew they were not insects. They were not really animals, either, according to the xenobiologists. They were more like mobile portions of the ground plants that scooted about doing their thing before returning to the mother stalk.

Olivia had watched him flick off the fungus-bug. "You think we're gonna see a Dragonfly?"

"If we're here long enough, then yeah. They're not rare. But if they come, we're ready," he said, patting the Bristol at his side.

Dragonflies were big enough and vicious enough to be a danger to a human, but the Volantites had dealt with them long enough to know how to handle them. A beam weapon was very effective against all Volante life. One blast would scramble its ability to move.

Every Marine had a Bristol-90 in a holster at their side. The Bristol-80 was used in crowd control. The 90 was the same model as for civilian use, but with a larger-capacity power source.

Olivia was about to respond when Link came back.

"Another CCM?" Pax asked.

"Nope. Something better."

Pax's ears perked up. "What?"

"Get the shovels out. We're preparing fighting positions."

All six of the Marines groaned, Pax maybe the loudest of them all.

One of the benefits of being in special ops was that they'd almost never had to dig fighting positions. And on the few occasions when it had been necessary, they'd had engineer equipment to help.

Soldiers had been digging fighting positions since the Roman times, but Pax hadn't dug a position with a shovel since he was a lance corporal in the grunts.

"I knew you'd love that. So get going," Link said.

"I suppose we're going to have to dig you one, too?"

"I wish. No, the gunny told me specifically to dig my own, so I'm doing this with you. All our positions are marked over there."

It didn't make any difference in the long run, but somehow, that made Pax feel a little better. With a sigh, he expanded one of the shovels, located his assigned position, and began to dig.

33

"Any word, L-T?" Pax asked.

"Still nothing," she said as she looked out into the forest.

One of the advantages of not trying to hide their position was that they had full comms with the Planetary Guard, and the lieutenant was getting continual updates of any movement picked up in the surrounding area. There was plenty of native life activity, but no Tucanans.

No one knew if the top command of the Guard were briefed on the company's mission, but they were obviously aware that the company was there, and they'd been giving full support.

"Maybe we're too big of a unit," Pax said.

None of the three Guard units to be wiped out had been over eighteen soldiers. As a platoon, Second had forty-eight Marines and Doc.

"Could be," the lieutenant said, non-committal as usual.

"How long do you think they'll keep us here?" Olivia asked.

"Up to them," she answered. "Well, you know the drill. Keep your eyes peeled."

"Always a mount of information," Olivia said as the platoon commander moved onto the next position.

"Font of information," Pax said automatically, which Olivia ignored. His corrections had become just part of the background noise.

"And she doesn't know any more than we do, Liv. I can tell you this, though. I don't think the overlords are going to keep us here forever. Something else is going to pop up that will get them excited to see what their grand experiment can do, and we'll be yanked out of here."

"I wouldn't complain if that happened. This is getting pretty old, staring at fugly, smelly trees for nothing."

"Not exactly nothing. That dragonfly was pretty cool, right?"

"That was two days ago, and if I want to see one of those things, I can watch the nature channel."

"I can't believe you're complaining, Liv. Here we are, in an exotic location with exciting native life, lounging in luxurious accommodations," he said, sweeping a hand to indicate their fighting hole, "while chowing down on the best food the Marine Corps can buy?"

He kicked the combat ration strap at the bottom of their hole in emphasis.

The LoH Marines didn't have their own rations. They bought them from the contributing units, and for this mission, the company had been issued the Hangul Republic Army "Long Rats," which the Marines had started calling "rat turds."

Pax generally liked Korean food, but there was a weird aftertaste to the Long Rats, which was surprising as they didn't really have much taste at all at first bite. They were designed for the wrapping to be eaten as well, which most folks thought was unpleasant, so that the Hangul soldiers wouldn't leave trash, but then the bars were bundled together by straps that weren't biodegradable.

"You are certifiably crazy, Pax. You know that?"

"And that's why you love me."

She snorted. "In your dreams."

They settled into silence until ten minutes later, Pax said, "I wish I had one of those E-Club Ostrich Burgers now."

"Shut the hell up, Pax," Olivia said, punching him in the upper arm.

"You sure?" Pax asked Olivia.

"I'm sure," Olivia groaned as she squatted over the slit trench, her utility trou down around her ankles.

Her statement was emphasized by a burst of splatting.

"Can you just leave?"

Being in the military desensitized soldiers to the simple biological processes. That was just a fact of field life. But extreme situations like this pushed that acceptability.

"Got it. I'll send over Doc."

She waved a dismissing hand.

"Fucking rat turds," she muttered as Pax went to find Link.

They'd all been injected with nanos that were supposed to fight off infections and deal with things like gastrological issues, but sometimes, nature just won out. Hopefully, Doc Grant would have something to give her nanos the boost needed to get her back into fighting trim.

He found Link with the gunny where they were both eating the Long Rats. Pax gave the bars a hard glance, but despite Olivia's parting comment, he didn't think they were the culprit.

"Liv can't make it," he told Link.

Both SNCOs looked up and waited for something more.

Pax lowered his voice and almost apologetically. "She's got the shits."

Link grimaced, but the gunny didn't miss a beat.

"Take Taufua."

"Uh . . . really?"

"FNGitis, Pax," Link said.

"It's not that . . ."

Both SNCOs just stared at him, waiting for his excuse.

"Right. Taufua," Pax said.

Lance Corporal Taufua was a former Royal Charter Marine Commando, and one of the new joins. As a commando, then an LoH Recon Marine, Taufua was probably capable. But it was the "probably" that got to Pax. That, and more importantly, he'd never trained with the man.

Given the choice, Pax would rather have had Blue Knopf or Lily Bartok if he was going to take someone from outside of his team. At least he'd worked with them on Lemon's Hold.

He asked Link to send Doc over to Olivia, then crossed the CP and collected Taufua from Staff Sergeant Byeon. He led him to where Wolf and Panda were waiting.

"How's Liv . . ." Panda started when he spotted Taufua. "Oh. That bad?"

Pax ignored him, instead saying, "Lance Corporal Taufua is joining us in Liv's place. It's no big deal."

He turned to Taufua and asked, "How up are you on the CCM?"

"Not very," the lance corporal said. "We don't have them in the Royal Marines."

Which is what he expected. "You and Wolf will be security. Panda, you're with me on the CCM."

Panda gave a disappointed frown. What Pax had done was to put his trust into Wolf for security. When push came to shove, Pax would rather have Wolf than Panda covering his ass.

Panda would understand that. It was commonly accepted that Wolf was one of the most capable Marines in the platoon. But that didn't mean Panda wouldn't feel a little hurt.

"OK. This is not a big deal. We've done it before," Pax said, more for Taufua than for the other two.

"We patrol out and run the checks on the CCM. Wolf, you and Taufua are security. I want you twenty meters in front of us, but in sight at all times. Wolf, make sure that draw to the left is covered."

Pax was pretty sure that the systems check wasn't absolutely necessary. The remote checks on the CCM were all green. And it had alerted on dragonflies and yellowjackets, which were a slightly smaller carnivore. But no Tucanan alerts.

Which meant that there were no Tucs to alert on. But on the slight chance that the system had trained itself to ignore the enemy, the lieutenant wanted to have the system checked.

That was the official reason, at least.

Gunny Akai had told them that either the overlords or the command—probably the overlords—had prohibited patrols outside of the platoon camps. That was a little troubling for a number of reasons.

Either the captain, who was with First Platoon, or the lieutenant had decided that the scanners had to be checked for operability. So there was a continual check of the systems that were set up surrounding the camp. As a result, at any given time, there was a four-person patrol out there.

That wouldn't provide that full manned extra layer of security, but it was something. And it had the additional benefit of keeping the Marines sharp.

After almost three weeks in the bush, just getting out and moving around was a welcome break.

Pax motioned for Wolf to take the point when Taufua said, "I can take the point."

Pax was going to say no—he wanted the Ghost Walker—when he saw the eager, almost anxious look on the younger Marine's face, and he realized that Taufua knew he was the FNG, and he wanted to fit in.

It wasn't that far, and there were no reported Tucanans in the area.

Yet.

He held up a hand and checked in with Mongol, who had CP duty. "We're getting ready to kick off. Any sign of activity?"

"A few dragonflies, but nothing else," Mongol passed back.

"Roger. We're passing through lines now."

"Roger. I'll let the L-T know."

Pax motioned for Taufua to take the point. Wolf looked surprised, but he moved behind Pax.

In one way, this was more SOP. Wolf liked to be both point and navigator, and he almost never looked back to make sure he was on the right track. With Taufua, who didn't even know where they were going, Pax could navigate, which was how it was supposed to go, while the lance corporal focused on spotting any threat before it spotted them.

"Find us a couple of pedes to shoot," Ogre said as they passed his and Fridge's fighting position.

"Any preference what kind?" Pax asked.

"I like 'em big. Bag a mule."

The camp was on a slight high ground with a mixture of Earth and native trees. As they started down the slope, the Earth vegetation gave way within a hundred meters to the native life. Not much direct sunlight made its way through the trees, and small flying creatures flitted in the shadows. It was pretty much as it had been on every other patrol.

They were taking a parallel but different route to the CCM control. Marines tried to avoid moving in their own footprints as those were the most logical place to emplace booby traps and mines. The Tucanans didn't use those types of weapons as much as humans did, and there'd been no sign that the enemy had been in the area, but an overabundance of caution became smart decision-making the first time the enemy decided to mine a prior route.

Taufua kept glancing back to make sure he was on the right path. Each time, Pax pointed with an outstretched arm. The lance corporal should be picking a landmark farther ahead and moving toward it—not looking back every ten meters. Pax was beginning to regret making him the point.

The four Marines wended their way to the bottom, then across the lower ground. It had rained the night before, and the ground was a little muddy, which made for slippery footing. And it wasn't just the rain. It seemed as if the slime patches were bigger, some even forming alongside the tree trunks. Pax brushed against several and had the slime on him.

He turned around, and Panda was also somewhat slimed. Wolf, of course, was spotless. Once again, Pax wondered if maybe he really wasn't Undead, but a real Ghost Walker.

He turned back just as Taufua jerked his Denon up. Beyond him, charging out of the trees, was one of the largest dragonflies Pax had seen. It buzzed a meter off the ground, its eight wings propelling it quickly.

Taufua fired a burst from his weapon. The dragonfly jerked, and it looked like a gossamer wing came apart, but the thing kept coming.

Pax bolted ahead and shoved Taufua out of the way and onto the ground as he drew his Bristol-90 and fired a two second burst that hit the dragonfly in the head. The native carnivore tumbled in flight and hit the ground, splattering slime and mud over the two Marines. It bounced twice and slid to a stop and Pax's feet.

"Your Bristol, not your Denon, Taufua. That's why they issued them to us."

"Sorry, Sergeant. I . . . I . . ." the lance corporal said as he tried to get up.

"Sergeant Alejo, what was that firing?" the lieutenant came over the net.

"Dragonfly. Came at us. Lance Corporal Taufua fired on it."

"That's not the correct weapon, Sergeant."

"I know. I dropped it with my Bristol. It's dead."

Taufua could hear Pax's response, and he looked suitably chagrined.

"Should we continue with the check?" Pax asked the platoon commander.

There was a pause, which Pax understood. By firing the Denon, they might have alerted any Tucanans in the region.

Finally, she said, "Continue. But hyper alert."

"Roger that."

It was the right decision, Pax knew. First, there was still no sign of any Tucs in the area, and second, they were *trying* to attract their attention. They wanted to be a target. A trap with no prey is just a waste of time.

"We're still on," he told the others.

Wolf and Panda closed in, and Pax looked at the almost two-meter-long creature. Close up, the similarities to an Earth dragonfly were remarkable given totally different evolutionary journeys. The compound eyes, in particular, were almost the same, except for the size, of course. The shell was an iridescent mixture of colors that were already beginning to fade. A huge, pincher-like apparatus at the fore seemed too big for the body.

Pax toed the thing, then flipped it over. Here is where it diverted from the Earth insect.

The Volante dragonfly didn't have legs for one. In place of the legs were opposing rows of grasping fangs—there was a more scientific term he'd heard in the briefs, but he'd long forgotten it.

From what he did remember, the hunter would grasp its prey by piercing the skin with its fangs, and then, like a spider, inject the body with digestive juices. Then it would fly back to its mother tree, alight into depressions in the trunk, and with one row of fangs still in the prey, it would bury the other into the mother and transfer the semi-digested prey into the tree.

Pax hadn't seen any prey yet that would require such a large predator, but they were out there.

"I still don't understand why they come after us? I thought

aliens and humans aren't food for each other," Panda said. "That's what they keep telling us."

"Carbon atoms are carbon atoms," Pax reminded the corporal. "The carbon in these fungus trees is the same as in, like a carrot. The reason we can't eat them is because of other stuff in their body that'll poison us."

"And even without the poison, we can't digest the stuff," Wolf added. "We can't break it down."

Always got to throw your two cents' worth, Wolf?

But he was right, and Pax continued, "But that doesn't go both ways. Earth life doesn't poison this stuff. And the trees can extract what they need from our organic matter."

"And the dragonflies happen to know all of that?" Panda asked.

"Who knows? The brief said they don't have much of a brain. Maybe they're just reacting to movement. Maybe they can sense those juicy carbon atoms. But the bottom line is that they will attack humans, and people have been killed and absorbed."

Taufua had been quietly listening in, but suddenly, he jumped back.

"What the . . ."

Several small, pill-bug-looking creatures were emerging and heading to the dragonfly with single-minded purpose. As they watched, various other critters started climbing down off trees and plants.

"And here come the scavengers," Wolf said.

"They might be small, but I don't want any of them to decide to sample my ass, so, let's get moving," Pax ordered.

Already, the first of the pill bugs had reached the carcass. A tube snaked out of one and attached itself to the dragonfly's body. Pax thought it was both gross and fascinating at the same time.

The patrol left the Volante nature to do its thing and moved through the forest. Pax didn't holster his Bristol-90 but kept it ready. Dragonflies weren't known to congregate, but if this was good dragonfly territory, then he figured there might be others.

The canopy opened up slightly, and more sunlight reached down to the ground. Almost as an aside, Pax noted that there were fewer slime patches here, and what patches there were were smaller. He didn't know if that was at all pertinent to them, but as Sergeant Danit, his first squad leader in the grunts had continually pounded into his head, situational awareness.

A Marine had to be aware of everything around him at all times. It was too late when the shit hit the fan.

They passed the semi-open area and went back into the heavier canopy. These trees were a deeper purple with much thicker trunks. As he passed one of them, Pax saw a brown, woody vine of some sort climbing one of the trees. He craned his head, and toward the top, bright green leaves were spreading.

Kudzu!

There was no other sign of Earth life in the area, just this lone vine. Pax didn't know how kudzu spread or how this single vine established a foothold all the way out here. But it gave him a mental lift.

"You go for it," he told his fellow Earth-life.

And then it was time for a change of course. They'd been crossing terrain features, but now they needed to adjust to the left and follow the slight rise, which, after another 400 meters, would lead them right to the control box.

But Taufua, who'd been continually looking back at the beginning of the movement, was now focused on the front.

Pax bent down to pick up a small clod of dirt and threw it at the lance corporal, hitting him in the back. The surprised Marine looked back, and Pax used his arm to indicate the new direction.

Taufua nodded when there was a crack, and his throat seemed to explode, spraying blood in a red cloud. The Marine collapsed into a boneless heap, while the other three Marines immediately took cover.

"What do you see?" Pax shouted as he tried to spot the enemy.

But there was nothing. No movement, no more incoming fire.

"Give me a target!"

"I don't see anything!" Wolf said.

Pax signaled Wolf to move to his right flank and then Panda to his right. He had both his Bristol and his Denon at the ready as he scanned the area to the front.

There was another crack, and Panda went down hard, but he rolled to his side and gave Pax a thumbs-up.

Pax thought he saw a branch flicker at the shot, and he poured several bursts into the spot. Wolf joined in.

An explosion rocked the forest—Panda had just tossed a grenade.

Pieces of trees liquefied, making a mist. The two Marines ceased firing, and Pax lifted his head as the mist slowly fell away.

There was nothing there except torn up vegetation.

"TIC TIC TIC.[1] This is Papa-Three. We're under fire, and we've got one down," Pax passed, his blood pounding.

"Give me a SALUTE," the lieutenant said, her voice calm.

That snapped Pax back. There was a reason the Marine Corps

---

1. **TIC TIC TIC**: Troops in Contact. Used to clear the net and establish reporting priority.

had standardized reporting. Just saying they were under fire didn't help the platoon commander much.

He kept scanning the forest as he reported. "Size of enemy—unknown. We can't see anything.

"Actions—we took two incoming rounds. I don't know what kind.

"Location—from the front, but I don't know how far. We're heading three-one-five."

Pax didn't need to establish their position. The lieutenant already had that.

"Uniform—can't tell what kind. We haven't spotted them."

While Marines still used the term "Uniform," for the Tucanans, that meant what type of the enemy.

"Time—now.

"Equipment—it sounded something like a Buzzer, but I'm not sure."

As he gave the report, he realized that he really hadn't given the lieutenant much. That's because he didn't know much. But just giving the report had calmed his pounding heart somewhat and let his training kick in.

"Who's down and what's his condition?" the lieutenant asked.

"Taufua."

He gave the lance corporal a glance. Two thirds of his neck was gone, and blood was flowing evenly from the neck, pooling on top of the damp soil. His entire head was bent backward.

"KIA."

"I'm sending out the reaction team. Stand by."

"Roger that."

But Pax wasn't just going to sit there. It would take a reaction team at least thirty minutes to reach them, and there was still one more of the pedes out there.

Using hand-and-arm signals, he ordered the other two forward. Together, the three low-crawled ahead, using every bit of cover. As Pax reached Taufua, he took the opportunity to pull out the lance corporal's injector.

SOP was to wait five minutes, but with an unknown assailant, there was a chance they might lose the opportunity. It had to be now. Only, with much of the neck gone, there wasn't a good spot to inject the zombie juice. So, he went to the secondary location, which was right under the temporomandibular joint. The injector activated, and Taufua's head jerked.

"Myc, do your thing," he muttered as he continued forward.

His stress level rose again as he crawled, expecting another shot to ring out at any second. But the forest was silent, not even the low whine that some of the native creatures made, like the cicadas back on San Marcos. Pax had gotten used to them, but now, that made the silence even more impactful.

It seemed to take forever to low-crawl the thirty-five meters to where they'd poured their fire. The area had taken a beating between the Denons and the grenade. The ground was pulverized with splattered mud and dirt surrounding a crater where groundwater was already seeping in. Two smaller trees were toppled, and plants had been scattered everywhere. Chunks had been blasted out of several of the larger trees.

What wasn't there was any sign of the enemy. None.

Pax signaled for them to stand up.

"Wolf, see if you can spot anything to tell us that they retreated."

With their foot-arms, the Tucanans would have left prints in the damp soil that any of the three of them could recognize, but Pax wanted the Ghost Walker in case there were subtle signs of anything at all.

He and Panda searched the pulverized area, searching for something that would help them figure out what had just happened. There were no Tucanan body parts, and Wolf confirmed that no pedes left the site.

"Could it have been a sniper?" Panda asked.

The Tucanans didn't do much along the lines of human spec-ops, but they did employ snipers. Pretty good ones. But they were in a dense forest. Whatever had hit them had been close, *and* it had left no sign.

"I just don't get it," Pax said as he scanned the surrounding jungle.

The low whine of native life had resumed, but that didn't make him feel any better. Some unknown entity had just killed Taufua, and he had to assume it was still out there given the lack of any evidence to the contrary.

He shifted his gaze back to the lance corporal as if Taufua could give him answers from beyond the grave and then gave an angry shout as he charged the body. He reached down and grabbed two of the pill bugs, yanking them out of Taufua with a sickening pop as the tube pulled free. He tossed the creatures as far as he could into the trees.

Even the slime had gotten into the act. A patch of it was taking on a pink tinge as it absorbed some of Taufua's spilled blood.

"We're not sticking around," he told the other two.

"But the—" Wolf started.

"We've done what we can do. If the lieutenant wants to keep

poking around, that's up to her. Wolf, you're point. Panda, Tail-end Charlie."

Pax reported back to the lieutenant what they were doing. He trussed the lance corporal in his harness, securing Taufua's wrists together, and sticking his head between the arms, he stood, lifting the Marine with a grunt.

Taufua was not a small man.

Pax gave one last look around, hoping he'd see something they'd all missed. But there was nothing.

He gave the order to Wolf, and they started back to the camp.

34

"You had to have missed something," Gunny Akai said.

"I swear, gunny, we searched the area," Pax protested. "And it isn't just us. The damn CCM didn't alert. According to it, there shouldn't have been anything there."

He looked to the lieutenant, who so far hadn't said much.

"That isn't a Buzzer wound," Staff Sergeant Byeon said, hooking her thumb to where Taufua's body was laid out on the ground. "Could it have been some native life? There's more than dragonflies here."

"I saw his neck get hit," Pax said, feeling like he was being ganged up on.

"If you weren't expecting it, it might not have registered with you."

"We heard the shot," Wolf added. "Twice. And Panda got hit, too."

"But you said it didn't sound like a Buzzer. Animals can make different kinds of noises," she said, but without much conviction.

Panda getting hit ruled out some sort of creature, Pax thought. The corporal had taken an oblique hit that tore his utility sleeve and scored the armor on the shoulder, but it wasn't a big enough hit for them to determine what the weapon was.

The gunny turned to the lieutenant and said, "I think we need to send a patrol. Like I said, something had to have been missed."

Pax started to protest again, but the gunny cut him off. "This isn't a ding on you, Q-B. I know how things can get in the heat of battle, and you had Taufua there to worry about."

"It wasn't in the heat of battle. It was afterward," Pax said, but the gunny was waiting for the lieutenant's response.

"I've made my report to the skipper," she said. "He's passed it up the line. Until then, and until we know what the threat is, we're staying put. Seventy-five percent alert until further notice."

Pax could see that the gunny didn't agree, but if he was going to discuss it with her, it wouldn't be in front of the platoon. Pax didn't know what the right course of action was, to be honest. Despite the three of them searching the area, they might have missed something. And the platoon had some gear that had more capability than the naked eye.

"Lieutenant, the CASEVAC is inbound. ETA five mikes," Doc came over and said.

"Let's take care of Lance Corporal Taufua. We'll get our orders soon enough," she responded.

The group of them went over to where Taufua's body was ready, already trussed up in the extraction harness. Doc had bandaged him up before he was slipped into the bright orange bag, but some blood had leaked out, turning the fabric brown.

No one said a word until they all seemed to hear the incoming bird at the same moment.

"Here they come," Doc said.

A few moments later, they caught glimpses through the trees as the big Pelican slowly crabbed over their heads.

The Pelican was technically a HT-405 when configured for military usage, but "Pelican" was widespread on the civilian side, so that was what the bird was commonly called. A tilt rotor with a huge lifting capacity, it had been a favorite of both the military and civilians for over sixty years.

What it wasn't was stealthy. The big blades made a racket as they "beat the air into submission," as the saying went, as opposed to flying like any other aircraft.

But that was still part of the plan. If there were Tucanans out there that had somehow escaped detection, the Pelican was a huge, neon arrow pinpointing their location.

If they didn't before, the Tucanans now knew exactly where they were.

The Pelican couldn't land at the camp, hence the extraction harness. It came to a hover over their heads, the rotor-wash sending the treetops whipping back and forth. A line dropped from an opening in the underside of the craft, which snaked its way down through the trees as if it had a mind of its own.

Which it did. The line could twist and turn, making recoveries in this type of terrain much easier. To Pax, it looked like a long, live snake was being lowered, and that was slightly disconcerting to him.

The end of the rescue line came to a stop directly above Taufua's body, barely moving in the rotor wash. Doc grabbed the end and slapped it hard to get past the static electrical charge the line would have built up.

"Lift," Doc said, and the five Marines grabbed the carrying straps and stood. "Keep it steady."

He checked to make sure that Taufua wasn't caught on anything, then touched his throat mic and spoke with the Pelican's crew chief. A moment later, Taufua started rising.

"Release!"

The Marines stepped back to watch the line do its thing, bending and twisting like some sort of convoluted industrial assembly line. Taufua brushed a few branches, but within a minute, he disappeared into the belly of the Pelican. The bottom hatch closed, the twin rotors started to shift into forward, and the big bird disappeared.

"Fair winds and following seas," the lieutenant said.

"Good xerox," the gunny added.

The Guard had been more than happy to provide the lift for what they were told was for transfer to a LoH Navy morgue. Only, as the gunny had mentioned, Taufua was heading back for reanimation.

Hopefully. What happened to Nani Vesta was ever in the back of their minds.

35

"Checking in," Pax passed on the net. "Nothing happening."

It was hardly proper comms procedures, but after two days of staring into the forest, he'd left some of that behind.

"Roger that. I've got you logged in. Uh . . . the gunny said that your relief might be two hours late," Kaleetha Morgan, who was the duty, said.

"Of course, they will. Why wouldn't they?"

He cut the connection before Lance Corporal Morgan could answer.

"We might be here for another two hours," Pax told Wolf.

"Here, there, it doesn't matter," Wolf said, sounding far less frustrated than Pax felt at the moment.

And not just because of the late relief. Pax had a deep-set feeling that he and the team were being blamed for what happened on their patrol four days ago. Into every look, every comment, he read an accusation. And it was wearing on him. Panda was the same way, and he was acting out, telling people off a few times.

But for Wolf, it seemed like water off a duck's back. It didn't seem to register.

Olivia told him to let it go, that no one blamed them. Pax didn't believe it.

He realized he might be being a little paranoid, but the more he thought about it, the more he wondered if they had missed something. He wracked his brain a thousand times until he wasn't quite sure what he actually remembered and what he thought he remembered.

Not even the fact that the patrol the gunny finally got approved didn't find any answers provided him with some relief.

And being out here on an OP, with only the taciturn Wolf for company, probably didn't help.

With an audible sigh, he reached into his cargo pocket and pulled out two Long Rats, then nudged Wolf in the thigh. When the corporal saw the rats, he frowned but took one.

There really wasn't much for the two of them to do except look out into the trees. They'd finally received their orders, and these were all the way from Cape Town. The overlords had evidently decided that whatever had killed Taufua might be the same entity that had wiped out the three Guard positions. Whether it was all related to the unexplained attacks on the other four planets remained to be seen, but they were treating this as a big fishing expedition, and what happened to Taufua was just a nibble. They wanted to set the hook, and the platoon was still the bait.

Not just Second Platoon. First and Third were in the same posture.

The platoons were supposed to continue, business as normal. Captain Kjellberg, however, made his own modifications, probably without reporting them. The platoons were to increase their close-in surveillance, and that included manned OPs situated on the most likely Tucanan avenues of approach.

Pax actually approved of the move. But that didn't mean he had to enjoy the boredom of sitting in a camouflaged fighting hole for eight hours at a time—and now, this was going to be a ten-hour post.

The normal SOP called for OPs to be four hours long. Past that, minds tended to wander a bit, and effectiveness dropped. But too much travel back and forth increased the chance of being spotted.

The company wanted the platoons to be attacked, but after what happened with Pax's team, they didn't want to leave an OP hanging. So, longer watches were emplaced.

There were four OPs around the platoon. Pax and Wolf's was roughly in the same direction as the CCM they'd been going to check when they were hit. It was a narrow, meter-wide, meter-and-a-half deep hole placed under a fallen tree trunk. Entry was from the rear so as to leave no sign from the front, which was then camouflaged with local vegetation.

Pax was getting sick of the fungus-looking stuff, but it didn't wilt like Earth plants did, so they didn't have to be replaced. In fact, some seemed to be taking root.

They were merely relying on passive camouflage. The CCM was still working, of course—not that Pax trusted it. But they'd emplaced a series of SM-156 "tripwires," which were tiny receivers that were aimed at each other. If anything disturbed the air between them, an alert would be sent to the OP.

They could alert on one of the little native creatures, so the 156s were set about half a meter off the ground, which was perfect for Tucanans. One had gone off the day before when Olivia and

Panda were manning the OP, but it had been one of the larger forms of mobile life passing between.

Pax peeled the wrapper off the ration. It was edible, but he thought it tasted bad. He pocketed it and slowly ate the bar while he watched his AOR.[1]

One of the little scavengers crawled through the camouflage, tiny antennae-looking things waving as if tasting the air, and headed to them. Pax just watched until it fell into the hole. It would be too difficult to bend over to retrieve it with both of them there, so Wolf crushed it with his boot, to join the twenty or thirty smashed bodies already there.

They'd already discovered that letting them live was a painful mistake. The little creatures had a righteous bite.

Pax finished off his bar, wiped his hand on his trousers, and leaned forward when it seemed like there was a small ripple in the ground in front of them.

Pax elbowed Wolf and started to say, "Did you see that . . ." when a sinkhole, about a meter in diameter opened up—or rather, flipped over.

"What the . . ." Pax said as he raised his Denon when shooting up as if from a catapult, a Tucanan scout flew out of the ground. And like an action holovid out of Bollywood, the thing fired two Mini-Buzzers, one in each second section foot-arm, the rounds aimed right into their OP.

Pax didn't expect to have to aim up, and his rounds chased the thing in the air. The scout's fire was on point, the rounds tearing into the camouflage. There was a grunt beside him, and Wolf collapsed.

---

1. **AOR**: Area of Responsibility

But pedes couldn't fly, and as it started to fall back, Pax's rounds caught up with it, stitching the body on the way down. And at six or seven meters away, his darts had no problem with the scout's armor. Three sections were hit, and the Tuc landed heavily, then bounced to its side where the foot-arms of the remaining sections struggled to right itself.

Pax knocked aside the camouflage fronds and peppered the remaining sections of the spasming enemy, dispatching the thing. He fired on instinct. His mind was still in shock from what he'd seen.

A Tuc, shooting out of the ground like an ICBM? It just wasn't . . . it never . . .

Liquid was dripping down his face, and he automatically wiped at it with his left hand while he kept his weapon trained on the mortally wounded pede.

"You OK? Wolf?"

He glanced at his hand. It was covered in blood. For a moment he thought it was his, but then he saw Wolf. The Marine was slumped inside the hole. Pax tried to push him upright, but that revealed a gaping hole through his upper chest, his armor cleanly cut.

The close range hadn't only helped Pax.

"Shit!"

He keyed his comms and started to say, "This is OP 3. We've just been—" when a barrage of fire erupted behind him, back toward the camp.

"Morgan this is OP 3. What's going on back there?"

There was no answer, but the volume of fire increased.

"Shit, shit, shit," he said as he jumped out of the hole, then dragged Wolf out as well.

The corporal was gone, that was evident. Pax fumbled for Wolf's injector, dropping it back in the hole in his haste. He stuck his head inside and reached, feeling extremely vulnerable, but he managed to grasp it among the dead scavengers.

Calm down. By the numbers, Pax.

He popped the cap, charged the injector, and placed the tip at the top of Wolf's throat. Once in place, he triggered the zombie juice.

Wolf's head jerked under the pressure of the shot.

"Good xerox," he muttered as he laid Wolf out on his back.

"Morgan, this is OP 3. I have a scout at my pos. Wolf is KIA."

His comms remained maddeningly silent.

The pede scout was just about gone. He could administer the coup de grâce, but he had other priorities.

There was a full-fledged battle going on back at the camp. He knew then that this scout was just a side action. And if the Tucanans had managed to tunnel into the camp before emerging like demons from the Underworld, then . . .

He didn't want to think about that. But he knew where he needed to be.

"I'll come back for you, Wolf," he said before keying his comms.

"This is Alejo. I'm coming in from OP 3."

He hadn't expected an answer, but he didn't want to fall to friendly fire, either. That wasn't going to stop him, though.

He broke into a run, dodging through the trees as he tried to reach the platoon. Branches and fronds slapped at him, swiping away some of Wolf's blood, but also sliming him. He didn't care. His mind was on the fighting ahead as he tried to make sense of what he was hearing.

That inattention was almost his doom. He saw the scout a split second after it spotted him, Pax dove for the ground as the rounds whizzed past his head.

He slid to a stop behind the trunk of one of the purple trees. Slamming into the ground had knocked his breath out, and he struggled to breathe again without gasping. Pedes, especially scouts, had excellent hearing this close in, better than humans'.

He tried to listen, too. But there was no click-click-click of segmented joints.

I've got to spot it.

He had started to edge his head around the base of the tree when two rounds slammed into it, centimeters from his face.

Fuck!

His heart was racing, adding to his breathlessness. He looked around him. This was a fairly flat section of ground. Flat and almost muddy, like where they'd killed the dragonfly. But it wasn't completely level. It dropped down a little where there was a glacially slow drainage, the water barely moving. He followed it with his eyes. If he could get to that, then maybe he could low-crawl to the right far enough to be in defilade to the scout. Then, if everything went right, he might be able to flank the Tucanan and surprise it.

He listened again for any sound of movement. If that had been a soldier, it would have charged him by now. They were not patient fighters. A scout?

Pax really didn't know. Scouts could defend themselves, just as some had done during the ambush on Hale's Refuge, but as far as he knew, they were never offensive troops. The scout that had burst from underground, though, had definitely been in attack mode.

He may not know what this scout was doing, but he did know

he couldn't just hunker down behind a purple tree. Already, the volume of fire from the camp was dying down. He didn't know what that meant, and he was afraid to try and figure it out.

Pax shifted to his belly, and with his Denon aimed forward, he started slowly pushing himself backward keeping the large trunk between him and the scout. The mud helped, greasing the path. Within a minute, he was in the creek, and he'd seen no sign of the Tuc.

Much of the native land smelled bad to humans. The fetid creek was worse. Bits of chitin analog of different creatures were in the water and mud, and every movement seemed to raise a cloud of putrid gas that hung around him. He kept his head mostly submerged, lifting his nose and mouth only to breathe.

As long as it kept him out of the sights of the scout, though, he'd bathe in it, if that's what it took. After about fifteen meters, he risked raising his head. There was barely any deviation in the topography, but being partially submerged helped. He couldn't see the spot where the scout had been. And a little farther on was a raised mound, the kind that existed in the swamps on San Marcos —little islands of solid ground among the mud.

That was his target. If he was right, he could use that to keep most of his body in defilade while shooting slightly down at the Tuc fighter. It wasn't perfect, but it was the best he could come up with.

And if he didn't have a shot? Well, he'd deal with that then.

Behind him, toward the platoon, there was a distant volley of exchanged fire, Marine Denons and Tucanan Buzzers, then silence. He didn't know what that meant, but worrying about it was out of the question. He had to concentrate on what was happening in this small section of Volante jungle.

He stopped his progress every few meters to listen, then pushed forward.

Stop, push. Stop, push.

Finally, he was at the base of the mound. Lying behind it, the mound wasn't as significant as he thought, maybe fifty centimeters high. And it was at least three meters long, with a dense patch of pinkish vegetation that looked like human fingers trying to claw their way out of Hades.

Here goes nothing.

He pulled himself up to the front part of the mound, easing his body out of the water. The fingers were semi-mobile, and they swayed out of his way the best they could. Pax crushed those directly in his path, pink fluid dripping down and running into the water. Once he had his whole body on the dryish ground, he could see his plan wasn't going to work. The crest, if you could call it that, was not high enough to give him any cover. The top of his head and body would be visible to the scout, if it was still in the same spot, before Pax could get far enough to engage his weapon. He'd have to either get to his knees to fire or just push forward and target the scout fast enough while avoiding being engaged himself.

His mind suddenly flashed back to NCO School, just before he was sent to the LoH Marines. Master Sergeant Tennessee Almaty, a small, petite SNCO with a chest full of fruit salad that would put a four-star general to shame, was teaching a class. He didn't remember the class, but he remembered a phrase she'd said one lazy afternoon after chow where most of the class was fighting to keep their eyes open.

"Any action is better than no action. Don't be frozen for fear of making the wrong decision."

Pax had no idea why that popped into his head.

Maybe it's an omen.

He gripped his Denon tightly and pushed his right knee up along his side. And without consciously making a decision, he used that leg to thrust himself upright, while he screamed his battle cry and sprayed the scout's position.

The scout was not where he'd last seen it, though. It was on the opposite side of the same mound he was on, not two meters away.

Pax didn't know who was more surprised. It took him a moment to adjust his aim, bringing the burst down and across the pede's body length.

The scout reacted as well by lifting the muzzle of its Buzzer, and firing just as the first of Pax's rounds started stitching it.

The cutting round hit Pax low in the belly with the force of a sledgehammer. He staggered, but through pure force of will, he kept firing, even as the world closed in on him until there was no more.

PAX DIDN'T KNOW how long he'd been out. A minute? Two? Ten?

The pede!

With a groan, he tried to sit up, but his body screamed in protest. He managed to twist his head, afraid of what he'd see. But the Tucanan scout was not standing over him, ready to administer their version of the coup de grâce. He couldn't see the whole thing, but at least the third section was cracked open, yellow fluid running out.

He couldn't see damage to the second section from his vantage, but only one foot-arm was moving, and just barely at that. It might be still alive, but it looked like it was in worse shape than he was.

Or was it?

His gut was both on fire and numb, if that was possible. With effort, he tilted his head down, and then wished he hadn't.

At this range, the round had torn through his body armor like tissue paper, and the damage was extensive. Half of his lower belly was missing, and bloody sections of his intestines had slipped through the destroyed armor.

He'd been in shock before, but the sight hit him in a stronger wave, and nausea overcame him. He felt like he had to vomit, but his body wasn't cooperating.

"I've got to get help."

He raised his right hand, surprised that it was untouched and functional, and touched his throat.

"Platoon, this is Alejo."

Silence.

"This is Pax. I need help."

Silence.

And suddenly the effort to try and contact them seemed too much. He let the arm fall back.

Pax had been in battle. He'd seen belly wounds like this. Get him back to a hospital, and the docs and autodocs could work wonders. But he was out here in the middle of nowhere, and the platoon might have been overrun.

The thought brought tears to his eyes, and for a moment, he welcomed joining them.

I've got no family to care. I should just go for real.

One thought gave him a perverse sense of satisfaction.

At least Greg won't get another death payment for me.

The thought made him laugh, which caused him to cough up

blood. He was filthy, covered in mud, slime, and rancid water, but somehow, the bright red blood made him angry.

And anger was a shot of determination.

I do have family. The Immortals.

Even if the platoon had been overrun, the company would come. The Tucanans didn't abuse the dead. Whoever had been killed would be where they fell. Even if they hadn't been injected with zombie juice, if the company got there soon enough, they could be xeroxed.

Him? They'd have to know he was out there and find him. The OP's position had been reported to the company, so he hoped Wolf would be recovered. And Wolf had been jabbed.

He'll make it.

As far as himself? Probably not.

Here's where I needed that autoinjector.

He'd known it was needed, and he'd had a perverse sense of pride that even if they'd be too late to save him, they might save some of his fellow Marines someday.

That's a good legacy.

He was drifting. Shock and blood loss were taking a toll. For a moment, he thought he had to finish off the scout, but he couldn't get up. And that was all right.

Something tried to make itself known, but the fuzziness was too strong.

Then, with an almost physical blow, he remembered his talk with the gunny about injecting oneself.

"No, that will kill the myc," he scolded himself.

"What have I got to lose?" he answered back.

"You can . . ." but it was too hard to come back with something.

And that seemed like the argument was won.

He couldn't sit up, but his arm was working fine. He reached his right cargo pocket, but the closure was too strong. He kept worrying at it, though.

There was no sense of urgency. The argument had been won, so it had to be done. That's all.

Somehow, the closure opened, and somehow, he managed to pull out the injector. Getting the cap off one-handed was difficult—he never considered bringing his left arm around his chest to help. He kept trying until he realized it was off.

There. Done.

But somewhere from deep inside, part of him screamed, "No! You're not done! You need to inject yourself."

Pax just wanted to go to sleep, but the voice kept yammering away. And more to just shut it up, he twisted the safety, arming it.

There was one more thing, he knew. But he was exhausted. At the urging of his inner voice, however, he raised the injector and brought it to his temple instead of his throat.

He was at the end, he knew. Real death was beckoning him, and he was curious to see what was next.

"You're Undead, not dead!" his inner voice screamed. "You can come back!"

Shit.

With one last effort, and as the tunnel of light opened up in front of him, he activated the injector.

An intense, excruciating explosion filled his skull, and Pax knew he'd made a mistake as his existence disappeared into the dark.

36

"He's coming around."

Pax dragged himself up from the comfortable embrace of the darkness. With extreme effort, he opened his eyes to the familiar lights of the rehab center, complete with the pale blue monitor at the foot of the bed.

Guess I made it.

"How are you doing, Sergeant Alejo?" the same voice asked.

"Still dead," he said automatically.

There was a shuffle of movement, and the voice said, "That's one of their pet phrases. And that's a good sign as to memory recovery."

Pax tilted his chin to his chest, and to his surprise, there were eight people in lab coats and one in scrubs, all staring at him.

"What's . . . what's going on?" he croaked.

They ignored his question, and a tall, skinny, older man stepped up and shined a light into his eyes while peering, as if he could see into Pax's brain and spot the mycelium.

Pax never knew why every doctor did that, even for a twisted ankle. It must be some weird doctor-thing.

The doctor snapped off the light and turned to the others. "As you've been briefed, the problem with Sergeant Alejo is that he injected his stasis gel while he was still alive, so his mycelium hadn't reverted to capsulation, and the shock was enough to create cell death. To compound that, for some unknown reason, the sergeant injected the gel directly into the squamous temporal instead of his throat. The injector compensated for the skull with increased force, and that damaged the hippocampus and amygdala, as well as the mycelial body that had infiltrated it."

What the hell is he talking about?

"The initial diagnosis and prognosis indicated that a reanimation was contraindicated . . ."

What?

". . . but as project head, I realized that this was a unique opportunity. The sergeant here is our own Henry Molaison, giving us an opportunity to study not only the ability of an uncapsulated mycelium to recover from trauma but how the mycelium regionalizes its data storing process within the hippocampus."

"Ah, Henry Molaison," one of the younger doctors said in a knowing tone. "The historical epilepsy patient whose temporal lobectomy resulted in him not being able to form new memories."

Some of the other doctors rolled their eyes, and the head doc just stared at the one who'd interrupted him for a moment.

Pax didn't care about some other patient, historical or not. But the doctor had used the term "contraindicated," and that was not a good term. Pax was suddenly worried, and he took the pause to jump in.

"Sir, what's this about my reanimation being contraindicated?"

For the first time since asking how he was, the doctor seemed to notice that there was a living—well, undead—breathing person in the hospital bed.

He placed a hand on the sheet over Pax's foot. "You are a very lucky person, Sergeant. Your injuries, done by your own hand, placed you outside of the program parameters. But I realized that your unique circumstances created a wonderful learning opportunity as we move to ramping the program up, and as the project head, I made an exception and approved your reanimation."

He turned to face the others and said, "The initial tests show significant mycelial integration with the original implant, and there is increased activity in the hippocampus. Now that the sergeant's been brought out of his coma, we'll be able to see how much of his memories have been recovered. This is the key, given that the initial hyphae located in the sergeant's hippocampus were among those that died."

"Do we have any indication that the secondary implant has recovered his episodic memories?" one of the others asked.

"That's what we'll be finding out over the next few weeks, and over a longer period, whether the tagging process is also affected. Remember, though, while we do have a baseline on the sergeant's cognitive abilities, there is also the reanimation degradation to contend with, so we'll try and determine any decline in the sergeant's abilities is from this specific incident or the normal reanimation degradation."

Pax just lay there in the bed, trying to make sense of what he was hearing. He was confused, and he wasn't sure that was just the effects of coming out of a coma. Something was going on here that he just couldn't grasp.

The doctor turned back to Pax. "Sergeant, do you know why you're here?"

"I was killed. Now I've been xeroxed."

The doctor gave another smile. "That's what they call getting reanimated."

"As in the Xerox Effect?" one of the others asked.

"That or just being copied, I imagine. The effect itself is named for one of the first machine methods of copying documents, after all, invented back in the Twentieth Century."

He glanced at a machine beside the bed, and for the first time, Pax realized that there were sensors attached to his head.

"Do you remember how you were killed?"

"Uh . . . yeah. I was with the Boracay militia, and we . . . no, wait. That was before. I, uh . . . I'm sorry. My mind's a little fuzzy right now. Let me wake up all the way, and it'll come back to me."

He felt embarrassed, like a schoolboy unable to answer the teacher's question on the previous night's homework.

The doctor pointed to the display on the machine, and the other lab-coated people crowded around.

"You can see that the hippocampus is firing almost normally. That's to be expected, given that the concussive damage was within workable parameters. The question is twofold. One, are the episodic memories stored within the hyphae located within the hippocampus? And two, if they are not, will the introduction of his second implant recover enough from his initial mycelium to then be reintroduced into the hippocampus. Or to be tagged and moved to the prefrontal cortex as eidetic memory, for that matter."

Pax started to ask, "Can someone please explain—"

But the doctor said, "Exciting times, exciting times. When

we're finally able to publish what we've accomplished here, it's going to make some people's brains explode."

"No problem that a little mycelium can't fix," one of the women said to the laughter of the rest.

"And I'll deny saying this to my dying days, but if a certain G. D. Namusa at Raynor Research is left out in the cold with his line of research, well, happy days. Now, we'll let the sergeant rest up for a couple of hours before we start the testing. I'll have Doctor Jain compile the initial results and get them out to you. I'd like a meeting to discuss them, say, Friday? Two PM? Does that work for everyone?"

There were some vigorous nods, and the doctor said, "Let's get back to work, then."

No one spoke to Pax as all of the lab coats filed out. The guy in the scrubs stepped up to the machine and made some inputs.

"Can I ask you what's going on?"

"Yeah, it's all probably confusing with all that medical speak. But you rest up. I'll be back in a few hours to start some testing, and I'll try to answer your questions then."

"But the doctor said they weren't going to reanimate me? Is that true?"

The tech shrugged. "Probably. Your brain was pretty messed up. Why'd you do that, anyway? Injecting your brain before your myc capsulated?"

"I . . . I don't remember doing that."

He vaguely remembered talking to the gunny about injecting oneself if they knew they were going to die, but nothing about actually doing so.

"Well, maybe those memories will come back. Doctor Miller seems to think they will, at least"

"Miller? Is that the guy who was doing all the talking?"

"The one and only, God's gift to the medical profession."

He didn't sound sincere, and the tech looked around suddenly, as if he were afraid of being overheard. "OK, you rest up now. There's water on the nightstand if you're thirsty, and you can page a nurse if you need anything. I'll be back in a few hours, and we'll do your initial post-reanimation levels, then add some additional memory tests Dr. Miller wants done.

"Any questions?"

About a million.

But all he asked was, "Is Kelli here?"

"Kelli Paramont? The physical therapist? Yeah, she's still on the staff."

"Can you ask if she can see me?"

"You're still a week away from PT. You've got a lot of testing before that."

He must have seen Pax's expression because he softened and said, "But I'll see if she can stop by and say hi. Now you get some rest. My tests are going to take a while."

"What's your name?" Pax asked as the tech started to leave.

"Korian. Korian Tyne. And we're going to be spending a lot of time together," he said before stepping out.

Pax leaned his head back and stared at the ceiling as he tried to process everything. Last time he was in this bed or another just like it, he didn't understand anything that had happened to him. It should be easier now. He understood the program.

Or at least he thought he did.

The loss of memory on how he'd been killed again was worrying, but not as much as he'd have thought it would. Memory could be recovered. At least that is what he'd gleaned from what he'd heard.

But, he didn't like being a test case, a Guinea pig.

Not that he had any choice. With a loud sigh, he settled in to wait.

37

"Knock-knock?"

The door to his room cracked open, and a welcomed Olivia stuck in her head.

"Still dead?" she asked.

"Still dead."

She slipped inside the room and closed the door behind her.

"You're still not cleared for visitors, but I was checking on Wolf and heard one of the techs say you were awake. Are you up for a visitor?"

"Damn right, I am. You were here to see Wolf? What happened? How is he?"

"He was KIA, with you, at the OP. But he's going strong on his xerox. Already in rehab. It's only his second, you know. Like you."

That he was with Wolf on an OP was news to him.

Olivia approached and sat at the foot of his bed. "I know you're still dead, but how are you doing? For real, I mean."

For a moment, Pax was going to give her the rote assurance

that he was fine and not burden her, but seeing Liv there raised the realization that he needed to share what he was feeling.

"I don't know, Liv. A bunch of docs were in here an hour ago, and they were in crazyland. Said I wasn't going to get xeroxed at first because my myc and even my brain were so messed up."

Her eyes got huge, and she asked, "What are you talking about?"

"They were going to keep me dead. Like Nani."

"Holy shit, Pax," she said breathlessly. "Why? Your gut was gone, but that's about all."

"They said I injected myself, and I guess I blew out my brains or something. Killed my myc, too."

"We figured you'd done that after we found you. But you're here, so whether you did it or someone else did it doesn't matter, right?"

"Well, I'm kinda fuzzy on what happened, to be honest. I don't remember much. From what Doctor Miller told the others, that's got to do with most of my myc dying and then me messing up my hippocampus."

She paused a moment, and Pax could see the gears turning.

"You had an injection mark up here," she said, pointing to the side of her skull. "That fucked up your hippopotamus?"

Despite himself, Pax had to smile. Olivia was Olivia.

"That's what he said. Too much with the zombie juice."

"Hell, then maybe Bozo saved your life twice."

It took a moment for that to register.

"What did you just say?"

"Bozo. He might have saved your life."

"Bozo? Lance Corporal type? Hasting Lymon?"

He wondered if his brain had been damaged so much that he was hallucinating.

"Well, yeah. After the battle, the lieutenant sent me, Panda, and him out to your OP. We found Wolf, and Panda humped him back. But you weren't anywhere. And we aren't Ghost Marines. We couldn't track you.

"I swear, Pax, we looked. Into the night. The lieutenant sent out more people to look for you, but then the platoon got recalled in the morning. And with Wolf being zombied, well, you had to have been the one to do that, which meant you were alone when you left him."

"And no one thought I'd inject myself, so the clock was ticking."

"Gunny said you might, but no one knew. Anyway, we had to get back, but Bozo, he wanted to go into that marshy area. I wanted to check the direct route again, thinking we might have missed something, so he insisted. And there you were with a dead pede."

I wasn't with Wolf? And a marsh? Why don't I remember that?

"I can't believe it, and I'm grateful, but what was the second time?"

"Well, when we found you, that was almost fourteen hours after the fight."

And beyond the time limit to get the zombie juice.

"But, you know, what was the harm? Might as well give it a shot. So I tried to get out your injector, but we couldn't find it. I took mine out—"

"You're not supposed to do that," Pax said. "Then what happens if you need it?"

Olivia blushed, coughed, then, in a quiet voice, said, "We were getting extracted. I figured I wouldn't need it." She gathered herself. "Anyway, I was about to give you the juice when Bozo stopped me. When we moved you so I could do the injection, he found the depleted injector under your arm, then he pointed to what we'd thought was the wound on your head. He was the one that figured you'd done it yourself, just like the gunny said you might."

She swallowed. "If you got too much zombie juice, and that almost did you in, then with another, you'd have OD'd. I might have killed you if it weren't for Bozo," she said, her voice cracking at the end.

Pax didn't know if it worked like that. From what the doc said, it had been more of the force of the injection. And the location. But he didn't know. If him knocking out most of his myc had stopped the encapsulation, then maybe another shot would have finished it off.

He motioned her closer, and she scooted over.

Taking her hand, he said, "Both of you saved my life. Otherwise, I'd be still on . . . where were we?"

"Volante. You really don't remember that?"

"I'd still be on Volante, rotting away."

"You really think so?"

"I do."

He didn't remember much, but that was obvious.

"So, what were we doing on Volante, anyway?" he asked.

"Acting as bait. There'd been some attacks, and the overlords thought we'd be good bait. Bait that can turn the tables and catch the fish when they came nibbling."

Pax didn't remember that, but it seemed right. He wasn't surprised at the news, at least.

"And what happened? I assume it worked."

"Nothing happened for three weeks, and everyone thought it was a bust. But then you, Wolf, Taufua, and Panda—"

"Who's Taufua?"

A look of concern crossed her face, and she said, "A new guy. I got . . . I was indisposed, and he took my place for the patrol."

"FNG," Pax muttered.

"Yeah. Well, the FNG got wasted. But you didn't know by what."

Pax raised his eyebrows in disbelief. "One of my Marines got killed, and I don't know how? I doubt that. And how is this Taufua?"

"Just hold on. And Taufua's in the next room. He's gonna be OK. But the thing is, we were told to keep acting like bait. The L-T, she wasn't going to just sit there, so she put out OPs."

Pax nodded. That was smart thinking.

"Now, I told you I was indisposed, so I'm talking to Doc, and he thinks that my—"

"Liv! I just came out of my coma. Can you get to the point?"

She flushed again. "OK, OK. We were in the camp when we heard your OP get hit. That gave us just enough time to get our heads on straight when the pedes, they came bursting out of the ground—"

"What? They were under the ground?" he asked in astonishment.

"Yeah. From under the ground."

Pax held up a hand to stop her for a moment as his brain grasped at something.

An image. Something bursting from the ground like a demon. A pede. Not a soldier.

He tried to concentrate.

"Were they scouts?" he tentatively asked.

"Yeah, scouts. Almost took us by surprise. We were just ready enough, and we got some as they were coming out. The rest, well, it got to be hand to foot-arm. If not for the attack on your OP, well, it would have been a lot worse."

"How bad was it?" Pax asked, dreading the answer.

"For us? For Second Platoon? We had six KIA and seven WIA."

"Who?"

"Byeon, Bartok, Fridge, Josiah, Wommack, and Tonya."

"And? What's their condition?"

"All in reanimation."

"Thank God," Pax said. "But you just said 'Second Platoon.' Were there other platoons with us?"

"First and Third. And Third got hit at the same time as us, but they didn't have a warning."

Pax grimaced. "How bad?"

"Overrun," she said, her voice barely audible.

"And . . . ?"

"That's why we weren't extracted right away. First had to get to Third and clean up."

Pax knew that meant saving as many as possible, and they couldn't very well be injecting throats with the locals there to see.

"What was the damage?"

"Four were still alive. The rest were zombied. Most are in the process now."

"Most?"

"Two were shut down, like Nani. And then there was the captain. KIA."

"Are they going to—"

Olivia shook her head. "He's an officer. Not eligible."

Two more Immortals gone for good. And add in Captain Kjellberg? This was all a gutshot, and Pax suddenly felt tired. He needed to find out about the operation he'd just been on, and hopefully that would jar his memory. But not at the moment. He was emotionally drained.

He wasn't sure what else to say, and from the look on her face, neither did Liv. She sat beside him in silence, her face turned to the floor past the foot of the bed.

"Liv, I'm exhausted," Pax finally said. "I'm glad you came. Really, I am. But can you leave for now?"

"Are you sure? I can just sit over there in the chair and keep you company."

"I'm sure. Maybe tomorrow?"

"Well, OK. We've got field training, but I can come over in the evening. Is that OK?"

"That's fine."

She slid off the bed and stood over him for a long moment, worry evident in her eyes.

"Thanks for coming, Liv. I appreciate it. See you tomorrow," he said with forced cheerfulness.

She nodded, turned, and left.

As the door closed behind her, tears started rolling down Pax's cheeks.

38

"How does it look?" Pax asked.

Korian studied the numbers for a moment, his head tilting back and forth as if that would help.

"I'm not one of the docs. They'll study these before they decide what's happening."

"But you've been doing this for a while. Can't you tell?"

Korian glanced at the door. Pax didn't know what the working conditions were for the civilians. He'd never even considered it. But the tech always seemed to be wary of being overheard.

"Well, and I'm stressing that I just give the tests, but I think your mycs are integrating. Your numbers are slightly up, and I can see growth as the mycelia is already spreading. Then there's you telling me earlier that you remember a recent E-club with good chow."

That E-Club could have been anywhere, years ago, but he didn't correct the tech. Then he caught onto the "s" in "mycs."

"Isn't mycelium singular? I mean, there's a lot to them, I know. A lot to it."

"To be honest, I don't know," Korian said with a laugh. "I just work here. But you've had two separate myc implants. The first time that's happened that I know of."

"Two. I'm a little confused."

"Doctor Miller explained it when you came out of your coma."

"He said a lot of stuff, but most of it went over my head."

Korian frowned. "I'm sure he explained it."

"I swear, I don't know anything about two mycs. Can't you just tell me?"

The tech looked at the open door again.

"I mean, it concerns me. Is there something the docs think I shouldn't know?"

"Well . . . I guess not."

"So?"

Korian hesitated, then began. "That's what makes you a test case. You're the first person who got two implants."

"But why?"

"When you blew up your first myc, what little survived was in bad shape. Call it shock. Fungus shock. And it wasn't responding to protocols. It wasn't really dead, as I understand it, but it was, like, in cold storage. Nothing was happening. With your hippocampus in such bad shape, that's why the decision was made to drop you from the project."

Kill me, you mean.

"But then Doctor Miller decided to play God." He spun around to see the door. No one was hovering there. Korian walked around Pax's bed so that he could watch the door while he spoke.

"He thought that with a new myc, it might integrate with the old and absorb your memories by proxy, as it were. The big thing he wanted to see was with the myc in your hippocampus destroyed, would your serial memories—that's your most recent memories that haven't transferred to your frontal cortex yet—be recovered. Those guys are always arguing about how the mycelium works, and whether it works like a human brain with different sections doing different parts is a big bone of contention. If you regain your serial memories, and if your hippocampus had been wiped out, then those memories had to have been stored elsewhere in your myc."

"And did it?"

"As much as I hate to admit it, I think Doctor Miller is right." He saw Pax's raised eyebrows, and he hastily corrected, "Not for you. For you it's a good thing. I mean, it's just . . ."

"And so now I've got two mycs. Are they both storing my DNA?"

"DNA? No, the data sharing, the memory is stored in the RNA," he said, as if correcting a child who just called a lion a puppy. "And you don't really have two. One is a lattice."

"I'm confused."

Korian paused. "You know what sourdough bread is, right?"

"Yeah."

"And you know how it's made, with a mother saved and used to turn the new dough sour."

"Yeah, like yogurt. What's your point?"

"Think of your old myc like the mother. Only a small portion of it survived, and it was essentially inert. But another myc culture was cleansed and introduced to the first. From what I heard, Doctor Miller and the rest knew the first one would probably integrate into the second, using it as a lattice to grow in. The question was how much of *you* would it carry with it."

"And now?"

"Not much happened at first. You've been in a longer coma than most of you who came back from Volante so they could heal your hippocampus and amygdala. But with you conscious now, I can already see improvement, and it's only been two days.

"No one knows what the long-term effects are. You may lose a few of your reanimations, but it's better than the alternative, right?" he said with a chuckle.

"A few of my reanimations?"

"Probably not many. One or two before you reach the max degradation."

Pax just stared at the tech, trying to decipher what he meant. The words were clear, but what the heck was he trying to say?

"One or two?" he said stupidly.

"Yes. You probably get the full eight, if the computer models are correct. No one's reached that yet, of course, so we don't know exactly how many you should end up with."

He started feeling anxious, and he wasn't sure why.

Eight reanimations? What the hell is he talking about?

Then it hit him.

Oh. Eight animations. Nine lives. Ha-fucking-ha.

"That's about the fifth or sixth time I've heard that, and it wasn't funny the first time," he groused.

"What wasn't funny?"

He's keeping a straight face. Give him that.

"The whole nine lives thing, like a cat."

"A cat?"

"Yeah, a cat. Ha-ha."

"What the hell are you talking about, Pax?"

The tech seemed more confused than Pax had been, and that gave him a funny void in the pit of his stomach.

"The joke about us Immortals having nine lives."

Korian just stared at him for a long moment. Too long.

"It's, uh, not a joke, Pax. You know that."

"I don't know what you're talking about."

"Your incoming brief. When the program was explained to you?"

"There was nothing about nine lives there!" he said, a little too forcibly.

"There was. This is your memory problem." He thought about it for a moment, then said, "No, that was almost two years ago. That should all be in your eidetic memory by now, and your prefrontal cortex and the myc there were fine."

He stared at Pax again, his mouth starting to say something, then shutting.

"Korian, can you just tell me what's this about? Why do I only have nine lives?"

"Eight reanimations, and that's an estimate," he softly corrected before saying, "I need to get someone," as he started around his bed.

Pax lunged forward, his healing belly screaming in pain, and locked his hand around Korian's wrist, stopping him cold. The tech tried to pull away, but even in a hospital bed after having half of his gut blown away, Pax was a powerful individual.

Korian recoiled in fear until he saw the pleading look in Pax's eyes.

"Just tell me."

He slowly nodded, and Pax released the wrist.

"I don't know why you don't know. It's in the inbriefs. Maybe your eidetic memory was lost, too."

Pax knew that wasn't the case. It was true that he wouldn't remember something if his memory was wiped, but he *did* remember wondering why Marines referred to "nine lives" or noted how many times people were xeroxed.

He stared at Korian with a force that the tech couldn't avoid.

"The reanimation isn't perfect. There is some nerve and tissue degradation that adds up over time, like how bending metal over and over makes it weaker."

Pax wanted to say that from how he understood things, when a bone breaks, it heals stronger at that point, but he didn't want to interrupt the reluctant tech.

"But it isn't just the body. The data transfer, your memories and all that makes you *you*, isn't perfect. Each time, there is a little bit of a loss, call it biological lossy. It's barely noticeable for the first reanimation, but not only does it build up over time, the lossy increases for each procedure, and it's cumulative."

Pax tried to wrap his mind around what he'd just heard.

Korian must have taken his silence as confusion, because he said, "You guys called the procedure 'getting xeroxed.' Do you know why?"

"A Xerox was one of the first practical machines to make copies of documents, way back in the Twentieth Century," Pax said.

That was one of the things he remembered Dr. Miller saying. It was one of the few things he'd understood.

"Well, yeah, a Xerox is a machine. But it's how that machine worked that gave rise to what was called the 'Xerox Effect.' When a document was copied, the copy was not quite as good as the original. It was a tiny bit fuzzier and not as sharp. And if Copy 1 was then copied, then Copy 2 was not as sharp as 1, and so on. So, after ten copies, Copy 10 might be significantly degraded to the point that it might not even be usable."

The analogy was not lost on Pax.

"So, you're saying that each time we get reanimated, the new me is not quite the same as the previous me, and we lose what, our memories?"

"More than just that. The brain does a lot more than remember. The midbrain controls coordination and movement, so that suffers. Vision, hearing, and balance are controlled by the pons. The medulla controls the things that keep the body humming like heart rate, breathing and all of that. So, it's not just memory. Get reanimated too many times, then all of those functions suffer."

Pax was surprisingly calm about the revelations. Maybe that's because once Korian explained what was happening, Pax had to admit that the signs were there. He couldn't quite get the PFT scores he had before. Link forgot all about Tinkerbell. And then there were all the nine lives comments.

But that thought blew away his calmness, and anger took over.

"So, once we're not as good as we were, you kill us?"

"We're not killing you. The enemy is."

All the frustration of not being a legal entity, of being a simple weapon for the overlords to employ, of not being the captain of their own ship, and now, the knowledge that once their use was over, they'd die for real, came bursting up like lava through a volcanic vent.

"Bullshit. It's murder!" he shouted, springing to his feet. "Sergeant Alejo? His arbitrary score's too low. Pull the plug!"

Korian froze in place until the sympathetic expression that he'd had morphed into one of pure, unadulterated anger. He jumped up, shoved his chest into Pax's, and brought his face to within centimeters of his.

"SHUT THE HELL UP, you arrogant prima donna!" he shouted, spit flying from his mouth and hitting Pax.

Pax took a step back and almost reacted, which would have been to take the tech to the ground. But shock stayed his hand.

"Why don't you realize how lucky you assholes are? You get to come back? Who the hell in the history of humankind has had that opportunity?"

Pax's mouth gaped, but nothing came out.

"Don't you think we would like to have that insurance policy? All of us here isolated on this godforsaken planet, we're the ones developing the process. But can we be reanimated? When Doctor Sun got killed by the loader, did she get reanimated? Hell no. Because she wasn't special-fucking-ops, and the process is too expensive for a mere mortal, even one developing the damn program. And yet, here you are. You screwed up your myc, and what happens? You get a new one!"

The onslaught took Pax by surprise. The tech never made physical contact, but Pax felt like he'd just been beat up.

"I didn't . . . it wasn't my choice," he protested while the enraged tech took huge breaths, his eyes ready to pop out of his head.

"And they took away our rights. We're not even legally humans anymore!" he said, regaining a little of his verve.

"Too bad, so sad," Korian said with a sneer. "Boo-fucking-hoo. Yeah, your legal condition sucks. But it sure beats the alternative, right? It sure beats having your body rotting in the ground."

He stared at Pax, hate in his eyes.

"You whining, ungrateful pukes make me sick," he said before wheeling about and stalking out the door.

Pax just stared at him, his hands trembling. His rage had been a fire, about to consume everything in its path until Korian dumped an ocean on him. The range of emotions in such a short time was almost too much for him to take.

He sat back down, lightheaded.

"But we're not even people," he muttered, trying to justify what he'd said. "At least Korian's got rights."

But he wasn't even convincing himself. His thoughts were a mess as they tumbled around his brain. And for a moment, they latched onto Captain Kjellberg.

The officer was an Academy grad TU Marine before coming over. A Gold Beret. He'd been awarded a Navy Cross. If anyone was on the fast track to eventually pinning on stars someday, it was him. And he was equally as skilled and capable as any of the Immortals, if not more so.

But he wasn't eligible for reanimation? In what universe was this fair?

Not the one where one of their unseen and unknown overlords made the political decision that officers were not to be trusted as the Undead.

What made it even worse was that with the Undead being tasked with the most dangerous missions, the four officers were at the same elevated risk of death, but for them, it would be final.

He was still upset with Korian's attack. He'd never chosen to become Undead. Maybe he could have had more empathy with the staff, which, to be honest, he'd considered more as jailers than anything else.

How Korian's bottled-up resentment exploded was uncalled

for, in his opinion, and for a moment, Pax considered reporting what had just happened. But he realized that was just him being butthurt. There was some basis for that resentment—it just should be aimed at those at the top of the program, those that made the rules.

Pax crept back into his bed. He had a lot to think about. The easy part was coming to grips with the knowledge that there was a limit on how many times they could be reanimated. That flash of anger had been doused by Korian. He just had to add that to his considerations in future operations. Maybe not be as reckless.

Maybe not, he thought with a chuckle.

Even with only one life, before he'd been killed, he'd always pushed the envelope.

The real question was what he should do going forward. He terribly resented having his legal status of being a human being stripped away from him, and he resented having the unknown overlords controlling every aspect of his life . . . or death, as the case may be.

He resented calling them the overlords because he had no idea who they really were.

What he didn't resent was serving with his Marines. For someone who'd never had a family life worth a warm bucket of spit, the Marines had always been his family—first, with the SMMC, then with the LoH Marines, and now with the Undead. Olivia, Wolf, Panda, Link, and all the rest. They were the people he cared for. The people he loved.

But there was something else, something greater.

Right now, humanity faced an existential threat to its very existence. None of the masses had put Pax in this position. They were blameless as far as his situation. They weren't the overlords.

And then there was the fact that when Pax had raised his right hand to become a Marine, he'd sworn an oath to defend the people of San Marcos. And when he'd transitioned to the LoH Marines, the oath had been to all of humanity.

He could argue that his dying released him from that oath. Hell, he might actually win that argument in the courts, if non-humans could even make use of them.

But that wasn't him. Undead or not, his word was good.

It had taken him the last half hour as he ran everything through his mind to come around to it, but he was a Marine, and his purpose in life was to help humanity survive. If he was a little slower now with two reanimations, if his memory wasn't quite as good, then all that meant was that he was going to work all the harder to ensure he was the best Marine he could be. The best protector of his fellow humans.

He fluffed up his pillow and lay back, at peace with himself. If this was his life after death, he was good with it.

Besides, Korian wasn't wrong. It sure beat rotting in his grave back at Cape Town.

EPILOGUE

"Twenty-nine, thirty!" Kelli said. "Good job. Now let me check the numbers."

Pax stripped the sensors from around his upper arms and sat up. It had been a tough set, but he felt pretty good for a dead man.

Around him, the rehab center was a hub of activity. Almost two-thirds of those killed on Volante had already been returned to full duty, but with the influx of FNGs, the place was packed with Marines. If the current surge in creating the Undead continued, then they were going to have to expand the facilities.

"Looks like you're firing on all cylinders," Kelli said as she studied the readout.

"So . . . ?"

"You still need to keep up with your rehab, but I'm going to recommend a return to duty. Uh . . . how about the . . . ?" she asked, tapping the side of her head.

"Are you asking if my myc's got my brain working? Got the check yesterday."

The speed at which his old mycelium had taken over the new one's lattice had been nothing short of amazing, according to Doctor Miller. And with that, most of Pax's short-term memory had flooded back. He knew what had happened prior to and during Volante. There were still some gaps, and some things were a bit fuzzy.

Doctor Miller had told the other doctors and scientists—with Pax sitting there like a prize specimen—that some of that may never come back due to the inherent Xerox Effect, but Pax could live with that. There wasn't a giant, gaping hole in his memory.

"Great! I know you've been itching to get back. So, if you don't have any questions?"

Pax laughed. "I'm fine. Go to your flock."

With the influx of Undead, the staff was pushed to their limits. Kelli and the others had their hands full with multiple patients.

"Right. And congrats," she said before reaching into her bag and pulling out a purple-wrapped rectangle. She waved it back and forth teasingly.

"You're a godsend, Kelli," Pax said, snatching the GooeyBar and holding it to his nose. "I can't believe you got this for me."

Without someplace to shop or the money to buy anything, the Undead were limited the two vending machines in their barracks for a limited selection of snacks and drinks. Pax had mentioned to Kelli that he missed various childhood favorites, with GooeyBars topping the list. The clinic staff had money and a store, and to his surprise, she remembered the conversation and bought the candy for him.

"You deserve it, Pax," she said while patting his shoulder, then rushed off to where one of the FNGs was at the hand station doing finger dexterity exercises.

He watched her for a moment, then kissed the GooeyBar. He'd save it for later, when he could give Olivia a taste.

Well, we did it, Mike.

He knew his mycelium wasn't an actual being, but as his short-term memories started to return, he wanted to thank his myc for the gift. And if Rachel Josiah could treat her sniper rifle like a sentient being, then why couldn't he treat his myc as one? *Mike.*

Pax didn't immediately get off the bench. He stuffed the candy bar into the pocket in his issue exercise shorts, pulled out a small notebook, and activated it.

The screen had the date on the top: September 2. He removed the attached stylus and wrote, "Received my physical check. I'm ready to get back to the unit."

He contemplated writing more but decided that was good enough. He tapped the bottom to save the page, then tapped it three times to send it back into the diary, leaving a new blank screen at the front before he slipped it back in his pocket.

Going through a significant memory loss, and knowing that each time he was killed, he'd lose a little more of himself, he decided to keep a written diary of his thoughts. He didn't want to wake up and question his commitment to serve humanity again.

If he woke in confusion, maybe reading his own words would make a difference. It probably wasn't necessary right now, but after six, seven, or eight reanimations? He figured it was better to have it, to help him adjust.

Pax looked up and spotted Byeon watching him, so he stood and sauntered over to her.

"Still doing that diary thing, I see."

Pax nodded.

"I still don't know why you just don't make a recording. It'd be easier."

Pax shrugged. He didn't have an answer that he could articulate that made sense. It was just that having something he could hold in his hands somehow seemed more real. It was probably why there were still people who wanted a physical book to read instead of using their screens.

The idea of a diary hadn't even been his. It had been Korian's, of all people. It had been a very stiff and withdrawn tech who'd come in to see Pax the day after their blowup. Pax had taken the opportunity to apologize, and Korian had done the same. That broke the ice, and for the next half hour, instead of Korian testing his progress, the two had opened up with each other, laying their souls on the line.

Pax learned a lot about the politics and undercurrents of the program, and he hoped Korian began to understand what the Undead were going through.

And when Pax had expressed fear that if—when—he was killed again, he might forget his renewed commitment to humanity, it was Korian who'd recommended the diary. Not only that, but during the next session, he gave Pax the device, which he'd bought at the staff store.

Whether it was ever used or not, it gave Pax a sense of security. And peace.

"I've been thinking, though," Staff Sergeant Byeon continued. "Maybe I should start a diary, too. Can't hurt, right?"

"No, Staff Sergeant. It can't hurt."

She shifted the subject. "I saw you and Kelli on the bench. And after all the other tests. Well?"

"She's giving me an upcheck."

Byeon slapped him across the shoulders. "Way to go, Quad Bod. Back to the platoon."

"How about you?"

"Not yet," she said with a frown. "I'm still down in three tests. Hopefully, in two more days."

"You'll make it."

She sniffed, then said, "So what are you doing still hanging out here with the rest of us sick, lame, and lazy? Get on outta here!"

"I, uh . . . there's one more thing I hafta do. And I need this place to clear out, first."

She looked confused for a moment until it dawned on her, and she said, "Oh, you mean your . . . Look, Pax, the brain techs say you're good to go. The bod techs say you're good to go. You know what that means, right? You're frickin' good to go!"

"I know, but I want me to say I'm good to go."

She shook her head. "You're one crazy dude, Pax. The millisecond I get the go-ahead, I'm outta here. But you do you. And with that, I need to get back to the grind if I wanna pass in two days."

Byeon turned back to her rehab, and Pax inconspicuously wandered around, slipping into various stations as they became open. Slowly, the gym emptied out.

"You still here, Pax?" Kelli called across the gym as she and her last patient started to leave.

"You said I still had to do my exercises, so I thought I'd get one of the sessions out of the way now."

"That's the dedication I like to see. Just turn off the lights when you leave, OK?"

"Got it," Pax said, giving her a thumbs-up.

It was time.

Pax walked over to the track that circled the gym. His twenty pull-ups might have been slightly strained, but he'd never been in danger of not completing them, and he managed to get in four more. He wasn't really satisfied with his sit-up time, though. One minute and fifty-six seconds. He still maxed the score, but with only four seconds to spare.

More importantly in some ways, it was eight seconds longer than what he'd done after his first reanimation. That could be within normal variation, but it could also show how much he'd lost.

Now came the run, and he'd see if he was still a 300 PFTer.

Most people thought the historical PFT, the one the San Marcos Marines had reinstated, was not a valid test of combat fitness. And maybe they were right. But it was a link to the past, and more importantly, it was a base-level for Pax, one that he could do on his own no matter where he was.

He took a few minutes to stretch his legs, then stepped up to the track.

Well, Mike, here we go. Let's see how much you saved of me.

He hit his timer, then took off. Twenty-seven laps. Three miles. Eighteen minutes.

As his adrenaline surged, he started off like a jackrabbit for the first lap before he settled into the easy lope that thousands of kilometers of running over the years had ingrained into his muscle memory. He knew he was on a good clip.

Or he thought he was. Given the test numbers, he knew there had been some degradation.

Is that affecting how fast I think I'm going?

That gave him a little bit of a panic, and he increased his pace.

Maintaining his status as a 300 PFTer wasn't an ego thing. Well, maybe ego was involved. But that wasn't the main thing. Korian and the others had only given Pax generalities as to the degree of his losses, and when he overheard numbers, they didn't mean anything to him. He wasn't sure what the actual percentage loss was that would occur around his eighth reanimation that would trigger his no-more decision. But his PFT scores would let him keep some sort of tally. And if he was losing his capabilities, he wanted to know how much he was losing them before the program staff got their hands on him.

And knowing that, maybe—just maybe—he'd be able to figure out what to do to limit or slow down that march into his final go-round.

By lap four, he'd settled back into a . . . not comfortable pace, but one he thought he could keep up. He'd already switched to mouth-breathing. All of the real runners seemed to breathe through their noses. Pax tried, but that wasn't him. His mouth would drop open, and he'd be sucking in air like a vacuum cleaner.

By lap fourteen—halfway—his legs started to tire. That usually didn't happen until the two-mile mark. But tired legs weren't going to stop him. He knew how to power through.

His mind went blank as he let his pounding feet take over. He rounded each turn, then looked ahead down the length of the track, his eyes locked onto the start of the next turn on the other side of the track.

Ten more laps. Nine more laps. Eight more.

He could feel himself slow down, and that surge of panic sped him up for half a lap before his body told him he couldn't keep up the pace. He had to dig down and find motivation.

This is for you! he promised all of humanity. *I'm doing this for you.*

But the problem was, he didn't know humanity. He'd had some friends back on San Marcos, but there really wasn't anyone there who he was still in contact with. And among the trillions of humans alive, they were more of a concept than actual individuals.

But there were people he loved.

"Immortals!" he shouted. "I'm doing this for you!"

I've got to be able to fight for you. I need to be my best self to cover you. I need to be able to take on the pedes. I can't let any of you down!

Five laps. Four laps.

It was his responsibility to his fellow Marines, his fellow Undead Marines, that drove him. That pushed him past the pain.

Three laps. Two laps.

His legs were breaking down. His lungs were on fire. All he could do was focus on each turn, fooling himself by telling himself that was the last turn, that he could quit.

He knew he could slow down. Heck, he knew he could stop right there. It wouldn't affect anything. He'd be back with the platoon tonight no matter what. He could quit with no ramifications.

But that wasn't Paxton Alejo.

Link, help me. Wolf. Panda. Olivia. Captain Kjellberg!

And then he really was on the last half-lap. He forced his final gram of strength to keep his legs pounding. He gasped for air.

Ten meters. Five meters. And he was falling across the finish, landing hard on the track.

He wildly stopped the timer, then lay still, sucking in the air.

Finally, as he began to rejoin the human race, he slowly raised the timer to his eyes.

Seventeen minutes and eight seconds. Twenty-eight seconds

slower than last time, and more seconds lost than he'd hoped. But a full fifty-two seconds quicker than the eighteen minute minimum.

He broke out into weak laughter. He was still a 300 PFT'er. He received the max score.

"I'm still the toughest son of a bitch out here, you bastards!" he shouted at the overlords. "You can't shut me off yet. And I swear, I'm not going to make it easy for you. Nine lives? Hell, I'm talking about ninety lives!"

He knew that was probably an idle boast, but you can't succeed unless you try.

Pax stayed on his back for several minutes before he turned over and slowly got to his feet.

It was time to rejoin his platoon.

Amazon won't always tell you about the next release. To stay updated on this series, be sure to sign up for our spam-free email list at jnchaney.com.

Sergeant Paxton Alejo will return in Proof of Concept, available on Amazon.

Continue reading for SITUATIONAL AWARENESS, a short story in the Undead Marine universe…

A SHORT STORY IN THE UNDEAD MARINE SERIES

SITUATIONAL AWARENESS

"Do we just go in?"

Private Paxton Alejo looked at his fellow Marine, Private Len Nijima. "The door, uh, *hatch,* is closed. Maybe we should knock?"

Neither one of them knew what they were supposed to do. Six hours ago, they'd been standing tall at the School of Infantry graduation, proud that they were finally infantry Marines. After a magrail ride to Camp Maria Morales and reporting in to camp receiving, they'd been told to draw their gear and then report in to India Company, Second Battalion, Sixth Marines.

Through sixteen weeks of boot camp and another twenty-two of SOI, it had been drilled into their heads that Marines always completed their mission. And now, they were standing in the corridor, stymied by a closed door.

Len tentatively reached out and softly rapped on the doorsill.

There was no response.

With raised eyebrows, Len looked at Pax, who then scrunched

his face up as he made his decision. Pushing the door open, Pax spied a single corporal sitting behind a desk as he worked on a pad.

The office was Spartan, with three desks and two benches along the wall—*bulkhead*, Pax reminded himself. There were five more doors on the back bulkhead. The only art, if you could call it that, consisted of posters depicting first aid for heat-related casualties, a warning about drinking while driving, Mount Popocatépetl, the highest mountain on San Marcos, and of a Marine low-crawling through the mud with the caption, "I Love the Suck."

Pax marched over and centered himself in front of the corporal, who looked on with a bemused expression.

As soon as Len stepped alongside him, Pax shouted, "Private Paxton Alejo, reporting in as ordered, sir!"

"I'm not a 'sir.' I work for a living," he said, as he'd probably done a thousand times before.

Pax winced. He knew better. But boot camp habits were hard to break.

"And you are?" the corporal asked Len.

"Private Len Nijima, reporting as ordered, sir."

"What the hell did I just tell your buddy here?"

Before Len could answer, the corporal said, "I've got both of you here on the roster change sheet. I don't know where the skipper wants to assign you, and all the Os are down at battalion for some brief. Uh . . . I could send you to the armory for your weapons draw, but that's supposed to happen after you're assigned. Let's see. Why don't you go report in to the first sergeant? She's in that second office there."

Pax didn't know if he'd actually been dismissed. In boot, all DIs were explicit in what they wanted done. So, he did the recruit "rabbit," freezing in place at the position of attention.

"What the hell are you waiting for, Alejo. Go."

Pax broke the position and hurried over to the designated door where a brass plaque said, "First Sergeant E. L. Potts." Two San Marcos Marine emblems flanked either side of the name.

This hatch was closed as well, and both Pax and Len looked back at the corporal, who rolled his eyes and said, "Knock, then go in when she tells you to."

Pax nodded, then reached out and tapped on the sill.

"She has to hear you, Private!"

He rapped harder, and a voice called out, "Enter."

Pax led the way in, his eyes locked on the first sergeant, barely noticing a gunny and sergeant sitting there as well. She was nondescript and wouldn't look out of place waiting tables—if she didn't have a buzz cut and piercing, ice-blue eyes that looked like they never missed a detail.

"Who are you two?"

"Private Paxton Alejo and Private Len Nijima, reporting as ordered, ma'am," Pax stumbled out, knowing he wasn't supposed to address her as "ma'am," but unable to stop himself.

In both boot camp and infantry school, he'd never actually spoken with a first sergeant and had merely seen them as they lurked about the area.

"And Private Nijima doesn't speak for himself?"

"No, ma'am," Len squeaked.

She just raised a single eyebrow in question.

"I mean, yes, I speak."

The gunny bit back a chuckle.

"Good," the first sergeant said. "That helps in being a Marine."

She tilted her head back and seemingly asked the air, "Colbert, has the skipper decided where these two boots are going, yet?"

Pax recognized the voice of the corporal from the outer office, which seemingly came from empty air in front of him. "No, First Sergeant. Not yet."

He realized this was probably easy tech, but coming from his background with next to nothing beyond what he needed to keep alive, it was pretty cool.

"Well, then, I guess you two will just have to cool your jets until the skipper gets back. Chow goes in another twenty-five minutes, so head on over and come back after you eat. Any questions?"

Pax was excited to finally be in an actual unit, an infantry company to boot. Couple that with a sudden desire to impress the first sergeant with his enthusiasm, he opened his mouth and inserted his foot.

"When are we going to go kill some Tucs, First Sergeant, ma'am. I'm ready!"

Both the gunny and the sergeant broke out laughing, and the first sergeant opened her eyes wide in surprise.

"That's probably not going to happen," she said after a moment.

What?

Pax was confused. One of the reasons he'd joined was to escape his prior life. It was either the Marines, jail, or end up dead, just one more statistic of the Lago de Oro megaplex. But there was also the patriotism and sense of adventure with the Tucanan Incursion.

An alien race, technologically on par with humanity at best, more advanced at worst, had invaded human space and killed people. They'd taken several planets. What red-blooded person wouldn't want to defend humanity?

"Won't happen?" Len asked, sounding just as shocked as Pax was. "But we're at war with them."

The hostile aliens were the major topic of discussion among their fellow recruits at boot camp and fellow privates at the School of Infantry. He and Len, along with four more privates that were reporting in to different companies, had a long discussion about the Tucanans on the magrail to Camp Morales. All of them were eager to face the alien menace and do their duty.

"Just where do you think the pedes are?" the first sergeant asked, using the "pede" nickname favored by the military to describe the vaguely centipede-like aliens.

"Um . . . " Pax had to try and recall one of the planets the Tucanan's attacked. "Oh! Carruker's Hold."

"That's Carruther's Hold. Tell me, where is that?"

Pax exchanged glances with Len, but it was obvious he didn't know, either.

"It's a SagFed planet, and that means it's on the other side of the galaxy. A long, long way from here."

"But they attacked humankind," Pax protested.

The first sergeant patiently explained, "The SagFed Navy and Naval Infantry are engaged, and now the LoH's Navy and Marines will be taking over. That's why they were formed, after all. Right?"

Pax hadn't heard much about the new League of Humanity military until he arrived at boot camp. Somehow, a lot of what made it down to the Lago was filtered out by censors. That, or maybe Pax hadn't paid much attention to what didn't directly affect him. The fact that aliens had arrived was headliner enough. The workings of humanity's central organizing body, which had only grown in power since the Tucanans arrived, were far less interesting to the public.

But they'd received several briefs at boot camp, both on the League of Humanity as a whole and specifically on the LOH Navy and Marines. Militaries from throughout humanity were contributing to this combined force, and soon they'd be throwing the Tucanans back to where they came from. It was very probable that should the situation with the Tucanans continue, some of the recruits would be transferred to the LoH Marines before all was said and done.

But Pax wanted to fight the aliens now.

"Aren't we going to be part of that?" Pax asked. "That's why I enlisted."

"Unless you've got your own spaceship, you're here with us. The pedes might be probing the edges of human-held space, but there are a lot of bad actors right here, and they don't receive a get-out-of-jail pass just because the pedes are here."

"In fact, that's where our officers are now," the gunny said. "The natives are acting up."

Pax turned to the gunnery sergeant. Short, dark, and broad-shouldered, he exuded relaxed confidence.

"You could see action sooner than you think, Private. You might not be quite as eager then to face a determined enemy as you are now."

"Anything else?" the first sergeant asked.

She'd been patient with them, but Pax knew there was a limit to that. And he needed time to digest what he'd just been told.

"No, First Sergeant."

"In that case, you go—"

Situational Awareness

The office was suddenly filled with the buzzing of personal pads. The three Marines looked at their pads in unison.

A moment later, the gunny looked up from the message. "When I said sooner than you think, I didn't fucking mean now."

The first sergeant stood and shouted, "Colbert! Start the recall. I want every swinging dick in formation in ten minutes."

She started to the door, when Len asked, "What's happening?"

The first sergeant seemed to remember them.

"Shit. Uh . . ." she said before her eyes fell on the sergeant. "Danit, with Eagleton in the brig, you're short. They're yours until the skipper says different."

Pax looked at the sergeant. Average height, average looks, average everything. The sergeant didn't stand out in any obvious way. And he didn't look happy to be given two boot privates.

But a Marine didn't question orders. He motioned the two privates forward.

"What's going on, Sergeant?" Pax asked.

"We're going into battle; that's what's going on," he said. "So, right now, you stay on my ass but out of my way."

Sergeant Danit spun about and bolted off at a run. It took a moment for that to register before the two privates chased after the sergeant in a dead sprint.

Pax nervously gripped his SMM-8 magrifle—the "SM" designating that this was the San Marcos-licensed version of the ubiquitous Denon family of military rifles—his hands unconsciously squeezing and releasing the stock. He'd been gung ho in the first sergeant's office just nine hours ago, but that was to sally forth and meet the Tucanan threat head-on.

Whether it was the fact that they might be facing humans or just the realization that they were going into harm's way was something he didn't know. He was still excited but with a fair amount of trepidation. As an SOI graduate, he was technically an infantry Marine, but he knew he was sadly lacking in experience and knowledge. He'd done exactly zero training with his new squad, and he had no idea what he was supposed to do.

Even his weapon wasn't ready for combat. All magrifles were tuned to the individual Marine. There'd been no time for him or Len to have that done. Their weapons would fire, but their capabilities and effectiveness would be drastically diminished.

The two privates' presence was probably why Third Squad had the reserve assignment. More than that, they'd both been told to stay back if there was contact. Stay back and out of the way.

At the moment, that sounded fine with Pax. Fear was a powerful motivating factor.

He wasn't afraid of dying. Well, not completely. Dying was part of life, whether that was in the Lago or as a Marine. He could accept that fear.

But what he was really afraid of was screwing up and letting his fellow Marines down. Except for Len, he barely knew any of them. Half of them hadn't even acknowledged his and Len's presence. As the FNGs—the Fucking New Guys—no one wanted to get close to them only to have them killed on their first mission. But even without knowing the other Marines, Pax felt a responsibility toward them, and he was afraid that his lack of experience could get one of them killed.

And that's why he was more than willing to hang back where

he couldn't screw up. Especially since they'd be facing Rohr and Fasheed Security.

R & F, as it was known, was registered on Acoron 3 as a private security corporation, but it was common knowledge that they were nothing more than a mercenary force. Made up almost exclusively of various ex-special-forces units, their reputation exceeded that of many of the top forces like the Royal Charter SAS, Hangul Black Berets, or Terran Union Navy SEALs.

Pax hadn't enlisted to fight humans, particularly the R & F, but when they came in and took over the New Horizon seat of government, the San Marcos Parliament decided to honor their treaty and send in the Marines to return the capital to the New Horizon citizens.

Pax wasn't particularly well educated, but he wasn't naïve. The decision to make the crossing to New Horizon wasn't strictly because of treaties. New Horizon was a sparsely populated organics factory, a huge agricultural planet where a mild climate and chemically enhanced soils produced a significant portion of the raw materials that fed this region of human space. And with ninety percent of that processed on nearby San Marcos for further distribution, not only to the factories needed to create food for the billions there but also to the food factories on various planets, the relationship between the two planets was tight.

The government of New Horizon controlled all exports of the organics, so when Golden Harvest was turned down after they requested to ship to other processing destinations, they hired R & F "for security purposes," then took over the capital and installed a new Board of Directors.

The old board, now in hiding, requested that San Marcos

honor their defense treaty, and the Parliament, anxious to protect their golden goose exclusivity, agreed.

The mission might be justified to support an ally, but all of the Marines knew that it was at least to a degree self-serving to protect San Marcos's largest industry. And now, Pax was off San Marcos for the first time and descending on a foreign planet. He'd be stepping foot on alien—sort of—soil.

"You boots still with me?" Sergeant Danit asked over the P2P, or person-to-person, circuit.

Pax turned to look down the line of seated Marines and gave the sergeant a thumbs-up while Len answered, "Yes, Sergeant."

"We'll be touching down in about fifteen minutes. You two just hang back and follow in trace of the squad. Nothing to it."

I get it, Sergeant. I get it.

This was only the tenth time or so that the sergeant had told them that. Pax was pretty sure it had sunk in.

But maybe the sergeant had reason to keep repeating it because Len said, "I'm ready, Sergeant," as he patted the M-52 Bushmaster that was in his lap. "If those R & F assholes want a fight, I'll give it to them."

"Damn it, Nijima, you're just humping the Bushmaster. Do not engage. You'll just shoot the hell out of your own squad," Sergeant Danit hit back.

"I won't."

Pax didn't know if Len meant he wouldn't fire or he wouldn't hit another Marine.

"Do not fucking fire that thing. You're just humping it until someone else needs it," the sergeant said.

"Got it, Sergeant."

Len turned to Pax and said something to him, but he failed to connect the P2P, and with his helmet sealed, Pax couldn't hear a thing.

Someone else must have because Len suddenly stopped speaking, and his eyes got large with panic. Pax could lip-read a "Sorry, Sergeant."

You dipshit, Len. Make sure you've got the right person on the net.

But his fellow private's mention of R & F reminded him of who the Marines were facing. He knew he should leave the sergeant alone, but he couldn't help himself.

"Sergeant Danit, have you ever faced the R & F before?" he asked on the P2P.

For a moment, he thought the squad leader wasn't going to answer, but after a few seconds, he replied, "Not against them. Relieved them on Tippy once. Why?"

"I was just wondering. I mean, they're all SAS, Recon, Black Berets and stuff. Aren't they supposed to be the best of the best?"

"Hell, Alejo. Don't get freaked out even before we land," he said, and Pax knew he'd screwed up.

He probably thinks I'm a coward now.

Pax could feel his face burn red, and he was glad he had his helmet sealed and face shield down.

But then the sergeant said, "Look, Alejo. There're probably no more than three hundred of them on New Horizon. Do you know how many of us are being committed?"

"No, Sergeant."

That information had never made it down to the two newbies.

"We're landing with a regiment-plus. Over three thousand Marines. And all those snake-eaters? They might be studs, but they're not organized for infantry operations." He paused for a moment, and almost as if in an afterthought, said, "'Sides, sometimes their prima donna arrogance can write chits their butts can't cash."

That took Pax by surprise. As far as he knew, special operators were the cream of the crop. They were almost superhuman. The Royal Charter SAS had that long-running holovid series. And not just that. His ex-girlfriend had been addicted to Romance novels where the love interests were always SEALs. She'd been quite disappointed when he'd enlisted into the Marines and left him before he was even sworn in.

"But if there're only three hundred of them, why would they try and take over New Horizon? I don't get it."

Sergeant Danit turned his head to Pax, who couldn't tell by the sergeant's expression if he was getting annoyed with him or not.

"Politics. Gamesmanship. Who knows? Maybe they were betting on us not coming. Maybe they want to negotiate a settlement, figuring our command wouldn't want to waste lives."

Marine lives. So, they are pretty badass.

"We may never even engage. Our show of force might be enough. It wouldn't be the first time."

The open net came alive with the five-minute warning, and the sergeant said, "Don't get wrapped up in the whys, Alejo. Just keep your head down and do what you're told. Now, get off the net and get ready to debark. Put on your warrior face. We don't think they'll engage the shuttles, but a good grunt is ready for anything."

And with that, Pax's adrenaline surged. This was it. This was why he'd enlisted.

He just hoped he wouldn't screw up.

Situational Awareness

"Don't turn around, you two. Tell me, how many floors are on the building directly behind you," Sergeant Danit asked the two privates."

Len started to turn, and the sergeant barked, "Eyes on me. You've been here for almost two hours. Tell me how many stories."

"Uh . . . five?" Pax said.

"Four," Len said with much more confidence.

"Turn."

"One, two, three, four, five, *six,*" Pax counted. "Shit."

"Situational awareness, boots. That's what keeps Marines alive. You have to be aware of everything around you because if the shit goes down, it's too late."

"But we're in the rear," Len said.

He'd complained to Pax often enough about that over the last two hours with more than a little bitterness.

"Oh, so the mercs don't know that? They're gonna play by our rules?" the sergeant said, slapping Len across the top of his helmet.

"Look, I know you've been left here cooling your jets. But you need to be constantly thinking about what you're gonna do if this happens, or what if that happens. Keep your mind busy working out the scenarios."

He must have caught Pax's and Lens's expression, because he said, "What happens if the rest of the squad eats a Piranha? What are you going to do then?"

"They've got Piranhas?" Len asked.

That surprised Pax, too. The Piranha was a Terran Union ballistic missile. A pretty powerful one.

Danit rolled his eyes. "Was that in our brief? No, they won't have Piranhas. I was just using that as a what-if. But the question remains. If anything took out the rest of the squad, what would you do?"

"Go to the platoon CP?" Pax asked.

"See there? That's a course of action."

"Is it the right one?" Pax asked.

The sergeant shrugged. "Maybe, maybe not. It depends on the situation. But the important thing is to game it out."

It took a few seconds for that to gel, but Pax could see the squad leader's point. Back in boot, his senior drill instructor had a habit of reminding them that any action was better than inaction. Pax and Len might not be skilled in actual combat yet, but it couldn't hurt to have some plans in their hip pockets.

"Do you think we're going in?" Len asked.

"If you mean 'we' as in our squad, no. We're pretty far back, so unless this breaks out into an all-out war, this one might pass us by. But there could be some action. The mercs won't want to waste manpower, but they might think they need to make a statement. They've been paid a lot for this, and they have to show some sort of bang for the buck."

This was still something Pax couldn't wrap his head around. The R & F mercenaries had taken over the government complex. If they were the enemy, then send the Marines to take them out. Why all the posturing and negotiating?

But all of that was so far over his head it might as well be in another solar system.

"Other than that, are you two doing OK?" the sergeant asked.

"Yes, Sergeant," both privates said in unison.

They were what was known as an OP, or observation post, keeping an eye on the rear of the squad's position. Sergeant Danit had placed them in a window well that provided daylight for the basement floor of the building. They could stand there with only their heads exposed as they watched down both sides of the road. To the left were more buildings. To the right, the city extended two more blocks before giving way to agricultural fields.

There was no sign of mercs beyond the government center two klicks away, so the two privates were really looking for nothing. It was obvious that they were simply being stashed, with their backs to a building that stood between them and the mercenaries.

Pax didn't like it, but he accepted the logic. Once he had time to train with the squad, though, he'd demand to be more involved.

"If you need anything, pull me up. I'm just two decks above you. And you, Nijima, you be ready to bring up the Bushmaster if we need it."

With that, the sergeant strode over to the steps and climbed into the building.

"Why give me the Bushmaster if I can't fire it," Len groused.

Frankly, Pax was a little jealous about the weapon. Pax wasn't a small guy, but he wasn't a giant, either, like Len was. And when Sergeant Danit had brought over the extra Bushmaster while they were still back on San Marcos, he'd barely given Pax a glance before handing the heavy weapon to Len.

If Pax had to wager, he'd bet that he was the stronger of the two, yet the sergeant had automatically assumed Len would have an easier time with it. And Pax really liked the weapon. He'd fam-fired it in SOI, and fallen in love with it. The truck hulk he chosen as a target had been demolished, giving him a rush.

"They just wanted a mule to carry it," Pax said with a little more bitterness than he'd intended. He softened his tone and then said, "Let's go over some of the contingencies Sergeant Danit told us to work. Like he said, the mercs aren't playing by our rules."

"Come on, Pax. I'm tired of this shit."

"Sergeant Danit said—"

"Do you see Sergeant Danit here? He doesn't care what we do. We're just safely stashed out of the way. So why do we have to make all these plans that'll never happen?"

"But if the mercs do—"

"Then I'd use this bad boy to teach them not to mess with me."

He raised the Bushmaster out of the window well and mimicked blasting away a regiment of mercenaries.

"How many rounds you got in that thing, anyway?"

Len frowned. "I don't know." He activated the readout and then said, "Fifty. That ain't shit."

"I'm surprised they even gave you that. They were probably issued before Sergeant Danit decided to have you hump the weapon."

Len frowned. "Still, I could take out a bunch of mercs with fifty. Or pedes."

Pax wasn't so sure. He'd fired the Bushmaster during SOI. The Bushmaster was a heavy machine gun, firing big 15 mm hypervelocity darts. Unlike the much smaller SMM-8 Denon magrifle, the Bushmaster's darts were fired in bursts, aiming at areas or vehicles, whereas the Denon was designed more for the one-shot, one-kill line of targeting.

At ten darts per second, it would only take five seconds to run the Bushmaster empty, so taking on more than a squad or fire team with only fifty darts was somewhat of a non-starter.

Still, the Bushmaster could take out most vehicles, so against an enemy fire team, even fifty rounds could mess up their day.

Pax watched Len raise and lower the Bushmaster as he kept saying "Budda, budda, budda" while he sent imaginary enemies to Valhalla.

"Hey, how about letting me hold—" Pax started before a scraping noise caught his attention.

"What was that?" he asked Len, who was still dropping the imaginary foe. "I heard something."

"Yeah, that was me, saving humanity."

Pax reached out and pushed the barrel of the Bushmaster down. "I'm serious. I heard something."

Len looked at him, his eyebrows scrunched together. "What did you hear?"

"I don't know. Some sort of—"

This time, the sound was clearer, like a heavy piece of metal being dragged across the ground. It seemed to be coming from down the street to their left. Pax leaned over to get a better view, but he couldn't see anything.

"Isn't Second Platoon down that way? Maybe they're moving around." Len said.

"Yeah, you're probably right. But I'm going to tell the gunny."

"And make it look like we're jumping at ghosts?" Len asked.

Pax hesitated. Len was correct in that. They'd look even more like boots. But their orders were to report anything.

"I'm still going to let them know. If it's Second, then no harm, no foul."

He keyed to the platoon HQ, where he knew the gunny would be monitoring, but as soon as he opened the circuit, a high-pitched squeal stabbed into his brain.

"What the hell?" he asked as he lowered the volume. "Gunny?" he asked. "Can you hear me?"

The squeal drowned him out.

He started to tell Len that the comms were down when the private lunged for him and pulled him back and dragged him to the bottom of the well.

His elbow cracked hard on the floor, making his arm go numb.

"What the fuck, Len?"

"There're people coming!"

"Civilians? They're probably getting out of the way."

"People in combat suits!" Len hissed.

"Second Platoon?" Pax asked as he got his feet under him.

He started to raise his head before he remembered the snake-eye he'd been issued. It was a flexible optical cable with magnifying capabilities. He put a crook at the lens, rigidized the body, and while looking through the eye-piece, slowly raised the sight.

Possibly 150 meters down the road were three combat-suited figures, all facing outboard from each other and obviously alert for any danger. And while he watched, almost blocked by a building, he could see one more emerge from seemingly underneath the road. That figure turned back, and a moment later, hauled out a piece of gear that Pax didn't recognize but screamed weapon. And a big one.

Intel told us the old sewer system had been sealed.

How they got behind the Marines didn't matter as much in the moment as the fact that they were here.

"I think they're mercs," Pax told Len. "I don't recognize anything about them, so they can't be Second Platoon. See if you can get through to the platoon or Sergeant Danit."

Two more figures joined, making six of them. And with sure, controlled moves, they unfolded what was now obviously a weapon. About a meter and a half long by a meter high, it had a short stubby barrel protruding from the top. Tracks ran along each side. It powered up, and at an unknown signal, the six mercs started to quickly move, the weapon trundling behind.

"They're coming this way," Pax said.

He started to raise his Denon, then stopped. The magrifle was excellent against soft targets, and it could be effective against body armor. But they'd been told that for full combat suits, much less mecha and armor, they weren't much good.

"I can't engage with this," he told Len, his eyes locked on the Bushmaster. The image of the truck hulk he'd shredded with the Bushmaster at SOI had been burned into his mind.

"Are they mercs?" Len asked.

"Have to be. They're not Marines, and I don't think they're NH police. Wait."

He looked through the eyepiece again and zoomed in. He didn't recognize any of the equipment, but just as someone didn't have to be able to identify the species of a coiled, hissing snake to know not to mess with it, he was sure they were R & F mercs.

Then he saw it—the small black Gryphon on the collar of the suits—the R & F symbol.

"It's them."

He looked up alongside the building's wall. There were windows above him, but would the squad be looking out them instead of toward the government center.

Pax had no idea how powerful the weapon he'd spotted was, but it looked bad, and if they targeted the building . . .

I've got to do something.

He hadn't gamed this possibility out, but they had a Bushmaster, and that gave him a little more confidence.

"Hey, Len. Give me that Bushmaster," he said, but instead of complying, his fellow private scrambled out of the window well, screaming at the top of his lungs as he raised the weapon.

Pax felt the shock wave in his bones the instant Len's head just disappeared, and his friend's body was flung back a few meters to lie on the ground.

Pax stared in shock as blood spurted from Len's neck and stained the road an impossibly bright red.

Len's right fingers twitched as if they didn't know he was dead.

Awareness hit him that he was exposed, so Pax dropped back into the well, his heart racing, his breath coming in gulps. He felt nauseous, and he had to fight to keep from vomiting.

Pax knew that being a Marine was a dangerous proposition, and it wasn't as if he'd never been exposed to death in the Lago, but this . . . this wasn't what he'd imagined. Len, who'd gone through boot and SOI with him, with whom he'd shared hours and hours of conversations, was dead, just like that.

His head is gone, damn it!

He had no idea what the mercs had used. But he did know one thing—the mercs were coming toward him.

Pax scooted as low as he could and up against the street side of the well. He hadn't thought he was afraid of getting killed, but after seeing what happened to Len, fear washed over him.

I don't want to die here.

And then he heard footsteps approaching. He had a death grip on his Denon, but even knowing it wouldn't be effective, he vowed not to be killed cowering in the window well. He'd go out fighting.

Still trembling in shock, he twisted his body around, weapon ready. The instant he saw anything, he was going to light it up and hope for a lucky shot.

The sounds of treads got closer, and he had to consciously slow down his breathing for fear he'd pass out.

The footsteps got louder and louder, and he could now hear the dull clunks of mechanical joints.

"By the Light, help me," he whispered, his finger on the trigger.

But instead of a looming combat suit coming into view, the sounds started getting quieter. Hope started like an ember being coaxed into a flame. Then he was sure of it. The mercs had passed him by, which he didn't understand.

At SOI, it had been drilled into their heads that when in a combat situation, the area had to be cleared of enemy before moving on. Len was lying on the street just a few meters away. The mercs knew there were Marines there, so why didn't they clear the window well?

Was it the arrogance Sergeant Danit had mentioned?

Whatever it was, Pax was grateful. He was still alive.

Part of him would be content to just hunker down and let the battle play out. But a bigger part had to know what was happening.

He scooted to the other side of the well and raised his snake-eye. The mercs had stopped at the corner of the building, not exposing themselves. Three were in some sort of conversation, with two gesturing and pointing to the building above.

They know the squad's in there.

After a few moments of arguing, the third seemed to acknowledge what the other two were saying, and they pointed at the mobile weapon. A few seconds later, the weapon began to crawl away.

Trying to get a better angle to fire on my squad.

Pax wasn't sure how he knew that. Maybe it was his subconscious working. Or maybe Sergeant Danit's lecture on situational awareness had sunken in after all.

He didn't know what the weapon could do, but he had to expect the worst. They wouldn't be deploying it unless they expected it to have effect on target, and that meant his squad was in danger.

Pax tried to call them up once more, but the jamming was still going strong. He considered for a moment simply standing in the well and firing with his Denon, but he knew that would just be throwing his life away.

The Bushmaster.

He turned the lens toward Len and the big weapon. Whatever had taken his friend's head off didn't seem to have damaged the machine gun. But it had fallen beyond Len and was at least four meters away. Pax couldn't grab it, pull it back to the well where he'd have some protection, and engage the mercs. He'd be spotted and cut down.

There was essentially only one choice. He understood that if he was really going to do this, he wouldn't have time to get back to cover. He'd have to fire from out in the open and hope the mercs couldn't react in time.

I could go prone. That might help.

But at SOI, the prone position for the Bushmaster wasn't the most effective for aiming. The front edge of helmet got in the way of the sights.

Pax didn't want to think through everything. He didn't want to give himself a chance to second-guess what he was about to do.

He unlatched his helmet and dropped it to the ground, and before mentally telling himself to go, his muscles were already working. He jumped out of the well, his eyes locked on the Bushmaster.

Expecting to be cut down, he leaped over Len's body, then went into a roll, and grabbed the machine gun as he went over it.

Firing the weapon on the range had been extremely controlled, with safety paramount. This wasn't that. He swung around the weapon, his finger questing for the trigger even before he had a sight picture.

It shouldn't have worked. But this time, the gods of war must have been smiling on the ignorant because as he came to the prone position, his weapon was almost already trained on the mercs, who suddenly seemed to realize what was happening. A group of five were tightly packed, and they started to dive away from each other as the stream of heavy darts blasted into them.

Pax wasn't sure if the Bushmaster's rounds would be effective.

They were.

Bodies were blasted, with three down immediately. Two more managed a few steps, one firing their weapon before Pax's sweep caught up to them.

That left the sixth merc, the one who'd been operating the weapon, which was now raising the barrel to its previously programmed target. He spun around and spotted Pax.

Time seemed to go into slow motion as the merc started to charge Pax while bringing up his personal rifle. Pax instinctively started to shift his aim to the mercenary, when the image he'd formed of the battle site became crystal clear. Every aspect was imprinted on his brain.

Pax knew he was in mortal danger from the merc, but the rest of his squad was being targeted by the mobile gun, and the barrel was already on target.

He reversed the sweep of the Bushmaster while pressing the trigger and walked the rounds to the enemy gun just as it fired.

A shock wave expanded past the muzzle of the gun, and Pax thought he could see his darts penetrate the wave and hit the weapon.

The merc stumbled ever so slightly as the wave hit him, bringing his rifle slightly off-target.

The round impacted the roadbed alongside Pax, sending bits of cerrocrete pinging off his body armor. Besides making the merc miss, that stumble gave Pax his opening. Still spewing darts, he swung back and stitched the merc until his magazine ran dry.

He kept pressing the trigger for a few more moments as chunks of building rained down around him before he realized the fight was over.

Holy shit. What the hell just happened?

To his right were five prone bodies. One, at least, was still alive, an arm raised in the air as if feebly reaching for something. In front of him, the merc was on their back, motionless. Pax raised himself to one elbow, almost overcome by dizziness before he spotted the mobile gun. It looked in decent shape, but the muzzle had sunk to its lowest elevation.

There weren't any lights to indicate operability, but Pax knew it was dead.

Pax let himself fall back down. His head was spinning, and he wasn't sure why. He raised a hand to his left temple, felt something warm and sticky, then lowered it again. It was covered in blood, and more was dripping down his face and neck.

Maybe my body armor didn't catch all of that cerrocrete.

He was vaguely aware of shouting from the building, but his mind was fuzzy. He tilted his head and laid his cheek on the street.

Just twenty centimeters from him was a gouge in the road. Pax reached out with his bloody hand and touched it.

That's how close I was to getting shot.

His fingers almost caressed the edges of the gouge as he imagined what the round would have done to his skull.

Words began to register with him. Someone was saying, "Shit, shit, shit," almost like a litany.

Someone else said, "Hey, Alejo's alive! Get a corpsman!"

Gentle hands turned him over, and Pax groaned. Marines stood around him while the corpsman, whose name escaped him for the moment, ran a scanner alongside his head.

"Concussion for sure, but the skull's intact. Scalps bleed a lot, though, so that's probably what we're seeing."

Sergeant Danit knelt beside Pax's head.

"You with us, Alejo?"

"I guess so. What happened?"

"What happened is that the mercs wanted one good strike to strengthen their position for negotiation," the lieutenant said. "You helped stop that. And you saved our asses while you were at it."

"Sergeant?" Pax asked.

What the platoon commander said was a little much for him to grasp at the moment.

"You took out six R & F mercs and a Ballentine Gun, all by your lonesome. I've got to ask, Alejo. How the hell did you do that?"

Pax looked around to the dozen Marines standing over him, waiting for his answer. Beyond them, another corpsman was attending to the still-living mercenary. Two more were covering Len's body, which left a pang in his throat.

Sergeant Danit was still looking at him expectantly.

"I just remembered what you told me, Sergeant Danit."

"What did I tell you?" he asked, obviously puzzled.

"Situational awareness, Sergeant. Situational awareness."

Amazon won't always tell you about the next release. To stay updated on this series, be sure to sign up for our spam-free email list at jnchaney.com.

Sergeant Paxton Alejo will return in Proof of Concept, available on Amazon.

CONNECT WITH J.N. CHANEY

Don't miss out on these exclusive perks:

- Instant access to free short stories from series like *The Messenger*, *Starcaster*, and more.
- Receive email updates for new releases and other news.
- Get notified when we run special deals on books and audiobooks.

So, what are you waiting for? Enter your email address at the link below to stay in the loop.

https://www.jnchaney.com/star-scrapper-subscribe

CONNECT WITH JONATHAN P. BRAZEE

Visit his website

www.jonathanbrazee.com

Sign up for Jonathan's Newsletter

http://eepurl.com/bnFSHH

Follow him on Amazon

https://www.amazon.com/Jonathan-P-Brazee/e/B007E4W0GC

Connect on Facebook

https://www.facebook.com/jonathanbrazeeauthor/

JOIN THE CONVERSATION

Join the conversation and get updates on new and upcoming releases in the awesomely active **Facebook group**, "JN Chaney's Renegade Readers."

This is a hotspot where readers come together and share their lives and interests, discuss the series, and speak directly to J.N. Chaney and his co-authors.

facebook.com/groups/jnchaneyreaders

ABOUT THE AUTHORS

J. N. Chaney is a USA Today Bestselling author and has a Master's of Fine Arts in Creative Writing. He fancies himself quite the Super Mario Bros. fan. When he isn't writing or gaming, you can find him online at **jnchaney.com**.

He migrates often, but was last seen in Las Vegas, NV. Any sightings should be reported, as they are rare.

Jonathan P. Brazee is a retired Marine colonel now living in Colorado Springs with his wife Kiwi and twin baby girls, Danika Dawn and Darika Marie. He was born in Oakland, CA, but has lived throughout the US and the world, and has traveled to over 100 countries.

About the Authors

He has more than eighty-five titles to his name in six different languages. He is a two-time Nebula Award and two-time Dragon Award finalist as well as a USA Today bestseller. Find out more by visiting his website at http://jonathanbrazee.com.

Printed in Great Britain
by Amazon